THE SCARAB AND THE CROSS

Andy Garza

Energion Publications
Gonzalez, FL
2016

Front Cover Design: Andy Garza

ISBN10: 1-63199-225-2
ISBN13: 978-1-63199-225-4
Library of Congress Control Number: 2016934478

Energion Publications
P. O. Box 841
Gonzalez, FL 32560

energion.com
pubs@energion.com
850-525-3916

PROLOGUE

It has been said by greater thinkers than I, that a person's destiny is fixed or established by Divine decree. And so it would seem for a stolen child to suffer pain, amnesia and a haunting sense of loss and then to overcome oceans of despair and as fate ordained, rise to be a first hand everyday witness to the works of the Nazarene. Therein to recover his lost memory by the Healer's presence. Find a love to last a lifetime and send the works of Jesus flying free across the lands of Europe.

DEDICATION

Mary, my love –
This one's for you

TABLE OF CONTENTS

Introduction

A boy named Jesus

The search goes on
from long miles they stood weary
on a sandy crest.
The wise-men three
pushed and pulled to here,
on words of dubious seer.
The star they followed left no doubt,
what they sought was near.
From distant borders
they came to see
the living word of prophecy.
A king born in lowly quarters.
No crown, no kingly robes, no royal line.
Can this be the will Divine?
Did they find what they sought?
Time is wise. Some men are not.

*And the angel said to her, "Do not be afraid, Mary,
for you have found favor with God. And behold, you will
conceive in your womb and bear a son, and you shall call*

his name Jesus. He will be great,
and will be called the Son of the Most High;
and the Lord God will give to him the throne
of his father David,
and he will reign over the house of Jacob for ever;
and of his kingdom there will be no end."   Luke 1:30-33

Now the birth of Jesus Christ took place in this way.
When his mother Mary had been betrothed to Joseph, before
they came together she was found to be with child of the
Holy Spirit; and her husband Joseph, being a just man and
unwilling to put her to shame, resolved to divorce her qui-
etly. But as he considered this, behold, an angel of the Lord
appeared to him in a dream, saying, "Joseph, son of David, do
not fear to take Mary your wife, for that which is conceived
in her is of the Holy Spirit;   Matthew 1:18-20

In those days Mary arose and went with haste into the
hill country, to a city of Judah, and she entered the house
of Zechariah and greeted Elizabeth. And when Elizabeth
heard the greeting of Mary, the babe leaped in her womb;
and Elizabeth was filled with the Holy Spirit and she ex-
claimed with a loud cry, "Blessed are you among women, and
blessed is the fruit of your womb!   Luke 1:39-42

And he rose and took the child and his mother by
night, and departed to Egypt, and remained there until the
death of Herod. This was to fulfil what the Lord had spo-
ken by the prophet, "Out of Egypt have I called my son."
Matthew 2:14-15

JESUS WAS ONCE A CHILD

Difficult though it may be, we must accept the fact that Jesus was once a child.

Like all children he frolicked around the yard and even played with the sawdust where his father plied his trade. Like any other kid he was forbidden to swing upon the gate. But just like you and I, he did.

From there one can only guess, he felt a sense of joy greeting and talking to people as they passed.

He was a guest of childish pleasures, often lying on the grass like you and I liked to do.

From this point of view he saw how a bird flies and often squinted when the sun got in his eyes.

Birds know a kind heart even today and they often perched close by to watch him play. Alone he gathered flocks that had no fear. No one can name the birds he drew, but they were more than just a few.

They sensed his childish love; they seemed to know He was God's own dove.

How painful it is to accept that his sweet, innocent brow would wear thorns and suffer agonies on the cross that you and I may be forgiven for our wrongs.

> *And he went down with them and came to Nazareth, and was obedient to them; and his mother kept all these things in her heart.*

> *And Jesus increased in wisdom and in stature, and in favor with God and man.*   *Luke 2:51-52*

> *In those days Jesus came from Nazareth of Galilee and was baptized by John in the Jordan. And when he came up out of the water, immediately he saw the heavens opened and the Spirit descending upon him like a dove; and a voice came from heav-*

en, "Thou art my beloved Son; with thee I am well pleased."
Mark 1:9-11

THE BAPTISM OF CHRIST

Silent upon the green and sloping bank the people sat, and while the leaves shook with the birds dropping early to their nest, and the grey eve came on, within their hearts they mused if he were Christ. The rippling stream still turned it's silver courses from his breast, as he divined their thought. "I but baptize," he said, "with water; but there cometh One, the latchet of whose shoes I may not dare E'en to unloosen. He will baptize with fire and with the Holy Ghost." And lo! While yet the words were on his lips, he raised his eyes and on the bank stood Jesus. He had laid His raiment off, and with his loins alone girt with a mantle, and his perfect limbs, in their angelic slightness, meek and bare, he waited to go in. But John forbade, and hurried to his feet and stay'd him there, and said, "Nay, Master, I have need of thine, Not thou of mine!" And Jesus, with a smile of heavenly sadness, met his earnest looks, and answer'd, "Suffer it to be so now; for thus it doth become me to fulfill all righteousness." And leaning to the stream, he took around him the Apostle's arm, and drew him gently to the midst. The wood was thick with the dim twilight as they came up from the water. With his clasped hands Laid on his breast, th' Apostle silently followed his Master's steps – When lo! A light bright as the tenfold glory of the sun, yet lambent as the softly burning stars, enveloped them, and from the heavens away parted the dim blue ether like a veil; And as a voice, fearful exceedingly, broke from the midst."This is my much loved Son, in whom I am well pleased," a snow-white dove, floating upon its wings descended through and shedding a swift music from its plumes, circled and flutter'd to the Savior's breast.

Nathaniel Parker Willis, 1806-1867

The next day again John was standing with two of his disciples; and he looked at Jesus as he walked, and said, "Behold, the Lamb of God!" The two disciples heard him say this, and they followed Jesus.   *John 1:35-37*

The next day Jesus decided to go to Galilee. And he found Philip and said to him, "Follow me." Now Philip was from Bethsaida, the city of Andrew and Peter. Philip found Nathanael, and said to him, "We have found him of whom Moses in the law and also the prophets wrote, Jesus of Nazareth, the son of Joseph."   *John 1:43-45*

One can only imagine the wonderment and perhaps bewilderment that could dwell in the mind and heart of Jesus. Since after all is said, he was human. A young man in the budding stage of manhood. Does it ever occur to us that he may have yearned for a wife and family? A love to hold close to his working body? To take his child by the hand and walk in the sunlight? We have grown accustomed through years of spiritual association to regard the young carpenter from Nazareth as always having been the savior, Jesus the Christ. We choose to ignore that in his community of Nazareth when he spoke; deaf ears were openly turned away. He was only the son of Joseph, the deceased carpenter. Like us he suffered through youthful failures. There was a common saying at the time, "Nothing good can come from Galilee." In the cities, people from Nazareth were publically regarded as blockheads for their rustic ways of speech and manners. It was even said that he was a prophet without honor in his own country. The baptism by his kinsman, John the baptizer in the Jordan was without doubt the key to his future. Jesus knew his repentance and cleansing ritual was the acceptance of his tribulation. The public baptism and trial by fasting and temptation he endured for forty days and nights gave him the strength to proceed. By now he knew the course of his life far more clear. With heavenly assurance the grown boy issued forth, gathering unto himself the followers that would bear first hand witness to his accounts and carry on his work at the end of his earthly journey. A mother help-lessly resolved to the future of the fruit of her womb was in the final word only a woman, with far less say than most men. She may have sensed with that wondrous inner feeling that all mothers possess, the hesitation in her son. Even the princely dove must suffer a gentle motherly nudge out of the nest on its first flight. And so it may have been with his first miracle. At a wedding in Cana from water he made wine to save face of his mother's friends. It was the first flight of the princely dove.

On the third day there was a marriage at Cana in Galilee, and the mother of Jesus was there; Jesus also was invited to the marriage, with his disciples. When the wine gave out, the mother of Jesus said to him, "They have no wine."
John 2:1-3

Now his parents went to Jerusalem every year at the feast of the Passover. And when he was twelve years old, they went up according to custom; and when the feast was ended, as they were returning, the boy Jesus stayed behind in Jerusalem. His parents did not know it,   *Luke 2:41-43*

JESUS IN THE TEMPLE

With His mother, who partakes thy woe, Joseph, turn back; see where your child doth sit. Blowing, yea blowing out those sparks of wit which himself on the doctors did bestow. The word but lately could not speak, and lo! It suddenly speaks wonders; Whence comes it that all which was, and all which should be writ, a shallow-seeming child should deeply know? His Godhead was not soul to his manhood, nor had time mellow'd him to his ripeness; But as for one which hath a long task, 'tis good, With the sun to begin His business. He in his age's morning has began, By miracles exceeding power of man.

John Donne 1573-1631

At eighteen years of age, it is virtually impossible to imagine Jesus. And yet for several years he had been the head of his household. Joseph died and Mary still a young woman was left with four sons and a daughter to raise. Jesus spent his entire childhood in Joseph's carpenter shop. There he learned his earthly father's craft from daily lessons without pause. Jesus then taught his brothers James, Simon and Judah all he learned. And so they managed to keep food on the table. From all over the country the sons of Joseph hard-earned their reputation daily as carpenters, builders and repairmen of all implements of labor. A modest house has been described resting alongside the carpenter shop. Close to the road it gave all clients easy access to the skills of the sons of Joseph. At any time oxen could be seen waiting for a new yoke or harness to be mended or a farmer patiently waiting for a plowshare to be fixed. Even a shepherd with a broken crook to be restored – these were all common sights at the shop. The brother's greatest fame came from their ability to build the lightest, yet the strongest yoke. The eldest brother was given credit for its invention. Furthering their already favorable reputation was the shop's ability to repair any given item, be it furniture, shepherd's staff or farm implement. Often repaired items returned to the owner better then when they were new. A mystery that was never solved.

There was repeated dissention among the brothers stemming from the charitable nature of their eldest brother, who often gave away the shop's work for a simple "thank you."

"How long, do you think the thanks of farmers and shepherds will keep our family in bread?" Judah asked on numerous occasions.

The oldest brother was a repeated source of near violent irritation to Judah. But, that was the way of Jesus. In his free time he visited the bed-ridden to console them and brought them food. He spent hours helping neighbors every chance he could. The destitute received clothes and some of their daily needs from the generous young carpenter. He visited the jails and spoke to the incarcerated in need of a friend. His unselfish sense of giving was widely known and spoke of. His acts of charity often put his own family in want. His mother, as no one else on earth, knew her son's destiny. And though she may have worried about her never to be rich state, she never reprimanded her son's unrequited generosity.

"He gave of himself, of his labor out of love for those in need." she was known to say more than once in answer to complaints from the other brothers.

"The wood was given to him by God. His time and ability is his to give as he pleases," she was heard to say other times. There should be no doubt that her deep motherly love and knowledge of her son's future were always foremost in her mind. Can we not imagine the heart clutching agony she suffered in silence from that knowledge? Can we not believe she secretly hoped that prophecy would prove to be false?

Jesus had heard that his cousin John, the baptizer, was doing work for the Lord in the wilderness. John was the son of Mary's cousin, Elizabeth and her husband Zechariah. It was openly said that a certain mystery surrounded John's birth, due to his parent's old age. Others would say that John was destined to be "the prophet of the Most High." Others would tell of countless people that John gathered to hear him speak. All this must have intrigued the young mind of the carpenter from Nazareth. As he grew up the news of all this occurrences reached the attention of Mary from passerby as well as local gossip. It would be natural for her to repeat and discuss these things at the supper table with her family.

It was during these times that young Jesus spent many nights in isolation a mile or so from home, on a jagged mountain ridge overlooking Nazareth. After work, he slipped away to be alone, to meditate and to chart the course of his life among men. It becomes clear that even in those younger days he was certain of his mission on earth. It is not by chance that he understood scriptures, ancient heroes and old time laws recited by the elders at the temple where he surprised even the most learned with his astounding answers. Only three days did he spend in the temple of knowledge where one could speak to God. In that short time, the knowledge that took the elders years to gain, he knew as a boy. These things may have crossed his mind during the cold nights of isolation on that jagged mountain peak, a mile or so from the warmth, love and safety of home.

On a clear morning, as the light of day glowed softly on the eastern horizon, he arrived home from the mountain to find his mother at the door. He embraced her warmly and long held her in his arms.

"The time has come," he whispered softly in her ear. Imagine, if you can, the tearing agony she must have felt that his destiny as the sacrificial lamb was now at her front door. A cold dagger punctured her heart and the terrible pain choked her into silence. Since she could not speak, she must have clutched her hand by her lips as the flood of tears raced down her face. He walked her to the edge of the porch and together they marveled at the sunrise. Once again he embraced her and kissed her forehead.

"I must go forth and do the work my heavenly father has ordained. I must join John, the baptizer and do repair to the broken spirit of man. The sick must be mended and made well again. The poor must have the word of the heavenly kingdom brought to them. My time has come."

For a fleeting moment that nobody can confirm or deny it is only reasonable to believe he would hold his loving mother close and draw attention to the early birds fluttering about to ease her aching heart. The sun barely cleared the peaks and reached the home of Mary, shining softly on the glory of the dawn. Silent clouds drifted on the desert breeze as the only witnesses to that fateful day. With certainty in his stride he walked away from his parent's home to become the Son of Man.

A VOICE IN THE DESERT

A voice from the desert comes awful and shrill:
The Lord is advancing--- prepare ye the way!
The word of Jehovah he comes to fulfill,
And o'er the dark world pours the splendor of day.
Bring down the proud mountain,
Though towering to heaven;
And be the low valley exalted on high;
The rough path and crooked
He made smooth and even;
Sir, Sion! Your king, your redeemer is nigh!
The beams of salvation his progress illume,
The lone dreary wilderness sings of her God;
The rose and the myrtle shall suddenly bloom,
And the olive of peace spread its branches abroad

William Drummond   1585 – 1649

CHAPTER ONE

WELCOME TO JERUSALEM

Onofrio, a stranger in Jerusalem, was arrested for stealing two smoked fish and a honeycomb and sentenced to three years at hard labor. He was a craftsman and field worker, earning a few coins, food and keep for short durations. Then moving on with no regard to where the road would take him. He harbored few regrets over where he had been and even fewer for what he did, in the private places of his life. His relationships were all of a loose nature. No family ties, political alliances or religious convictions impaired his moves to any direction his meager earnings would provide. Not a large individual of brute strength but a mature boy nearing manhood with the grace of hard work and moderate diet. Clear white teeth shown with every smile and sound bones within his body. Not a shifty eyed person but keen to any opportunity that may benefit his current state. The light tone of his skin suggested some northern tribe from beyond the Mediterranean, while his premature beard showed a touch of grey as did his hair. It was his bluish green eyes that brought second looks as well as his admirable slender physique. He was a free soul living off the land and the sweat of his labor. He claimed his love of fresh air and sunshine as his allies in life. He loved to bathe in country streams surrounded by trees and there he found a joy that sang within his soul.

In a foul-smelling dungeon he stood alone with thoughts that often meandered to his parents during his childhood. He saw himself as a young boy working with his father in the fields back home. But where was back home? Persistent dreams often visited him of long ships with dragon heads, stone castles on misty isles, wide fertile valleys and clear blue lakes. Perhaps in Italia, or Iberia. Even Greece somewhere beyond the sea. Which sea? What valley? He sometimes questioned if his visions were true or a product of wishful thinking. Such nocturnal visions always dissolved at the first light of dawn. As they did on this day in dim lit corridors of vaulted stone, iron gates and steel doors that held him without hope of escape. In the incarcerated state of his life, he dwelled longingly in the faded memories of a childhood that seemed so far away and so long ago. On the brink of tears he heard his father speak as once he did after a minor childish mishap,"But, men don't cry. They accept what fate the gods dole out with masculine grace." Within his heart resided an unfathomed love for the parents that lived in his mind and he hungered painfully to be again in the circle of their love. One day he would return to them when he discovered where home was. Somehow he would find it.

As a very young boy, he fondly remembered following his father into the fields, the barns and animal keeps. He got in the way while additions to their modest home took place. He saw furniture being built. Trees felled in the forest and dragged by oxen to the home site, then split into lumber for all their needs. Onofrio had never been a stranger to work. He may have been a nuisance to his dad and uncle, but to him it was work. And it filled him to the brim with happiness. Where he lived in those days was a paradise lost in time. How he came to be in this country was a perplexing riddle that haunted his mind almost constantly. Occasionally he remembered bits and pieces of the last ten or twelve years. From those mental flashes he knew with dogged determination that one day he would find his way home. Although, he had no inkling as to how or when. When the time came, he would remember and find the way to his beloved land. Only then would he find peace within himself. Mentally he fondled the moment he would see his parents again.

Officers and guards stood at wide assembly as prisoners were herded forward with rude shoves and bellowed commands. Some detainees were in strong chains from wrist to ankle. Others were kept with forearms in retainer staffs and chains behind their backs. A modest set of cuffs held Onofrio secure. Hands before him hanging low, he bowed his head out of respect for the powers that held him and not from fear. He was resolved to pay his due since he clearly knew why and where he was.

On the awkward command of a centurion, new to his rank and clearly intoxicated with wine or power, soldiers lined up the prisoners in the center of the torch lit rotunda. Chains rasped on crude flagstone floors as each man was pushed and shoved into position. Cells and sealed confinements lined the walls of the circular enclosure. The chiseled rock walls were a deep, hellish black above and below the yellowish smoking torches. A strong odor of urine, sweat and putrid human feces hung heavy in the air. It smarted the eyes and rudely offended the nostrils of Onofrio, having long been accustomed to open air and field scented breezes. Little or no fresh air ever visited the depths of this dungeon. Even the stones wept with a heavy mucous that sluggishly crept down the rough-hewn walls. Dark green, like something deadly and faintly glistening in the weak light of the flickering torches.

"By all the gods known to those that grieve and despair, show me a glimmer of hope I can cling to. For in this hell-hole I will surely die," Onofrio prayed in earnest silence.

A man of secure station entered the enclosure followed by two armed guards that flanked him. Each placing themselves carefully so not to invade his space. He came to the center of the rotunda where the light was strongest. Here was a large, tall man physically strong and openly showing a flair of authority, with polished brownish grey skin, well robed and groomed. He was decorated with jewels, gold and enough baubles to ransom a princess. His eyes were those of a hawk, wise to what they sought and each one was pin dagger sharp. A clear brown, his eyes were with a black shinning point of light at each center. Leisurely he walked among the prisoners, confident in his stride. Inspecting each detainee as one would examine goats or cattle to buy. He held a release scroll in his left hand, which he used to gain each prospect's attention like a weapon. He showed no regard for size of man. He was above them all, in rank and power. He knew it and they all knew it. Every detainee in the room knew that this man, whoever he may be, had the power to do as he wished. To whom he wished.

Onofrio stood resolute. He did not fear the three year sentence, somehow he would survive it. His mind was busy questioning how this man would affect him? Did the man have the power to send him to the dreaded copper mines? Or as a chained oarsman on a Roman ship?

A gold scarab the size of a man's thumb with a clear blue stone held the man's outer robe in place. He imperiously flushed the robe behind him to demonstrate the shinning symbol of his office hanging from an elaborate gold chain in the middle of his ample chest. The rich garment beneath the medallion dimmed by the brilliance of the glowing emblem.

"I am Serou, Master of Public Works. By the direct order of Rome, Herod and now Pilate," he said with a nondescript gesture of his hand. To mention Herod, the king and Pontius Pilate, the new governor from Rome without proper title was a show of flamboyant power. Or positive conviction of self importance. Neither one to be challenged. "I have the task of improving living conditions in Jerusalem. With the powers vested in me, I am to pick from among you, the dregs of humanity a work force to make a better place for Pilate to live in and Herod to rule." He strode among the convicts as he spoke, carefully choosing his words, while he inspected prospects. He wanted strong backs with weak minds to do his bidding without questions. If the workers performed according to Serou's demands, the better his position would be with whoever may govern rebellious Judea in the future. Twenty years he had been at his post, an unprecedented length of time to serve the moods of Jerusalem. Through civil unrest, political upheaval, a few wars, some friends that were enemies and enemies that proved to be friends. Serou was no stranger to adversity or to the social whims of time.

With the release scroll, he pointed to the new centurion, who was holding firm to a slimy metal rail lest, he stumble or worse yet take an embarrassing fall in view of all those present. "You!" Serou commanded. "Centurion Clemidius, is this the best you have stored in this rock box of rats and parasites? Have you no better to offer other than yourself?" Serou toyed with the new centurion, confident the word game would end in his favor. The game was common to Serou and his long experience with short-term officers. They all came, then they all went away. Sometimes, alive.

"Sir," the centurion's voice already colored with a tone of apology. "I am new to this post. I am not familiar with these convicts or with your needs. Given a few days, I will have a prime selection of workers to fit your needs."

"In short," Serou rebutted, "you ask from your iron balcony and intoxicated condition that King Herod and Governor Pontius Pilate simply wait? Until you feel better?"

The centurion smarted from Serou's sting and jerked himself erect as his rank demanded. With borrowed dignity and a Roman set of his jaw, he curtly bowed to his tormentor. "I simply ask for time to find a stable before I unsaddle my horse, sir. I am newly arrived and weary from the journey."

Serou lifted his arms imperiously. His hands open and waving in a mock gesture of peace. "Let us not debate the quality of your convicts, for now. Instead allow me to make your arrival more pleasant." Serou still played with the centurion. He now chose to release him, like a cat does a mouse, to play with again at a later time. "Come to my house tonight, with your officers and I will lay before you feast, drink and pleasure such as can only be found in Rome or far away Greece, whichever you prefer."

With a bright, sincere smile and widely gesturing hands, Serou continued facetiously, "Let me be your friend. We are both foreigners here and will have many projects to work on together. Come to my house tonight. You may even find my house your home away from Rome. We'll celebrate your promotion and safe arrival in Jerusalem." The centurion smiled weakly and nodded in docile agreement.

As Serou slipped the release scroll back into his outer garment, the gold scarab that had not escaped Onofrio's keen eye came loose and flew silently behind the tall Egyptian. The scarab barely touched the floor and Serou was hardly a step away, as Onofrio cupped the precious bauble in his agile hand. Before he stood erect, his voice was clearly heard throughout the chamber.

'Sir," his voice quavered a bit as his hand came between himself and the hawk-eye of Serou. "You dropped something that may be of value, sir." The scarab firmly planted in his open hand shone brightly in the dim light so clearly that no one in the chamber failed to see it. Cuffed as he was, Onofrio bowed awkwardly bringing the precious bauble up to the tall Egyptian. The scarab was solid gold and felt heavy, taking up most of his palm. The stone on its back was a huge clear and faintly blue diamond, the size of a large thumbnail.

There they met, eye to eye. Neither flinching from the other. Serou looked down to his scarab then back to Onofrio, visually measuring the distance of its fall. He then walked around Onofrio, examining him carefully. With the scroll he jabbed Onofrio's muscles tenderly, annoying but not injuring. Onofrio stood rigid, tolerating and pretending not to be offended. He stood as proud as the handcuffs would allow. Never flinching, not even once.

"What is your name, convict and what is your crime?" he asked in a modest tone.

"I stole two smoked fish and a honeycomb, for which I am sentenced to three years at hard labor, sir. And I am called Onofrio."

"For that I would put you in my fields for three days and not feed you for three years." Serou retorted, still appraising the young man's physique and manners. "Why did you steal?" Serou continued.

"I stole from hunger, sir. Not from profession." the young man answered still looking straight ahead into the oblivion of dungeon darkness.

"And what is your profession, convict Onofrio?" the Egyptian asked with obvious interest.

"I do woodwork, sir. I work in the fields when work is available there. I know something of metals and the making of tools and weapons." Onofrio answered as if suddenly having something valuable to sell.

"Why did you return the scarab? You could have kept it. No one in chains would inform on you. In this dim light, only you saw it fall." Serou was looking closely at the young man's face.

"I wasn't hungry. I've been here almost a month and they feed us very well," Onofrio answered with a dim smile on his face and an eye cocked at Serou's peering glare.

"The hell you say." Serou chuckled looking amused at the young convict. Serou had not made an effort to recover his property while Onofrio held the bauble before him. Now Serou gestured for the return of the scarab and asked," Are you returning it because you expect a favor in return?"

To which Onofrio quickly answered, "Yes, sir. It is. I prefer the open fields over copper mines, Roman ships or smelly dungeons."

"Your wit and honestly will serve you well, convict Onofrio." Looking at the scarab Serou gestured Onofrio to pin his robe properly so not to lose it again. Onofrio heeded the silent demand carefully pinning the rich garment together.

"Sir, may I suggest you take this piece to your jeweler and have the clasp replaced. It is worn and will slip away again. It would be a considerable loss, since you obviously favor this expensive bug." Onofrio commented with casual sincerity.

"It is not a bug. It is a sacred scarab. Revered in my country and favored by those blessed with good fortune, such as I. But, I will heed your advice." The Egyptian stroked the scarab, as if in prayer then briskly walked away. "Centurion Clemidius, bring this convict with you tonight. He will be the first of our work force." Serou pointed to Onofrio as he left the chamber followed by his personal guards. "Uncuff him." he commanded over his shoulder. "But keep a watchful eye on him." In a shuffle of padded feet and swirling robes, Serou was gone.

Alone again, Onofrio experienced a ruthless sense of isolation. In this odorous place of no sunshine, he had no friends. Home and family were a far away dream. Reality was here and now. He had only fleeting memories to keep him company. He knew instinctively, that his most powerful ally was his will to survive this ordeal.

Late that afternoon an unruly guard called Onofrio out of the communal cell that held him. An officer under Clemidius had come to collect him before departing for the home of Serou. He was a civil fellow with blondish brown hair and sparkling eyes. But, he was unshaven and his uniform was visibly worn. He studied Onofrio momentarily with a knowing eye and asked."- Do I need to keep you in chains or can you be trusted without manacles?"

"You have nothing to worry about. I want to go where you're going," Onofrio answered joyfully. Without added comment, they were on the way out of that hell hole and into the freedom of the outside world. The young convict rejoiced to see the amber gold sun over the fortress walls. The warm desert air, a refreshing balm and he took long breaths of the liberty that rode on the life restoring breeze.

At an encampment not far from the city gates, they met a group of officers and foot soldiers. Onofrio was made to trot alongside tired horses and a somewhat ratty chariot. Several soldiers ran with him, making him feel as though he was being watched. The pace was not hard, but he welcomed the rest, sitting on a flat stone not far from an officer's tent. Campfires were already burning and men were busy cleaning weapons, seeing about supplies and equipment. Even though the camp seemed undisciplined and chaotic, there was order and method in the men's activities. Horses and gear were all being tended to. Some men were sharpening lances, while others cared for bows and arrows. Meals were being prepared in the midst of what seemed to be confusion. From somewhere in all this activity the sound of softly beaten drums and string instruments found attention in his ear.

Chapter Two

In the Gardens of Serou

Onofrio asked for permission to join the men in the stream not far away. There the men, and now Onofrio, came to the water to bathe, clean and groom the horses and some of their clothes. Amidst much masculine jocularity, splashing, dunking and joyful wise cracking, they managed to get the job done. Onofrio was sure he could develop friendships among the bunch and prove useful at a later time. And so, he played their games and exchanged friendly insults with them. More importantly he worked hard at the task at hand, making certain that his efforts did not go unnoticed. He even helped shave a trooper suffering from wounds on his right shoulder and left leg. Having long been accustomed to a clean body and being well shaven, he was pleased to use a razor and clear the stubble from his face and have someone help to trim some of his unruly hair. His meager rags were thrown away and some old but clean robes given to him by a soldier. In spite of all the effort, it was a scarred, road-worn assembly of officers, men and horses that rode out of camp. It seemed unfit to go calling in such a ragged condition. His rummaged attire could be acceptable but these men were the living representatives of the mighty empire of Rome.

Onofrio rode in a rickety chariot with the officer that collected him. The pace was relaxed with an unseen assurance prevailing since their destination was unquestioned. Soon blood-filled episodes filled their conversations. Wild descriptions of man-to-man conflicts at various battles ricocheted from soldier to soldier in graphic gestures and gory details. Onofrio rode in silence listening to their bloody tales and appalled at how easy blood baths and murder came to these Romans.

Arriving at Serou's estate they were met with armed guards at a strong gate. An officer spoke to the commanding guardsman and promptly the party was welcomed into the vast compound that was the home of the Master of Public Works. Torches and fresh runners brightened the way to the main house. A palace of graceful arches, well-crafted balconies, admirable stone works and a sense of opulent power. Trees, foliage plants and plush grasses made the place seem like a paradise within a blistering desert. Small streams and many ponds appeared from behind clusters of lush plantings. There was a constant hum, like that heard when birds roost in flocks together. Doves cooed to each other in the darkness while ducks and geese quacked their day's final song.

There was damage to the outer walls of the city requiring heavy physical labor to repair. Clogged sewage canals needed clearing and enlarging. The stench blew over the city on the prevailing desert breezes. Serou, the Egyptian knew this condition not to be healthy and demanded attention. Although he was politically strong and could institute many changes, he could not change Rome. For now Rome was only vaguely interested in Jerusalem smelling bad. Securing the outer walls, repairing government buildings, reinforcing the garrison, restocking army depots and rebuilding military stables held priority. Centurion Clemidius and the Master of Public Works discussed all these things into the night. Rotating business talks with pleasure was controlled by the Egyptian. He made the transition from pleasure to business virtually unnoticed. Pleasant music from Rome, jugglers, provocative dancers and acrobats mixed with exotic foods and drink were well taken by the centurion and his officers. Several officers retired to secluded corners of the large banquet hall and were resting or soon asleep. When the moon was at its summit, Serou and Clemidius met on a balcony overlooking a large clear pool surrounded by vegetation. Dim oil lamps illuminated the garden from strategic points, creating interesting areas of light and shadows. The scent of gardenias and his homeland's geraniums filled the surprisingly cool and moist night air. From somewhere in the shadowed foliages began to wisp out the fanciful sounds of a well-played harp. An alluring feminine voice joined in with songs he had heard long ago. Tunes familiar to the homesick centurion. His mind wandered away to the fruitful valleys of his youth and a time in which he lived a happier life. Savoring the tunes in his head and humming ever so softly to himself, loosely gesturing, as if conducting an invisible musical group.

"Clemidius, in that garden are two lovely young women. One favors the legendary Helen of Troy. She has golden hair, the body of Venus with skin as white as cream and smooth as warm silk. I am told she is a student of Athena and the art of making love. The other could be a twin to Cleopatra with raven hair and skin the color of polished copper. Almond-shaped eyes and lips like scarlet roses. She could be the voice of a lonesome nightingale. Her schooling in the far East can make a man happy beyond his wildest expectations. They are instructed to be illusive but not impossible to find. They are to be coy but willing to comply with your pleasure, if you find them fairly. You can't set the garden on fire." Serou added laughingly. "Oh, they'll hide to evade you. They know the garden better than I. If you choose to only find one, it'll be alright. Or you can choose to catch both of them, after your long, exhausting journey. Good luck! Beyond that rise in the trees is a villa on the south shore of the lake. I had it fully prepared for your stay. A slave man and woman are in their quarters, should you have need of them. Your horse is fed, watered and in the stable behind the villa." Serou placed both hands on the centurion's shoulders, "Let my modest house be your home in Jerusalem." With a nodded expression of gratitude, Clemidius proceeded down the stairs to the garden below. Serou noticed a modest sprint to the centurion's step and stored a private thought in his mind, *"That randy devil is sure to breed problems in the future."*

Onofrio met Serou at the stairs to the upper floor. He wore a fresh tunic, his hair was neatly clipped, his fingernails manicured and was freshly bathed, smelling of scented oils. New sandals graced his feet and he obviously had a few cups of wine.

"I had somebody secure their chariots and see about their horses. Slaves are cleaning up their Roman mess from the great hall. Some of those men need to bathe," he added, sniffing on the cuff of his tunic, his eyes slightly off balance from drink. Serou praised him for his efforts, unsure of the end result. Onofrio raised his cup to hail the Egyptian. "As the lovely red haired, green-eyed Ruth Ann always said, all it takes is – money."

CHAPTER THREE

NEW HORIZONS

E arly the next morning Serou heard complaints from his household staff. Each charging that Onofrio had taken over and changed many things throughout the night.

"I just made it difficult for them to steal so much. I had untouched food saved for themselves, instead of using fresh food. Leftover wine is now contained in earthen jars and covered for cooking. Day old wine is wonderful on fish, vegetables and other seafood. Leftover bread is wasted on birds and wild animals. That bread with leftover honey and milk along with shreds of cheese makes a delicious cake, edible for many days longer than the individual ingredients. These people have gotten spoiled to only fresh food and steal food items which they hide in their clothes or sneak out the back door. They have forgotten they are slaves and entitled only to what a slave deserves. Not the first cut of meat, the top of the milk or the best loaf from the oven." Onofrio's sincere oration was cut short by the rise of Serou's hand.

"Onofrio, these are my slaves. This is my home. No one gave you the right to do what you did," Serou said in earnest. "I've known these people for years. I've known you less than a day." Serou's patience was cool and clear as he pointed a finger of authority directly at Onofrio's chest.

The young convict felt the ice in the Egyptian's suppressed mellow voice. He knew he had exceeded his visitor's privilege. He also knew he was right. Slaves are slaves. Thieves are thieves. Thieving slaves are yet another matter. Resolved to give ground but hold to his convictions, he said, "Sir, I apologize for my transgressions. I will apologize to them if I offended anyone in your home. I was trying to reduce the thievery that goes on when your back is turned. I will not intervene with slaves drinking your wine without consent. I will do my best to overlook all these things. When you instruct me in my duties, I will adhere to them specifically. Please do not subject me to witnessing open thievery from he that has been kind and protective to these people. I will do all you ask of me until my debt is paid. After which I will depart to find my parents and homeland." His head still bowed, he waited for Serou's stern reply.

"And the wine you drank last night, was that with my consent?"

"No sir. It was not with your consent. But it was wine fit for slaves and not from your guest's reserve." The young man still held to his sense of righteousness.

"And how much did you save me with all your tampering, last night? What price do you put on the loyalty and tenure these people have with me?"

"Loyal slaves do not steal from their master. As for tenure, none of them have a choice. They belong to you until you say otherwise. With last night's savings, there is enough food, drink, sweets and bread to feed the entire kitchen staff for three or four days without having to spend any more money." Onofrio concluded firm in his conviction.

"By what right do you condemn the stealing of food? You stole food, that is why you are here." Serou stated, seriously studying the young man from parts unknown.

"I stole from hunger. These people are not hungry. They all have homes and clothes on their back. Their only task is to please you; all else is provided by you. They have what is yours, for the asking. There's no reason to steal." The Egyptian gave thought to the young man's impressive defense. A seed of guarded admiration was planted at that moment. What fruit it would bear was too soon to know. Just then, the centurion entered the room and noticed the men talking. He called to a pretty slave girl entering an opposite door for some warm tea and freshly baked breads dripping with melted butter. Every guest was treated to sliced cantaloupe, fresh berries and sweet milk on the tray of another girl. Ripe quartered dates over warm bread topped with butter and toasted kernels of wheat. The aromas filled the room and the conversation between Onofrio and Serou came to an immediate halt. Simple courtesy would not allow the Egyptian to continue. Instead, Serou hooked Onofrio's arm and turned him away from the arriving guests. In a voice of complete authority barely above a whisper, he ordered the young convict," You will serve breakfast this morning. Get proper instruction from the kitchen immediately. Other guests will be arriving soon. Drop one crumb, spill anything at all and you will dance to the sting of my lash. Now go! I have more important things to attend to." And with that Serou turned to greet his guests with waving hands and a broad smile on his burnished face. Onofrio knew these harsh commands were punishment for his behavior. It was also clear that Serou wanted him close by. Although, it did not escape Onofrio's attention that Serou sent him to the kitchen to witness the morning thievery. He could have been sent to the fields.

The day was barely started. He accepted his punishment with zeal. It was far better to be in the cool comfort of the house than out in the blistering fields. So serve breakfast he would. And spill not a drop. Should he be jovial? No, be happy in his work. Perform it well. But, jovial be not. Courteous? By all means he would be courteous. He had pride and he would hold on to it with the best of his ability in these strange surroundings. He was a servant to no man. Except today, today was the first light of a new horizon. He sensed it. He felt it. He knew it.

Figs and dates cooked in wine over fresh bread and covered with melting butter came on a large silver tray, which he struggled to balance with dignity. Oat, wheat and millet porridge in large steaming bowls with bits of fowl and honey mixed with cream was a familiar breakfast food for him. It was a field hand's treat. It smelled delicious and made him anxious to have some. He bore it all with good grace and made the best of his situation. Something within him rebelled, but he remained calm and performed his work better than he expected of himself. He had never been a servant before and resolved never to be again.

Antonios, the chariot keeper and officer under Clemidius entered the room and went directly to the centurion.

"Sir, it appears we have been raided during the night or we have an open case of theft here. The chariots, supplies and horses have been stolen. Where the chariots and horses were posted last night is an area of military debris now. All else is gone. We searched the immediate vicinity and found nothing." Antonios had been quick to surmise that thieves had scoured the area taking what was most valuable. Roman chariots and weapons brought fancy prices from the local rebels. Quick glances were exchanged between Clemidius and Serou.

Onofrio being free of hand at the moment and in his servant's apron was hardly expected to speak. But he broke from proper procedure to address Antonios with a knowing and sincere smile.

"Sir, all horses and chariots were moved to the round stable beyond the olive grove last night. The horses are in better pasture there. As for your supplies and weapons, I had them stored in the warehouse adjoining the round stable. I had some people clean the chariots and groom the horses as best they could in the dark. I'm sorry they didn't pick up everything, our torches were inadequate and we most likely missed some items since your men came so well equipped. I'll be glad to lead you there so you may see that all is well." It was at that moment that Onofrio caught the eyes of Clemidius and Serou, whose attention was riveted on him. He was surprised to feel their gaze so intent on him that it felt like a physical blow. For a split instant he felt the sting of Serou's lash and the wrath of the centurion. But Antonios rescued him.

"I should have known to ask you first. You were a busy young man last night tending to us, the kitchen staff and now the horses. This fellow is a golden addition to your household," Antonios addressed his comment to Serou.

Serou was now at Onofrio's side with a calm composure but a question gleamed in his hawkeye, like a polished jewel. Then quietly he added, "Perhaps you should lead us to the horses and chariots. I pray for your sake, all is well."

"It will be, sir. It will be." And it was. When the horses, chariots and army gear was found, the group was soon busy sorting out the collection of items all thrown together in one pile. The horses got a token grooming and the chariots as well. It was nonetheless a noticeable effort by a lot of people that were apparently orchestrated by the young convict.

"Serou, I admit being apprehensive about coming here last night. I came as evidence clearly shows, ready for anything. However, now that I've been here, thank you, for all you've done for these field weary men and myself. It's been a night in our own homes. One thing mystifies me. You have no guards posted. The grounds are not patrolled. Yet, there is a sense of security here I cannot quite touch on. I felt no need to sleep armed last night. It felt good." the centurion commented, surveying his men's progress.

"Around this entire compound is a wide canal fenced in by poisonous African thorn bushes, from the outer side. Intruders attempting entry must first fight the thorn bush to get into the canal. Once in the canal, they only have the crocodiles to worry about. The same obstacles apply to anyone leaving this place without my consent. A similar barrier on the inner side of the compound prevents crocodiles from invading the populated grounds. With the exception of a few choice areas of waterfront we use for washing and other needs, there's a few open areas on the outer barrier that wild animals use for drink and some become crocodile food. A solitary guard patrols the entire area with dogs at night. The people here all know not to go out of their homes once the dogs are loose. And there is no need for a heavy force at my gates. I have many legitimate visitors and they consider that force quite adequate."

"About this prisoner, Onofrio? I want to buy him," Clemidius stated openly. "Will you arrange papers so I can have him? At a fair price, of course. I can use a clever fellow like him."

Serou thought about it for less than a second, and before he knew his own thoughts he answered in an unsteady voice, unfamiliar even to himself. "It is with some regret that I must tell you that I arranged to buy him for me. Seems we both have need of a clever fellow like him. But, let me have him for a while. If he does not comply with my expectations, I'll give him to you to take into the field or do with him as you please. What do you think?"

"Seems I have no choice for the time being," said Clemidius, not liking such an obvious lie. He would wait, knowing slave owners are known to tire of new toys quickly. For the time being, Onofrio was a novelty.

Days turned into weeks and Onofrio had the run of the entire compound. He was under the tutorship of Tremiyo, the Chief Steward of the sizeable estate of Serou. Tremiyo was kind, but stern in his teachings of how the house and compound all functioned. He knew every slave by name, their duties and how they came to be here. No tidbit of information escaped his attention, the slaves and home he governed with considerable attention to detail.

It was a new experience to wear clean clothes almost every day. It was a great novelty to bathe on a regular basis. At first he enjoyed being bathed by the same slave that bathed Serou. To be shaved, his hair washed and clipped often were exciting events. To be anointed with fresh smelling oils, to feel clean. To not be concerned with smelling foul were all new experiences. He soon tired of being bathed by another person and was perfectly happy to lounge in comfort when he bathed. He still enjoyed being trimmed, groomed and fresh clothes brought to him. He played with various tools and enjoyed searching through Serou's large collection of books, although he could read very little. His free time and evenings were spent in Serou's extensive craft shops. Potters, weavers, leather and harness shops and a complete bakery adjacent the huge kitchen. There was a receiving station to handle produce and other vital supplies that fed the army of slaves and servants. Choice items were hand selected by Tremiyo for Serou's family and guests. A slaughter house and butcher shop produced many fresh cuts of meat for immediate use and also provided cuts to be dried, smoked or made into various kinds of sausages. The storage smokehouse and the area where chickens and other fowl were penned reminded Onofrio of his early childhood. Each section had a responsible person in charge answerable to Bonaz. Bonaz, the general overseer, was a huge man of massive strength. Gentle, yet firm when he needed to be. No one argued with Bonaz.

Serou's multiple investments in high yield endeavors, his enormous salary, bonuses and uncounted riches left to him by his father and mother made the Master of Public Works a very wealthy man for life.

The shop that held Onofrio's attention more than all else was the carpentry shop. Master craftsmen produced many elaborate pieces of furniture, fixtures and home decorating items, some pieces for Serou's many guest rooms and his family., beds for the slave quarters, storage cabinets for edible goods and countless items of every day necessity. Fine woods were used by men that were not only freed slaves but masters of their craft as well. Some of these men were paid a salary while others were paid by the finished work they produced. Here were many things that gripped Onofrio's interest. The smell of paints, glues, resins, varnishes and shellacs mixed with the keen odor of fresh cut pine, cedars, oak and exotic fragrances he could not identify. All this blended within his senses and sparked his curiosity intensely. Clamps, vises, all sorts of hammers and cutting tools stimulated a strong desire to work with these things. Soon he was working on small projects, overseen by the masters of the shop. Everyone treated him with a certain respect, some of which he earned and because he was a favorite of Master Serou. His dexterity soon won him the right to use carving tools and pick choice scraps of wood for his projects., always receiving advice on how to get the best results from the scraps he used. He learned much about varnishes, stains and finishes.

The thought of being bought by Serou bothered the young convict. Even though he knew he was serving a sentence, nothing more had been said about him being sold. He did not want to belong to anybody. He belonged to himself. Other than these occasional troublesome thoughts, he was happy working in the shops after completing his duties with Tremiyo.

It was not uncommon to go many days without seeing Serou. He often saw the centurion coming or going to the villa by the lake. It was openly said that two young women kept him company most of the time. The centurion's drinking all night, parties and gambling sorties into the city were much talked about. It was also rumored that he often discharged his female companions to spend time with two young boys. Many elaborations adhered to these stories. All of which Onofrio decided only to vaguely listen and not contribute or repeat.

His many projects reached the attention of Serou by slave report. Since Serou had not objected, there was no reason to stop. His sleeping quarters were a short distance behind Serou's home, away from the guard dogs that patrolled the slaves' quarters nightly. The slave that helped clean his rooms and brought him fresh clothes and food Onofrio felt was his chief informer. She was a somewhat attractive, kind-hearted middle age woman, whose name was Camia. A helpless servant simply doing what she was told to do. She was an experienced mid-wife, having brought many compound children into the world. In a motherly fashion she often told him when to eat and lately when to wash the sawdust, sweat and grime from himself. She complimented the pieces he carved, some of which she asked to keep. But Onofrio always told her the wood was not his to give.

One evening Serou and Tremiyo paid him an unexpected visit. Serou slowly surveyed the comfortable quarters Onofrio lived in, leisurely walking around as if looking for something stolen. Tremiyo placed a dinner tray and a decanter of wine on a table Onofrio had built. The table boasted ornately carved legs that supported a beautiful marble top. It was made from a fine grained wood and gleamed almost majestically in the fluttering candle light.

"Master Serou, I wanted you to see this table. It's a masterpiece of woodwork." Serou studiously approached the table and slowly glided an experienced hand on the marble surface and edges of the tabletop.

"Did this splendid piece of marble come from my scrap?" he asked, not accusing but simply curious.

"Sir, the marble is actually five fragments cleverly pieced together to appear as one."

Tremiyo enthusiastically took the dim light and moved his fingers along the almost invisible joints. The marble had been carefully cut along its natural seams then skillfully matched and fitted to appear as an inherent line in the stone. Tremiyo was openly anxious to hear Serou's comments.

After closer inspection, Serou raised an eyebrow at the piece of work. "Very clever," he finally said. "Did you do all this yourself, Onofrio?"

"The shop masters guided my hands with their experience, sir."

"You've learned your lessons well, young man. The legs on the table, did you carve them also?"

"No sir. I found a discarded bed in the scrap pile, whose posts I rescued to become the legs on this table. I then embellished the curves and swirls to better exhibit the quality of the old wood. By letting some of the stains sink into the crevasses the high and low points show up more dramatically, don't you think?" asked the young convict, anxious to hear a favorable response.

Serou looked on without comment or expression, seemingly deep in thought.

Tremiyo failed to get the response he wanted from the Egyptian, adding in an unusual apologetic tone, "The table if not worthy of your keen taste and appreciation, sir, I simply wanted you to see the efforts of this novice craftsman."

"I knew he had talent, that's why he's here." Serou's voice was unusually cold and seemed to grope for words. "I lost a wager to the centurion and you are the prize he has wrested from me. You will move your things to the slave quarters at the villa by the lake, sometime soon. Don't make the centurion happy by appearing anxious to leave here. Make him wait as long as possible, within reason. It is evident you are content with your working conditions and living quarters." Onofrio felt an icy hand grip his heart. It finally came. The dread of being sold was showing its ugly head. He felt betrayed. He shook inside. With all the power within him, he managed a weak smile.

"How long will I have to serve the centurion, sir? Or have I been lost to him permanently?" Without prior knowledge of this Tremiyo was shocked. He stood motionless, his mouth agape unable to speak.

"Enjoy your dinner," Serou smiled. "I shall win you back. You are only temporarily in his keep. And don't hurry to change quarters. I like knowing you're here." Serou had a strange gleam in his eyes, it was in fact the plan to win Onofrio back and keep him, permanently. It did Onofrio good to feel Serou's hand on his shoulder followed by a pat or two."Don't worry," Serou added removing his hand swiftly as though it was not proper. The fleeting sign of affection went deep into the young man's senses as a needed balm. He had not fully digested what he heard. He was only keen of being sloughed off like a faulty coin or a used-up old horse.

Serou made a genuine effort to ease the young man's anxiety. "I only lost you in Jerusalem, Onofrio. You are still a prisoner and I am responsible for your whereabouts and safety. If the centurion gets transferred out or goes into battle, you will remain here. Besides the experience may do you some good." Tremiyo reserved all comments, making his objection obvious by his silent presence.

Clemidius palmed a set of winning cards and held them in his outer robe then kept mental track of the cards played. In a carefully chosen moment he switched his winning collection for the dead hand that fell to him. And so it was that he won Onofrio. Never giving the method used a second thought, it was simply the thing that men did to other men. His philosophy was that winning took first place. The road to victory was secondary. As for honor? Honor had a price and could be bought with gold. With enough gold, a man could buy all the honor he wanted and then more. Serou was a keen player, having chanced his luck with some of the best gamblers in the area. The Egyptian knew when the centurion cheated and was firsthand witness to the centurion's sense of honor. His honesty was no longer a debatable issue.

At last Onofrio was alone and the dinner that smelled so delicious moments ago, no longer held appeal. He wondered what the centurion wanted with him. He envisioned himself on the battlefield, picking through cadavers for the gold and valuables the centurion wanted. He felt sick at his stomach. He drank a small cup of wine. It didn't help. He knew he could not sleep, so he decided to wash the sweat of the day from his body, hoping it would make him feel better. Should he bathe in his new quarters? It wouldn't matter. There was the lake. Maybe he could drown there. Maybe Serou would win him back next week. He bathed and put on fresh sun-dried clothes. Then went for a walk on a secluded garden path he knew, away from the main house and other quarters. This was a section of garden seldom used. He often meditated and enjoyed his dreams of going home here. He had almost decided to walk to the villa and let the centurion know how soon he would be moving over. He then noticed two figures in the moonlight behind him. He stopped to see who they were. Not afraid, just curious and cautious. The figures were dark and shadowy. They shuffled slowly on the graveled path, seeming to float rather than walk. He searched himself for a weapon. He had none. He looked for a fallen branch. There were none. Could it be someone the centurion sent to collect him? It most likely was. Nobody used this garden path. A gauzy grey cloud momentarily obscured the otherwise bright moon as the shadowy figures continued to approach.

Chapter Four

A Past Revisited

The familiar voice of Tremiyo called out. Instantly Onofrio breathed a sigh of relief.

"Onofrio, wait for us, we'll walk with you." The old man had a companion and Onofrio was in no mood for conversation. He wanted to be alone. Confronted by Tremiyo and his companion, the young convict acknowledged them out of courtesy and planned to move on. He had to rearrange his life and he could best do that alone. Tremiyo laid an arm over Onofrio's shoulder as he often did. Before Onofrio could shake it off, the old man spoke softly, "I know how you feel. I have been sold off three times. I've been here fifteen years. It is my home now. Serou is a good master. He will keep his word and find a way to get you back. You shouldn't worry. After all, the villa here is far better than the dungeons. Listen, the centurion will either go on campaign or lose you back to Serou. Whichever happens, you will still be here. So, why worry? Make the best of it and the best will come from it." Tremiyo concluded with conviction.

Onofrio felt a spark of hope in his heart. He went from deep grief to inner jubilation in one breath. The old man was right.

"Three times! You've been sold off three times?" Onofrio was incredulous. "How did you survive it?"

"With God's help, faith and a lot of patience," the old man answered in earnest.

"Amen." Tremiyo's companion added without further comment. A head cover and body length cape of a russet, shiny material concealed any identity. They walked a short distance in silence. Onofrio was stirring the old man's revelation in his head. Tremiyo was right. Anything was better than the dungeons for three years. They came to an open circular area with stone benches and a fountain bubbling into a clear brook that disappeared into the bushes not far away. In the center of the park-like enclosure was a round garden house. A circular high peaked roof topped the six columns that held it up. It was quiet and private. It was a place for lovers. The fountain provided a peaceful rhythm to the serenity of the spot. The moon shone down with no regard to anything that fell into its light. It was daytime in a dim and subtle fashion. It was peace on earth. From the darkness echoed the songs of night singing birds.

After a long silence appreciating the serenity and glowing beauty of the place, Onofrio finally spoke. "Tremiyo, tell me how you came to be in bondage and is there any hope of you ever being free?" The old man's head bowed a bit from admiring the moon. He thought for a long moment as if searching for the words, and finally spoke, "I killed two men and my judges sold me to a slave ship on which I served two years, before I was traded to a rich merchant in Macedonia and Serou bought me."

"I cannot see you as a killer." Onofrio injected, unbelieving what he heard.

"There were valid reasons; you are too young to understand."

"I could not make myself kill another man. Killing two is even harder to understand." Onofrio was struggling to see the mild mannered kitchen master as a hardened killer.

Tremiyo took a deep sigh, cleared his throat and put his arm around the shrouded figure beside him. "I had an inn some three hundred strata from here. My wife, young son and baby daughter lived over the inn. We served food and drink, stabled and fed animals, also rented rooms to merchants and travelers. We had a good business from which we would never get rich, but it made us a comfortable living. I was very much in love with my wife and I was the happiest man in the world. I labored every day, but there was no weariness from my work. There was only the unity my labor won within my home. My children were cared for. My wife loved me and was happy with our lives. She labored with me every day. Together we forged our home and happiness therein." Tremiyo paused again and it was clear in the moonlight that the old man was crying.

Onofrio had been sitting on the grass in front of the old man and stood up to pat Tremiyo on the shoulder. "You need not go on, if it causes you grief. I'm sorry I asked."

"It's alright; it all comes back in my dreams. It is best I speak of it now and perhaps tonight I can rest from it." From his robe, the old man produced a wine skin and took a sizeable swallow. He shared the skin with Onofrio and they drank symbolically, like striking a secret pact.

"One night three men came to my inn around midnight. They asked for food and drink and wanted their horses fed and sheltered. It was obvious they had much to drink and smelled foul. They asked for a room and beds to sleep on and appeared not to have money to pay for our services. I told them that at this late hour it was customary to pay in advance. I hoped the tactic would make them leave.

'Don't worry Innkeeper; we have gold to pay you with. Now get us food and drink.' The two people we had working for us had been discharged for the day. My wife came down to help me when she heard guests downstairs. She was very beautiful and came here with her parents from Greece. Her name was Sintia and had long golden hair which she often wore in braids and pinned them on top of her head. I can still remember her saying,

'My dear husband, be not so tart with late night guests. Please forgive, my husband. It has been a long day and he is tired. There is some lamb on a spit, plenty of lentils and hot bread.'

From the cupboard on the back wall, she brought a pitcher of wine and put it before them with cups from which to drink. 'We will bring you food in a few moments. While you eat we will tend to your animals and make ready a place for you to sleep. We will provide for your comfort as best we can.' She told them this in her usual polite manner.

The older man appeared to be their leader. He was foul and out spoken. 'You can be my comfort the rest of my life.' And he reached out for her with an awkward grab.

She was swift and had her wits about her all the time. "Sir, I am a happily married woman. And only strive to make your stay as pleasant as possible. However, I have a widowed great aunt. I can speak to her about you. She is a grand and lovely lady with her own home and raises donkeys to sell from time to time. She's quite well off, in fact. You could be happy there. And never be lonesome.'

We put food before them and went to see about their animals and prepare the only room we had available. When we returned, the older man was joyful and over friendly. He wanted to pay for our services now, before he got more tired. He had a handful of coins. I quoted him a figure and he counted out the money on the table. I told him about their animals and where they could sleep.

When we entered our quarters, I could smell their stench. Our rooms had been searched. Small coins lay all about. Our belongings scattered throughout. A trail of lesser coins led to our son's bed. He was sound asleep and in his tiny hand was a heap of coins. I knew in my heart that our son had not done this. I knew from the odor in the room and the fact that our son was not a thief. Besides, the boy knew where we kept the money. I often gave him coins to put in our safe place. He had no reason to ransack. From the look on her face, Sintia's thoughts were equal to mine. Sintia started picking up money from the floor. I was in a rage, quandering over what to do. Sintia came to me with a handful of coins. 'They took all of value and left the lesser coins,' she told me trembling and crying. We didn't have long to wait.

All three men were at our door, their presence threatening. The chief spoke first. 'I demand our money back,' he said with his arms crossed and his hand griping the handle of a long knife at his waist. Sintia was shocked. She came behind me and I was unarmed.

In as calm a fashion as I could, I spoke directly to their chief. My heart fluttered but I did not dare show them my fear. 'You've been in our quarters. Stole our money, paid for our services with it and now you want it back. What manner of man, are you?'

My question incensed him and he looked at me with bloodshot eyes filled with hate. 'You accuse me of being a thief? We're not thieves!' With a wave of his arm one of the men went to our son and blatantly pointed at the sleeping child. 'There's your thief,' he announced for all to hear. 'Seems you run an untidy house, Innkeeper. You have an insulting wife and a thief for a son,' their chief seemed proud to announce.

'My wife never insulted you and my son is not a thief. You are the only thief here. While we saw to your animals and your quarters, you came up here and stole our money. The boy did nothing but sleep.'

'Your wife said I would be happy among asses. I am insulted and I want our money back. We refuse to stay in such a place. Now, are you going to give us our money back? Or do we have to take it from you?' Sintia pointed to my purse on the table by the door. 'There!' she said. 'There is the money you paid us. Take it and leave us in peace. You could have the decency to pay for what you ate and drank. That is a rightful debt.'

'You see, Innkeeper, you have an insulting wife.' Sintia was behind me again. 'She assumes I do not know what is right and accuses me of being indecent,' he retorted with a sinister mask for a face.

'Take the money and be gone with you.'

I had resolved to call the evening a bad experience and let it go at that. Our peace and welfare were far more valuable than a handful of coins.

'No,' the thief insisted. 'I want to hear her apologize for saying that I would be happy among asses.' I was truly surprised at the accusation.

'She never said such a thing in that manner,' I defended Sintia, with a rage smoldering within me. 'I'm not easily fooled, innkeeper. She lied saying she had an old aunt that raises asses and I would be happy among them,' the thief continued.

'But, it's true. I do have an aunt that raises and sells donkeys. I only meant that a strong man such as yourself and a lovely lady such as her could be happy together,' Sintia defended sincerely.

The chief looked over his shoulder to his companions. 'What did I tell you?' he sneered. 'I told you she laid eyes of desire on me.'

'Sir,' Sintia said her pride the only source of strength. 'I only noticed how much you needed to bathe. After I thought of it, I remembered our hired help was not around to fetch water for you. So, I didn't mention it.'

'You need not lie, I can see in your eyes that you desire a man such as I. Come, go with me, I will show you the wonders of the world.' As he spoke, he gestured Sintia to go to him.

The rage within me broke loose. I struck at him with all the strength within me. He knew when to expect the blow and was prepared for it. He fended off the blow smartly, but left his waist exposed. In a flash I had the knife he carried well in my grip. I saw one of them close the door behind him.

'Take the purse from the table and leave now. This has gone far enough.' I was deeply concerned about my family's safety. 'You leave this place now and go in peace. Nothing more will come of it. We've had a misunderstanding. Let it go at that.'

'I think not, Innkeeper.' His arms spread open gesturing his men to surround me. Sintia had a pottery jar ready to throw at whatever moved. He made a mocking move at me and I slashed at him with his knife, just barely missing him. There was a neat slice on the sash around his waist. In the ensuing fight I managed to cut him on the forearm. I was no match for three men whose business it is to fight. Soon they overwhelmed me. While one held me from behind, I saw the hand club coming. It struck the side of my head very hard and the lights went out. When I came around a few hours later, it was to the cry of our baby daughter. My son and Sintia were gone. So were the men, their animals and gear. I searched the house and grounds in tormented anguish and in vain. I was covered in dry blood from the blow to my head. And I reeled when I tried to walk. It was close to dawn when our hired help arrived. They alone believed me. The authorities noted that my wife had run off with another man. Nothing serious, it happens all the time. As for the missing boy, his mother simply took him with her. And the robbery? There was only my word to say there was money missing. Runaway wives with children need money. It was all dismissed as a family argument. It would settle itself. I took our daughter to Sintia's parents and told them what happened.

I then started asking questions about the three men. After a few days and a lot of questions, I had their names and where they came from, also where they may be going. I armed myself fully and left the hired help to manage the inn. I went in search of my tormentors and my family. They were an elusive bunch. I spent many nights searching inns, taverns and dens of iniquity for them. Always missing them by days and sometimes by a few hours. After weeks of pursuit, I tracked them to their camp in the desert. I could see from my hiding place that Sintia and my son were not with them. I prayed to God that Sintia had escaped them and was now safely home with our son. I convinced myself of exactly that, as I waited for them to fall asleep. When I felt sure they were in deep slumber, I unhobbled their animals and led them away, then released them. With the stealth of a snake in the darkness, I rounded up their weapons and buried them in the sand. I took their boots and water. I took their food and anything they could use as a weapon. Knowing that my wits were a better ally than my ability to fight three men, silently I tied their ankles with a knot that would only tighten more with every pull. There was murder in my heart and it beat furiously within me. I decided to reduce the opposition even more. Walking upright, I shot the first man in the throat with a strong bow. This one may get up, but he wouldn't live long. I knew it. I heard the arrow pierce the sand beyond him. The gurgled scream woke the others. By that time I had a lance buried deep in the stomach of their chief. Even in the darkness, I saw his eyes shine in terror when he felt the lance. He looked at me, he recognized me and his horror grew as he tried to pull the lance from himself. He stepped forward with his arms reaching for me and I pushed the lance further, until I knew he was punctured clear through. I held the second lance ready for the third man. The hobbles stopped him in his tracks and he knelt with his hands raised in submission. He looked at me in total shock, shaking his head. Their chief was making an effort to remove the lance when I struck him with the scimitar across the neck. It is absolutely terrible to remember his head flying off his shoulders to roll in the sand like a large ball of hair. The mouth and eyes wide open in horror. His body continued to walk a few paces towards me then fell to jerk and shudder for a while. Blood rushed from his neck like a scarlet fountain. The third man saw all this and was in sheer panic. He knew he was next. The more he pulled on my hobbles, the tighter they got. He searched himself for a weapon, he had none. With the bloody scimitar, I came to him and told him to renew the campfire.

'But, I can't walk,' he pleaded weakly.

'Then crawl or die where you are.'

I felt no remorse. The revulsion of seeing a man gurgling for his life and the other beheaded, past quickly in my haste to know about Sintia and my son. This man had the answer and I wanted that answer. It was when the man spoke that I realized how drunk he was. I had gotten lucky because they were all drunk beyond reason or control. He soon had faggots blazing while I stood behind him the whole time. Somehow he knew to keep his back to me and be submissive.

'Sir, could I have something to drink?' his voice quavering.

'I don't have anything for you to drink.' I came around the campfire to see his face. For a horrible instant my conscious wanted to be sure I had found the right men. The look on his face assured me.

'The innkeeper! You're the innkeeper. How did you find us? We left no trail.'

'You left your foul stench behind and it was enough to find you. Where are my wife and son?'

'If I tell you, will you spare my life?' The thief was gaining sobriety. He was very afraid of me now. He knew it and I knew it.

'I don't know. Perhaps. In any event I intend to cut off your fingers one at a time then watch you bleed. You won't die, but you'll hurt a lot. Or I can make it quick and be done with it. If my wife is not with you, she is looking for a way home and she will bring my son.'

'You're too clever for an innkeeper,' he snorted back with a sneer.

'I was not always an innkeeper. I've known battle and scum like you. Now get ready to lose your first finger.' I wanted to prolong pain. I did not thirst for death just then. I wanted to ration out as much agony as I had suffered. The death of the other two men came too easy. They had not satisfied my driving hunger for revenge. 'Is it true, that if a limb is cut off a living body with a hot blade, the wound will not bleed as much? Have you ever heard that?' I continued. I enjoyed his look of helplessness. 'You will live a long time. You'll hurt and bleed from the wound, but you will take long to die.'

'Your son has been sold into slavery," he slobbered in panic. 'He is at this moment on a ship bound for Athens, or Italia or up the Nile. I do not know for certain. It was not my business to know.'

For an instant, I wanted to wield the sword at his face. It was all I could do not to. I had to know about Sintia. The shock hit my heart like a boulder of ice. Something with an awful taste, I cannot describe rose in my throat. Whatever it was, gagged me fiercely and forced me to vomit. Putrid phlegm with a terrible odor spewed from my throat. I finally gained control of myself through tremendous effort. I drank some wine from my tunic flask and rinsed the awful taste from my mouth. I was torn and the thief wore a contented look on his face. He knew how much his words injured me and took pleasure from it. It was all I could do not to swing the scimitar at him. With God-granted calmness, I looked at him and slipped the scimitar into the fire for him to see, without saying a word.

'I've decided to cut off a whole limb at a time. First will come one of your feet. You can stick the stub in the sand to help stop the bleeding. I've seen brave men do that in battle. You can do the same.' With that I pulled one of his legs out from under him and when he fell back, I swung the sword with all my strength. He screamed and I stopped the blade at the skin of his ankle. The red-hot blade singed his flesh. He smelled it and felt the burn.

'You smell better while you're cooking,' I said. I grabbed his beard tight in my hand. 'You have one more chance to tell me where my wife and son are. If I find them safe, you will live.'

His face was total terror. And I enjoyed it because he would never leave that camp alive. I had decided to leave him alive for the buzzards.

'It is absolutely true. Your son was sold by the headless one over there to an outbound ship. I do not know where the ship was going and he didn't bring very much, so it won't take very much to buy him back.'

'What about my wife?'

'The only way I will tell you is if you give me your solemn oath to spare my life. I too have a wife and son awaiting my return. If you kill me now, you will never know anything about your wife and son.'

I walked around the fire for a moment. 'You stay here,' I told him. 'If you make an effort to escape you forfeit our agreement. I will fetch us something to drink. We will then talk like two intelligent men faced with a serious problem. Be calm, you're safe in my word. I won't kill you.' I brought wine, bread and meat. I ate a cold meal with my wine and he only drank.

'Where was my son sold?" I calmly asked, not wanting to sound anxious while my heart wept blood.

'There was a caravan of precious goods heading for the coast. He, the headless one, had done business with the caravan leader, Amin Hassan. The boy was very scared, but he was obedient to instruction. This caught the attention of the caravan chief and he offered to buy the boy on the spot. We were getting low on money, so he got sold.'

'Where was my wife through all this? Had she tried to escape?'

'You will not want to hear what I have to tell you, Innkeeper. I must first know that you will keep your word and not break your promise. I fell into bad company and never did anything to harm the boy or your wife. The worst thing I do is drink too much.'

'I'll keep my word. I solemnly swear. I will not kill you. Now tell me about Sintia.' All the while, I fought a violent urge to destroy this man.

'He killed her.'"And he nodded towards the headless carcass. 'The first night out. She fought like a wild cat. Although he beat her without mercy, she managed to sting him several times with his own knife. He finally kicked her out of camp with the boy, knowing, she would not run with the boy into the desert without food and water at night. He planned to starve them both until she submitted. During the night, he stole his way back to her to get what he wanted. In the morning, she was dead. He claimed it was a shame to die for nothing and had scratches on his face and one eye shut. We buried her and nothing more was said. The boy had seen it all. He grew fearfully silent and far more obedient. He was steadily crying.'

'Where is she buried?' I asked, taking deep breaths to keep myself from screaming. The pain in my soul was tearing me apart. My mind could not accept her death. Sintia had to be alive, somehow.

'You ask too much of me, Innkeeper. I've been drunk for two years. She's out there, in the desert somewhere. I have no idea where. I could not find her if you gave me gold to drink. You followed our trail here, follow it back. Maybe you'll find her. But she's still dead and buried. There's nothing you can do about it. Accept it. It's a fact. Do you have anything else to drink? We need to bury these bodies. We can't just leave them for the jackals and the buzzards.'

The name Amin Hassan hit me like a bolt of light. A trader and caravan chief called Amin Hassan stayed at my inn several times. I could find him. I no longer needed the thief. I bound his hands and feet and left him there to witness the animals feasting on his companions then on him. It would prolong the agony. I kept my word. I did not kill him. I had no time to dig graves. I gathered everything of value and useful to my journey. I would first go to the coast. I would find the ship the trader was on and eventually find Amin Hassan and my son. There was the possibility that the thief lied and Sintia may be with the boy. She would ask to be sold with her son. She would not part from our boy. I never thought anybody would rescue the thief. However, he survived his ordeal and lived long enough to make a final statement. He lied all the way to his grave. He even said Sintia had gone with them of her own free will and allowed all three of them to enjoy her body. I could not prove my son was kidnapped or my wife's refusal to go with them. Although I spent my entire fortune on defense, the word of a dying man convicted me.

Almost fifteen years ago, Serou bought me in Macedonia to be his cook. Soon I was kitchen master. When I felt secure in my position, I asked Serou for an audience, which he granted the following evening. I left out no detail of my ordeal and how I came to be here. He was reluctant to grant my request. In his mind, I was still a roadside bandit and murderer. I'm sure he had someone verify my story. You see Onofrio, the only thing I had in the entire world was my daughter Senobia, whom I left with my wife's parents. In a few days, Serou arranged for me to bring my daughter here. He sent a strong-arm man along with me. He wanted to make sure I came back. He gave me clothes, money and advice.

'Give what you think is fair to your in-laws for the care of your daughter. Be a slave in their eyes, if you think it best. But be well dressed and appear to prosper in your new position. It will make it easier for you. The girl's grandparents would not let you have her, if they think she too would be a slave. The strong-arm guard will do your bidding. His instructions are to help you in your quest and to keep you from running off. So he will watch you closely. Your papers give you leave to travel only in the areas you mentioned. Outside of that vicinity, you're a runaway slave. The authorities will return you and I will sell you to a sea captain or a Roman ship.'

I discovered how sly Serou really is. To keep me from running away, he helped me bring my only family with me so I would stay and serve his house," Tremiyo concluded taking a deep sigh.

Onofrio finally had an opportunity to speak. "Your daughter is here, in the compound? I never knew that." It was only then that the old man realized he had not introduced his hooded companion. "We've grown very accustomed to walking and talking to ourselves," he said in apology. "I assumed you knew about Senobia." He gingerly eased back the hood from his companion. "This is my daughter, Senobia."

The pale moonlight grew brighter by the glow on the face of an angel. Senobia's tarnished bronze hair cascaded to her shoulders in soft flowing strands. Her large eyes sparkled and her smile shone brightly before a background of dimly lit shadows. She had high cheek bones and appeared Grecian. Her skin was very light in color and seemed supple and warm. She was absolutely beautiful.

"I already know who you are," she said in a young, sweet voice. "My father speaks of you often. He says you are a hard worker and you are not a thief." Her graceful hand reached out to touch Onofrio. It was a light pat on his forearm and a totally harmless, but friendly gesture. The touch was warm and wonderful. The spot on his forearm seemed to glow. He felt an electrical charge pulsate through his whole body. And he knew not what to do or say. He looked into her eyes and they smiled at him. He looked at Tremiyo only to see the old man innocently smiling at the moon or counting stars.

"But, I am. I stole two smoked fish and a honeycomb, for which I was given a three year sentence. I stole them because I was out of work and hungry. I've been ashamed of it ever since. The good thing is that I've had work to do every day since. And I'll be free in the near future," Onofrio jetted enthusiastically. For reasons unknown to him now, he wanted to make a good impression on the daughter of Tremiyo. He didn't know how to acknowledge the sense of joy he felt.

A few hours were happily spent in conversations pertaining to their lives. Onofrio indulged in idyllic images of his childhood. Tremiyo was content to be where he was. He wished for the sound of youngsters playing in his own courtyard. He felt he had been denied the activities of small children. He longed for grandchildren and was not shy to let Senobia know it. Senobia in a reserved fashion reminded her father of his promise. "You promised to give me the liberty of choosing a man I felt in my heart would be the right man for my life. My dear father," she continued, "you've made me the jewel in your life. It will be difficult to find a male jewel that you will accept. I am the one left with the task of finding my lifemate and a rightful happiness for your old age. I know for a fact that not just any brood of brats will make you happy. I've seen how you avoid children that you think are brats." And she made a funny face to mimic his refusal to recognize unruly children. Tremiyo's openly false denial only won his daughter's open laughter. A joyous, youthful laugher that soon had her male companions in equally joy-filled chuckles.

The mystery of the evening remained with Onofrio, not remembering how he came to be here. The time of his childhood up to a point was very clear. Recollections of the life with his parents were vivid and he talked of it with genuine affection. He felt reasonably certain that his ability to work with the many tools he was now using stemmed from those days on the farm with his father. Although he was too young to know exactly where that farm and home actually were. He suspected Iberia, maybe even Italia or Greece. Probably Greece. Then there was the blank area of his memory. The memory of the last five or six years seemed clear enough. The present came into the conversation with Tremiyo's concern for his many projects, which he would soon have to leave behind. Tremiyo promised to have Senobia look after his treasures while he was in service to the centurion. Carefully avoiding comment on his plans to go search for his home.

They finally decided to walk back to their quarters since the moon was settling over the trees and the once illuminated park was now gloomy and awash with many forbidding shadows. Tremiyo casually motioned for Senobia to walk between Onofrio and himself. The couple fleetingly brushed against each other as they walked causing sparks to warm their souls. Tremiyo stopped twice to straighten his robe and tie his sandals, while the couple faced each other groping for things to say. It was an opportunity for their eyes to explore each other in the failing moonlight and neither one lost the chance.

"I'll come to your quarters tomorrow and collect your treasures for safe keeping," Senobia quietly said, exploring his shadowed features closely. "I have just the place in my rooms to store them for you," she added as she reached out for his hand.

And Onofrio found reason to help Tremiyo get up from tying his sandal. He was afraid of offending the old man.

Senobia smiled and softly said, "That old man is not near as helpless as you think."

In the next few days, Onofrio moved to the slave quarters behind the villa. His small windowless room was far less inviting than his previous accommodations. He shared a bath with other slaves and preferred the lake in which to bathe. He felt at home there. The villa became an armed camp with weapons, armor and military supplies heaped in various places. Riding gear and a chariot under repair were unruly dumped in a corner of the once elegant courtyard. Maps, field observations in scrolls, military orders in disarray all over a once handsome family table now serving as the centurion's command center. The disorder annoyed Onofrio. But the centurion left specific orders not to disturb his desk other than to remove leftover food and drink. All else he wanted left as is. It seemed to the young man that the villa was suffering the damage of barbarous men far more at home around a campfire. Already there was visible damage from lances aimed at shields crudely hanging on the walls. The entire place, although somewhat clean, had a foul odor hanging in the air. Onofrio with some reluctance accepted what he saw and resolved to live through this also. He would serve the centurion, he would return to Serou, he would win his freedom and he would find his way home. One day at a time.

CHAPTER FIVE

RUMORS OF THE NAZARENE

*For Herod had sent and seized John, and bound him
in prison for the sake of Herodias, his brother Philip's wife;
because he had married her. For John said to Herod, "It is not
lawful for you to have your brother's wife." Mark 6:17-18*

And so it came to pass that out of spite, feminine revenge or a simple drunken whim, the price of John the Baptist's head was a single dance. Salome, the niece and stepdaughter of the fox, Herod Antipas was a vision of masculine desire. And Herod admired her much. It was at a birthday celebration of Herod that he asked Salome to dance for him. Offering her anything she wanted, including half his kingdom if she would only dance for him. A king cannot go back on his word, especially before a large audience. On her mother's prompting, she asked for the head of John the Baptist served on a platter. After considerable debate and sobering regret he granted the young temptress, her mother's wish. It was widely said that Herodias conspired to have John destroyed because she could not gain his attention. His devotion to God and his work were his only love. Add to the rejection, the fact that John the Baptist had the audacity to publically reprimand the puppet king for putting away his wife to marry Herodias.

Lifting up his eyes, then, and seeing that a multitude was coming to him, Jesus said to Philip, "How are we to buy bread, so that these people may eat?" This he said to test him, for he himself knew what he would do.

One of his disciples, Andrew, Simon Peter's brother, said to him, "There is a lad here who has five barley loaves and two fish; but what are they among so many?"
                                                                          John 6:5-6, 8-9

For all the blind to see, Jesus fed the five thousand. They came from Bethsaida and from Capernaum and from all places in between to hear Jesus teach. As the sun began to make its exit from the sky, a young boy was seen with a small basket in which he had two fish and five loaves of fresh baked barley bread. One of the disciples went to the lad and after a few words took the basket and gave it to Jesus. He looked to the heavens and soon thereafter started to pass out fish and loaves of barley to the multitude. Many people came back again and again and each time their baskets were filled. His followers among them and they also helped to distribute food to so many. For the miracle was just as great to them as it was to the vast crowds. To see such abundance when moments ago they were destitute was to say the least, disarming.

And when evening came, the boat was out on the sea, and he was alone on the land. And he saw that they were making headway painfully, for the wind was against them. And about the fourth watch of the night he came to them, walking on the sea.   *Mark 6:47-48*

Such were the miracles the local newscasters vocalized to the long distance traveler, passer-by and next door neighbor. The deeds and words of Jesus went out in all directions spreading like fire in a forest, from tree to tree and from soul to soul. Men of many languages and individual beliefs came from numerous distant kingdoms to hear him speak. The Jewish council at every opportunity had scribes present to record the words that fell from his mouth. These records would prove useful at a later time.

All this is not to say that everybody heard of Jesus. There were an equal or larger number of people that lived in those days without ever hearing or paying attention to the name or teachings of Jesus. It seems hard to grasp but there were countless people deeply involved in other religions, sects and beliefs that went on with their lives without the slightest concern for the carpenter from Nazareth. This man Jesus had to be a great trickster with an armload of accomplices to successfully do some of the things he did. The world had much business to conduct and many lives went untouched by him. To the Jewish council, he was a troublesome individual that was effectively making them look bad. They chose to let him speak hoping he would eventually accomplish his own demise with the words he spoke. As for miracles, each one had a logical explanation and their mystery would solve itself in time.

During that time many other gods and deities existed, revered and held in the uppermost levels of faith and adoration. The god Dionysus was said to prevail in a wide area of the Mediterranean and gained people's favor somewhat by force. It is written that Zeus came to earth and fathered many sons. Rome itself was crammed full of gods enough to spread around to all.

And so it is possible that a select group would simply shy away from a humble carpenter from Nazareth to pursue their established faith.

Onofrio was soon carrying messages to Serou and back again regarding the many repair and refortification needs of the city. Sometime during all this, Onofrio noticed other men and sometimes women wearing slave bracelets like his own. Any person having removed such bracelets without written authority was doomed to severe punishment. The bracelet Clemidius made him wear was loose and did not impair his movements. However, just knowing it was there was sufficient discomfort for one so used to absolute freedom of movement.

Evenings were regularly spent in the company of soldiers and officers. It became normal for discussions or games to run into midnight and after. The guests at the villa were of infinite variety, ranging from city officials to loose women, horse traders, politicians and street dwellers with information to sell. It was a taxing time for the young man whose morals were unaccustomed to such blatant doses of Roman behavior.

His newest interest arrived at his attention without being announced. He suddenly discovered that he was able to decipher various words and symbols written on orders or scrolls. He did not fully understand them all, but he could read in a limited fashion. The centurion took notice of this, and knowing full well that it would increase the value of the slave, took time to explain and after a fashion taught Onofrio to read Roman text and numerals. The spark to learn was quick to ignite in the mind of the young man from parts unknown. His eagerness to learn more urged him to unscramble everything written that he encountered. Street signs, shop names and addresses became his daily quest. Soon he was making comparisons and associating Roman images to the graceful arabesques of the local languages. From the soldiers, officers and guests frequently at the villa he learned many phrases and ideas new to the mind of one accustomed to the rough language and mindset of field hands and common laborers. New horizons opened up before his eyes, as he understood more of what he could read. It became an adventure like no other.

On an unusual afternoon when the centurion wanted only his own company he dismissed Onofrio with instructions to stay close to the villa. "In fact," the centurion emphasized, "there's a new set of rules or regulations pertaining to the taxation of herd animals. Read it. See what you make of it and let me know. I intend to read it myself later. Your views will acquaint me with it in advance. I am weary. I want to bathe in leisure, lounge, drink in solitude and relax. Send someone with fresh robes and sweet smelling oils. I also want someone to trim my hair and beard. Have someone bring fresh fish and garden vegetables for my dinner tonight. I'm tired of burned meat and stale bread. I posted guards to discharge any would be visitors I don't want to see." Then he looked at Onofrio with a questioning gesture of his hands. "Do you think this place smells like sweat, old leather and horse manure?" And he walked around a little bit, sniffing the air.

Onofrio was obliged to answer casually, "Not very much today, sir. The odor is mostly when the breeze stops in the afternoon." Having done as requested Onofrio retired to his solitary room, which he chose to call "the trap" since it had no windows and one small door.

Having made himself comfortable in the company of a full bottle of wine and reading the set of rules, he came to the commonly seen Roman numeral II. He knew it meant two. A deeper meaning struck his head like a hard slap and he felt a numbing cold in his chest. Two is synonymous to second, he realized. In his homeland the word second was Segundo. His full name was Onofrio Segundo. He was named after his father. He was Onofrio the second. He cheered a mixed thrill in the discovery. He remembered what he was called as a child in his homeland. But exactly where was his homeland? He read and rested, sober and not in great comfort.

Serou was not indifferent to what the young man was learning and the lack-luster company around him. He saw the changes in Onofrio's walk, his demeanor and colorful language he adopted. Serou was also concerned with Onofrio's acquired taste for wine in abundance. Such was the topic of discussion with Tremiyo in Serou's private garden, a sanctuary of solace and meditation for the wealthy Egyptian.

"You promised to win him back," Tremiyo reminded with respectful hesitation. "He's been around thugs and misfits entirely too long. He will never be the same as before after this exposure." Tremiyo stated openly concerned.

"That is partly what annoys me. The centurion has deliberately avoided us playing a new game. It seems Clemidius wants to keep the young man permanently. I do not want to press for the boy's release for fear of appearing to renege on my word. However, it will soon be time to rectify that situation. The time is near to deal from a new deck. I'll have to implement some of the ploys and tricks I've learned from the not so honorable centurion." Serou then turned the conversation to other areas of concern having to do with his home and general condition of the people for which he was responsible.

CHAPTER SIX

THE SCHOOLING OF ONOFRIO

I t was early evening and Onofrio found himself bored from inactivity. Alone in one of the many balconies, he collected dishes and miscellaneous objects scattered about. Dishes and related items he returned to the kitchen. All else he dumped into a large shallow bowl in the center of the centurion's desk, the safest place in the villa. Among the many things he found was a large scarab on an elaborate gold chain with a clear faintly blue diamond the size of a thumbnail on its back. He picked up the item examined it and checked the clasp. It was weak and worn and he knew the piece belonged to Serou. Had he lost it again due to the weak clasp, dice or cards? He thought about taking it to Serou then decided against it. Instead he took the precious bug and slipped it inside a damaged arrow quiver hanging high up in the corner of the room collecting dust. What if somebody asked for it? He would decide what to do then. Until that time Serou's property was safe. And he would watch the quiver very closely.

Being allowed to roam the compound at will, he chose to go visit his friend Tremiyo and perhaps find something to do in the workshops. He was not surprised to find young people along the trail, walking and talking, hand in hand. A few couples, in amorous closeness, whispered softly within the circle of their arms. Finally he reached the secret overlap in the hedges leading to the separate section in the garden where Tremiyo and his daughter, Senobia took evening walks. He expected to find them seated where they chatted once before. His pace hastened, inspired by hope and even an unrecognizable sense of longing. They were nowhere along the labyrinth of hedges and exotic plants. The garden enclosure Tremiyo called "Wisher's Paradise" was cold, empty and appeared lonely. The moon was still far from its summit and glorified the area with its mellow golden light. He wished they would materialize from the shadows and suffered silent disappointment when they didn't. Even in the pleasant warmth of the early evening he felt uncomfortable and cold in their absence.

The wood shops offered no solace. He saw a few men he knew working on a project. As he visited with them he managed to ask about Tremiyo.

The men looked at each other hearing the inquiry and went silent, busy with their project. His question visibly ignored, Onofrio repeated his question. This time the men busied themselves with sweeping off their work area as if finishing their day. Finally one of them answered, "We haven't seen them today. We don't know where they went. They often disappear like that. They always return by morning. They'll be here tomorrow." The man concluded with obvious finality.

A young man, a stranger at the shop slowly swept so not to raise too much sawdust. While the other men got busy finishing their work in silence, the young man brought himself close to Onofrio, away from the view of others. He took a stick and on the sawdust covered floor drew the outline of a fish, comprised of two inverted arcs overlapping each other at one end, forming the tail of a fish. With a skillful thrust the young man dotted an eye on the fish. He looked at Onofrio as though expecting an answer.

"Do you know what that means?" he asked slyly looking over his shoulder at the other men. Onofrio was ignorant of the symbol's meaning and shook his head.

"*That* is where they are. If you know where they meet, that is where you'll find them." Just as Onofrio started to question the young man further, a veteran worker approached.

"You two take your conversation outside. We're closing shop for the night." And he proceeded to extinguish oil lamps. In a rush the young man ran his broom over the symbol and the fish disappeared.

Once outside Onofrio waited for the young man to question him further. The doors went shut then locked and the men Onofrio knew were all walking away in separate directions. The young man was not among them. Onofrio looked for him in vain all around the shop and even stood in the moonlight to make himself be seen. Finally tired of waiting he started walking back to the villa and suddenly the distance seemed enormous. The incident continued to disturb him and he concluded that Tremiyo was on an overnight fishing trip. He would not leave Senobia alone and therefore she was with her father. He failed to see the need for so much secrecy unless the other men were envious of Tremiyo having so much liberty. These thoughts tumbled through his mind as he made his way back to the villa. But hard as he tried to accept his theory, it didn't fit. He would have liked to see Senobia again. He wished to hear her voice and see her smile at him, with trust and childish innocence in her eyes. He acknowledged to himself that he had missed being close to her and he felt pleasantly warm thinking of her.

He slept lightly without rest. He longed to see Tremiyo and Senobia. He felt a deep longing for their presence. He would find a way to get invited to their next fishing trip. He envisioned a campsite on a riverbank or lakeshore. He saw a bright campfire and sleeping mats with warm blankets all around it. He could almost smell the cooking pot. He wished to feel the cool damp air from the water. He longed to hear the sounds of the night insects making music in the darkness. Croaking frogs calling to each other added to the sweet chirps and whistles of the night singing birds. The dancing flames made light and shadows on the trees. Fireflies flickering on and off in random places. A circle of light in a world of darkness with the moon waltzing peacefully on the water. Suddenly from some remote corner of his mind he remembered such nights with his father, a very long time ago in a very special place faraway. A wide beautiful valley clothed in many shades of green and wondrous mountain peaks on the horizon. A place he knew not where it was, worst yet how to find a way to get there. And the little boy within him cried in his troubled sleep.

A mauve and soft amber glow touched the eastern horizon announcing the birth of yet another day. He bathed and wore a discarded but rather new pair of sturdy sandals and fresh clothes. The scroll neatly tucked in the overlap of his corded tunic. He ate some wheat cakes with butter and honey, drank a hot tea made from citrus tree leaves and adjusted his mind to another day in bondage. He would do the centurion's bidding, run his errands, allow the abusive military jargon to roll off his back and in general make the best of it all. From that he gained the peace and strength he needed for now. Tomorrow depended on how well he used that power today. Wispy strands of amber clouds softly tumbling in the sun among themselves reminded him of Senobia's hair.

The days went uncounted, the work unending and the evenings often busy with visitors of all kinds coming and going. His nights grew longer and more lonesome. His physical need for female company palpitated strongly within him. It was with him every day. These emotions were further enhanced by the liberal sexual acts on constant display at the villa, any time of the day or night. He felt compelled to isolate one of the available maidens for a night of needed gratification. But he was repulsed by the malodor some females carried with them. And where he did not reject their flirtatious advances, he nonetheless avoided further indulgence and he often hurt from his need. In his agrarian past he had indulged and enjoyed the courtship and lustful chase of willing girls in the harvest moonlight. The chase ending in the exhilarating exchange of anxious embraces, lusty kisses and the stimulating exploration of willing flesh. The union of two people that had an undeniable magnetic attraction for each other. For the young people that fell into that web of physical longing, nothing short of total fulfillment would suffice. Be it love, be it the call of nature, simple lust or anything else people have labeled it through millennia, the powerful call to recreate one's own kind. Moonlight and shadows bathing the wheat fields while willing bodies writhed and clung to one another in repeated ecstasy were images that visited the mind of the young man from parts unknown. There was power in the aroma of honest labor. There was beauty in the simple wild flower garlands the girls wore around their heads. The sweet smell of them and the odor of honest sweat coupled with the scent of ripened wheat was a lusty tonic of love. That ardent interest was a moving force that often led to lifelong unions. It was the way of nature and Onofrio strongly believed that nature was the Divine ruler of man. And man either studied the rules of Divine nature, abided by them and did well; or disregarded nature's dictate and suffered the consequences.

What he saw in and around the villa were human bodies given or traded to anyone the masters had in mind to. People were like cattle or swine to be bartered for favors or money and used as tools. The practice of it repulsed him. It was a way of life he could not accept and so he refused the favors of the women at the villa, always thinking they were instructed to ensnare him into their way of life. The centurion laid out the rules by example and the rest of his bunch followed the lead. Onofrio chose not to tag along. He preferred the love found in the fields. It was cleaner in some sense of the word. It was of free will by free willing people.

And so his nights continued to be deeply lonely as he refused the company offered by several young women at the villa. He frequently emptied a skin of wine after a long day's work, awaking late at night to eat and drink again. Long ships with square sails and dragon head bows, stone castles on misty isles and panoramic views of peaceful valleys often visited his troubled sleep.

Senobia came to his bedside one night and stood before him a long time, just looking at him. A golden light danced behind her. There was a swirl of glowing clouds all about her. In the silent breeze that swelled the soft pink gown she wore was the scent of wild flowers and ripened wheat. It was a delicate fragrance long absent from his mind. Her body silhouetted in the glowing light, she danced slowly to a music he knew was there but could not hear. Her dance was like a graceful willow swaying in a gentle breeze. Her moves were totally feminine in every way, but not seductive, rather childlike and fumbling a step occasionally, like a young girl in need of practice. When her head tilted skyward, her hair fell free to become glowing strands of molten gold and amber. Her arms extended straight out from her body and the light behind her transformed her silhouette into an upright beam and her arms a crossbar. From where her body and limbs crossed, her hair flowed and swayed as if in gesture to come forth. He could see her plain and sense her presence but could not wake to go to her. He anxiously inhaled the scent of ripened wheat and the perfume she wore when last he was close to her. She seemed to move forward only to recede a step or two. Willing to come close yet afraid to get too close. He tried hard to wake up and go to her side. Finally with a mighty effort he awoke and sat up straight in a single motion. But Senobia had only been a dream. An illusion forged from loneliness. A vision that danced before his wide awake mind the rest of the night.

> *And he went about all Galilee, teaching in their synagogues and preaching the gospel of the kingdom and healing every disease and every infirmity among the people. So his fame spread throughout all Syria, and they brought him all the sick, those afflicted with various diseases and pains, demoniacs, epileptics, and paralytics, and he healed them. And*

great crowds followed him from Galilee and the Decapolis and Jerusalem and Judea and from beyond the Jordan.
Matthew 4:23-25

And they came, bringing to him a paralytic carried by four men. And when they could not get near him because of the crowd, they removed the roof above him; and when they had made an opening, they let down the pallet on which the paralytic lay. *Mark 2:3-4*

And when Jesus entered Peter's house, he saw his mother-in-law lying sick with a fever; he touched her hand, and the fever left her, and she rose and served him.
Matthew 8:14-15

Then came one of the rulers of the synagogue, Jairus by name; and seeing him, he fell at his feet, and besought him, saying, "My little daughter is at the point of death. Come and lay your hands on her, so that she may be made well, and live."
Mark 5:22-23

Now there was a man of the Pharisees, named Nicodemus, a ruler of the Jews. This man came to Jesus by night and said to him, "Rabbi, we know that you are a teacher come from God; for no one can do these signs that you do, unless God is with him." *John 3:1-2*

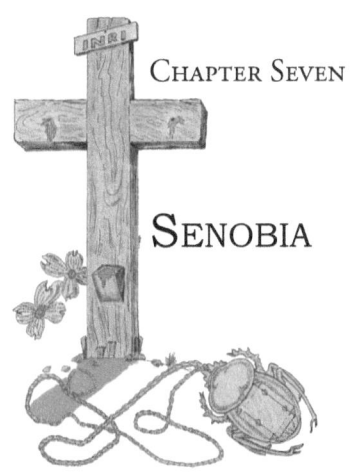

CHAPTER SEVEN

SENOBIA

BLIND BARTIMEUS

Blind Bartimeus at the gates
Of Jericho in darkness waits;
He hears a crowd – he hears a breath
Say, "It is Christ of Nazareth!"
And calls, in tones of agony,
"Jesus, have mercy now on me!"

The thronging multitudes increase;
"Blind Bartimeus, hold thy peace!"
But still, above the noisy crowd,
The beggar's cry is shrill and loud;
Until they say, "He calleth thee!"
"Fear not, arise, He calleth thee!"

Then saith the Christ, as silent stands
The crowd, "What wilt thou at my hands?"
And he replies, "O give me light!
Rabbi, restore the blind man's sight!"
And Jesus answers, "Go in peace,
Thy faith from blindness gives release!"

Ye that have eyes, yet cannot see,
In darkness and in misery,
Recall those mighty Voices Three,
"Jesus, have mercy now on me!
Fear not, arise and go in peace!
Thy faith from blindness gives release!"

Henry Wadsworth Longfellow (1807 – 1882)

In a room filled with the aroma of fresh melons, grapes and oranges, Senobia and her father peacefully sat having dinner. Tremiyo routinely had wine with his meals, showing a preference for a copper cup hammered out by a local craftsman. A religious leader from Nazareth was said to have used the cherished cup. Their conversation was sparse this evening and mostly circled around their immediate lives. There was always a new story about a slave in trouble for one reason or other. A new flock of goats and sheep had recently been acquired by Serou for his many tables. The usual gossip of the centurion and events at the villa had long ago become stale news at their dinner table.

"I heard the centurion has taught Onofrio how to read and is now teaching him to use a sword. Serou is happy the young man is learning to read but he is not happy to know Onofrio is sparring with real weapons against seasoned men." The old man carried his conversation between working troublesome pomegranate seeds in his cheek and disposing of them in a jar used for leftovers. The sound of Onofrio's name tingled like little silver bells in Senobia's heart.

"Is he well?" she asked quietly not wanting to sound overly anxious. "Is he coming back here soon? When he comes back, we must ask him to have dinner with us." Suddenly and without warning she was no longer concerned with sounding anxious. When her father raised an eyebrow and looked at her with an eye more typical of Serou, Senobia felt a blush rush to her cheeks. Her graceful hand covered her mouth and her eyes sparkled like a child caught in mischief. The old man took a handful of pomegranate seeds from his mouth and gently dropped them into the container. He wiped his lips and chin with a fresh linen towel then looked intently at his daughter in silence for a long moment. Senobia busied herself with the remainder of her meal while her heart beat in fury. She set her jaw and looked into her father's eyes expecting a reprimand or whatever came.

"He is well." the old man finally answered exhaling a captive breath. "In fact, he is too well. The work and regular diet has done him a lot of good. He is developing into a handsome young man. He is now educated to a degree and there's changes in his mind happening at a rapid pace. He would make a good addition to our group." the old man concluded, evaluating what he said.

"Then you've seen him?" Senobia's eyes beaming brightly and no longer worried about hiding her excitement.

"Yes, dear daughter. I've seen him; he even minimized his interest in you. So there!" He took more pomegranate seeds to munch on and appeared deep in thought for a few moments.

"He did? Then he remembers me." Senobia was elated with the news. Filled with an excitement she never felt before.

"My dear one," the old man sighed, "only a blind old man would not remember you." He reached out to lovingly caress his daughter's excited face. She was indeed the jewel in his life. A part of his lovely wife Sintia, still alive and bubbling over with excitement over some boy whose parents, background and intentions Tremiyo had no knowledge of. None whatsoever.

"I will speak to Serou tomorrow about your young man's return to the main house. I will use the excuse of needing him in my work. The slave I have now is simply not doing well. He is stupid and slow to move about. Senobia, this individual is so used to chains on his ankles that he walks like they were still on him," Tremiyo chuckled pleasantly.

"Father, we must get something very special for his homecoming. It has to be above and beyond anything he's ever had. And he must be made to know that it is to welcome him home. After all, for the time being this is his home. And for now, we are his only family, aren't we, Father?" The young girl's bubbling enthusiasm shined on her face as only true happiness can. While her grayish green eyes sparkled brightly in the candlelight, like beacons of total joy.

"Senobia," her father intervened. "You must remember that there are many other girls at the villa. In fact, theres entirely too many women in that place. It's become a hellhole of open prostitution. While Serou has looked the other way, it became a den of evil iniquity."

"But, you said that he asked about me." Senobia stated somewhat deflated.

"He may have been trying to be polite. After all, he was never rude."

Instantly there was deep trouble in Senobia's eyes. The sparkling joy that moments ago raced through her anxious heart was now a rage of dark, uncertain clouds dashing against jagged rocks. She put her hands together before her pretty rounded lips as though in prayer, closed her eyes for a moment then looked at her father with complete resolve. "We will still prepare a homecoming meal he will never forget. If he asked about me, it's because he truly cares. He would not ask otherwise. I know it and my heart knows it. Whatever evil lurks at the villa is like dust around his feet. It will not harm him and it can be washed off with no after effects. There is nothing in that place that can claim his attention for very long." she finalized with complete confidence.

Among the things that young Senobia treasured was an old drinking cup made of copper and porcelain. An image of the Grecian god, Apollo, graced the old cup and until recently had always been – just Apollo. In her young mind the image magically became Onofrio. She did not tire of looking at it and it received many cleaning, caressing strokes. Her young body pulsated in unfulfilled anxiety at the sight of Onofrio weaving and swaying in the candlelight. She studied the tiny hands and arms of the image and transformed them in her mind to be

Onofrio's. She wanted to see Onofrio wearing a blue loin cover as the image did. She imagined how it would feel to be in his arms and shivered at the thought of his hands exploring her eager body. And the intimate things he would do to her and with her. She was not at all repulsed by the thoughts. Instead she wistfully longed for reality, which she knew would not materialize unless they were properly married according to her father's dictatorial rule on the matter.

Within her many childhood treasures was an assortment of dolls she collected over the years, most of which decorated her bed as pillows. Boy dolls, girl dolls and even animal dolls. And they all had names. There was rag and bone, made with a strong twig skeleton inside of cotton and cloth. Rag and bone's head was a small gourd, handsomely painted and boasting an ample wig of kid goat hair. There was a long haired beauty she called Salome. "Smokey" was a black boy doll with a permanent grin on his face. Her father had long ago found the head of a stone statue missing its body. He recovered the handsomely carved head and someone in the compound found a way to make it into a doll for Tremiyo's baby daughter. He was called Apollo, now became Onofrio, and slept on her pillow. She even covered him when the nights got chilly and lay on her breast all night. Jokingly her father often called her dolls his only grandchildren. Perhaps it was a kind and loving way to remind his daughter that the time for toys was almost over. She was no longer a little girl. She was a beautiful young lady. In a fatherly fashion, he was always careful to select clothes that did not over expose her young figure. However, it was getting increasingly difficult to hide her facial beauty. And she was filling out her clothes too well, to try to avoid masculine admiration. Her father was not anxious to lose a daughter, whom he loved immensely. In his heart he wanted her to have security and more so, the joys of true love. He wished for her the kind of love he had with her mother, the long deceased Sintia. It would be a strong, mutually sincere love; a love to overcome all barriers. He could not think of bartering her off for his own security or for anything of value in the world. He wanted for her a love that would last a lifetime.

Tremiyo had a different kind of love with the slave woman, Camia. It was a fulfilling relationship, mutually beneficial and embellished with mature affection. It would never reach the proportions of a full-unmeasured love such as he had with Sintia. Camia knew this. She also knew his kindness, knew his heart and mind and knew his devotion to her would suffice for her lifetime. Camia had raised Senobia from childhood, the girl was her own in her heart and mind. And she made no secret of it. She showed pride to be called Senobia's mother. It filled her heart with joy. Together, they were a family undivided. Camia held all the feminine answers to Senobia's questions regarding her monthly cycle and anxiety she suffered. It was Camia that guarded her during these times. It was Camia that help bathe her and provided scented oils and perfumes to obscure the telltale odor during her cycle.

Many girls in less fortunate conditions lost the jewel of their youth during these times. In spite of the mild hardship it imposed, both Camia and Tremiyo wished for Senobia to be a virgin on her wedding night. They provided diversions during these times. Let it not be said by anybody that they did not raise a right and proper daughter. All matters of love and reproduction were explained to the young girl in closed sessions with Camia. All questions dealt with in a proper and motherly fashion. Matters of personal hygiene and all that Camia knew of male expectations, most of which she learned attending and listening to women in the compound. Her own experience in matters of love had always been of a limited fashion, until she met the girl's father, Tremiyo.

Senobia learned to cook and clean house at an early age. She learned to wash her own clothes and care for her father's quarters, all with Camia as a nearby coach and quality control engineer, so to speak. It was Senobia who now managed her father's house. Young compound girls were always willing to help

Senobia keep the house clean and neat. Her father always found ways to compensate his daughter's eager helpers. And although he was genuinely kind to the young mob, he always managed to reduce their visitations to a minimum. Not maliciously, but as a precaution. He did not want his daughter to learn anything he did not deem fit for her.

Chapter Eight

The Scarab of Serou

When Serou entered the villa escorted by his personal guards, the dice game in the corner of the large room ceased. The card game between officers and lesser dignitaries was soon concluded. Partially dressed girls were seen scurrying into the darkness. Two of Serou's dog trainers held four salivating animals on strong leashes. Serou's assembly of dogs and armed personal guards made a respectable force, not here on pleasant business. The crowd of people spread out to the outer walls in unison, leaving a clear path to the room where Clemidius was. The centurion was teaching Onofrio a fencing lesson surrounded by women and a collection of familiar as well as unknown faces. The centurion appeared hard pressed to convey his instruction, while Onofrio seemed calm and was handling the weapon and himself impressively, indicating lessons well taken. He was sparring, thrusting and slicing with admirable skill and performing his defensive moves equally well. The cheers going to Onofrio were not to the liking of the stressed centurion. Obviously the wine had taken its toll on the seasoned warrior, turned struggling teacher. Both men had been sparring at length, judging from their glistening bodies and obvious exhaustion.

"Hail Serou, the righteous Egyptian has arrived." The centurion raised his right arm in a Roman salute and clearly in jest.

Sober, Onofrio came to Serou and extended his hand in friendship expecting a handshake. To which Serou raised a dignified hawk eye and eyebrow. Instead he put his hand on the young man's shoulder and spoke clear enough for all to hear, "Get cleaned up and gather your things. I've come to take what is rightfully mine."

There was instant indignation in Onofrio, at being so coldly regarded as simple property. His pride had grown with his physical strength and a sword in his hand. His reasoning had expanded often beyond his own comprehension. His eyes went directly to Serou's calculating look with a seething rage within them. "I prefer it here," he said in slow syllables. The white edges of his teeth barely visible and he gripped the sword firmer.

Serou looked at him with indifference and disregard for the weapon. Calmly he spoke to the angry young man, "Do as you're told and don't argue."

The heat from Onofrio's body was waved off by Serou's hand as though it was offensive. From his robe the Egyptian produced a fragrant silk scarf with which he waved off Onofrio. He brought the scarf to his nose, waving the scented wisp as he walked through the room refreshing the air. Not being a stranger to trouble, the centurion prepared to do battle allowing the wine to be his guide. He made a fruitless effort to appear more sober than what he was. He came to Onofrio's side and addressed Serou as he walked away, both men with swords in hand.

"Serou!" Clemidius gruffly called out. "I won this man fair and square. We agreed that if I could improve his mind, I could keep him. I intend to make him a Roman officer following the same pattern I did." Only then did Onofrio notice people scurrying away in haste.

In the brief walk through his own villa Serou evaluated the defense of the place and was sure of his next move. Or Plan Two, if need be. "Centurion Clemidius, we also agreed that we would have to be in accord with the improvements you implemented. Is that not true?"

Confident in his accomplishments, the centurion replied adjusting the sword across his chest, "We agreed to that, yes." A whimsical smile creasing his rugged face and he looked around for backup support.

Serou applauded in mockery, the wisp of silk muffling the clap of his hands. "There are greater lessons than reading, counting and wielding a sword, Centurion." With a motion from Serou, a group of servants came into the room with the table Onofrio had so painstakingly built. The table was brought before Clemidius and Serou as the servants bowed out of harm's way, exiting from the air heavy with conflict. On the table were numerous curves, swirls and carved pieces made of wood that Onofrio did as lessons. "Centurion Clemidius," Serou began calmly. "the man is naturally inquisitive and already knew how to read from his visits to my library. (And Serou knew he stretched the truth, a good bit.) The man was raised in the fields where counting seeds per row is essential. Therefore, the man already knew how to count. Your claims are baseless. The man is here because he is a thief. These things were taken without my permission. I have several witnesses outside these doors to convince you of that." And the centurion knew without asking that the witnesses were all armed to the teeth. "The most valuable lesson you could have taught is honesty. In that you failed. Therefore, I am here to take what is rightfully mine and not injure the relationship between us. I am responsible for this man to the ruling governor. If you have further claim, take it to the governor. We can't have cheats and thieves running around loose, can we, Centurion?" The low key barb stung Clemidius and he made a move towards Serou, tightening the grip on his sword. Simultaneously the dog trainers got ready to release the beasts. A low growl gurgling in their throats clearly heard across the room. A move not missed by the battle scarred centurion. Onofrio stood riveted to the unfolding scene, not knowing what to do. Clemidius looked at Serou and then the dogs, evaluating the situation.

"They are trained to eat only Romans," the Egyptian said softly but convincingly. On the balcony above, Clemidius saw several of Serou's armed guards and so did Onofrio. No doubt ready for action and the young man noticed more people slipping out of the doors in fearful silence.

"Serou, that is what I like about you. Most times you are ready for anything that may or may not happen," respectfully injected the sobering centurion. He tossed the sword onto a nearby table making a loud metallic sound when it landed. To which the dogs responded with a deeper growl. They pranced vigorously, straining their leashes, wanting to be released.

"That is precisely what makes me Serou, the righteous Egyptian."

Clemidius came to him with open arms and embraced the Egyptian. "I would rather have you as a friend," he said in earnest. Then with a single knuckled finger he thumped Serou on the chest smiling admirably, "Complete with battle armor, huh?" chuckled the centurion.

"Complete with battle armor," chuckled Serou.

Dog latches were secured and the men on the balcony dissolved without a sound. Servants vanished into the night with Onofrio's table and treasures. Serou and Clemidius spoke in whispers both men looking at Onofrio occasionally. Onofrio seethed inside. His mind was a storm of vengeful anger. He would not be bartered like beef on the block, tossed back and forth like so much meat. He loathed the position in which he was a helpless captive. Caught between two powers, he could not fight. With great difficulty he bowed to Serou in obvious irreverence. "I'll get my things and we can go," he stated curtly. Serou looked at him with guarded disregard.

"Don't keep us waiting too long," he demanded and dismissed the young man with a single look. Shortly Onofrio reappeared with a bundle of things over his shoulder. "Would you like to inspect what I have here? I don't want to be accused twice in one night." Almost in unison both men waved a silent "no" with their hands, and continued their whispered conversation. Onofrio remembered the scarab in the quiver. It would be a great way to get even with Serou. Instantly he resolved to take it and in pretended humility addressed the centurion. "Centurion Clemidius, may I have that old quiver hanging in the corner? I'd like to attempt repairs, in my free time," and pointed to the dust covered old quiver.

Clemidius gave the quiver a quick glance and told Onofrio to get it down, it was his. He then added, "Take it as a gift," as if the old quiver alone had value. "You need not return it when it's mended."

"And, what a gift it is," rang silently in the young man's mind. He could tell the scarab was still inside when he brought it down gently, hoping the contents would not make a tell-tale sound. And it didn't.

The group under Serou's command left the villa in orderly fashion. The storm still raged in Onofrio's mind as he silently walked behind Serou like a goat in tow. *"Serou may have his way tonight but his precious bug is going to buy my freedom and help me find my way home. He has condemned me to being a thief. So, what's the difference? His trinket or his wood? In his mind I will always be a common thief."*

It never occurred to the young man from parts unknown that Serou may have simply done what was most expedient to rescue him from a den that was now showing its end result. A result that brewed a vengeful storm in Onofrio's mind. An ugly environment always fosters an ugly result.

At the main house Serou discharged his escort and posted extra guards. The centurion smarted from tonight's exercise and may create some mischief during the night or early dawn. "Onofrio, come to the house with me. We need to talk," Serou commanded. Once inside, Serou proceeded to remove his outer robes. Only then did Onofrio see the armor beneath. With an awkward gesture, Serou motioned for the young man to release the latches that secured the protective chest plate. Reluctantly

Onofrio obliged. His rude moves and gestures obvious to the time wise Egyptian.

"Your hate does not become you, young man. You behave like a man that prefers the dungeons to the comfort of my home. Or perhaps, it is just now that you show the true color of your character."

"I would not be in the dungeons very long. Clemidius would have me out by morning." Onofrio stoutly replied.

"That, my young friend, is absolutely true. And you would belong to Rome for the rest of your life. You would never know the real you." Serou placed a friendly hand on Onofrio's shoulder, which Onofrio fended off in a not too gentle a fashion while his eyes were still on fire. Serou discharged the rejection without emotion or concern. Then softly chuckled, "Your wits have abandoned you and left you blind. It was the wish of Tremiyo and Senobia that I bring you back, whichever way I could. I personally wanted to show the centurion who is master here. It's been made known that the young Senobia favors you and her father seems to approve. And I did promise to bring you back, remember?" the Egyptian spoke over his shoulder pushing cushions around a luxurious couch to make a comfortable spot for himself.

From beyond the seething rage flowed a stronger force. It was like a soft cooling mantle that gently settled over his anger. He had not allowed himself to think of Senobia for days. Her image eased into his mind like a soothing balm over a lonely heart. He purposely wearied himself with work and self-imposed his isolation at night. Ample opportunities to satisfy the need that beat within his young body were not always gently turned away, giving the willing girls the right to call him cold hearted, stuck up and other unfavorable names. They even boldly asked, "What are you saving it for? Spread it around, you might like it." The anger he felt tonight did not dissolve immediately; instead it ebbed away slowly with the image of Senobia slowly easing into the eyes within his mind. Memories of reddish, golden hair cascading to her shoulders drifted into view. He saw her as he did in all his dreams, softly swaying to a music he knew was there, but could not hear. And a gentle calm began to settle upon him.

But the work of devious minds so rampant at the villa left their mark on the young mind of Onofrio. People were subject to do anything and say anything to get what they wanted. People use any kind of bait to trap you. This too could be a people game Serou was playing with him. Testing him, to see if he cared and would openly displayed it. Serou would have an added grip to ensnare him for his own purpose. No! He would not play the game. He had the scarab. He knew people would pay handsome-ly for it. He had access to a horse to take him far from here and fast. Once on shore he would remember to what port he wanted to sail. To sail? Sail to where? Where would he go? He did not know the way to his valley or where that valley was. In a flash his mind became a battle field of conflicting thoughts. Time. He needed time to sort out the disarray playing havoc with his mind. One thing stood out, clear and without question. Senobia. Senobia was peace. Wisher's paradise was a fine place to air out the conflict in his mind. As before, he was again forced to deal with the dictate of the moment. He would be patient and appear to go along until the time was right. Then he would make his move swiftly.

With Onofrio's anger visibly receding, Serou pointed to an elaborate pitcher on a gleaming tray with drinking cups around it. "Let's have some wine. This comes from a secret reserve, I keep and use only on special occasions." With a full cup in hand, he began laughing hardily. "By all the gods I know, I would have loved to see what the centurion would do with four of my dogs chewing on his butt. I can see him now, hanging from the chandeliers, screaming holy hell, eyes bulging out while my hounds bit off little pieces from his skinny buttocks." Serou's hardy laughter soon affected Onofrio and soon he too was laughing, though not as vigorously as the Egyptian. Serou gestured Onofrio to sit next to him while his laughter simmered to a quiet chuckle. "Onofrio, I swear I have no idea what makes you so special. Tonight, I came close to killing a man and had just cause to do so. Now, here you are sitting in my presence, drinking my most special wine, I do not serve to guests of royal distinction. Not one slave in this entire compound has ever sat on this couch as you and I are doing. I'm not sure I like my attraction to you. There is something about you that I do not quite understand. You stand out from other men. You have the ability to think. You have the ability to take control and yet you do not use this power selfishly. It is ability, rare among men. Tonight, I saw you almost master your teacher with a sword. Centurion Clemidius is no doubt a formidable foe. He has killed in battle and personal conflict. Yet, tonight I saw you toy with his lessons as though you already knew them. You have made a place with me from our first encounter. I saw you in chains meet my scrutiny with dignity and strength, in a dungeon where men live in fear."

Onofrio's anger mellowed to a relaxed comfort. He felt free of the tensions that he felt at the villa. The wine was excellent, the surroundings inspired awe and he was being paid honor. He felt welcomed. He felt the genuine sincerity he forgot existed within the Egyptian. Serou was not maliciously devious. He would never say anything he did not mean.

"Stand up; I want to look at you. Peel off your robes," Serou ordered his hawk eye gleaming. Onofrio had never been accustomed to inspection and felt like a lamb at the auction block, but he slowly dropped his clothes to the floor. Serou appraised him from a sitting position. "That is another of your admirable qualities. You have pride in yourself and the intelligence not to fight a force you cannot overcome. That is a sign of deep seated wisdom. You have developed into a strong and handsome young man. The hard work and regular diet has served you well. The sun has favored your skin and the gods have graced your body with admirable qualities. Dress and come sit with me. Drink my wine and let me show you the Serou, you have never known."

The storm of anger had drifted away with the third cup of wine. He decided to listen to the wisdom of Serou, who seemed more than willing to talk. Onofrio learned that often times, one finds a solution to a problem by listening to the problem. And Serou was a big problem. As Serou spoke, Onofrio would sort out his entangled mind and by morning he would have a partial solution. He knew going home was not going to be easy. There were forces here that laid a claim on him and he did not have a way to dislodge their grip. He was unaccustomed to being bound. The life within his memory had always been free to wander in any direction he wished. He longed to be free again, but more so he yearned to be home with his mother and father. Serou was being a gracious host. He drank considerably, eating fruit from an overloaded tureen. "I noticed how discreetly you've avoided talking about Senobia," the Egyptian spoke with an open smile. "There's an important matter I must settle with you before I feel free to speak of anything." He went to the quiver and brought it to the table before Serou. Gently he shook it until the scarab slipped out. He picked up the precious bauble and dusted it off on his robe then handed it to Serou. The Egyptian with his hawk eye questioning, looked at the young man for a long moment. "Where did you get this? How did it get in the quiver?" Serou thoughtfully inquired taking a deep breath.

"I found it at the villa one night when a troupe of entertainers was there. I came across it while rounding up dishes, clothes and other things. I put it in the quiver for safekeeping."

"Why did you not return it sooner, or had you decided to keep it this time?" Serou was intently studying the young man and waiting for the answer.

"I was unsure of the consequences if I returned it. I feared it might implicate the centurion in some way and cause friction between you."

"And you never thought about keeping it?"

"Tonight, in a rage when I felt like a beef on the auction block, tossed between two men I cannot oppose, I decided to

keep it. It would buy my freedom and secure my way home."
Onofrio confessed as the last shreds of anger slipped away.

"It would do far more than buy your freedom and take you
home, my impetuous, young friend." Serou said in a near whisper as a knot rose on his jaw and his eyes glistened. He poured
them each another cup of wine and motioned Onofrio to sit
on a cushioned stool before him. Onofrio felt unsettled sitting
before the Egyptian. Was this the last drink before going back
to the dungeons?

"Why are you returning it now?" he asked, knowing the
answer, but wanting to hear it.

"Because it is not mine to keep. I am not a thief at heart.
I'm not able to keep what is not truly mine, earned by my labor
and the power of my mind."

"I told you once before that your honesty will serve you well,
young Onofrio. You should learn restraint in certain areas and
not be so open with your truth. The man from whom you took
an unpaid meal has taken payment plus considerable interest.
The charges against you have been dismissed. The merchant has
posted a letter of apology to the magistrate and to you for the
inconvenience. He invites you to come eat at his place anytime
you wish at no cost. There is no legal claim on your freedom, as
far as I'm concerned. The centurion is yet another matter. Although, he has no legal claim on you, he will create mischief to
get his way. The man wants to make you a Roman soldier and
see you progress in his steps to higher rank. And he will accept
credit for enlisting you into the service of the emperor. Physical strength and clever minds have served the Roman Empire
extremely well for a very long time." Serou measured his words
slowly and clearly while he toyed with the golden scarab. He
checked and rechecked the weak clasp studying the angles of
the diamond on the trinket's back.

Onofrio suddenly felt a huge stone lifted from his shoulders
and even felt as though he breathed better. He was a free man
again. Although not able to speak for a few moments, his mind

was a kettle of bubbling joy. He was free to roam field and vale at his leisure, to explore and find the way back to his beloved valley where there were stone castles on misty isles, clear lakes of glorious blue and regal mountains. His mind could see the welcoming smoke curling skyward from the fires of home. He smelled the moist, dark earth when he and his father tilled the fields. Peeling back in dark furrows the skin of mother earth, to lay seed within the cuts and watch in happy anticipation the birth of another good harvest as his father often said. Senobia softly eased into his mind with a gentle smile on her rosy lips. Serou could not have known of the unfamiliar claim she had on his freedom. For even Onofrio was uncertain of the gentle tugging inspired by Senobia that seemed to have as much power on his soul as the urgent drive to find his way home.

Through many restless nights the gentle Senobia dreamed and fantasized of the time when she would again be close to the young man from parts unknown. While her father secretly counted and recounted his savings and continued to methodically plan his daughter's wedding, he wished he had made half as many wise investments as Serou. Tremiyo and the Egyptian had occasionally ventured their gold on assorted money making enterprises. Serou's well-informed investments in commerce had returned a huge fortune. Whereas Tremiyo's ventures were not as great as Serou's, he was nonetheless a rich man.

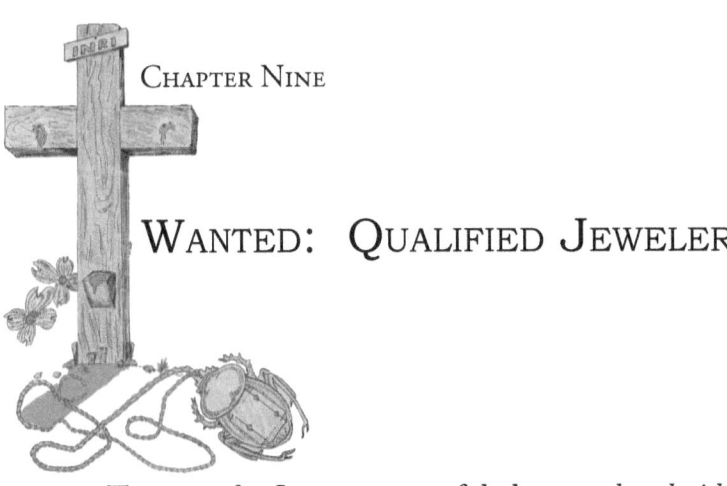

CHAPTER NINE

WANTED: QUALIFIED JEWELER

That same day Jesus went out of the house and sat beside the sea. And great crowds gathered about him, so that he got into a boat and sat there; and the whole crowd stood on the beach. And he told them many things in parables, saying: "A sower went out to sow.   Matthew 13:1-3

Then the disciples came and said to him, "Why do you speak to them in parables?" And he answered them, "To you it has been given to know the secrets of the kingdom of heaven, but to them it has not been given ...

This is why I speak to them in parables, because seeing they do not see, and hearing they do not hear, nor do they understand.   Matthew 10:10-11, 13

"And when you pray, you must not be like the hypocrites; for they love to stand and pray in the synagogues and at the street corners, that they may be seen by men. Truly, I say to you, they have received their reward. But when you pray, go into your room and shut the door and pray to your Father who is in secret; and your Father who sees in secret will reward you."   Matthew 6:5-6

Pray then like this:

Our Father who art in heaven,
Hallowed be thy name.
10 Thy kingdom come,
Thy will be done,
    On earth as it is in heaven.
11 Give us this day our daily bread;
12 And forgive us our debts,
    As we also have forgiven our debtors;
13 And lead us not into temptation,
    But deliver us from evil.   *Matthew 6:9-13*

"Onofrio, tomorrow I want you to make some open inquiries in the market place. Find a jeweler to come here with tools to repair this necklace. I want you to stand over him every minute. I do not want a single piece of this chain to end up among the missing. I want a clasp made as close to this one as he can possibly get. If need be, have the person bring equipment to manufacture one exactly like it. I do not need the most economical craftsman. I want the best. You decide who is most qualified for the task. But select a person on merit alone. Have them show you samples of their work, before you decide who is best for the work."

Onofrio briefly mulled over his own plans in spite of Serou's demands. Taking liberty from the wine he announced, "I was hoping to consult some charts and maps and start searching for my homeland. Once I know where it is, I can work my way through the fields until I find the crest above my parent's cottage. And I'll be home."

"Onofrio, do you believe me to be a fair and just man?" Serou asked looking directly into Onofrio's eyes.

"Yes. Yes, I do. You are one of the few men I know, whom I trust and respect."

"Then trust me a while longer," Serou pleaded. "Do as you please around my home. Pursue your woodworking skills, be a help to Tremiyo, but stay for a while longer. I promise, you will not regret it. There is only one request, stay away from the centurion and the mob with whom he runs. At the villa, as we speak, is the festering womb that will bring grief to the entire world. Do anything you wish, but stay away from there and avoid Clemidius." Serou was in earnest delivering a speech as though he knew things beyond Onofrio's comprehension.

"Master Serou, I feel a connection. I feel an obligation to Clemidius. He made a real effort to be my friend and never asked anything in return."

"Then respect that," Serou instructed. "Keep it in the back of your mind. I am not asking you to sever your regard for Clemidius. I am not asking you lose respect for your teacher. I am asking that you stay clear for a time. If things result as I believe they will, when the boil that festers there comes to a head and erupts, then choose where you prefer to be.

In the meantime weigh in your mind if you choose to serve the emperor or be free in the fields of your father's making. To not see your options clearly is not to be what I give you credit for being. I am by no means a great judge of character. But I know what brews in the pot before my hearth better than most. You being free now is due to my doing. It is due to my faith in the Onofrio I met in a gruesome dungeon. That young man stands before me now and I know him not. That man is now different in bodily strength, worldly knowledge and the ability to wield a sword. I ask you, whoever you may be at the moment, who would you be given the chance? Onofrio, the butcher? Will you be a replaceable piece of meat doing the Emperor's bidding? Killing, pillaging and laying a bloody path over which the Emperor will rule? Or will you be the Onofrio I know to be, an honest, sincere individual who can cultivate the land to feed the hungry, who can use his hands to create beauty? Onofrio who answers to a call within himself to be fair and just, with mercy and strength to help those in need? This Onofrio will see the Seven Hills of Rome be leveled with the power embedded within his future faith. The boil is close to erupting. The spew of its malice will stain the unfit and they will cease to be of this realm, while the spotless ones find grace in a new light that will shine upon the earth for thousands of years. There is a glory coming that will make students out of wealthy kings." Concluding his oratory he turned to find Onofrio calmly laid out on the length of the couch sound asleep. His empty cup dangling from a finger tip. Smiling at the peaceful scene Serou raised his head and arms to the sky in prayer. "Oh mighty keeper of all records and most gracious of all judges, be amply fair in thy judgment of this young man, who knows what is right even if he doesn't know why. There is a truth simmering among us these days, impervious to the grit that blows with the change of times. That truth is like a tiny dot of light across a dark and stormy sea. But it will become a beacon to mankind like a magnet drawing bits of steel. The sins of Rome will feed its own demise when honorable men within this new movement do what is honorably correct. Give this young man the strength to prevail through the holocaust that brews on the horizon." Serou had access to many gods and he revered them all with equal zest. His prayer would surely find favor among his many gods.

A cream-colored glow tinted the eastern horizon although the rest of the sky was an assembly of soft purple and lavender billowing clouds, meandering slowly in graceful motion before a gentle breeze as if seeking to be the first to touch the sun. From somewhere in the early morning dim crowed an off key, late rising rooster. Soon followed by the bleating of an infant lamb, most likely looking for its mother. Onofrio came awake warm and comfortable on the luxurious couch. His sandals had been removed and laid at leg length on the floor. Last night's fruit, stale wine and other edibles had all been removed. The vast receiving chamber was spotlessly clean and the aroma of sweet smelling flowers and aromatic branches placed at strategic locations. A working crew like silent fairies made their efforts clearly seen.

Galloping horses echoing away brought Onofrio fully awake, followed by the familiar, smiling face of Tremiyo standing before him with a tray loaded down with breakfast. Curling wisps floated from a bowl of spiced oat porridge. Aromatic, fresh baked bread with the scent of honey and butter had the young man salivating. A moist towel fell on his face as he heard Tremiyo instruct, "Wipe the sleep from your face and here's a bowl of warm water for your hands." Towels fell on the young man's lap and with little or no choice, he obeyed orders. The servant woman Camia, brought him fresh robes and tossed him a brush for his hair. He was overjoyed to see such friendly faces treating him like a long lost son. His happiness gleamed like a beacon in the early morning glow.

"Tremiyo, I am delighted to see you." The joy was visibly mutual as he ran a hand through the young man's tangled hair.

"Clean up, get dressed and eat your breakfast. We have much to do. The master has left instructions."

A two-seated cart with a pair of mellow-spirited horses were held at their ready by friendly servants for Tremiyo and Onofrio. On their way to Jerusalem they discussed their objectives. Tremiyo was in search of cooking oils, seeds, herbs and spices to enhance the flavor of meats. He sought fruits and vegetables not grown in the gardens of Serou. Onofrio had within him the happy spirit of a young man. Substantial coins provided by Master Serou jingled loosely in his newly acquire purse. His stride was a clear warning to mother hens. *Hide your young chickens, because this cocky rooster is on the prowl.* It was grand to a free man and not subjected to the whims of others.

There were plenty of jewelers everywhere. They sprang from solid walls at the jingle of gold coins. One or more of those hungry experts would materialize by a single word from him. Onofrio el Segundo, close drinking friend of Serou, the wealthy Egyptian. An unfamiliar boldness fanned the fire within him. He could do anything he wished. He could go anywhere he wanted to. If he fell in foul climate due to his misjudgment, he had two maybe three reputable friends to call on and he would be free of whatever befell him. Clearly, the liquor of power bloated his judgment. He sauntered into the market place and spoke to one of the first merchants he met, "Have someone fetch to me an experienced jeweler. He must be a master goldsmith and expert at repairing rare jewelry. I have no time to waste on amateurs or back porch workers. I want only the best there is." He soon found comfort in a cut willow chair not far from a fountain splashing a cooling mist on the immediate surroundings. The shop keeper, a maker of outdoor furniture was overly impressed and scurried around like a love hungry puppy to please the inflated Onofrio, who was not annoyed by the synthetic attention. With borrowed dignity and over imperious gestures he ordered the shopkeeper to bring wine. Not just wine, but good wine with suitable drinking cups. The shopkeeper, although miserly in personal worth, was keen at inflating market values. The overpriced wine arrived on a dingy looking tray with equally dingy looking cups. A second chair materialized and soon a table was provided and Onofrio sat pompously waiting for a jeweler to emerge from a bustling crowd in the market place. It was not long before he was swamped with no less than ten would be expert jewelers. All yelling, shoving and pushing to be first at catching the young man's attention. He was overwhelmed with offers and hands waving jewelry items in the air. Besieged with attention he struggled fruitlessly to decide who to see first. How was he going to select who to deal with?

While trying to answer questions and keep the more aggressive craftsmen from literally bowling him over, a middle aged man sauntered into the back of the mob. He stood tall and calmly crossed his arms over his chest, studying the focus of the unruly crowd. He was extremely well dressed with a handsome turban as a crown and a large jewel at the center of the headdress. He sported a graying beard and deep-set chocolate colored eyes. He focused his attention on the bewildered Onofrio. He had at his side, a muscular bare-chested man with a scimitar in the sash around his full waist. Given the signal the muscle man commenced to rudely shove jewelers aside, clearing a path to Onofrio. Yells, moans and objections rang out from bodies shoved aside without mercy. Nobody made an effort to stop the bully and most stood aside seeing the instigator of the assault. The man leisurely walked on the cleared path and stood before Onofrio's table to bow semi-courteously. Touching his chest, his lips and his brow in a graceful motion while surveying the young man with a certain disdain. His hand made a fluid arc to the east, while the muscular man stood off the crowd.

"I am Komar of the house of Jumansa. My father and his fathers before him have been jewelers, craftsmen in fine gold, rare metals and precious stones for a hundred years in Jerusalem and their homeland to the east. Perhaps, we can be of service to you." he offered from a semi-bowed position with his right hand over his abdomen. In a single keen-eyed glance, he evaluated Onofrio's wardrobe and obvious inexperience, surmising correctly that Onofrio did not have the money to pay for Jumansa's expertise in matters of gold. Abruptly he stood up as though he had bowed too long. He looked down at the seated, somewhat annoyed young man and asked loud enough for all to hear, "And how do you propose to pay for such expensive services? Is this some leftover, perhaps stolen bauble your grandmother left you as your sole inheritance?" And Komar turned around smiling at the whispers and giggles from the crowd.

Onofrio, never one to be outdone took a small sip of wine, put the cup down and ran a finger through his hair. Without bowing or leaving the comfort of his chair he clearly announced for all to hear, "In the name of Serou, Master builder of all Judea, I am to secure a qualified craftsman to perform a repair on one of his favorite pieces of personal jewelry. Perhaps your grandfather has the knowledge and expertise required. I am responsible for securing the most skilled individual for the task." Onofrio commenced to look around the few remaining craftsmen still lingering about. Most had left either injured or felt no need to stay. With a single look at Komar, Onofrio made it clear that the house of Jumansa would never touch Serou's precious trinket. Onofrio spotted a bearded individual in ragged clothes, worn out shoes and a lumpy leather bundle hanging heavy over a slender shoulder. But the man had intelligent eyes, even if he looked poorly. The leather bag on his shoulder indicated the man's devotion to his work. "You!" Onofrio called out, pointing an aimless finger at the dingy individual. The man's eyes flew wide open, pointing to his chest in shock.

"Me?" His voice quavered in disbelief. "I am a simple street goldsmith. Are you sure you want me?" He made a move towards Onofrio and hesitated, looking frightfully at Komar and his companion.

"Yes, you. Come here." Onofrio ordered, openly ignoring Komar's threatening presence. Some of the braver craftsmen began to filter back sensing they may have an opportunity to show their wares. "Do you have a sample of your work from which I can judge your qualifications?" Onofrio asked the dingy man. The man still in shock, gingerly brought out a lambskin bag from his inner garments. Carefully he shook out a long chain of delicately woven gold thread. Onofrio admirably examined the workmanship of the chain primarily interested in the clasp that locked the work into a necklace. The work of a talented craftsman shone brightly in his hand. Onofrio carefully inspected the clasp. He looked at the ragged jeweler, whose face was still beaming. "May I pull on this clasp?" Onofrio asked not wanting to damage the masterpiece.

The ragged man shrugged his shoulders and smiling quickly added, "Be my guest. It will not tear apart. It contains a tiny spring inside the circular sheath that holds the chain secure until you press this tiny stem and only then will the clasp open. I have made many of these locks in various sizes." The man beamed with pride justly gained.

Onofrio tried the tiny gold stem on the inside of the clasping circle and as he did, he gently pulled the chain. Magically it came open and laid shining gloriously in the noonday sun. "How much weight will this clasp hold, do you know?" Onofrio inquired.

"It will hold a tremendous amount of weight, sir, I assure you."

"Does your ability surpass this?" Onofrio addressed Komar who enviously admired the magical clasp. Protecting the ragged man's professional secret, Onofrio closed his hand and palmed the precious chain to the jeweler.

Boastfully and loud enough for all to hear Komar responded, "By miles, my good sir, by miles. The top artisans in my father's house can outperform any begging street so called jeweler in Jerusalem."

Onofrio eyed him coldly. "Had you said anything else sir, anything else at all I would have been pleasantly surprised. Your station in life has abandoned your civility, sir."

Spotting the menacing looks on the duo before him and fearing for the jeweler's safety Onofrio decided to take the craftsman with him to Serou's home. "I think it best you come with me, staying here may prove hazardous to your health and property," the young man stated. Komar apologized for his behavior while the muscle man extended his hand in friendship to the jeweler. Innocently the jeweler complied and the muscle man took his hand in a crippling grip reaching inside the man's robe for the lambskin bag. The jeweler howled in pain and the muscle man shrugged his shoulders as if he did nothing wrong. But the harm was done and the jeweler agonized from his crushed knuckles.

The trip home was uneventful. The jeweler slept in the back of the cart after taking bread and wine Tremiyo brought for himself. Events of the day passed through Tremiyo's ear several times before reaching the gates of home late in the afternoon. People gathered to care for the horses and unload supplies. All were anxious to hear news from the city, a treat that Tremiyo often embellished with colorful descriptions. Now he had a new story to tell, after finding a place for the jeweler to spend a few days. Tremiyo checked his hand and diagnosed a broken bone or badly bruised at best. In any event the hand would be useless until the injury healed. Already the hand was swollen and showed a faint discoloration. Tremiyo looked through the industrious crowd unloading the cart until he spotted whom he wanted and called out to him by name, "Chim-mi-yu!" and waved him forth. A powerful medium-sized man with strange yellowish-brown skin and dark slanted eyes came forth. He wore a kimono type robe and sported a black hair braid to the middle of his back. In a weird language, Onofrio never heard before, Tremiyo instructed the man. Chim-mi-yu bowed deeply and looked to the jeweler seated at the end of the cart. The alien man looked similar to Komar's bodyguard although this man had a friendlier face. Chim scooped up the heavy leather bag and slung it over his shoulder to the useless objections of the jeweler. He then picked up the jeweler in his arms and carried him off to his assigned quarters as if he were a mere babe. The jeweler could remain as long as he wished. No questions asked.

When the cart was unloaded, Tremiyo came to a perspiring Onofrio who had volunteered to unload the supplies. The scent of honest sweat, farm sacks, vegetables and grains stirred welcome memories in the young man's mind. He sighed deeply in the presence of Tremiyo and pointed to the western horizon. The early evening clouds gathered like heavenly eagles to frolic and mingle with their own kind. The billowing clouds touched each other in slow motion. Majestically painted amber-gold, lavender-bronze and tarnished copper in a way that only the gods can cast upon their day's departure. "The godly artwork is presented to man as a token gift for his labor," stated Onofrio's father at the end of their work. And Onofrio remembered it well. "My father always said of sunsets such as this, 'Be grateful that the helpers of nature have granted us more light to complete our work.' And we would work until the moon was above us.

There was much joy in our accomplishments. My mother and father sang happy love songs and sad ballads while we worked. I worked. I often tried to join in causing them to laugh at my efforts. Their laughter felt like a warm loving touch from each of them. Often we roused sleeping birds or startled rabbits in our furrows. My father checked various snares he had around our fields for rabbits and birds. What he snared was often times our dinner the next day. My father almost always carried me home on his shoulders. And I rode on the shoulders of the Master of the World. Nothing could touch me there. My father and uncle would send my mother and aunt home ahead of us. They needed time to clean up and prepare dinner. Walking home, my father and uncle spoke of what needed to be done tomorrow. We always bathed in the stream close to our cottage and when we came to the table, there were wonderful meals fragrant with the aroma of love and home. The fire in our hearth glowed brightly and it was the center of my world. I had toys my father or uncle made, my mother too. I remember a toy plow made from the fork of a hardy tree, with tiny leather straps for harness that attached to a horse, mule or donkey figure made of clay and painted. I played with it by our front door many times. I slept soundly every night in a bed my father made for me. My bed was close to the fireplace, but out of my mother's way. She could watch me, tend the fire and do her cooking. She was always up early, stirring the embers of yesterday and starting a new fire for today. Our cottage filled with the fragrance of bread baking in the side oven of the hearth. When my father came down from their sleeping room, he always embraced my mother by the fireplace and they would whisper things to each other I never heard. They often giggled and laughed like children. When they laughed, I felt like laughing too and often did. They would look at me as though embarrassed that I might know what they were laughing about. They always ate and drank their morning meal together and it was a joy to be in their presence. When my father would start to go, it seems to me they never wanted to leave each other. They clung to one another until my father would shut the door and resolve to go. He turned many times to look at our cottage before he disappeared into the fields or animal keeps beyond our view."

The once vivid heavenly eagles dissolved into early darkness. A gentle breeze from the desert warmed the evening while a mellow crescent moon hung low in the sky, reluctant to make its nightly journey. Tremiyo allowed the young man to speak freely, convinced that the more he spoke of his past, the more he would remember. "Come to my home, tonight," he was saying with an arm over the young man's shoulder. Entering the busy kitchen, Tremiyo was soon busy with the calls of his responsibility. The man had a commanding aura and nobody disputed his word. There was even a semblance of nobility in the way he pointed at various items and in the way he addressed the workers. His flowing robes, the way he walked and the huge medallion resting on his chest made Tremiyo undisputed master over his busy realm. Every food item was inspected no less than three times. Onofrio went around visiting almost every cooking station, taking samples everywhere he went as though he missed being here. An entire bakery was producing a variety of breads, cakes and multiple sweet things. The fragrance from the ovens drove him to swipe a hot loaf and slice off a generous chunk on which he poured a liquid kind of flavorable cheese. Onofrio was thoroughly enjoying the snack when Tremiyo found him. "Don't overload yourself on bread. Senobia and I have a special feast for your homecoming." When Onofrio took one last bite, the old man grabbed the remains and tossed it into his sample basket. "Go see about your jeweler. Make sure his valuables are secure and he is fed for the night. Then clean yourself up, put on some fresh clothes and be at my home in about two hours. My daughter and I have a surprise for you." In finality the older man walked away, with a faithful servant only one step behind him lugging the heavy basket.

Onofrio managed to snatch the bread from the basket and kept on munching. "Dictatorial old goat," Onofrio chuckled as he walked away from the old man's stern commands. But he said it in jest and soon found joy in being in his own bath. His assortment of fresh smelling oils were where he put them as though he never left or was expected to return. He welcomed but was not surprised to find a neat stack of clean clothes lying over a small bathroom bench. The ragged jeweler had washed off the road grime and was housed in a small workman's cottage. He had been given clean clothes and even a new pair of sandals. Camia was busy attending to his crushed hand and showed a happy smile when she turned to greet the young man from parts unknown. She commented on how well he looked and tenderly ran a hand through his hair. Onofrio felt a soothing balm warm his heart by such an unexpected show of affection. She moved away, allowing Onofrio to come closer to the jeweler. On a small bedside table was a washbowl, an assortment of strange smelling ointments and medicinal herbs. The injured hand was neatly wrapped and the jeweler was resting well.

"I made a poultice of ingredients a Grecian physician to whom I once belonged taught me to make. He routinely had me make this mixture in large amounts, which he sold in small covered jars to travelers and caravans for road injuries. It soothes the pain and mends injured flesh and the swelling will go down in a day or two," Camia stated with a degree of authority.

Impressed with her effort, Onofrio patted her amiably on the shoulder. "You've done well, lady doctor. You've done well. Do what you think is best for him."

"Oh, I think someone should stay with him," Camia anxiously volunteered, "in case he needs something during the night. I brought him some wine with his meal and he's resting well, but he may need someone to be with him later tonight when he wakes up." Her outer concern appeared genuine, but her haste to stay overnight in a small room with an absolute stranger was not like the kind and reserved Camia.

"I'm sure your company will do much to heal his hand," Onofrio smiled profusely as he left the pair for his dinner engagement with Senobia. Oh, and her father too.

The demand for his presence or invitation was about two hours old and he was soon at Tremiyo's front door. He reached up to use the door knocker and was momentarily surprised when the door came open before him. And there stood Senobia in the doorway illuminated by the oil lamp at her home's front entrance. Light within the house shone though her gown and the silhouette of her form was that of a young goddess.

"Please come in," she invited sweetly. "We've been waiting for you."

"Not I. I've been with him all day long" quipped Tremiyo from somewhere inside. Senobia wore a sky blue gown of some sort of shiny, flimsy material accented by a gold chain around her slender neck with a modest bracelet to favor her left wrist. A large well appointed room met his eyes in wonder. These were not slave quarters and he felt humbled by the unexpected opulence. Senobia had her lips faintly colored like a warm blush of pink while her hair cascaded to her shoulders in graceful swirls of bronze and gold. Onofrio heard the welcome voices but was struck by a sense of shyness. He didn't know what to do or say and seemed awkward in a boyish fashion. He toyed with his hands, exploring the home, furnishings and decorations in awe. Senobia saw his uncertainty and took him by the hand to a couch made in the form of two swans facing away from each other. Their backs were made to accommodate two people on appealing cushions. To promote comfort their wings spread upwards providing a pleasing back rest. Handsomely carved feet gave credence to their posture and assured strength. Here was something Onofrio could relate to and talk about to dismiss his uneasy feelings. Making every effort to regain himself, he walked around the couch in Senobia's hand.

"What a handsome piece of work," he stated running a hand over the highly polished white wings of the couch. A piece such as this was suited to the rich and powerful far more than to a mere servant. He was busy exploring the surroundings with Senobia as tour guide when he became aware of music softly floating into the room from somewhere. Harps, flutes, muted drums and string instruments blended harmoniously to deliver a sense of joy. Muffled voices and quiet laughter drifted to him from yet another room to which Senobia led him. Tremiyo stood on a raised floor encircled by handsome marble balustrades. He dressed elegantly, in flowing robes with embroidered neck and hem lines to the floor. He looked fresh and well groomed, as if this were a special occasion. The sparkling emblem of his office was on a golden chain planted at the center of his chest. Tremiyo was not a slave or servant as he often pretended to be. This was the home of the Steward of the House of Serou. A prestigious position envied by many, respected by all. As Tremiyo stood on that elevated floor, he looked every bit the part. Ease and self assurance radiated from him, derived from years of being in command of his domain. When Tremiyo descended the stairs coming to Onofrio with open arms, it was with warmth and genuine affection. Onofrio sensed it, he felt it. It was a presence unseen but powerful in its reality.

"Welcome home, son. I'm glad you decided to come. The only thing we have to offer you is good music, plenty of food, some old friends and my daughter's birthday, who I know is truly glad you came. Today marks the sixteenth year of her birth." Onofrio turned to looked at Senobia, but she had disappeared. Having gained his usual composure he walked with Tremiyo to the door from which echoed the sounds of activity and music. "Come, let's join the others in wishing my daughter her happiest birthday. People brought gifts to commemorate the event of her arrival. The greatest gift she wants is your presence. Come, we'll make her happy together." There was serenity in the old man's directive. No high tone dictates, just a peaceful willingness to make his daughter happy. He had often made it clear she was the truest love in his life. With ease the old man pushed the massive doors open binging into focus a melee of familiar faces having a good time. Senobia was surrounded by the people she had known since childhood, many of which regarded her as a daughter like their own. Tremiyo was always a kind taskmaster. Firm in the things his position demanded from slaves and servants but kind and considerate when their work was done. Happiness seemed to reign supreme with the admiration and respect for father and daughter on open display. Senobia stood before a table inspecting and caressing gifts brought by the only family she ever knew. From the distant view Onofrio had, her face was a portrait of delightful bliss. There was no room for him there and he accepted it with good grace. She was the focus of all eyes and her happiness was contagious. Instead of intruding in her circle of admiration, he chose to admire the beauty of her character. She was a child receiving praises in material form from people that held her in esteem. Above all, they loved her and he could too. With all the attention, praise and gifts the child within her behaved in a girlish manner. Yet, she was not a child. She was a lovely and desirable young lady. She was like a beautiful rose in the budding stage. A white dove of untarnished virtue. And as she inspected, received and thanked her guests she demonstrated all the things Onofrio was thinking of. She possessed beauty that queens would kill to have. She had poise such as can be taught only by expert teachers. All things wondrous to the world rested on her graceful shoulders. Painfully, reluctantly he arrived at the conclusion that her station in life, her beauty in known demand and limitless grace placed her far beyond his wildest expectations. He was a homeless, penniless convict in bondage to far deeper things than his masculine desires. A familiar resident of his mind reminded him that he must find his memory, his homeland, his parents and he must find a way to earn the gold for such an expedition. Senobia was a beautiful, wonderful young girl but, she was a dream in real life as well as in his sleep. Tonight the illusion was more vivid in its reality than ever before.

"Your troubles are showing on your face, young man. Lay your concerns aside for tonight and rest assured she is very fond of you." Tremiyo handed him a cup of wine and gave him a confirming look. And he allowed himself to simper away from his troublesome thoughts. But he felt ill at ease, as though his thoughts were read by the older man. He fumbled for something appropriate to say and nothing came forth. "She's a beautiful child," he finally managed almost to himself and slowly exhaled a long captive breath.

"She's a young lady never having known the lust of men, a child innocent of all sin. She's the walking, breathing reflection of her mother. And the most precious jewel in my existence. She's the fountain from which I hope will spring a deeper meaning to my life. To the rest of the world, she is just a young, exciting female. Not much more than an object of masculine desire."

The young man took a cup of wine from the older man and decided to keep his thoughts to himself, since he had no immediate answer. With the spiced wine in hand he raised his cup to the older man's daughter. "To Senobia," he declared inviting her father to join his toast. The words were barely away from his lips when he caught sight of the lovely birthday lady. The look from her eyes felt like a warm ostrich plume stroking his face. It was a beacon of soft light begging for his presence. He nodded to her in silence and transmitted his soundless reply, *'I'll be right there.'* while her father was handed an empty cup and left there. Onofrio glided though the crowd with ease and no obstructions. The force that propelled him was not a single cup of wine; it was a glorious feeling stemming from a joy he never knew before. He answered her summons without question or hesitation. He hastened with palpitating heart to be in Senobia's presence. To stand near to her and to breathe and to live in the aura of her magic. He felt a call to his inner soul and not just a call of the flesh. Onofrio was no different than any other randy young man of whom often first love answers with their physical bodies. His sense of longing was deeply embedded within his heart, but not his physical need alone. There was something more intense than his masculine desires. His physical need was real and throbbing within him. He acknowledged that his longing was not for just any body. It was for Senobia, and Senobia alone could appease it. Somehow he knew that beyond the physical call of mere humans lies a deeper and more profound way to amplify their love.

CHAPTER TEN

AN ISLAND OF FRIENDSHIP, IN A SEA OF SLAVES

Now as they went on their way, he entered a village; and a woman named Martha received him into her house. And she had a sister called Mary, who sat at the Lord's feet and listened to his teaching. But Martha was distracted with much serving; and she went to him and said, "Lord, do you not care that my sister has left me to serve alone? Tell her then to help me."
Luke 10:38-40

"I'm so glad you came," Senobia whispered close to his face. Her eyes filled with joy. She had a soft hand firmly planted on his forearm then passed her entire arm behind his back and clutched him close to her side, in a very matter-of-fact manner. She tilted her pretty head sideways and looked at him with a somewhat childish but nonetheless satisfied smile. He looked at her in amazement and her almost brazen behavior. He judged her to be simply an immature child and open with her happiness to see him. But, he struggled to accept that.

"Had you not come, the evening would not have been complete. You brought me more happiness than all the presents these people brought me. Today I am sixteen years old. Some say I am too old to marry. Do you think I'm too old to marry?" She genuinely wanted to know, especially from him. A puzzled Onofrio searched for the proper thing to say; in fact, he was glad to see Bonaz before him with his hand extended. But, responding to his salutation, seeing Onofrio's right hand busy at Senobia's waist Bonaz nodded amiably at the firm grip she had on Onofrio. "What a handsome couple you two make," and passed them by but looked over his shoulder a few times. Bonaz semi-disappeared into the crowd but Onofrio spotted him talking to someone and giving knowing looks in Senobia's direction.

Almost all that were present met the young couple and almost in unison expressed approval. As expected there were countless whispers and reserved opinions also. Senobia wanted the approval of her only family. It made her happy to know he was well accepted into their closed community, it being almost a private world. She was filled with pride that he was held in such high esteem and respected by so many. Exuberant with joy at having her arm around him and seeing her father's faded smile from a distance, she looked to heaven and thanked God. Slowly they made their way through many quick stops of "Happy Birthday" wishes to a huge table laden with an immense variety of foods. People milled around selecting choice items to place on plates or nibble on by hand. They spoke to, shook hands and greeted each other as long time absent friends and yet they were the same people they worked with every day. Socializing in an open manner as if the yoke of slavery did not exist. They were in the home of the Steward of Serou, on neutral ground so to speak. There was plenty of wine and Egyptian beer to be had and yet nobody over indulged. Most of them had a cup of wine or a goblet of beer. Fragrant fresh baked bread floated in the air along with the unmistakable aroma of roasted lamb. Half a beef was brought in from an outside grill and was being dissected into portions for all to enjoy. Trays of figs, grapes, dates and sliced cucumbers, a large tureen loaded down with Tremiyo's favorite pomegranates, roasted grasshoppers and locust swam in shallow bowls of honey, and sliced melons of various colors and sizes graced another tray. The ever present music waltzed in Onofrio's mind as he mingled and visited with the crowd while

Senobia followed suit but never let go of his arm. She seized it like a prized possession. Eventually Onofrio spotted Tremiyo occupied in speaking to a small group of women. When the women turned their attention on him and Senobia, he realized they were the topic of the group's conversation. He didn't care. He was happy. Senobia was happy. Add to all that the temporary dismissal of his more eminent problem. He would confront that problem tomorrow. As well as all these people would confront being slaves again – but tomorrow.

At last the trio was alone with only a few servants doing overtime duty. A large fish was presented on a silver fish shaped tray. It was baked to excellence and stuffed with a spicy dressing that filled the room with a delectable aroma. Along came assorted vegetables and the ever present fresh bread. The surprise meal would not be complete without Senobia's favorite wine mixture. Tremiyo carved out sections of the fish and transferred servings to his two guests. He raised his cup to Senobia, "Happy birthday, angel." Then to Onofrio, "Welcome home, son." He reached out for Onofrio's hand and to his daughter. United by hand he prayed. Onofrio was far more anxious to eat than he was to holding hands. He complied sheepishly with the old man's request and was not surprised to see and hear the servants join in.

"Thank you Lord, for the gifts we are about to receive from your generous abundance. Thank you for the company gathered at this table in your Holy name. Bless us with the strength to follow your rule. Give us this day the wisdom to always walk in the path of righteousness, Amen."

The meal was peacefully consumed followed by many compliments to the engineer of the feast. And as the hour had grown late, Tremiyo made ready to exit. Instructing Onofrio to sleep in a small room prepared for him by the front door. From there he would be close to the work before him tomorrow. To his daughter he said, "Senobia don't be up much longer. You need your rest also. When you come to bed, knock on my door that I may know you are in your rooms." Then with a knowing look, he addressed the couple before him. "Both of you have a lifetime ahead of you. Do not hasten the inevitable; it will come soon enough under the proper society demands. Enjoy your company but say good-night some time soon." With that said, he patted Onofrio on the shoulder and shook a knowing finger at him, as he walked away.

Once alone with Senobia, he again felt awkward and ill at ease. He fumbled for words and hesitated to look into her eyes. The feelings were new and strange sensations. He was never ill at ease with other girls. This was no ordinary girl. Senobia was not the daughter of some unknown field hand. Senobia was special. She was head and shoulders above any other girl he had ever known. She was taught to read and speak well. She generated respect to her person without asking for it. Her grace and charm were lessons she practiced without pretence. She was musically inclined and he had no doubt, her virtue was intact. Her laughter was that of a happy child but she was not a child. She was a young lady, fully developed. The silhouette of her graceful figure before the light of her door still glowed vividly in Onofrio's mind. Today was her sixteenth birthday. Without a word said, she declared she wanted to be in his arms. But she was the daughter of a man with whom Onofrio had an invisible alliance. Tremiyo was like a father to him and that imposed an obligation on Onofrio to stay within the lines of honor and respect. Which made Senobia, forbidden fruit. She was to be held at bay, a treasure to cherish and admire. The obligation prevented him from holding her close to his yearning body and touching her intimately as he so much wanted to do. As he so much needed to do.

"You act like you're afraid of me. Why is that?" she asked perplexed. A sadness filled her eyes as she waited for him to answer.

"I'm not afraid of anything," he answered too quick and too much like a little boy's defense. "It's just that, well, you don't know anything about me and I'm older than you are." Meaning he had experiences she knew nothing about.

"And what does being older than I have to do with us talking about things people our age talk about so we can know each other better?" She reached out and rested her hand gently on his forearm. He pretended not to feel the tantalizing warmth. But, his effort to ignore it was clearly visible to her.

"Well, I don't know. It's just that around you, I feel tongue tied. I don't know what things to talk with you about. You have servants around you all the time and a tutor to teach you things I don't know about. People in the compound teach you the art of baking, sewing, weaving and even cooking. You have dancing and music lessons and I've been told you sing beautifully." After gesturing wildly while he spoke, he stopped to catch his breath.

"Oh? And who told you I sang beautifully? she asked, amused at his boyish ranting.

"Well, I don't really know. I heard it around the compound. Everybody knows it."

"You were never curious to know for sure?" she toyed with his boyish manners. An inquiring smile rested on her lips and her eyes looked at his, while his avoided looking at her.

"I just thought that if you sang beautifully, you sang beautifully. That's all. How could it mean anything to me?"

"When I heard you were learning to use a sword and shield, I worried something terrible would happen to you." she allowed her concerns to show hoping he would reciprocate but, he continued his boyish manner.

"It's not at all the same. I do what all men do. There is nothing to worry about. Besides if I get hurt there's a lot of medical help within the compound to see about me."

She poured him a small cup of wine. "So!" she finally asked in a soft muffled voice, "you don't even like me a little bit, do you?"

"Oh, I like you a lot." He answered too quickly in an unfamiliar voice.

"Why then are you afraid to show you care about me?" she asked in earnest, looking directly into his eyes, in which she found hesitation and perhaps regret over his hasty announcement.

He found reason to get up and walk around the couch in silence. Looking at the room and furnishings he saw a dozen times tonight. He toyed with the cup of wine in his hand, clearly avoiding her closeness. Perplexed, his mind raced through what to say to the object of his dreams. Would this be the time to speak of his quest for his memory and home?

But Senobia understood it to be unmistaken rejection. Plain disinterest. Perhaps there was another girl or girls he liked better? With reluctant acceptance she raised going to her rooms as her father instructed. "Will you need me to help find your sleeping room?" she asked with kindness but firm resolve. She carried a terrible weight over her heart and she had trouble breathing. She felt like crying but a greater power kept her from it. She tried to smile but her mouth would not comply. She felt chilled in the warmth and comfort of her home.

"Senobia." he called out in his gentle ruffian voice. And she clearly heard him exhale a deep sigh. "Please come here. Don't leave yet," suppressed emotion clearly in his voice. She came to his side looking inquisitively unto his face from around his shoulder. He saw a beautiful young girl peeking around his bicep with a bright gleam in her eyes and strands of golden bronze hair cascading down in graceful swirls. As if in fear he would bruise her, he gently took her by the shoulders and brought her close. She waited for his lead but saw him exploring her face. The scent of her closeness, the sweet aroma from her lips, and the delicate touch of her hands on his biceps sent electrical charges throughout his body. Boldly he chose to state his case before emotions stampeded logic. "You must understand that I am here as a temporary item, by the will or dismay of Master Serou. I could be sold off or discharged to parts unknown any day. Your father is in an equal position. I am a transient field worker without a shack to call my own, a carpenter apprentice without a tool or a coin in my keep. Even the clothes on my back are subject to recall when I leave here. I need to find my memory and my homeland that I may sleep in peace. All I have that is truly mine is me." And as he spoke, sincerity sparkled in his eyes close to tears.

"You have yourself and that is all I want." she stated with heartfelt resolve. She trembled at the thought of him going away to search for what may not exist. She feared his drive be so strong that he may leave her, unfulfilled.

"That is not enough. You have a life of ease and comfort before you. All the things that any young lady such as yourself could want are resting at your feet. I could not live with myself if I destroyed that for you. Furthermore, I know that for now there is no chance of me coming into a fortune to carry us away from here. My parents, if they still live, would be a wonderful place for us. But, your is education here and the things you have before you may be better for you than the life of a peasant. However good the life of my parents may be for them and me, it may not be for you. That may cause you pain and me anguish."

"My place would always be where your heart is. Be it any-where in the world. I would be happy by your side. Whatever destiny has in store for you, I would share with you. Good or bad." and she said it from her heart looking straight into his eyes, unafraid of her commitment. In her father's presence she was quiet and demure. He never knew her to be so open with her thoughts. The revelation was startling to him.

"Your father would take you over his knee, if he heard you talking to a man in this manner." And he gently pushed her back, expecting Tremiyo to materialize from a dark corner with ax in hand.

"My father is well aware of how I feel about you. And he approves with conditions, of course." she said in a gen-tle whisper and smoothly eased into his arms. She took his face in both her hands and caressing his short beard she re-vealed, "I've loved you since the first night we met at wisher's paradise. You were a frightened boy trying to be a brave man then, as you are now." He was still uncertain of what was un-folding before him. Was this to be the night of his dreams? Wild thoughts racing through his mind, while searching for a secluded dark spot preferably with a couch. "I never knew you to be so bold," he managed to say in an unfamiliar voice.

"And I never knew you to be so logical, so clear of thought. You must care for me a great deal, if you would forfeit our lives together, so I may have the things our world has to offer. In all that, you overlooked one very important item. That is, if I am to have the things you so clearly described, then surely I will have to belong to somebody. And that somebody may be someone I would hate to live with and live for. So, for all your clear thinking, there's a view from my side of life. My father has rejected offers from wealthy men that would have me for themselves or to give away to some favorite son or distant nephew. There's been offers my father thought were suitable for me but he has the wisdom and kindness to always allow me the freedom of my thoughts. I know very well that he wants me to bear children. That he may have loving toys in his later years. I also know he wants children born of true love as he had with my mother and not through a fixed relationship. He wants children that will grow up to be like you and I." She took him by the hand and led him to a table where a candle glowed brightly. "Please sit with me a little longer, she invited. "There is more you should know before this night is over." With each a fresh cup of wine they sat close as though to start a new line of conversation. Only then did Onofrio realize the musicians were still there. Very possibly somebody was watching them and he smiled to himself. Somewhat happy over the prospect but distressed that his private time with Senobia may not be so private, after all. She took his hand in the warm enclosure of her own and spoke in a near whisper. "You must promise on your solemn word of honor that you will not disclose what I will tell you to no one." He saw deep loving affection in her eyes. He saw faith and expectancy also.

"I promise not to tell." He stated unsure of what he would hear, and expecting an unsavory story about her loss of virginity and with whom.

"Serou freed my father three years ago. On the condition that he stay and be steward to his house. Serou has complete trust in my father and that trust earns us a handsome salary and a comfortable home to live in. We have the freedom to go and come wherever my father's duty takes us without recall from anybody. Serou has given my father documents stating that I, Senobia, belong only to my father. I am not a bartering tool for the Master of Public Works. My father and I chose to remain here to help improve the lives of these people as best we can. My father is very aware of how it feels to bear the yoke of slavery and tries never to treat anybody as such. He treats them all with dignity and respect and I think he does well in that area. Dad would never subject me to a life where I would not have the freedom of my thoughts or worse be forced to submit to unpleasant things. Equally so, my father will do all he can to see you totally free. Should you choose not to have me in your life, he will still help you be free and find your home. He believes you to be a worthwhile young man. Nobody knows my father is a free man. Some may suspect it but, nobody knows for certain. Remember, you made a solemn oath not to tell that my father is a freed man."

"But, why should it be such a big secret," Onofrio asked.

"There is some resentment among the slaves that we are free to go and come as they think we please. Although most times we go on business for the house of Serou, we also run errands for some slaves. They are like children, they always want something. You are considered free and subject to resentment and even jealousy that you should be so favored by Serou and coveted by the centurion. The games Serou and the centurion play to win you to their side is common knowledge. In spite of all that, you are widely admired and respected among them all," she finally concluded.

"I never set out to win favor from anybody. I simply worked hard to make the best of my situation." Onofrio stated with sincerity and did not realize that his masculine desires of a few minutes ago had dissolved into a broader reality.

"I know that my love, but their point of view is different," she stated. He loved the light from the oil lamps glowing through Senobia's hair. She sat close to him in the circle of his arm as her warm breath softly caressed his face as she spoke. The spiced wine she sipped perfumed the small space between them, while her delicate feminine scent invaded his masculine senses again. The gauzy cloth separating the warm flesh of her breast from the side of his chest evaporated in his imagination. He fought the desire to cup his hand over the protruding garment while every nerve in his body rang for completion of his physical need. The innocent Senobia felt corresponding sensations coursing through her in alarming fashion and pleaded with her eyes for the ultimate satisfaction. He forced himself to stand up and break away from what he knew would happen if he let go of his senses. Gently her arms came to encircle his face as she stood on her toes to reach his lips. A wisp of light shone through his hair and, in her eyes, he became Apollo. She savored the mind spinning sensation of her favorite god holding her in his strong arms. While her eager body begged for culmination as she cast aside all lessons on feminine behavior,she knew well what the end result could be and still did not regress. She wrapped her arms around Onofrio's waist and on her toes pushed herself to him until their anatomies fit exactly where nature intended. She found his lips eager, hot and waiting. With her head tipped a bit sideways she crushed her lips to his with a feverish hunger that took long moments to achieve a partial satisfaction, then took a breath, and literally attacked his lips again and he responded with equal fervor but could not draw her close enough. They clung to each other in lip grinding kisses until they were intoxicated by their passion. He smiled at his realization that although she knew what to do, she had not done it enough to really know how. There was a mild inept grace in her kiss. Could it be, this was her first kiss? An odd thought to be having at such a time and he dismissed the notion to lose himself again in her passion for him and him for her. In the glory of a prolonged kiss and body grinding embrace he clearly heard the musicians pick up their tempo and the realization of being watched slapped him to sobriety. When he eased her away, her hair was in disarray and she looked stunned at his pushing her gently away, and made an effort to regain her position in his arms.

Taking a deep breath, he held a finger before her eyes and softy whispered, "Somebody's watching us. We need to walk around a bit." The man within him struggled fiercefully to relinquish a goal so near to completion. Perhaps the uneasy feeling of being watched by whoever it may or may not be was a blessing in disguise. And then they both heard someone drop a drum stick or a cup or a flute and they both broke out in childish laughter. Most likely the musicians were paid to keep an eye on them. They never suspected Camia, Senobia's long time chaperone. With an awkward controlled breath, he led her to the patio for the night air to cool their fever. He looked at her with longing eyes and hoarsely managed to say, "We must stop before I betray your father's trust and I make an ass of myself. I have dreamed of having you in my arms for too long to honestly say I can suppress my need of you for very much longer." And he released all holds on her.

She looked deep into his pain ridden eyes, simmering in her own agony. She took time to explore his face and slowly said in almost a whisper, "And do you thnk that your wishes and longings are reserved only for you? My love. I too have longed to be solely in your presence, to feel your arms around me, to kiss you and be kissed by you. I have wanted to caress you and be caressed by you, to feel as one with you. I have dreamed of you also. And I too fear that our desires will carry us beyond restraint. I trust we love each other enough to save ourselves for each other. I pray we have the strength to preserve what is considered precious by so many that no one can ever reproach us or speak ill of us. I want everybody to know that all is right with ourselves and for ourselves in the presence of Almighty God. As my father so aptly said a while ago, we have a lifetime before us. Leave us not rush the inevitable. Instead let us prepare for it with what is socially correct for both of us. I would wish for your first admission into my body to be a beautiful and unforgettable experience. I would wish for us to never forget our first night of love fulfilled. I wish it to be an event to glorify our lives as man and wife. You should know that tonight, I was ready and willing to concede to your needs and in so doing appease my own."

From somewhere in the darkness a rooster crowed long and unmelodious. Rudely it broke into the mellow tunes the musicians still played somewhere within the house. Onofrio had temporarily forgotten about them. "Oh, my heavens!" Senobia said with her eyes wide open and a hand to her mouth. "That is Bonaz's rooster, he's the first to crow." Giggling like a child she added," My father wants to kill that rooster so bad, most especially at this time of night. If he ever gets the chance to kill it, he will endanger his life with Bonaz. I'm sorry my love, but I have to go to my rooms. My father will worry."

She nodded in the direction of the private quarters upstairs, walking a bit awkward with her arms around his waist and her head on his chest. His arm around her shoulder made her feel blissfully happy. She never knew happiness could feel so wonderful. Only then did Onofrio hear the music come to a soft conclusion, followed by the unmistakable sound of instruments being put away. He saw no one but could feel eyes upon him from somewhere. They were friendly eyes so he dismissed them.

At the door to her rooms he kissed her gently on the lips first, then on each cheek. He took her by the chin and looked into her sleepy, weepy eyes that lit up brightly with his attention. "Happy Birthday," he whispered softly. "I'll see you sometime tomorrow." He opened the door and allowed her to pass into her chambers.

She touched his arm gently and whispered, "I miss you already, and you're not even gone yet."

He smiled at her and tenderly nudged her into her room, quietly pulled the door shut and walked away.

CHAPTER ELEVEN

HOME IS JUST BEYOND THE NEXT HILL

He awoke in pleasant surroundings by a glow of early morning that came too soon and immediately began thinking about what there was to eat. Quickly washing the sleep from his face and eyes, his mind started wondering what his workload would be for the day, a habit he practiced from childhood; then swiftly decided to address his workload when it arrived. He felt too good to bother with anything, besides food. Pleasantly enjoying the happy warmth that filled his sense of well being, his most urgent business remained to find the kitchens. And when he did, they were already busy with a melee of people doing what they had been doing for he didn't know how long. Metallic and wooden sounds banging, rolling and thumping, mixed with delectable aromas that filled the air. Onofrio, as usual had no trouble finding his way around the many cooking stations. Sneaking a snack here and a taste there. Not settling for any one thing, just being a boy playing with the kitchen staff. Here and there lifting a pot for somebody or stirring a skillet for somebody else. Someone pointed to a crate of eggs in a far corner and gestured him to bring it near. When he arrived with the fragile crate, he placed it close to the cook who nodded a silent *"thank you"* and pointed to a plate of hot bread, cooked eggs and some kind of sausage. The young man scooped up the plate, only to instantly put it back down with a loud bang. The cook threw him a towel from his shoulder and pointed to the hot plate, "Use that," and continued working, not missing a stroke. Tremiyo made his appearance, inspecting this, tasting that and correcting or approving something else. As usual he oversaw everything in a casual stroll like a general inspecting his troops. The previous hush of laxness turned into serious activity and Onofrio could see everybody doubling their efforts by Tremiyo's presence. When the older man came upon Onofrio, he invited the young man to come sit with him. They found comfort away from the noisy kitchen by an open window overlooking a large herb and vegetable garden. It was early morning and people were already working the patch, harvesting ripe items and culling out unwanted weeds. The agrarian scene, the moist odor of fresh tilled earth and growing plants in the mist of early day captivated Onofrio. He felt compelled to take a deep breath of all this as his mind swiftly traveled to another time. Before long a servant brought fresh juice, milk, hot tea, bread with butter and honey to their table. And a shallow bowl with a heap of pomegranates, Tremiyo's favorite breakfast materialized at their table. He claimed the fruit refreshed him and cleansed his teeth all at once. Generously the old man invited Onofrio to have some of the fruit.

"I never liked pomegranates," he slowly said, seemingly lost in thought. "Too much work for too little reward. These are granadas. That's what that fruit is called back home. My father spoke of a place called Granada when I was a child. It was a three or four day journey from home, depending on the cargo, my father said. He took farm goods there to sell in the market. My uncle and my father prepared for days to make the trip and they would go well armed against road bandits. Granada." Onofrio repeated several times as if to memorize the word. Totally lost in his thoughts he was unaware of anything around him. Clearly Tremiyo saw that the young man was struggling with the sudden revelation. Knowing well that it was good he was remembering an important part of his past, he allowed him to dwell in his thoughts. Tremiyo worked a mouthful of the trouble-some seeds studying the mystified young man's face. Disposing of the seeds out the open window, he finally asked, "Is this the first you've thought of that place called Granada?"

Emphatically the young man replied, "Yes." With a joyful gleam in his eyes he visibly shook with excitement. "I can find my way home when I get to Granada. People there will know my parents and give me directions home." For a fleeting moment, the young man felt his father pick him up and toss him over his shoulders to walk home. And he dwelled momentarily in the happy ambience of that time so long ago and so far away. The most urgent question was, do they still live? Are they well? Do I have added brothers and sisters? A rush of parental faces paraded through his mind in a hazy swirl. Onofrio's voice quavered unable to stop from shaking and eyes running over with tears. "Home is just over the next hill," rang clearly in his mind.

Gently patting him on the shoulder the older man spoke to him, "Easy now, son. Here have some tea and calm down." Tremiyo was struggling to do and/or say the right thing to a very distraught young man. "This is an important revelation that re-quires time to sort out and plan a solution." he surmised, pouring Onofrio some tea and doctoring it up with honey and a dash of milk.

As if realizing he needed to follow the old man's directive, he began to regain his usual composure. His eyes remained glassy and riveted on the distant horizon not really seeing anything around him. In his mind's eye, he saw wide vistas of forested hills in multiple shades of green. He looked through furrowed fields with long rows touching the faraway edge of his world. He felt that familiar breeze that swept down the mountain behind his home. His mind heard the splashing of wild water dashing over stones in the creek nearby. He felt the sting of cold water washing down his body when his father bathed with him in that creek after a day's work. He took a deep breath as his memory went to the warmth of the fireplace at home. Suddenly he felt dizzy and a throbbing pain was pounding at his temples. He saw his mother busy with her morning chores. It was all here, in this vast kitchen, the cultivated furrows outside the window and the fragrance of fresh baked bread. But this was not home. "Serou paid my debt and had the charges against me dropped," Onofrio stated making a continued effort to regain himself. "I am, in reality, a free man. I will speak to Serou and see if I can go. I would like to go home." His head still pounded and he seemed drained of his usual vitality. He wanted to run from this place and be free, to walk through his cottage door to find his parents in a loving embrace by the fireplace. His headache persisted and he sat gloomily with his head in his hands.

Guessing that random plans may be stirring in the young man's mind, Tremiyo spoke to him softly, "Now, that you have a better idea of where your home is, you must plan carefully to reach it. It will take money of which you have none. So be calm and let us do this day what we have to do. Give us this day to think. Tonight we will meet again. We'll talk about all this and together devise a plan to get you home. Don't do anything foolish. Instead busy your mind with whatever work Serou puts on you, and do it well. Be patient for today. This is not the place to discuss your future." Onofrio saw kindness and concern in the old man's eyes and nodded silently in agreement. He remembered Senobia saying," My father will help you."

Then Tremiyo went about his many duties leaving Onofrio to think and do whatever his day demanded. Although he worried in silence about the young man and the revelations that fell on him so suddenly. He felt reasonably certain Onofrio was too intelligent to foolishly try and go find Granada completely unprepared. Tremiyo knew a place called Granada was somewhere in Iberia across the vast Mediterranean sea. From the shores of Iberia, to the area of his homeland were countless miles over mountains and wide valleys to reach his goal. He had no way of knowing in which direction to start his search for his illusive home. There were also the emotions of his loving daughter to consider. Tremiyo's grandchildren were suddenly on the scale of balance. Senobia had confessed a growing affection for Onofrio and added that with him Tremiyo would have his anticipated grandchildren in due course. The beauty and talent of the young girl was widely known by the many daily contacts Tremiyo had in his capacity. Being Steward to the House of Serou carried many favorable privileges denied the ordinary business man and Tremiyo knew that well. He had respectfully cast off many offers from prosperous men to have Senobia for themselves or for a wealthy son, always allowing his daughter to have a say in her own future. Some offers, her father honestly wished she had taken. There had been opportunities to provide a handsome husband and a grand life of ease and comfort for her. He could not reproach Senobia for being drawn to Onofrio. After all was said and done, it was Tremiyo who inadvertently placed Onofrio in the light of her eyes. Without premeditation he brought them together for the first time. Senobia's interest had been sparked with each story her father told about the young man from parts unknown. Tremiyo knew the young man had merit. He was industrious. He was handsome and would make a good father. The old man imagined his grandchildren to be equally so. However, Onofrio was penniless, without a home to call his own. His future uncertain and no great fortune in sight. He could carpenter, do metal work, and raise crops. He was clever and would do well. In spite of all that, their lives would be difficult unless Tremiyo provided otherwise. Perhaps Serou would retire him and he could buy an old, well established inn to sustain them. But he could not see Onofrio carrying wine trays for the midnight drunks, let alone stirring pots to provide a meager living. So much for that idea.

Serou sent him to the wood working shops for the day. At the right moment Onofrio managed to ask for an audience sometime soon. Serou hawk-eyed him as usual, cleared his throat then nodded his head in reply. "I'll send for you when my time is right."

Concluding that too much wine last night gave him the throbbing headache, he resolved to pass the day as quickly as possible. He would use the day to find a way to Granada. This day would be a small step closer to home and family.

The usual hubbub of the woodworking shops was quiet this morning. Instead a group of workmen surrounded two men at the center of the shop, apparently in conference. One was a bearded man with a concerned look and slow motion gestures. The other man Onofrio recognized as the one that mysteriously disappeared a few nights ago. Workmen were posted at various places as if they were guards. Whispers and hand signals were swiftly passed among them as he approached the group. Bonaz met him before he got too close and immediately gave him orders to load some planks stacked by the door onto a wagon not far away. Since nobody argued with Bonaz, Onofrio chose to ignore the conference and the men therein. His mood and private thoughts taking precedence, he preferred to be alone. Soon the planks were loaded and although not tired from the minor chore, he found comfort in just standing idly by. Since he was noticeably not wanted among them he leaned on the wagon and daydreamed of being home. He gave little or no thought to the two mysterious individuals. It was not normal for these shop workers to gather around any man as he had just seen. It was even more unusual not be wanted among them. Shortly the two men came out of the shop and amidst many handshakes and waves of departure proceeded to the loaded wagon. As they drew closer, the bearded one nodded a silent "*thank you*" to Onofrio with a smile he clearly felt but did not see. The man dressed in tan and brown homespun with a light rope tie at his waist ending in the customary tassels. In minor disarray his rich brown hair came to his shoulders to join his full beard kept short. A peaceful gleam rested within his light brown eyes as he looked at Onofrio. His eyes did not scrutinize the young man of no memory but seemed to bathe him in a light mantle of tranquility. His graceful stride was clearly noted as he drew closer and although he was slight of build, there was a sense of strength about him. For some unknown reason and somewhat out of character Onofrio felt strangely compelled to bow to this man. Close to the wagon, the man placed his hand on Onofrio's shoulder and heaved himself unto the two-wheel vehicle. Onofrio experienced an odd sensation where the man laid his hand that seemed to softly sift through his mind and body. He had no choice but to look up to the man now making himself comfortable on the rough wagon seat. Questions went reeling through Onofrio's mind but he felt compelled to remain silent. The man looked down on him and raised his hand in departure or benediction. Silently watching the wagon leave the compound he quietly walked to the woodshop and met Bonaz. Strangely at peace with his headache gone, he asked," Who are those men?"

"They are the sons of Joseph, Judah and his older brother. They run a carpenter shop in Nazareth," replied Bonaz over his shoulder as he went back to work in a somewhat jovial mood. Whispered rumors and open discussions regarding a prophet from Nazareth had reached Onofrio a few times but he never paid heed. It was simply gossip in which he always chose not to indulge. These men were carpenters, craftsmen plainly clothed and far from being prophets of whatever god people chose to revere.

Around mid-morning Onofrio met the cleaned-up and better dressed jeweler of yesterday. His hand was still bandaged but he appeared semi-recovered. Smiling eyes foretold he was glad to see Onofrio.

"You're looking well,"Onofrio greeted.

"I haven't felt this good since I left home," he responded. They met with a cautious forearm clasp as the jeweler looked around for someone or something. "Have you seen the carpenter from Nazareth?" he asked looking concerned and with an aura of secrecy.

"Yes, Judah and his older brother were here earlier. But they left some time ago." Onofrio saw sheer disappointment in the jeweler's face.

"I have spent an entire fortune to find him. Now, I know he is nearby. Do you know if they will meet tonight?" he asked, desperate to hear a favorable answer and near to tears. Onofrio knew absolutely nothing about the jeweler's inquiry. It became obvious the man was of some importance since the workmen gathered around him in devoted attention. They appeared un-happy to see him go. Onofrio had experienced a vague sadness to see the bearded one leave. For no apparent reason, he felt a sudden compulsion to know, "Why do you seek this man?" he asked the jeweler."

The jeweler suddenly achieved a semblance of mystery and secrecy then looked around furtively as if afraid to be heard. "You mean you do not know who he is?"

Onofrio shrugged his shoulders in ignorance and sincerely replied, "He is the son of a man named Joseph, a carpenter from Nazareth. That's all I know."

The jeweler went down on one knee and with his finger quickly drew the outline of a fish on the loose soil. He looked up to Onofrio with a question beaming in his eyes. "Do you know what this means?" and he pointed to the crude symbol.

"No, I do not." Onofrio replied emphatically.

The jeweler passed his hand over the fish looking around as though in fear someone may have seen it. He then made a hasty departure in the direction Onofrio indicated the men had gone. He called out over his shoulder that he would return tomorrow to do the work for Serou.; that the precious bauble could wait one more day, much to the puzzlement of Onofrio. One did not just walk away from work. Especially work Serou wanted done. To rebuke the wishes of Serou was to invite his anger. Although now free he did not feel at liberty to disobey the Egyptian. In fact Onofrio did not feel truly free. Instead, he felt unexplainably committed to remain here for a time. Contrary to the powerful calls of home he experienced earlier. He would need a release form stating he was indeed free. He chose not to speak to anyone else about this. He would wait to make the announcement with proof in hand. A debt of honor had to be satisfied first. He owed Serou and he would pay him.

Even though he was kept busy with multiple petty chores Bonaz found for him to do, Senobia silently wandered into his mind several times during the day. Early evening finally came and the shops shut down for the night. As the men left their workplace the normal shouts and friendly insults went silent before a robed and hooded figure standing by a nightlight, in full view for all to see. Even fully robed, Onofrio knew as well as all the men that the figure was the young Senobia. When he came to her, she reached for his hand and led him away in silence.

After a short distance her first words finally came out from her pouted mouth and wrinkled nose. "You reek of stains, old wood and varnish. What's more you smell like a beast of burden." And she did a little dance holding her nose and laughing cheerfully.

"Thank you, Senobia. It's so nice of you to meet me after work to tell me I stink. What beast of burden do I smell like? A jackass?" And Onofrio pushed her gently away to arm's length smiling within.

She giggled some more, retrieved his hand and squeezed it gently. "Camia and I cleaned your quarters and arranged all your things in there, including the table and chair you built. I hope you like what we did. I also have a hot bath and a good dinner waiting for you. Serou sent some clothes. They're leftovers but still very nice and fairly new. He also sent an old arrow quiver and word that he would see you after dinner."

The promptness of Serou, Onofrio thought to himself, not sure he wanted to speak to the Egyptian tonight. For the present he was content with things just as they were. The scent of Senobia's freshly washed hair and the perfume she wore filled his sense of well being over the brim. He felt happy and complete in her presence. No parts missing. Just him, Senobia, some chirping crickets in the darkness and the refreshing coolness of early evening. Slowly they walked home, happy in each other's company. Camia waited for Senobia by his doorstep. A gentle kiss, a soft look of longing in her eyes and Senobia was reluctantly tugged along by Camia as they began to dissolve into the darkness. She stopped at the last shred of light to kiss her palm and blew the invisible kiss to Onofrio. An appeasement that fell entirely too short of his desires. He longed to be with her, but not in the lustful ways of the wheat fields in his past. He longed for her in a different manner. She had an aura of respectability that followed her everywhere and he wanted to maintain that status for her. If she was to be his, he wanted her in the most legal and righteous fashion. He would not violate the trust her father placed on them. He would not bring shame on her by forcing himself on her body. Even though he knew her wishes were equal to his. The man within him wanted to throw away all the foolish rules people hold in such high esteem. Virginity being such a precious element of high regard was reserved for those that lived in some other world. This was a world of slaves and bonded servants. That very thought gave sound reason to disregard the conditions of their existence and live for the moment. He wanted to forget Tremiyo's wish that his daughter be a virgin on her wedding night. He needed her more than he ever needed anyone before. His physical need for her had recently become painful at times. What would be the harm of being with her, just once? It would certainly relieve his agony. The whole world as he knew it indulged in satisfying their physical needs with no apparent harm. The fulfillment of personal pleasure between two people that cared very much for each other should not cause any problems. Why then did he feel as though he would be stepping on hallowed ground? What if he reached out and took what was being offered? His quarters would be the perfect place for the occasion. And if he took her virginity, what would happen to him? Who would come to do battle with him for having taken the blossom of her youth? Nobody, not even the great Serou and why should he? Lost in his thoughts he lathered himself with a sweet scented pumice, he found by his bath. Along with fresh towels and sun-dried garments. The wine concoction Senobia liked mellowed his mind, but did nothing to quell his physical needs.

Feeling fresh and clean he began to form his thoughts to discuss with Serou. His freedom would be the springboard to his future. Be it here with Senobia or be it with him and her going to his home land together. He remembered how his mother and father showed their love in his childhood. And he knew they would duplicate those scenes once they were at his home.

> *Now a certain man was ill, Lazarus of Bethany, the village of Mary and her sister Martha. It was Mary who anointed the Lord with ointment and wiped his feet with her hair. Whose Brother Lazarus was ill. So the sisters went to him saying, "Lord, he whom you love is ill." John 11:1-3*

By foot and mouth news moved rapidly among those knowing the whereabouts of Jesus. By this time he rarely traveled alone. There had been several attempts to disrupt his ministry by unbelievers stirred up by the powerful Jewish council. There were even physical attempts to dispose of him by hanging, another by pushing him over a precipice to certain death. Also by stabbing him in a crowd. Matthew and Peter armed with clubs prevented attackers from doing Jesus any harm.

What would the world be like today, if the attempts on Jesus' life had succeeded? That thought, that idea, that possibility has been the subject of conjecture for centuries by laymen and religious heads alike. The answer is awesome in its simplicity. The life and ultimate death of Jesus was preordained by his Heavenly Father. "For God so loved the earth that he gave his only begotten son, that man may have salvation." No other end to his life on earth would have achieved the same result. Evidence of that is more clear two thousand years later.

The common fear of the Pharisees was the near worship and adulation Jesus received from the many cures and miracles he performed wherever he made an appearance. Some members of the Jewish council feared that if his popularity continued to multiply, he could overthrow the council's grip on the people. If enough followers went to Jesus to be their sole religious leader he could in fact, become King of the Jews. No doubt an intolerable situation. Jesus knew the council plotted against him. He reminded them of their wrongful ways too many times to go unpunished. The open deviation from the laws of Abraham and Moses were too often skimmed over in lieu of what was presently more expedient. From that practice a rift of enormous proportions existed within members of the council. And so the bonding laws of Abraham and Moses eroded to a mere semblance of the true words. Be that as it may, they were in power and fully intended to remain so. They sent scribes to serve as spies to almost all his gatherings. Literally recording every word he spoke by more than one scribe, as one gathers evidence against a dangerous criminal. Patiently and methodically they wove the noose for his head from every word he spoke.

Four days after Lazarus died Jesus appeared at the home of Mary and Martha. Mourners and members of the council from Jerusalem were present as expected. Knowing that, Jesus took Martha away from the house and spoke to her. She greeted him with a title, "Oh Rabbi, dear Rabbi. You've come too late. Had you been here a few days ago, our brother would live."

"Have faith, my dear Martha. Your brother will walk again. Come show me where your brother lies." Having said that they walked from the house to the grave, freshly hewn from solid rock. When they made the turn on the road, Mary was given the word. Jesus and Martha were going to the grave and she decided to join them. By then, the crowd was trained to follow Jesus through every step, including the scribes, like hounds on the scent of something worth reporting. The grave had a massive circular stone serving as a lid to the hand-hewn cavern. None from the crowd could be forced to help roll back the stone. With considerable hesitation then strenuous effort the stone was rolled back by Peter, James and Mary assisted with a crowbar. Loud objections rose from the crowd as well as the grief stricken sisters. They strongly anticipated the stench of a body four days dead. Corruption had surely begun to eat away the flesh. Enormous apprehension and unearthly fear hummed from within the crowd as many took steps back anticipating the worse scenario. It is reasonable to say, that only the paid scribes remained at their post. Not far behind came members of the Pharisees serving as witnesses to the written record. It was heard from within the mob, "It is one thing to cure the sick. It is quite another to raise the dead." And if Lazarus did walk after four days in the grave, would this not be power far beyond that of the common man? Would this miracle not prove beyond doubt that this man, Jesus was truly the Son of God? Is it not reasonable to expect the flesh to be falling from the bones of Lazarus? The believers and the non-believers became one in apprehension and unprecedented fear.

Jesus looked to the heavens and prayed that the people may be made to believe that, He had been sent by his father. After a few moments of silent meditation, he called to the darkened orifice, "Lazarus, rise and come forth." Jesus extended his hand as if in a blessing at the grave's mouth. The crowd grew grippingly silent in unknown expectation. Silent fear expressed in every wide-eyed individual. Some mumblings and mixed language prayers uttered in haste by the bravest. Silence kept rhythm with each heartbeat in the crowd. Moments passed and nothing happened, serving to inspire the stone-hearted, "He's dead, leave him alone. He's dead." Still the crowd waited. After what seemed a lifetime of throat clutching fear a grey flutter of movement within the darkness of the cavern was seen by all eyes riveted to the grave. An almost inaudible rasp of sandals brushing over loose gravel. Then a second grayish movement put the crowd back two steps. Hands went to gaping mouths throughout the electrified mob. All eyes were now magnetized to the grave's opening. Without exception, it would be safe to say that a few scribes may have missed a few pen strokes. Sighs, moans and gasps rang clear from the mystified witnesses. A horrified silence gripped them all as Lazarus moved slowly into the light, wrapped in burial cloth. The wrapping cloth around his head fell partly away from his eyes. Lazarus, bound securely in burial cloth struggled to make the tiny steps the bindings permitted. Then with great effort he returned to the world of the living, one tiny step at a time. Lazarus smiled at the first person he recognized, it was Jesus standing before him unafraid. Those able to stand looked on in total awe. Several fainted while others ran away in absolute horror. Still others fell to their knees and some knelt with faces close to the earth. A number of the stout hearted disbelievers abandoned their previous convictions. Others became true believers on the spot where they witnessed firsthand the power of God. No man walks away from his grave. Lazarus did. So it is written and so he did; written records clearly show it.

When the news reached the Pharisees, plans were immediately formulated to assassinate Lazarus. It would discredit the uncredentialed teacher turned miracle maker, widely known as the dubious son of a carpenter from Nazareth. It was all so simple. A few gold coins discreetly paid and all the problems this ragged troublemaker was causing would go away. They considered the miracle of Lazarus rising from his grave as nothing more than a well-done magician's trick. Unexplained for the time being, but nonetheless a magician's trick. Lazarus was not dead, in the first place. There were very few witnesses at the burial. A switch of some sort could have occurred to fool everybody.

The sisters no doubt, played a part in the conspiracy. Conjectures, probabilities and reasonable answers ricocheted from councilman to councilman. While all the talk was finalized, Lazarus was home having dinner with his sisters and guests. The news that Jesus brought the dead to life spread rapidly throughout the countryside. The word went out by camel, horse, afoot and in more ways than one, by jackass.

Some council members considered the entire incident as being a serious affront by a tricky prophet against the Jewish seat of government and their religious convictions. It insulted their intellect. How dare Jesus add this to his list of torments against the Council? King Herod had done well to dispose of John. It was time to dispose of the troublesome Jesus. But, it had to be done cleverly. A way must be found to eliminate the problem and not be held accountable. The council must not have blood on their hands. Although the signs were all there, the council chose not to acknowledge the lowly carpenter born in a stable under mysterious circumstances as their Messiah. The savior they anticipated breathed hellfire and brimstone. The anticipated Messiah would strike the Roman yoke from the land with a single blow. This man, Jesus was soft bread dipped in honey. His tricks all had a logical explanation that time would reveal.

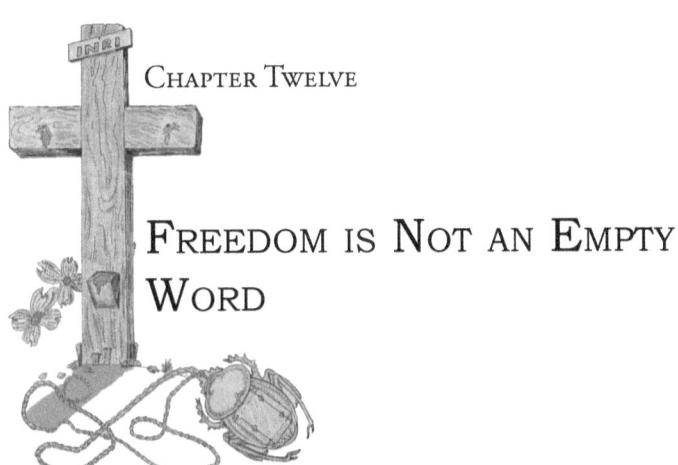

CHAPTER TWELVE

FREEDOM IS NOT AN EMPTY WORD

I t smarted the centurion to have Onofrio plucked from his grip and nearly being called a card cheat. Unaccustomed to accepting refusal he sought another approach to Onofrio's reluctance to join the Roman army under the tutorship of himself. It was inconceivable to Centurion Clemidius that someone of Onofrio's intellect would refuse such a grand opportunity to enrich himself at the expense of the fallen. He reasoned that once Onofrio felt the power of gold coins he could call his own, his attitude would change and he would come to his senses. There had to be more at the slave compound of Serou than what met the eye. The whole damned place operated entirely too smooth to be normal. There was no obvious dissention. No disregard for orders. No open opposition to slavery. Everybody seemed too happy to be there. It was not the common scene. Serou was a powerful man and the centurion now knew it. He also knew that Serou was not a magician able to generate contentment from enslavement. It was time to send in the spies.

On Serou's request a messenger promptly brought the young man into the great chamber to wait for Serou to lift his attention from the work before him. When Onofrio was noticed, he was motioned to sit and eat away from the documents Serou was studying. "There's food and wine over there you may like," the Egyptian invited with gestures. Onofrio refilled Serou's cup then his own and proceeded to indulge in the array of edible delights. When the master of the house was finally where he could stop, he sat and appeared to relax. He looked at his guest with his usual hawk-eye gleaming, "How did everybody react to your being free at the celebration last night?" he asked in a tone of genuine sincerity. It did not escape Onofrio that the Egyptian knew what stirred in his own backyard.

"I said nothing about it to anyone. There are still some matters to clear up between you and me. I have no document or release stating that I am truly free. Therefore there is nothing to say to anybody."

Incredulously Serou asked, "Do you doubt my word, young man?"

"No sir, I never doubted your word. But when I go home I will need proof that the law does not want me. I may encounter some promotion-hungry officer anxious to advance his career at my expense. Capturing escaped convicts brings a healthy reward. Without proof of who I am and what I am, I would be courting danger."

Serou softly clapped his hands at the young man. "Well thought, my young friend, well thought. I will see that you have the proper traveling credentials and proof that the law has no claim on you in a few days." And a faint glimmer of admiration sparkled in his eye for the young man. "There is also the matter of what I owe you for all you've done for me. I rest uneasy knowing I owe someone a debt." Straight faced Onofrio looked directly at Serou to punctuate his statement. From Serou he met a smile, "Onofrio, knowing that the world is not totally corrupt, knowing that in my house is a young man of principal is enough compensation. You have paid your debt plus interest with your presence here."

"Sir, that is not enough. You paid gold for me to be free. All I did is be myself. I will always be myself. You are still minus your gold," Onofrio stated his case.

"A little gold among friends is good," smiled the Egyptian busy sampling tidbits and sipping wine.

"I will need money to travel to my homeland. I would like to be in your employ for a time to earn that money," knowing that he needed twice the money to pay for Senobia and him to make the journey.

"Have you decided to reject the centurion's offer?" Serou asked, and then added, "He was very anxious to speak to you about it."

"He mentioned it several times while I was at the villa. And he was by my quarters not long ago to rekindle the offer" Onofrio replied. "May I speak freely here without reproach?" asked Onofrio with his eyes keen on Serou for reaction.

"Of course you may. Anything you say to me stays with me. You know that."

Somewhat reluctant to state his mind Onofrio coined out his words slowly, "I do not care to fight Rome's battles. I fear no man, but I will not do battle for causes that are not my own. It is also not my nature to answer to another man's beck and call. To fight and kill on orders from a man secure in his Roman bed sits foul with me. I will not kill or be killed for that man's ambitions," Onofrio concluded calmly.

The Egyptian listened intently, taking a deep breath and sipping wine as he thoughtfully gathered his reply. "The centurion bites like a Nile crocodile. What he has clamped in his jaw, he will not easily forfeit. He has you in his grasp to serve his purpose. He will not be easily dissuaded. I predict he will start twisting his body soon, to bite off what he wants. However, there is a simple solution to your double dilemma. Did you not say that a man convicted of a crime deserves his just punishment?" Serou asked with a strange look on his face. After a brief walk around his work area he settled down with a cup full of fresh water. "I have officially been given the extra assignment of overseeing that punishment facilities are properly equipped. There is much work to be done in that area. Such as detention cells, constructed in sections, then transported to be assembled on site. Iron gates, individual cages and many other incarceration needs. I believe you mentioned that you knew something of metal working. There are chains, cuffs and locks to manufacture. Plus large numbers of suitable stakes on which criminals are placed as a death penalty. Once convicted and sentenced to one of these crosses the criminal is publicly displayed until the sentence is fulfilled. There is no commutation of sentence and it may take days for the person to die. It is a slow, agonizing death giving the convict time to dwell on what brought him to this point. I believe the scene deters substantial offenders from committing similar offenses. Even for the love of Ra, I would not want to be committed to one of those crosses." As Serou spoke he looked skyward in private prayer to Ra or whatever deity the Egyptian revered. "There is much work to be done in wood. The assembled crosses are quiet tall, since a portion of the upright stake is planted in the ground. They are required to be tall, so the victim may be seen from a distance. It's all legal and proper; it's just not very pleasant work. The reward for the work is not enormous. But with a little careful planning you could soon have a substantial amount saved up for your journey home. The work would keep you out of the centurion's eye since the location of the manufacturing facility is not widely known. There is an entire staff of people working on all these projects with little or no public notice. It would be an ideal place to keep out of sight until you decide to journey home. Providing you ever discover where your home is."

Onofrio was a bit apprehensive about working in such a place but soon decided Serou was right, as usual. His situation had two choices, this work under the supervision of Serou or serving the greed of Rome. He would prefer an open field with fresh warm breezes harvesting some fragrant grain for a fair minded employer. Brief summation brought him to vaguely accept the work as doing some good for the community. There was a lot of crime on the streets of Jerusalem. The prosperity of the city of David drew unwelcome criminals to ply their trade on the streets. Onofrio witnessed many acts of violence, theft and even murder. Pickpockets were very successful on market days stealing from housewives and merchants alike. Crime and criminals had to be cleared from the streets, to make a safe place for people to live in and raise their children. Rumors and stories flew wild about a man called Barabbas at the villa and carpenter shops. Some said Barabbas was a Greek with ties to the Jewish council. Others added spice to their stories by saying Barabbas was a paid assassin working for the highest bidder. It was more commonly believed that he was an insurrectionist working for pay to fight off the yoke of Rome. Whispers indicated Barabbas engineered the highjacking of two military convoys, while witnesses would say he frolicked in a local tavern. Murdering bandit or self proclaimed mutineer made no difference to Rome. His actions were criminal offenses punishable by death on the cross. Onofrio had only recently heard these stories about the popular bandit. Based on those stories Onofrio decided to accept Serou's offer. Gold earned with honest sweat for a good cause made things right. With a warm handshake the deal was done.

The young man felt compelled to disclose his attraction for Senobia. "There is one more thing you should know, I found a girl I am quite fond of."

Having heard this, the Egyptian tipped his head sideways giving the young man an inquisitive look to slowly ask, "She must be the crown jewel of the world, if she has turned your head. Who is this girl that has converted the mischievous boy into a thinking man?" Serou smiled admirably at hearing the news.

"Her name is Senobia, the daughter of Tremiyo." The young man seemed proud to announce this. Serou's gaiety immediately dissolved. His eyes narrowed to gleaming slits and he looked deeply serious.

"Does her father know of this and how far has this affair been going on?" He paced the floor thinking and toying with his chin in a disquieting manner.

"We're not having an affair, sir. We like each other very much and we're happy being together. Her father introduced us so he knows we spend time with each other. I have nothing to offer her with my life here. If she should be willing, I would bring her with me to my homeland. If she would have me, she would be my wife." A more sincere statement could not be made by the young man and served to recapture the Egyptian's attention.

The hour was late and unexpectedly, a door to Serou's chambers upstairs came open. A lovely woman, richly dressed with a graceful stride descended the stairs going directly to Serou. The Egyptian's behavior made an immediate transformation at the sight of the lady. She came to him and affectionately kissed his cheek. His arms gently enfolded her and he looked pleased to see her. With her hands on his chest, she looked at his tired face with a glow in her eyes that only love can produce. "Must you be gone for days at a time and when you come home you spend the nights away from me and our daughters?" Her delicate feminine voice carried a tone of genuine concern.

Onofrio saw ample reason to end his discussion before Serou did. "Master Serou, I will be here in the morning and I will go where you send me," Onofrio stated and started walking away. He knew not who the elegant lady was but he also knew he was not needed in their presence.

"Wait!" Serou commanded and Onofrio froze in his tracks. "Come here for a moment. I want you to meet my wife." Onofrio was shocked by the honor. This was far more than he ever expected. He bowed his head as he neared her. The delicate scent of her female fragrances gently touched on his masculine senses before he arrived in her presence. With visible pride Serou made the introduction, "Onofrio, this is my wife Clavenia." Making every effort to capture what he knew of courtly manners, Onofrio bowed to the lady courteously with his hand extended to his back as far as he could. When he looked up, he met her smile and eyes in sparkling approval.

"You were right my husband, he is a handsome young man and well mannered. Has he had schooling in this, or is he naturally polite?"

"Master Serou, you do me honor beyond my worth. I am very happy to meet the wife of the Master of Public Works. And I would add that the Lady Clavenia is no doubt the true crown jewel of the world. If ever, I can be of service to the lady I would serve her with the best of my ability."

"My husband holds you in very high regard. It is easy to see why. You are a remarkable young fellow. If I should ever need a young man of your caliber, I'll send for you." Clavenia turned her full attention to Serou. "How much longer will you be, my love? The girls in your life require your presence." She caressed his face adding softly. "You look tired, have you eaten?" And she wrapped her arms around his waist to rest her head on his chest, "Come home soon. I miss you," she purred.

"I am tired. I need to clear a few details with Onofrio and I'll be finished." Onofrio noticed how gently he touched her, like something delicate and precious. In parting Clavenia courteously nodded at Onofrio and seemed to float across the floor with no effort to the curved stairway. Onofrio admired her graceful strides as she ascended the steps to their private chambers. "Clavenia." Serou called and she stopped to look at her husband with her hand on the door handle. "Do you think Senobia and Onofrio would make a handsome couple? They have been seeing each other quite a bit," Serou concluded. Onofrio felt spotlighted as Serou unfolded his hands in a modest gesture at Onofrio.

Within the study of a single breath, the Lady Clavenia responded with a faint smile, "Yes, I think they would comprise an attractive pair and I will add that it is about time she showed an interest in something else besides her father's home and her education." Clavenia directed her eyes at Onofrio and in feminine fashion had to ask, "Onofrio, do you love her?"

To which he promptly answered, "I don't know, my lady. I have not ventured beyond liking her very much and being happy in her company." Sincerity born of naiveness rang in his voice.

"You are very fortunate she favors your company. She is a lovely girl with a heart of gold. She is intelligent and worthy of much good fortune. But, you must be warned. You mind your manners around that young lady or else her father will serve your head to my husband's dogs." She smiled affectionately at the young man then added, "Good luck to you." She nodded graciously at Serou and disappeared beyond the door.

"Now," Serou started over, "in the morning I want to see your jeweler. I understand he's run off and will be here tomorrow. Get him here soon before he disappears for good. He is chasing trouble and he will surely find it. In about two days, someone will take you to your new station. There you will have accommodations to suit your taste. Only your guide, you and I will know where your new station is. Take only your immediate needs, leave all else, as is. We want the centurion to think you are still here. One more thing, I'll have Clavenia talk to Senobia about where you are. Two teachers come here every day. Clavenia and Senobia take music and voice lessons together but, I suppose you already knew that." And so Serou quickened his step to the curved stairway and Onofrio slipped out the door to his quarters.

Walking to his rooms Onofrio's heart was smiling. He now had a clear picture of how Senobia acquired her ladylike qualities. Her intellect, grace and decorum were effectively a reflection of the Lady Clavenia of the House of Serou.

> *And after six days Jesus took with him Peter and James and John his brother, and led them up a high mountain apart. And he was transfigured before them, and his face shone like the sun, and his garments became white as light.*
> *Matthew 17:1-2*

Moses and Elijah appeared to Jesus at the mountaintop. It is openly debated that it was here, they brought word to Jesus regarding the final days of his ministry on earth. John and James seeing these apparitions laid face down on the ground in absolute fear. Only Peter dared to stand and witness the event to the fullest. Brave Peter had seen other miracles. This would not be his last.

> *Six days before the Passover, Jesus came to Bethany, where Lazarus was, whom Jesus had raised from the dead. There they made him a supper; Martha served, and Lazarus was one of those at table with him. Mary took a pound of costly ointment of pure nard and anointed the feet of Jesus and wiped his feet with her hair; and the house was filled with the fragrance of the ointment.* John 12:1-3

The awesome burdens that Jesus bore would surely cripple the ordinary man for by this time Jesus knew well, the ordeal he must endure. He knew that Judas Iscariot would betray him. That Simon would deny him, not once but thrice. He knew his hour had come. He had not resolved to accept his father's demands on his life. Therefore it would be safe to guess that he harbored a deep hope that he too be spared by Divine intervention, as Isaac was spared from the knife of his determined father Abraham, at Jehovah-Jireh. And should have Jesus harbored that hope, he was certainly entitled to it. For the lamb had thus far done, the Master's bidding.

It did not seem possible that two days and two nights had passed by so swiftly. The jeweler had not made an appearance and Onofrio felt much like going in search of him. The jeweler's negligence was making Onofrio's choice look bad. But, in kindness, Serou said nothing. A new day was upon them and Bonaz's rooster crowed entirely too soon. The usual hubbub at the kitchens soon achieved full pitch as a new day faintly glowed on his personal horizon. Onofrio was not clear what his duties would be at his new station. Today was the day he would move to his new post. It honestly did not matter what work he was asked to do, providing he secured the funds required to find his way home with Senobia. Tremiyo was the usual general, overseeing everything that moved within his vast domain. Onofrio realized he missed this place while he was at the villa. He would miss it even more now that Senobia was a silent part of it all. He made himself useful with everybody in the vast kitchen. Anybody that asked for his help, got it. In return, he didn't fail to receive or swipe his favorite breakfast tidbits. He inspired laughter with his boyish antics and it made him happy to do so. It was a good life here, in spite of the fact that almost everybody was a slave.

It was still early morning when Serou made an unexpected appearance and spoke to Tremiyo in whispers and at length. After which Tremiyo disappeared. Serou gestured Onofrio to join him at Tremiyo's table by the garden window. The Egyptian dressed in elegant robes, freshly shaved and neatly groomed. His radiance made Onofrio feel shabby. A slave girl brought a giant tray of assorted edibles for Serou's choice. A second person delivered a selection of juices, milk drinks and assorted teas. Serou sampled almost all that was provided. Eating with graceful relish and obvious approval he invited bright eyes from the hard working kitchen crew. Soon a large, unkempt muscular man appeared. He was without question, a prison guard. His demeanor announced it before he arrived at Serou's presence. The Egyptian took a deep breath before he acknowledged the man with an abbreviated nod of his head. Cold gray eyes surveyed Serou and his breakfast companion.

"Is this the boy, I'm supposed to babysit?" With a leather strap secured to his wrist, he pointed the polished club at Onofrio. The man appeared to hate the world and exuded hatred like a skunk emits bad odor. Serou evaluated the man and gestured him to sit on the bench alongside the table.

"Sit for a while, have something to eat and give us time to know each other. The work will all be there, no matter when you arrive," Serou invited amiably. The man grunted an incomprehensible something and straddled the bench as one would ride a horse. Serou smiled at the man while working a plan in his mind. "Have some tea and anything that brings you pleasure," he invited. The man heaved some meats and bread onto a plate and set it before him, using the bench as a table. With unclean hands he fed himself, gulping tea from a pot in slobbering grunts as he chewed and swallowed. His head was constantly bobbing up and down in obvious approval. Onofrio remained silent as if learning from the game Serou was playing. He felt no fear of the man. He had seen his type before. They were a breed of dim-witted bullies and badgers. Usually equipped with a handle from which they are controlled, by those that know how. Finally Serou spoke in short clear phrases.

"Your reputation arrives ahead of you. You are a hard worker. You know your craft better than most men and your price is too high. But, we can discuss it and come to a satisfactory agreement," calmly stated Serou waited for the man's reply.

"I won't work for less." Eyes wide open and a mouth full of food, the man responded with something grisly and shiney hanging from his chin. Only then did Onofrio notice that the kitchen was mostly vacated. At one entrance stood Bonaz, holding two muscular dogs with muzzles over their jaws and strong collars attached to chains around their necks. At the opposite door stood Serou's dog keeper equally prepared. The man had not noticed what was happening around him. He was too busy feeding himself in large gulps and making strange noises. It was obvious the man believed he was in full command of the situation. He was here to dictate how, when and for how much he would work. He was here to tell Serou that he would not have an apprentice under him to steal his secrets. "I require a month's salary in advance to get my affairs in order. After which I will be paid in advance every month, in gold." He passed his chin over a leathered wrist and belched loudly to show fine manners and appreciation of good food. With a black fingernail he picked his teeth and spit out something on the floor.

Silently Serou produced a scroll from his inner robes, took a deep breath and quietly stated, "Here I have a petition for your arrest. It comes from Syria. You are wanted there for stealing from your building fund. It seems you paid yourself several months in advance, and cleared out the remainder of the budget account. In addition you are wanted on several assault charges. Also for stealing some horses and countless wagon loads of tools and supplies." Then Serou laid out the open scroll for the Syrian to read.

"That's a dirty lie." the man yelled pointing his club at Serou's nose. Serou hawk-eyed him calmly lifting his hands as if in surrender and leisurely rose to his feet. In a calm singular motion he summoned a silent "*come here*" to his back up team. The ugly Syrian looked completely surprised to be surrounded so quickly. Two men and four dogs is a fearful apparition. When he started to get up from his awkward straddle, Serou casually pushed him back onto his bench with one easy motion.

"Stay seated," the Egyptian ordered with calm authority. "I will now tell you, the conditions under which you will work for me. I will tell you the salary you can expect and when it will be paid. If you ever address me again without calling me "sir" you will answer to these dogs. I will further tell you here and now that I will not tolerate the slightest insubordination from you. Each offense will find you minus one appendage. First an ear, then a nose tip, then a finger and any other appendage that gets in the way of my cutter's knife. Are we clear, so far?" Serou said in a near state of anger.

"Yes, sir" answered the wide-eyed Syrian but harbored a simmering dislike for Serou. Serou waved the men and dogs away with a nod and faint smile of gratitude. Only to have them stand at a fair distance. He then put out his hand to the ugly Syrian, now somewhat docile.

"I am Serou, the only Master of Public Works." The man understood the authority of Serou much better now. "I would want us to have a solid understanding from the very beginning that we may have a good working relationship. I have no argument with you. I know you are a master of your craft. Overzealous in some areas, but I think you have a better picture of your position here. You will perform your highest quality work for half of what you demanded, which is twice what you earned in Syria. You will be paid at the end of each month in gold. No advances. The lack of quality in your work will be deducted from your earnings. Jerusalem has no extradition agreement with Syria. Here you are a free man and presented with the opportunity to remold your life. With a fair salary, reasonable living quarters and a portion of your food provided, you could do well here. When you break the law in Jerusalem, I will do what I can to help you, providing you are in the right."

The jeweler made his presence known and was eating something on a far away table. Serou addressed the ugly Syrian again, this time with a wide smile, "Now that we understand each other, do we still need these damned dogs in my kitchen?"

The man not given to total submission was quick to respond, "I understand that I am a prisoner here. I am to do your bidding without my say so or no so."

"That is not entirely true. In Judea, you are a free man. If you wish to decline my offer, that is up to you. Go with my blessings and good luck. There's other craftsman anxious to work for the Master of Public Works. If you decide to stay, it will be of your own free will and you will adhere rigidly to what is demanded of you. Do we still need these dogs here?" Serou had grown weary of their low growls.

"No, no we don't" the ugly Syrian answered digesting what he heard and feebly waving the dogs away. "Where does he come in?" the man asked, pointing his baton at Onofrio only to be swiftly whisked away in a flash of motion. Serou eyed the gesture with approval and signaled the dogs be removed.

"This is Onofrio. He is like my son. He will oversee your work. Every piece manufactured will meet with his approval. He will be the keeper of your building fund. He will negotiate for whatever you need to buy and pay for it. Your earnings will come through him. You should understand that his word is the word of Serou. His command is the command of the Master of Public Works. In the event that something tragic should befall him, I will hold you responsible for the welfare of my son. Treat him as you would me and all will be well between us." the wily Egyptian concluded and he never raised his voice.

The Syrian looked at Onofrio with disapproval, but agreed to the conditions with an extended hand to Serou. "I've been told you are a fair man. I will put trust in what I've heard. But, I feel unsure about him." the man snorted.

"Allow me to put it another way. He is my son. Are you clear on that yet?" Serou stood before the man with his fists planted on his waistline.

"I understand." The man answered still rebellious. "You can't hold me accountable if he runs a splinter into his hand or hammers his nail."

"If he runs a tiny splinter under his fingernail, see to him and report to me. If you in any way allow harm to befall him, you will first answer to me, then to the authorities, then to the law in Syria. Need I say more?" Serou had grown weary of toying with the craftsman.

The ugly Syrian was forced to see Onofrio in a different light. The young man was to be in full charge. He would hold the purse strings to Serou's gold. However, a sly old craftsman, such as himself could fool this young man. It might even be better for the young man to carry the whole load of responsibility. Any shortages would befall the young man. Having adjusted to that, the man put out his hand to Onofrio. Their handshake and looks into each other's eyes was a clear understanding of mutual distrust. With an artificial smile, not resting well on his face the man patted Onofrio on the shoulder, "Come on, boy. Let's go to work."

But the Egyptian intervened. "You go wait in the wagon or eat something if you wish. I still have some business to clear with my son." The man grumbled something inaudible and shuffled away. When he was clear away, a baffled Onofrio had to speak.

It was choking him not too. "Master Serou, do you realize what you have done? In one morning you have named me your son and delivered more gold than I can count into my hands. Are you sure you want to do this?"

A smiling Serou had to ask, "Would you prefer things be the other way? I can arrange it, if you so wish." And he laughed openly. "Let that ugly Syrian simmer in the wagon 'til noon. The sun will burn some sense into him. If he decides to leave, so be it. I have a list of craftsmen anxious for the position. Now, call your jeweler." Sipping tea to cool his brow Serou made an open declaration that would change Onofrio's life forever. "I would have chosen a better place to say this. But if I was to have a son, I would have him be like you. You have much to be admired. You rank high in my esteem as a man. I know I can trust you to do what is fair and just. In the event you come upon something you do not know how to handle, find a way to postpone your conclusion and send for me. I will never be far away. I promise to come by the building plant on a regular basis. Help me through this project and you will have more gold than you need for your journey home." He patted the young man's face and pointed to the approaching jeweler.

Chapter Thirteen

Treasure in the Desert
and Flowers on the Cross

"The markings on this diamond are known to be star positions," declared the jeweler carefully inspecting the large gem with awed admiration. "A diamond this large is enormously valuable, providing a man with much comfort for a very long time. It has only one tiny flaw and the craftsman cleverly used that flaw as an added reference point. Remarkable, absolutely remarkable." The jeweler was completely taken by the size of the stone. As he inspected the gem from every angle he asked, "Do you know the significance of these precisely cut notches and punctuations?"

Serou shrugged his shoulders in guarded ignorance. "I welcome what you contribute, since I know little about the gem. It was my father's before me and I came to it by chance after his demise."

The jeweler continued to examine the gem and finally spoke, "The markings are precisely cut to coincide with known stars in the night. They could be a guide to a secret location pointed out to the bearer of this stone. The stars indicated come into this position for only a few days every few years. So one has to know exactly where to position the stone to coincide with the stars and get the exact location the stone indicates. It's safe to say that the stone is a secret map to a secret location." He proceeded to take the necklace between his first fingers and thumbs and allow the scarab to hang from the center of a golden triangle. "This is a possible way to have the diamond's markings coincide with the stars indicated. Very clever work. My guess would be the location of something of great value. The work is not local. It is the precise work of a superior craftsman, possibly Egyptian in origin. If it were Egyptian would give me cause to guess the notches will coincide with a particular star and the length of the chain would indicate the distance to a Pharaoh's hidden tomb or treasure trove. It is equally important that the length of the chain be kept intact. Since the length would indicate distance to the secret place. Master Serou, this is all speculation, knowing as little about these things as I do. My business here is to repair or replace a faulty clasp." The jeweler rummaged through his bag and came up with a small wooden box not much bigger than his hand and from it extracted a clasp very similar to the old one. In short order he replaced the worn clasp giving it to Serou. "Keep this safe, in case my calculations are incorrect."

"Name your price, jeweler," Serou offered with a satisfied look.

"There's no charge, master. Your kindness and hospitality are more than fair compensation. I must leave you now. I am searching of something far more valuable than gold," the jeweler stated repacking his beat-up old bag.

"Do you know a man named Lazarus of Bethany?" Serou asked with a strange look on his face.

The jeweler thought, and replied, "No sir, I don't recall knowing anybody by that name. Why do you ask?"

"The carpenter you seek recently raised Lazarus from being dead four days in his grave. Many people witnessed the event and there is much talk about it on the streets. The carpenter you seek has been here on his way to the hills. He travels with three other men." Serou concluded while Onofrio was astonished at hearing such things.

How is it possible to make the dead walk and breathe after four days dead? This could not be true. Surely it was a trick or illusion created by which the witnesses were fooled. No man walks away from the grave of his destiny. Onofrio was totally mystified by the story, whereas the jeweler, in a modified calmness, simply stated, "This is no ordinary man, young Onofrio. This man has a unique destiny to fulfill, as you yourself will see." Anxiety returned to the jeweler's face, looking at Serou in amazement. "Master, how do you know these things? Please forgive my asking. It is simply that such a miracle is of great significance in the life of this carpenter. Are you familiar with the writings of the Jewish prophets?"

"Yes, I am fully acquainted with the prophecies and the coming of their Messiah. My people have had a relationship with the Jews since before the time of Moses. It is part of my inherited knowledge to know these things."

"What hills are they bound for? Do you know?" the jeweler inquired looking frantically at Serou from a kneeling position as he secured his work bag and launched it to his shoulder. "I must follow this man and see him to his final destiny. He has much to fulfill."

"Only if he is the real one," interjected Serou somewhat in disbelief. "As for his destination, I am not certain. However, if you follow the pattern of his predecessors, it would be safe to guess, the hills around Mt. Carmel," and Serou pointed vaguely in their direction. Hastily the jeweler said his farewells and mumbled blessings then disappeared into the horizon.

Chapter Fourteen

A Love is Born

Serou acquired a new chariot made of study willow, skillfully secured with strong leather thongs. Swift wheels expertly painted gold and red gave the vehicle a handsomely rich aura. Emblazoned on the rounded front of the two-wheel glorified wagon was a bold eagle with its wings spread open against a scarlet lacquered background. Two well-matched white horses with grey spots on their rumps pulled the vehicle with ease. To ride in such a conspicuous announcement of Roman authority was a thrill to the young man from parts unknown. To ride alongside Serou through the streets of Jerusalem was even more exhilarating. It quickened his heartbeat to see venders and pedestrians scurry out of harm's way as the handsome coursers galloped by. At the foot of the driver was a wood and metal box secured to the oaken floor with chains. Onofrio assumed it contained work plans for the multiple projects in Serou's mind, and possibly money. Perhaps valuable instruments of Serou's profession. Leather wine flasks hung on either side of the inner carriage. Measuring devices, some levels and such things rolled loosely on the floor from side to side, never igniting a spark of concern from Serou. Finally they dashed into a very large enclosure of high timbers, iron gates and locks. Gates were held open anticipating the chariot's arrival. Once the chariot cleared the gates, two muscular black men glistening in the sun struggled to close those heavy gates, and Onofrio suddenly felt captured inside the foul smelling bowls of an ugly iron barred prison. Huge stacks of oaken timbers, piles of iron bars, huge lengths of chain heaped in wild abandon to look like sleeping serpents greeted the new director of the establishment. The young Master, Onofrio of the house of Serou. Silently Onofrio thought to himself, *"What in the world have I gotten myself into? They certainly don't raise wheat here and there's not a girl in sight."*

Expertly Serou guided the chariot to a handsome two-story building of hewn stone. Around the edifice two men waited to meet the chariot and tend to the horses. Serou stepped down from the chariot with ease and quickly led the way through an open garden area before entering a rear door to the building, while Onofrio followed in reluctant silence. Once inside the young man was truly surprised to see a wide work room full of tables and men working out details of projects on paper. Stacks of books, sheaves of paper, measuring devises, abacuses and a world of knowledge laid before his eyes in total disarray. It occurred to Onofrio that Senobia knew how to read and write far better than he. But, if he applied himself and gleaned knowledge from these learned men, he too could master the art of ciphering, reading and writing. But now was not the time to voice his thoughts. A scholarly middle aged, well dressed man came before Serou.

"Shalom," he greeted cordially, bowing to Onofrio and Serou. He was clearly Jewish, complete with skull cap and a thin well kept beard. Without fear of reproach, a bronze Star of David on a gold chain rested at mid chest. "Is this the young man you spoke of?" he asked courteously.

Serou nodded in reply and rested his hand on Onofrio's shoulder. "Onofrio, this is Eljazar. He is chief engineer and head designer of the work we do here. He will be your mentor in my absence. You have much to learn and he has much to teach you. Listen well and a whole new world will open before you," Serou smiled.

Eljazar shook Onofrio's hand and commented, "We will work well together. After we get you settled, I'll go over the work expected of you. There are many details to keep up with but no heavy labor involved for you." Then he addressed Serou, "Sir, if you have no need of me now, I will take the young man to his quarters and show him around."

Serou stopped him pointing to a pair of muscle men carrying the heavy box Onofrio had seen on the chariot floor. "These men bring the funds required to operate this place for the next two or three months. The box will be in your safe keeping and requires three keys to open." He handed Onofrio two keys on a small chain and one to Eljazar. "The lock requires all three keys to be used in proper sequence. Without using all three keys the lock will not release. If the wrong sequence is used, it will jam the lock and a locksmith will have to come and reset the sequence."

After a long tour of the facility Eljazar and Onofrio took a light lunch of cold fish and vegetables bathed in rich tasting oil. Their wine was cooled in earthen jars resting in a nearby stream. Relaxing under a shade tree Onofrio dipped bread in the cool wine with the distant hills in view and decided he was going to like it here. Senobia played hide and seek with his heart all day and he wondered when he would see her again. She seemed so far away for the time being. His living quarters were spacious and well kept. The furnishings although sparse would do for now. There was ample light from a pair of doors leading to a large wrought iron balcony. The view of the colorful country side he enjoyed was amplified from here. An iron stairway led down to a secluded garden giving his quarters a private entrance. It was the time of year when the God of renewal touched on all plant matter and made them live and bloom again. The invigorating breath of new life filled the air as he and Eljazar crossed the garden area in view of the stables not far away. Serou's chariot was neatly backed into a stall and the prize horses were sheltered in a large section of the barn. They had space to stroll around in, fresh straw and feed was laid out for them and a trough made of wood and stone sparkled with fresh, clear water.

"Is Serou still here?" Onofrio asked.

"No, he left with one of the men in charge of an irrigation project Herod wants done to please the Pharisees." Eljazar responded with a conspicuous tone of displeasure.

"He left his new chariot here?" Onofrio asked in disbelief, altering his course and going to the horses with Eljazar in tow. The animals sensed his admiration and responded to his mellow voice, scratches and stroking hands. Both horses seemed to want his attention.

"They like you. That's good. You should get along well with your new means of transportation," Eljazar quipped smiling broadly. Onofrio's eyes and mouth flew wide open in disbelief hearing Eljazar's casual announcement.

"You mean Serou left these fine animals for me to use?"

"Not exactly like that, but close to it. You are to exercise them daily within the compound. Have them groomed and fed properly. You are not to go into the city with these animals. Only in an extreme emergency are you to go out of the compound with these animals. You see, Serou won this team and chariot from the centurion in a high stakes card game. The centurion is still simmering from the loss. To see you sporting his new chariot and team of horses about town would ignite the centurion into a blazing torch," Unable to contain himself, Onofrio broke out into roaring laugher. To be joined by Eljazar and soon thereafter, the horses. Their cheerful neighing and stomping around their enclosure rekindled the men's merriment. And both men agreed the horses were extremely intelligent and had a great sense of humor. "If you are to go visit Senobia in the night, the chariot and horses must remain out of sight of the centurion," Eljazar added.

"Why must it be that way? If Serou won the prize fairly, it is his to do with as he pleases," Onofrio wondered.

"Those men bet horses and people like you and I bet grape seeds," Eljazar plainly stated. "And understand this" he continued, "Serou takes his losses and gains like a man. The centurion takes his gains to heart; they help bolster his ego. He, by contrast is a very poor loser. To see you, one of his losses proudly riding his second great loss would ignite a rage that would scorch his beard."

"I suppose it was Serou that told you about Senobia and me?" Onofrio inquired.

"Yes, and Tremiyo and I have been friends for a long time. You are a lucky young man. The beautiful Senobia has never shown favor for any man, young or old." Eljazar concluded.

"All you say is true. The centurion would not be glad to see me riding his fancy wagon," Onofrio surmised having given thought to Eljazar's perceptive comments. In a flash ofr realization, Onofrio accepted how Serou always surrounded himself with righteous men. Mighty in spirit, strong in will and never poor in judgment or personal character. He recognized the privilege of being in such company. Without saying it, Serou had accepted him as being cast from the same honorable mold. He was glad to know Serou chose him because he had some worth. It gave him reason to feel good about it and resolved never to disappoint the Egyptian.

Smoke spiraled from the triple chimneys shutting off the sun and turning the immediate area gray with its billowing exhaust. Small wonder the location was chosen this far from the city. Inside, the work was divided into many sections. One work station produced ankle shackles by a huge open hearth. The fire made hot enough to melt iron bars into bracelets by a glistening man working to the unceasing beat of hammer on anvil. A second individual powered a large bellows, keeping the fire hot. Immediately nearby, a locksmith fitted each piece with a lock and tied the keys with a leather thong. Then carelessly tossed the completed unit into a large wooden crate. Another section hammered out crude handcuffs and received equal treatment from the robotic locksmith. Not far away with a hearth of their own, several sweaty men worked on sections of iron jail cells.

Iron cages, to transport slaves or prisoners were the sole project of three grisly men awash with odorous sweat. Their genital area covered by a filthy rag. Piles of metal links were joined into chains by the ringing beat of hammer on steel at yet another station. Onofrio was surprised to see work being done on helmets which prison guards would wear. The noise was the beat of a constant hammer, the heat was oppressive, the stench obnoxious, working conditions hazardous and still men laughed and cut up with each other. Foul language and ugly names slung at each other in carefree abandon. Prisoners serving a sentence labored shackled to their work area. In all, they made a productive work force. The end result of their labor was Onofrio's chief concern. Guards and their dogs provided security and section foremen plodded their men to maintain production.

In a detached ventilated section, the wood workers made whipping posts and long wooden crates that looked much like coffins. Clubs stood at attention in a box while a hole was drilled through the handle for a leather tong. Countless instruments of detention decorated the walls. Some were models for future workers to duplicate. None won Onofrio's approval until he would have to inspect the item as his responsibility required. Having seen a look of abhorance or apprehension on Onofrio's face, Eljazar suggested they leave the place.

"Some convicts are untamed beasts. Some become civilized only after suffering physical torment for their unwillingness to obey the law. Still others will reject the laws of civility completely and live their entire lives as uncultured brutes. This facility provides the tools needed to keep those criminal minds in check and some of them successfully find their way back into civil order. It's a hard fact to accept and as horrible as this facility may seem, it is nonetheless a necessary outlet of justice." Patiently Eljazar tried to ease Onofrio's anxiety. The young man at his side listened carefully, genuinely trying to accept what he knew to be unquestioned reality.

Walking back to the office building, Onofrio was stopped by an odd sight. From a long squared timber lying in the sun, a small green twig sprouted. A noble almost white four petal blossom bravely faced the sun, causing Onofrio to stoop and pluck the valiant little flower. With childlike curiosity he admired the bloom's efforts to survive. "What is this timber?" he asked Eljazar.

"It is a timber from the dogberry tree, known as dogwood. It's a good, sturdy wood. Well suited to our purpose here." Onofrio made a final observation and discarded the slowly wilting flower. Even as the blossom rested on the grass, it seemed to call him for one last look. Soon the blossom drooped its head as if doing penance.

In the following days he was subjected to inspection tours of all working stations. He learned to accept top quality pieces and return inferior work for improvement with cold indifference. As shadows began to grow long one day, Eljazar nudged him and pointed to the office building. They took a welcome detour to the stream for a cup of cool wine and comfort under the shade tree. The lushness of springtime, birds twittering about and a meadow of wild flowers provided an excellent place to rest from the oppressive heat of the manufacturing facility. Eljazar took off his sandals to wash his feet in the cooling stream. Onofrio dropped his clothes and went for a full dip. He could not resist the inviting cool element of life. Discovering a pool amidst the center of the stream, he swam to it and back frolicking like a young boy on the stream's edge.

Early evening found the young man engrossed in study. His attention riveted on illustrated plans for an instrument of punishment consisting of an upright beam and a cross bar. The convict was publicly displayed on these crosses until he died. In some cases the end result would take a day to occur. The young man accepted that it was just and fair punishment for hardened criminals. Eljazar came to his rooms with a scroll and handed the message to Onofrio.

"What is it?" asked the near illiterate young man.

"I would guess your freedom papers that Serou promised. He wants you to stay of your own free will. It's his way of testing you. From your actions he will know precisely where he stands with you," Eljazar stated clearly and proceeded to open and read the contents to Onofrio. It was a release form exonerating him of any crime. It was an enormous relief to the young man whose studies of a few moments ago dealt with a gruesome penalty for convicts. A form of adoption was included and it required Onofrio's signature in the presence of a witness. Slowly Eljazar related all this to the young man, studying his reactions. "Were I you" he continued, "I would want to share this news with Senobia and her father. You know, they both care for you very much. The centurion is in the city at a known brothel and gambling den. He will not be at the villa until late tonight and perhaps not at all. It would be safe for you to ride a horse to Serou's compound and hide it well from prying eyes. From a distance you can have the night guard take a message to Tremiyo announcing your arrival. Tremiyo should be told first. Keep it legal, so to speak." the Jewish elder concluded smiling amiably. "I'll have someone saddle a horse. You make yourself presentable. You smell of fishy water, chimney exhaust and your hair is full of soot. You don't want the fair Senobia to see you like that. You are filthy and you'll find clean clothes in that hamper in the corner."

He left the facility by a little known route told by Eljazar. He rode like a free spirit sailing on the wind. The evening was warm and the breeze felt good on his body. He did not ride at a full gallop and the horse soon adjusted to a steady rotating pace that reduced the distance in graceful strides. He was filled with the excitement of being close to Senobia, feeling her hands on his face and his arms around her warm, tender body. The horse seemed to feel the young man's excitement and responded with unprompted zeal. Man and horse united on a mission. Well familiar with the grounds within the compound, he rode directly to the dog keeper's cottage, knowing the man did not keep dogs close to his home, wife and children. The cottage was lit and the man sat by his front door. As Onofrio rode up, the man stood up to greet the rider. He was surprised to see Onofrio riding such a fine horse and knowing such a prize animal had to belong to Master Serou. The dog keeper still bowed out of customary respect. He was known to be trustworthy but Onofrio chose to only say that he was working on an important project with Serou and was here to see Tremiyo.

Stroking the horse, the dog keeper asked, "Is this one of the horses Clemidius lost to my master?"

"Yes." Onofrio replied with no added details.

The dog keeper went into his cottage and soon emerged with a boy of eight or nine years of age. "My son will carry your message to Tremiyo just tell him what you want him to say."

Onofrio spoke to the boy, named Micah in slow words and extracted a promise not to speak to anyone but Tremiyo. Onofrio brought out two coins of minor denomination and gave one to the boy saying, "One is for carrying my message to Tremiyo. The second is for keeping this a secret and bringing an answer back." Micah's eyes beamed with excitement and he looked to his father, asking permission to accept the offer. His father nodded a silent *"Yes"* and the boy ran down the path on his mission. The men proceeded to care for the horse behind the cottage and Onofrio asked that the horse be kept saddled for his departure later tonight. They chatted and admired the animal until Micah returned followed by a creamy yellow puppy, panting for breath. "Master Tremiyo said you are welcome to come visit. He and Senobia await you, and Camia too."

"You're a good man, little Micah." Onofrio praised him and roughed up his hair then gave him the promised coin and one of greater value to his father.

Walking at a hurried pace, he suddenly realized he was coming to visit empty handed. He forgot to bring a gift of some kind. He soon remembered that the news he carried was a great gift to them all. However, it still didn't seem enough.

He was almost to Tremiyo's home when he was confronted by a robed figure coming to him in hurried paces. Her slender arms went swiftly around his neck, her fragrance and the magic of her touch captured his masculine senses instantly. Joyfully he surrendered to her embrace wrapping his arms around her like binding ties of human flesh. He pressed her to him almost fiercely and he heard her gasp as her eager lips found his and attacked them hungrily, burying her passion in total abandon in his arms and in her scorching kiss. Like two souls liquefying into each other to become a silent fulfillment of their physical needs. Gently, reluctantly she eased away from his lips to draw his body closer to hers and it was still not close enough. Hoarsely she whispered, "Ony, my loving Ony. I thought you would never get here. Papa is upset and is going to scold me for running out of the house to come meet you. He said it was not proper for a young lady to go running to her suitor." With her arms around his waist impeding her stride she asked him, "You don't think I'm improper, do you? I wouldn't want you to think that I am presumptuous or aggressive."

Her inquiry went unanswered as Onofrio only then realized she still wore the hood from her robe. Gently, he lifted the hood to see her lovely face beaming like a light in the night. In his eyes there was no darkness. There was only this lovely beacon of love so close to his eager body and yet so far away by circumstance and social dictate. Again he brought her close and kissed her with deep, longing passion. Grinding his lips into hers with such fervor that she gasped for breath. She gained his release then looked into his eyes, readjusted her position and aggressively returned to his fevered lips. Their lips bonding with a near crazed obsession as their need for each other simmered ever closer to total fulfillment. Slowly with regrettable pauses, he gently released her from the clutch in which he held her. His arms ached to recapture the sensation of her body close to his as each tiny space became miles of separation.

Trembling and difficult as it was to speak he said in short gasps, "We must stop now. If we continue - our honeymoon will happen tonight." Torment coursing through his fully aroused body, so long deprived of his manly needs, but, she refused to relinquish her hold on him.

"Let whatever the heavens ordain be ours tonight." she whispered in warm eager gasps. Looking at him with complete resolve and the soft touch of moonlight and love shinning in her eyes. "In my heart I have made all the vows we need," she proclaimed softly.

"And I to you," he whispered firmly. His warm breath caressing her flushed cheeks.

"Let us then fulfill our wishes and let the laws and rules of men have a merry chase. I will always swear I was a true and proper virgin on my wedding night. And nobody can ever prove otherwise." He leaned to kiss her again and she adjusted to his approach ready to let the doors of hell ring their bells. He eased her to where his body needed her the most and as their anatomies fitted to where nature intended, a loud clear voice called out from the darkness, "Oh, there you are. I'm so glad I found you."

Camia came to them from the darkness better dressed than ever. Tonight even in the gloom she appeared happy, well groomed and totally unwelcome. She approached them calmly and without being pushy inserted herself between the lovers entwining her arms with theirs and pointed towards home, needing to say no more. "Your father should not worry about you," she nodded to Senobia. By the light at Tremiyo's front door she gave him closer inspection and impishly commented, "My, how well you look. The sun has done you a lot of good," and she couldn't suppress a giggle. Onofrio knew it was Senobia's berry stain.

"Are you always so timely in collecting your stray lambs?" Onofrio chuckled wiping his lips and face on her sleeve.

Acquainted with his quips she smartly answered, "I would say that tonight, my timing was perfect. Had I wasted a single moment I would be using my walking stick across your back about now. And even that may not have stopped the proceedings." They laughed quietly while Senobia shyly hid her face in the folds of her hood giggling like a child.

Tremiyo greeted Onofrio warmly. Then quickly pushed him back to arms length inspecting his face in the light, "The sun has played hell with your face, son." Then roared in laugher seeing Onofrio's lower half of his face blushing further in red berry stain.

Camia ushered Senobia in a quiet retreat to her rooms to powder and rinse away the excited blush from her face. Senobia trembled from the arousal of her feminine senses; such as she had never known before. She felt incomplete and troubled. An urgent need demanded she run to Onofrio and melt into his arms again. Her lips ached and vibrated in tiny throbs that sent tingling pulses through her body. She ached physically with strange delightful warmth. Camia saw and understood the girl's mental state. She knew the girl from childhood and her history as an innocent adolescent. She was present when her father and the girl spoke of Onofrio. She also knew this was the girl's first claim to love and given time, it could change. Patiently Camia asked, "Are you sure you love him?"

"Oh, yes!" Senobia volunteered, "with all my heart. I would be his forever. Tonight, I would have gladly sinned for his love." Hearing that, Camia brought the young girl to her breast and held her close as one would comfort a child in pain. "He was strong for us both. I was ready to complete my body's demands. I was willing to do anything he wanted. It troubles me he didn't take me. I felt all of him through our clothes. He was ready to be mine and he pushed me away saying, 'We must stop before we go too far.' Oh, Camia does that mean he does not love me? Could it mean he does not want me like I want him?" Senobia was crying giant tears at the awful possibility.

Calmly Camia took the girls face and spoke lovingly at her, "It only means the time and the place was not right, little girl. Would you have him you throw on the dirt and have his way like a beast in the wilderness. Would you love him more for dishonoring your father's wishes and in so doing dishonoring you? Have you not said that you love his sensitivity and his logic? Was it you that said you love the way he keeps clean?" Saying all this, the mother in Camia comforted her child. "Would you destroy that image because he honored you and your father above his manly needs? He is a randy young man. Given the right time and place, you will be in bed for a long time. You will want for rest and sleep, believe me. In less than one year you will be a mother fighting off your father, from your child. You know how much he wishes children. Now, make peace with that thought and let's make our presence known among the men in your life." Camia helped her ward straighten up her clothes, combed her hair and allowed her to recolor her lips. Soon the girl regained her normal composure. She felt remarkably well even though she realized her tender face and chin were visibly brush burned. Her lips still felt tender, rhythmically pulsating to the beat of her heart. Simultaneously the men in her life raised their cups to salute the fair Senobia as she entered the room.

"You'll have to forgive my daughter. Her manners are in total disarray. She is supposed to be properly introduced to her suitor in the presence of her father. Instead she runs off without permission, meets her suitor in a dark alley and drags him home covered in berry stains." Her father gestured her to sit by him visibly discontent. "Everything I have spent years teaching her, she tosses out the window in one short evening." Tremiyo was chuckling softly shaking his head in disbelief.

Onofrio sat isolated on the opposite side of the table with three pair of eyes looking at him. He plucked the scroll from his inner robe and handed the document to Tremiyo. "Read that for all of us to hear." And his usual self began to reappear. "That is why I came. Serou sent it to me today and I could not wait to bring you the news." This time he spoke directly to Tremiyo and nodded his head. Briefly Tremiyo read the initial document and looked at Onofrio in approval.

"I will be working for Serou until I repay what he has done for me." Senobia again broke the rules and with bubbling happiness rounded the table to come to sit by Onofrio's side. Looking at him with adoring eyes she could not contain, "Ony, my loving Ony! You're free, and exonerated of all wrong doing. Oh my love, I always knew you were not a thief! We can go find your home now. We are free to go anywhere, we want to." Her excitement splattered over her manners and her father's feelings.

The thought of them going away came as a total shock to Tremiyo. He was counting grandchildren just a moment ago. Before he could think, he burst out in a near rage, "I'll not hear of this! Neither one of you is mature enough to consider such a journey, without a suitable escort. Senobia, you come sit with me and behave yourself or I'll send you to your rooms." His eyes were blazing while Camia patted him gently on his forearm trying to calm him down. It was Camia's soothing touch and words that reached through Tremiyo's rage.

"Simmer down, love. They are both young and need our advice and guidance much more than they need your anger. Please sit down and let's talk about this sensibly. It is entirely too soon to be making such long-range plans. Senobia, your father and I only want your welfare and happiness. Such a journey is extremely hazardous. Careful planning is required; our combined wisdom can arrive at a favorable plan."

Tremiyo was quick to agree. "Yes, yes. We need time to think on this. There is the matter of making all this proper. You cannot just run off like two jay birds from your nest. I look forward to a large wedding, with friends and acquaintances present and everything properly done. I owe that obligation to Senobia's mother and, by God, I will not fail in that commitment. I have not spent my years developing this young lady to see her run off with the first bow-legged goat that turns her fancy. I'm surprised she would even think such a thing. And you, Onofrio. You should have come to me first. I should have heard this plan from you initially." Although his rage had cooled, Tremiyo was holding his ground.

"I'm sorry, Papa, I've behaved badly. Please forgive me. It was my state of joy that made me speak as I did. Onofrio has never asked me to go with him to find his home. It was I that spoke out of turn." And as she spoke she caressed her father's face. The flash of anger mellowed and he gave her a gentle squeeze and gestured her to sit down.

"You should have had Serou play the part of your father along with a witness and ask for Senobia's hand in marriage. It would add much to make his arrangement correct. People here have little to talk about. Let them carry tales about how things are done in a proper and socially accepted manner. I want it all done without a blemish." Tremiyo waved a finger at Onofrio emphasizing his demands. "Men have asked for Senobia's hand in marriage and I always held that she would choose her life mate. I should not be embarrassed by her wedding being done in an improper manner. So young man, you will just have to bear with me."

"But Serou has already chosen to be my father, and I am not a bow-legged goat. He has included adoption papers ready for my signature and proper witnesses." Then he gently rolled out the document for Tremiyo to examine. The older man expressed astonishment bordering on skepticism as he slowly read it word by word for all to hear, while the ladies looked at each other in total surprise.

"And do you intend to accept the will of Serou? You will be hard pressed, living up to his expectations. He is a man with a brilliant mind, he will expect you to be equally so." Tremiyo expressed studious apprehension at the young vagabond field hand from parts unknown.

"I intend to accept his offer and do all I can to never disappoint him. And I will tell him as I am telling you; I intend to go search for my homeland, in due course. I desperately need to know everything about my mother and father. Only they can tell me how I came to be here. No doubt, there is much to learn from Serou but I will struggle through all he puts before me to a rightful end. I have no choice. This is the opportunity of a lifetime. I will earn the money to support my wife in the manner to which she is accustomed and my children shall not want." Strong resolve found a guide post in the mind of the young vagabond field hand from parts unknown, while Tremiyo's fit of anger took a complete turnaround.

Typical of a father wanting his daughter to be cared for, he was nonetheless pleased with Onofrio's good fortune. Onofrio was a young man with much merit; he would absorb his education and follow the rules of the Master of Public Works. Perhaps in due course become the right hand of Serou. The Egyptian had often stated he wished to have a son he could call his own; perhaps the gods he revered were answering his wish. In the older man's mind, he was certain Onofrio would live up to what he expected of himself. Carefully he replaced the documents in the canister and slid it to Onofrio.

"These are precious records. Be sure they are kept safe. Have your stepfather come to me for Senobia's hand. He need not bring proper witnesses, he knows me well enough to know I'm not going to simply give her away without some kind of harangue properly noted."

Senobia was beaming with overwhelming joy. Her father had just consented to her being Onofrio's wife. Adopted son of Serou. However, she was at a loss not knowing who to kiss first, her father or Onofrio. She chose Onofrio. Camia saw Senobia worshipping her future husband with joy-filled eyes. Equally so was Onofrio sandwiched between his future wife and father-in-law. The young vagabond field hand from parts unknown had accumulated quite a family.

The following morning found him swamped with things to learn, memorize and use as needed later. He saw the ugly Syrian several times yelling orders, badgering workers and applying his billy club to a man in chains. A sight he would not soon forget. In passing conversations, Eljazar assured him that proper witnesses would be present when he signed his adoption papers.

About mid-morning Serou made an appearance seemingly in a rush and ushered Onofrio into a private conversation. Not wanting to appear anxious, he only asked about his freedom papers. In Serou fashion, Onofrio made a bid to be heard. "Before you say anything, please hear me out. Rest assured I will honor and respect you as my father and never do anything that would stain your name. I promise to do everything within my power to live up to your expectations through all that lies ahead, be it triumph or strife. When Eljazar gathers the witnesses, I will sign the adoption." Serou took a deep breath and took Onofrio in a manly embrace, seemingly relieved.

"We will have a celebration and collect friends around me to acknowledge you as the son of Serou in a week or two. When will Eljazar round up the witnesses?"

It brought forth a chuckle when Onofrio said, "Father, he only heard of all this last night. He's hardly had time to think about it." *Father.* The word sounded good to both men.

"I want to ask you, by what authority does the ugly Syrian abuse and torment the workers in this place?"

Serou gave it some thought and quickly answered, "His position is to achieve results. Occasionally it may require some force, but not wanton force. That only creates dissention. However, the man works under your supervision and if he needs correcting, it becomes your responsibility to rectify the situation. If you need help in resolving the problem, send for me." Swiftly Serou unloaded a possible problem back on Onofrio. "I trust you can handle the situation but be careful, the ugly Syrian is a tricky bastard. You in turn are more quick witted and physically agile than he. That gives you the upper hand." He made a mental note to have someone keep an extra eye on his adopted son.

"Tremiyo requested you gather the proper witnesses to ask for Senobia's hand for me."

The swift minded Egyptian took a second to grasp what he heard. "You're saying you are going to marry Senobia?" He was incredulous but soon filled the room with laughter. "May the gods never cease to smile upon me and may they never forget my name!" It surprised Onofrio that Serou had no reply. Still laughing he walked away and left the compound.

On the third day a messenger delivered a handwritten invitation to have dinner with Tremiyo and Senobia that evening. After days of nonstop drudgery, this was a welcome invitation. With firm resignation he told Eljazar he would be leaving the facility early for a dinner engagement with Tremiyo. He asked that someone saddle the horse named "Hector" and added he would return by morning. He was in no mood for long explanations. His responsibilities would all be here in the morning, just as they had been for years before he arrived. He felt a need to be away from the inhumanity of the place. The peace and surroundings at Tremiyo's home offered exactly what he needed. And of course, there was Senobia.

He spent time scrubbing the grime from his body and the smell of the hell hole on earth where he worked. When he was through bathing, he bathed again. This time he made use of the fragrant oils and masculine scents that appeared by his bath the day before. Carefully he groomed himself and dressed in the best the hamper had to offer. As the day began to fade, he rode out refreshed and eager to feel the wind coursing through his hair. For a short while he let go the reins, spread his arms out, looked to a beautiful evening sky and happily reunited with the wondrous feeling of being free. He rode a fine horse, feeling fresh and clean in route to be in the company of the fair Senobia. And the rest of the world had no meaning.

Once again in the company of Tremiyo, and Senobia by his side, he glowed with happiness. Dinner was an assortment of delightful things to eat, the wine mixture Senobia liked tasted better than ever. Even Camia and the servants seemed happy to see him. The prime reason for the invitation faded out all other conversations. The details of Serou's request for Senobia's hand were repeated several times. All had gone well. Serou requested an audience at Tremiyo's convenience and brought three respectable witnesses. They had dinner, wine and conversation. A scribe recorded every word said, all of which were now ringing in Onofrio's ear. The Egyptian had not been seen in days. It was said he was a long distance away investigating a future project. According to a runner that brought messages and presents to his wife and daughters, Serou would be home in a few days.

And so he was, haggard from long hours of work, travel and short nights of rest. He saw nobody for two whole days and the entire compound worried. His work was a demanding mistress that never left him and tonight the lights burned into the early hours of tomorrow. His work did not allow him to be lonely, though lately he yearned for company more than ever before. He realized that it was partly the reason why he acquired a son and also knew he had in fact, bought a son. A son he would never have with Clavenia or any other woman. A son with whom to share trials, triumphs, experience and old age. He cared deeply for Onofrio in a strange and senseless way. Onofrio was Serou himself, once upon his youth. Where Serou had been confined to pursue an education, Onofrio had been free to roam over hill and valley. Free as the wind that took him where he wished to go. Eating, working and mating as nature declared. Dedicated though he seemed on the surface, his soul was that of a restless gypsy. A wife and family may well anchor his feet to the ground. And the ground belonged to Serou. The young man was honest, talented and a hard worker. He was true to his word. What else could a man want of his son? When the blood of kinship is not present, an unbreakable bond must be created with prosperity, honesty and mutual respect and from there love may blossom.

As they were gathering in Galilee, Jesus said to them,
"The Son of man is to be delivered into the hands of men, and

they will kill him, and he will be raised on the third day."
And they were greatly distressed.   Matthew 17:22-23

Chapter Fifteen

The Building of the Cross

Wedding plans and date were viewed and reviewed many times by an overjoyed father of the bride then shared with Serou. Extracting a promise from the Egyptian to act surprised if he heard the news elsewhere, Serou was to Tremiyo a brother he never had. Serou was not a master over him, he was instead a generous employer; an honorable man he admired and respected. Tremiyo never forgot that it was Serou's rescue of his life that made the happiness before him possible. A rescue that allowed him to anticipate grandchildren he could hold close to his loving soul and no doubt spoil them until their parents begged for mercy. He looked forward to those glory filled days with an anxious heart. In three or four years he may have a grandchild playing in his patio and anticipating more.

When Onofrio showed up for work the following morning, the ugly Syrian waited for him in a foul mood visible from a distance. "It's been a month now and I want my money. That slick tongued Egyptian promised me a month in advance to see about my obligations and he's sneaking out on his promise." He toyed with his club and angrily spat on the ground.

Onofrio eyed him with disregard and a cold grunt then spat on the ground also. "First of all, don't try your bully ways on me. Secondly, nobody promised you anything in advance. And finally you earn your pay or you walk. I need to see the work you've done.

If it meets the standards, you will be paid as promised. Until I see what your worth is, there is nothing to talk about."

A flash of anger creased the Syrian's face and as Onofrio paced away he swung his baton at the back of Onofrio's head. But the young man read the tell tale signs and smartly ducked as the baton whizzed by. As he swiftly recoiled he aimed his boot directly at the Syrian's crotch and he hit the target solidly with a resounding wallop. In a mini-flash the Syrian's eyes bulged open as he doubled up in pain. He fought for breath in short agonizing gasps and slumped heavily to the ground where he rolled over several times holding his crotch, but he never stopped cursing in inaudible spurts. Having witnessed the Syrian's brutality of a few days ago, he could not afford to give the man an even chance. Coldly he stepped over the slumped body without concern. Everybody within sight witnessed the event. Some looked at the young man with calculated respect. Others continued to work without a second glance or ounce of concern. Leisurely walking to a pile of scouring posts and crosses the Syrian had overseen, he called to an idle individual close by wearing a length of chain on his ankles making it difficult for him to walk.

"You work with me," he demanded. Cowering slightly the man finally answered, "Yes sir." Together they looked at the work done and Onofrio asked for an opinion. Obviously afraid to answer, the man went silent looking at the ugly Syrian struggling to get up.

"Don't worry about him. He'll talk like a girl for a few days, but he won't be any trouble. Now tell me what you think of this cross. It appears weak. These timbers are not oak."

"It's pine." the man finally answered in hesitation.

"The specifications call for oak," Onofrio calmly stated mostly to himself. "What is your name and why are you here? he asked the man now by his side.

"My name is Amparo, I belonged to a band of thieves and I got caught. The others got away." There seemed to be no reason for secrecy.

"Where are you from?" Onofrio managed the question in a more civil tone, still inspecting crosses and whipping posts, paying close attention to how the crosses fitted together. He hefted a cross unto his shoulder and was satisfied that the weight, and a long way to haul it, would encourage a man to beg forgiveness and a quick death from his god.

"I lived in a secluded farm in the hills of Andalucía in the heart of Iberia." the man's eyes sparkled with momentary longing as he stumbled over a fallen cross. Together they found the rigid parchment on which the timbers were recorded. The price was the same as it would be for hard woods or oak. Under closer inspection Onofrio noticed the price had been cleverly altered. Perhaps someone upped the price to skim a profit. His first suspicion fell on the Syrian but then he wondered, *"Could the man be that articulate?"* He would keep that in mind for later.

The Syrian limped into their presence, his eyes red with anger and almost yelled, "You have no business going through my papers! My record box is not in your area of authority. What I keep there is private." Onofrio faced the man squarely while Amparo made room to run. Onofrio took the Syrian's baton and politely brought it up smiling generously as he did. From his waistband came a quick flash of a blade and the thong that held the baton to the Syrian's wrist softly fell away.

Onofrio now had two weapons. He prodded the Syrian not too gently on his chest with the baton while he expertly slipped the knife back in place. "You're going to get in trouble with this thing. For your own protection, you will not carry one of these things any more while you work here. My authority in this place extends from the dirt on the floor to the birds that fly above it. It is my business when the sun shines, when it is cold, when it rains and all night long every night. My authority has no limit. You are courting dismissal in a rush. Best you get your priorities in order. Safety here or jail in Syria. Your choice." Still in obvious pain the Syrian semi-stood up before Onofrio. Convinced the young man was not going to be an easy pushover he decided the promise of "safety here" was better than a jail cell in Syria.

"The wood is easier to work with. It is easier to cut, it's lighter and less expensive. It all helps to increase production at a reduced cost. The vendor will not take them back. We bargained to buy from him and he wouldn't be pleased if we break the contract," the Syrian sincerely defended the choice of timbers.

"The vendor has already broken the contract by not providing what is required. When the vendor roars, send him to me. You need not concern yourself with my realm of authority. Have I not in my lifetime heard the lion roar?" Onofrio patted the man with his own baton and gave him a look indicating that a few moments ago the lion that roared was now limping. "About your money. Serou never promised you an advance. Your pay is governed by the acceptable items you produce. Due to your history, there will never be an advance. The timbers you spoiled will be deducted from your earnings at the price on the bill. Don't be looking for a lot of money at month's end. Be sure you understand what I am saying because I will not go through this money conversation again." Onofrio expected the man to object having the overpriced timbers taken from his earnings.

But he didn't, instead he appeared busy doing figures in his head. With an artificial smile not looking well on his face and in visible discomfort he announced, "I guess half a loaf is better than no loaf." And once again, Amparo's chains made him stumble over a finished cross lying at his feet. The Syrian, although still walking with considerable discomfort, called out a man by name. Loudly instructing him to "get some help and remove all the pine crosses and posts from the building." Looking around the spacious grounds, he pointed to a suitable location and ordered the wood be put there. They were his and he would sell them back to Onofrio for the right use.

Later Amparo, Onofrio and the Syrian walked to where some hard woods had been stacked for future use. Onofrio visually examined the timbers drying in the relentless sun, noting how rough and course they were. With a wave of his hand he silenced his companions and began to speak, "When a man is properly tried and found guilty of a criminal offense, a penalty is imposed upon him by the court. He then becomes a convict. Part of the convict's punishment is to dwell for a time in the fact that his crucifixion is inescapable. On occasion the convict is forced to bear the cross to the location of his execution. As he carries on his back the implement of his demise, he is continuously reminded of his offenses. The instrument of his death must feel equal in weight to the severity of his crime. There is no accepted repentance from those that sentenced him. He must bear the burden of justice. He has only a limited time to make peace with the gods of his choice. He is completely alone with his crimes and his punishment. Once a man is condemned to the cross, he lives in fear of it. Our work here is to meet those requirements." Onofrio was convinced that the worst offenders deserved a heavy cross. He harbored no reservations over convicted felons meeting such a death. They deserved it. It was the law. It was an effective deterrent to other criminals. Through all this Amparo, the thief silently looked into the distant horizon, gently tugging on his ankle chains.

"Have you ever built a cross?" the Syrian asked the young task master, deep in thought.

"No," Onofrio was quick to answer. "But I will. I understand that you started chipping wood and doing chores for men that taught you the craft. It would benefit our relationship if you coached me on how to build one of these things. I want to feel and see the work progress under my own hands, from rough beam to finished product." Onofrio was visibly ready to do physical work and it pleased the ugly Syrian. Surveying a stack of beams he finally made a choice. "See that long beam under the tree; we'll start with that one." The chosen beam boasted a tiny green sprout with a delicate four petal flower. The tiny creamy white blossom faced the sun with dignified boldness. Having no choice Amparo soon brought a donkey with some rope and proceeded to drag the chosen timber to where Onofrio would work.

"I'm going to enjoy the hell out of pulling a tiny splinter from your finger and sending for your daddy to see about his baby boy." And the men around them broke out in laugher at the Syrian's unexpected joke.

Onofrio hefted the beam. It was suitably heavy. The grain was close making the beam a quality piece of wood. Soon Amparo arrived with a second timber of the same wood. Eyes from all angles stole glances at the young task master's efforts. All of them knowing of the earlier confrontation between Onofrio and the Syrian now wondered if the conflict would continue since both men had saws and axes in hand.

"Every cross varies somewhat in width as well as height because the beams are not always precisely the same size. With a little time and your keen eye, you will learn to pick timbers close to the same size. You'll have less shaving to do to make a good fit. Talking about good fits, did you know that it is not uncommon to measure a convict's arm and leg length then find a suitable cross to fit him properly? Imagine how good the convict feels knowing his cross was carefully selected for him to die in comfort." And the Syrian laughed again while Onofrio hawk-eyed him in Serou fashion and Amparo the thief, remained absolutely silent. The Syrian was being instructive and falsely patient. He was accustomed to working with men that knew what they were doing. "That beam is well suited for the upright," he instructed, "while that beam there is better suited for the cross bar. Work on the cross bar first, get the feel of what you're doing." He picked up the lesser beam and tossed it onto the work table with no effort. "Have someone cut it to – better still cut it yourself to five cubits in length. That'll give you a good feel of how that wood is. I can see now, it's going to make a fine cross. Worthy of a finished craftsman," and he patted Onofrio on the shoulder. Amparo secured a sharp saw and pitched it onto the beam. Someone else provided a measuring rod and a metal marking tool. Even a large and small square found their way to Onofrio's work table. Some of the braver men became Onofrio's audience, anxious to see the well dressed and groomed young man do physical labor. It was an uncommon sight in this home of hellish productions. He would botch up the wood in no time and almost all looked forward to it. The Syrian was soon his usual self as he gruffed and shoved all idle hands back to work. His movements made it obvious he missed his club. The man could hardly speak without it. Standing over Onofrio, watching as he carefully measured the beam. After some fruitless moments, the Syrian urged him to hurry. "Lay the measuring rod out straight and mark the damned thing, will you?"

"Let me take my time. I want to know the measure is accurate. If I botch it up, it's going to cost you." Onofrio was almost smiling.

"Wait! Your meddling has cost me enough for one day. Let me build one of these things and you watch my every move." He added with marked emphasis, "I don't give *second* lessons and I don't demonstrate *twice*." Quickly he laid out the measuring rod on the beam and brusquely wiped off the creamy white blossom that so bravely hung on to its life. Onofrio saw the blossom fall, tumbling over twice before it lay still facing the sun. He looked around and spotted some equally suitable timbers not far away. "Look, use those beams, leave these for me to use," and he pointed the Syrian away from his work. The Syrian shrugged his shoulders and signaled Amparo to move the beams to him. Deftly the beam was laid before him and he gave it a quick look for squareness. He looked around and soon had a tool consisting of a sharp blade with a handle at either end. With the plainer and some short powerful strokes he squared the timbers to satisfy his experienced eye. Skillfully moving around his work with unexpected grace, his eyes never left the object of his labor. He drew lines in the air with his finger, directing him to where his cut was going to be and slammed the measuring rod on the spar. He measured five cubits and marked the spot. Using a square across the spot, he marked it with a marking knife; then turned the beam over and followed the same procedure on that side. The beam was then marked on the top and bottom. Using the marking knife he drew the lines together and the beam was clearly marked on all four sides. Large metal clamps secured the beam to the edge of the table. The Syrian eyed Amparo and Amparo obeyed with obvious reluctance took one end of the double handled saw. They positioned themselves on either side of the beam. The Syrian skillfully drew the first line and then they heaved and pulled the saw in unison until the excess beam fell away. The Syrian proved he was a skilled worker but the effort put a glint of perspiration on his forehead. The Syrian measured the length again marking the exact center of the beam. He measured the width of the upright beam. It measured two hands width. One hand width on each side of center and he marked the beam at that spot. Using the square he made sure the lines were straight. He turned the beam sideways and measured exactly to the center of the beam and there he drew a line lengthwise to form a box. Again they went to work with the two handled saw. With the cuts halfway through the beam he cut two diagonal lines across the middle to form an X. With a mallet and chisel he whacked out four triangular chunks of wood from the center of the spar leaving a neat square cut box. He chiseled out some splinters to make a level notch. The cross bar was momentarily set aside and the upright beam brought into working position. At three cubits from the top he laid the cross bar and pressed it onto the upright beam. It fit snug and he marked it to accommodate the exact depth of the notch on the crossbar. With the precision of experience, he duplicated his previous performance with no effort. He pushed the crossbar into place and it made a perfect fit. Taking a left over triangular piece of wood he applied it to the upright beam laughingly calling it a "foot rest." The cross was leaned against a roofline nearby while Onofrio and the Syrian admired the work. Except Amparo, he had hobbled away to kneel and cry, praying to a god somewhere in the sky. All around them the din and clangor of production never ceased. All else in the world did not matter. In this place hell reigned supreme. This was the birthplace of agony, instruments of torture and slow death. Manufactured at the swiftest possible rate by men that may one day test the quality of their efforts.

Onofrio was rightfully hesitant to commence work. He studied the timbers carefully. Then slowly but productively leveled the beams to his satisfaction as the Syrian had done before cutting. As close as he could, Onofrio methodically duplicated the Syrian's every move. The wood seemed rougher and harder than what the Syrian used. He struggled to chip out a precise box from the center. When the Syrian grew impatient with the snail pace progress he came to assist, but the young man refused the help and commanded, "Start another cross, we'll increase production and I can watch you to learn more." Although he worked harder and longer than his teacher, he completed a near perfect cross. He failed to groove out the vertical spar deep enough for a perfect fit. Knowing he would not accept such a defect from the Syrian, he pulled his work apart and chiseled out splinters and debris until the pieces fitted snug and perfectly level across the face of the unit. He found satisfaction with the fruit of his labor knowing the cross would pass his own inspection. The Syrian eyed the work and looked pleased. He did not voice it, but he was pleased. "In twenty or thirty years you might be half as good as me," he snickered and ambled away in no positive direction.

He returned with a red hot branding iron in each of his gloved hands and motioned Amparo to move the finished cross to the edge of the table. Looking at his branding irons, he put one of them down. Once certain he had the right one he pressed it hard into the bottom of the upright beam. Smoke billowed in frantic swirls and the smell of burning wood filled the air. When he removed the iron, it left a black smoking circle on the sole of the beam. Satisfied with his work, he looked at Onofrio with a phony smile. "That stands for Onofrio or for zero," he razzed the young man chuckling wickedly. He pressed the second hot iron onto his cross leaving a smoking letter "S."

"That stands for Syrian or for the number 5. Take your pick. I can make five of these things to every one of yours. And I'm willing to bet big money on it," he challenged.

Unperturbed Onofrio asked, "How long have you been making these things?"

"Twenty years, son. Twenty hard years," he responded with pride.

"If you're still here a year from today, I'll take that bet," Onofrio quipped.

By mid afternoon, Onofrio produced two more crosses from the same tough timbers that mysteriously sprung bright green sprouts and creamy four petal flowers. The Syrian branded his finished pieces, leaving a smoking "O" on them and even nudged the young man with his hairy shoulder in obvious approval.

His busy mind only vaguely thought of being Serou's adopted son although visions of Senobia visited several times. Eljazar came for him by late afternoon. He said two witnesses waited for him to sign his adoption papers.

He cleaned himself up as well as possible and dressed plainly in no haste to impress anybody. Suffered through the ordeal of introductions and finally settled to hear out the two men dressed in overall black and a silent scribe busy with his work. It annoyed Onofrio that the men seemed surprised to see the vagabond field hand sign his name. When the ceremony was complete, he was given a rolled up document testifying to what transpired that day. They explained that the incident would be logged in the hall of records. A third copy would be hand-delivered to Serou thus making the entire proceedings legal. And the only thing that touched his heart was a driving need to find his home in Granada., to be in the presence of his parents, to see them and to hold them close to him again. He allowed Senobia to gently drift into his mind and complete the trio of people most precious in his life. As they departed, one of the men said that Serou requested he come home for dinner tonight. The councilman did not miss the only show of emotion the young man displayed throughout the entire affair. "Come home for dinner tonight." Visions of an elusive Granada, its valleys and vistas, the cottage where he once lived all flashed into his mind. Then present day reality made its rude appearance. He was to use the chariot and horses Serou had the young man keep. He should dress and look his best since a celebration was waiting.

He bathed in luxurious comfort surrounded to capacity by an entire new wardrobe and all the necessities of being well groomed and dressed. Serou was fond of having his belongings look their best. Onofrio would not disappoint his foster father, he was resigned to that. Equally so, he would always be Onofrio. Better dressed but still only Onofrio. He did not know how to ask Serou not to give him money. He wanted only what he earned by his labor.

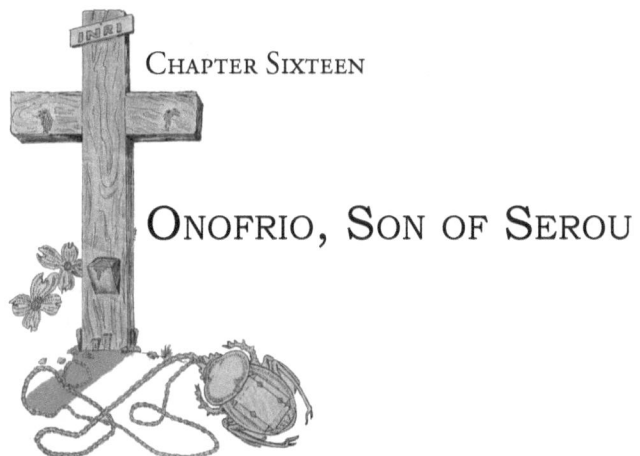

CHAPTER SIXTEEN

ONOFRIO, SON OF SEROU

Arriving at the palatial home of Serou, he was surprised to find a vast assembly of carriages, slave borne litters, chariots, camels and assorted horses in the adjacent field. He knew there would be people to whom he would be introduced whose names he must remember. There would be questions once inside those doors that he could not answer. He would meet them in due course. His life rested on making a good impression. And he would borrow from Serou's demeanor and self assurance to help him. He was the young Serou. He did not know how to control the anxiety that almost choked him. He would learn to expect his title be used to address him. *"Just don't strut it, Onofrio. Just don't strut it. Be humble, be gracious but don't strut your good fortune."* he kept hearing inside his head. Delighted? Oh yes, he was delighted to see Tremiyo and Eljazar (his momentary saviors) elegantly dressed waiting for him by the door. Gladly patting his shoulder and shaking his hand, they escorted Onofrio into the great hall.

The enormous room was made over to look like a hero's reception in Rome. He was soon the center of attention as countless people congratulated him and shook his hand. Serou diplomatically allowed for all this to happen. When he finally managed to catch Onofrio's attention through the milling crowd, he motioned for him to join Clavenia, his daughters and him where they were seated. They met on stage in view of all those present and Serou escorted his adopted son into the folds of his family. Lady Clavenia acknowledged him a warm smile and a graceful nod of approval. She was dressed exquisitely and groomed to perfection. Elegant jewelry adorned her wrists, fingers and swan-like neck. She extended a slender hand with fluid motion and bid him sit between her and Serou, politely commenting how well he looked. Onofrio was truly busy scanning the crowd to finally find Tremiyo at his seat – and there was Senobia. Her eyes focused on him from across an ocean of space and noisy people. Their eyes met in mid-air and each felt the satisfying glow of unity. She motioned for him to sit and wait. Then kissed the palm of her hand and blew the invisible kiss to him. He caught the kiss on the wing and put it to his heart. Lady Clavenia being a first hand witness had to ask, "Has our son so soon found reason to leave us?" and in a most feminine fashion, fluttered her graceful fingers at Senobia. Then she pointed an equally graceful thumb ambiguously at the handsome young man next to her. They were friends in a way that only women understand. Senobia acknowledged the gesture with a smile but her eyes were centered on Onofrio.

Without forethought Onofrio casually commented, "We're to be married, but I suppose you already know." Apparently not, because she looked at him in amazement, then to faraway Senobia. She nodded to Senobia, pointed to her wedding ring, then to Onofrio. The silent question got an immediate response from Senobia with bright eyes and a smile filled with joy, while her head nodded an enthusiastic *"Yes!"* Lady Clavenia's hand went to her mouth in surprise very close to shock. Senobia had made a choice. Lady Clavenia reached up to bring her husband's ear close to hers and whispered, "Have the necessary arrangements been made? Can we announce it tonight?" Serou was not the usual calm and coordinated Master of Public Works. Tremiyo and he may soon have grand children skittering around the compound. Both men had often discussed and looked forward to such an event never having been as close to their wishes as now.

He had recently imagined how beautiful the children of Onofrio and Senobia would be. They were a fine pair, thoroughbreds in their own right. Intelligent, righteous and civil people. Serou experienced emotions alien to his normal logical being. Could it be something on the edge of love?

"Her father and I spoke again last night and everything now hinges on setting the wedding date. To make an official announcement now could be a little premature. I believe you have enough to say for tonight, don't you?"

Onofrio spoke with a tone of command. "Tremiyo was very happy that you asked for Senobia's hand in such a righteous manner." Serou hawk-eyed him, cleared his throat and, with an arm over the young man's shoulder, addressed the crowd, getting their attention by his upraised hands and booming voice. The room slowly hushed until only the faded music was heard. All faces attended the Egyptian and the handsome lad by his side.

"We have some important news to share with you, tonight." When he saw Tremiyo seated by his daughter, he motioned him to come forward. "I am happy to announce that the formalities of adoption have been completed as of this day. It gives me great pleasure to present to you, my newly adopted son, Onofrio of Serou. From this day forward he will be my rightful son. Sharing with me all the benefits and joys a father and son can share. My wife, Clavenia is with me in this adoption. Both of us have done our parts to make this official. Onofrio Serou will be known throughout, as my legal son. I ask in the warmth of our friendship and business relationships to honor him as such. It would bring me great joy to know that he shares the same umbrella all of you have shared with me. Events are developing, in which I may be needed elsewhere. Onofrio will be the key to my attention." Serou motioned Onofrio to step forward and when he did, the room broke out in loud cheers and booming applause. Tremiyo stood by, not knowing why he was wanted. Serou invited the older man on stage and placed a friendly hand on his shoulder.

"Have you granted my son Onofrio permission to marry your daughter, Senobia?"

Knowing this gesture was for public notice Tremiyo was happy to respond, "Yes, I granted him permission. We were going to consult you regarding a suitable wedding date."

"You pick the date, old friend and leave the matters of finance to me." Serou looked behind him and addressed his wife, "Please bring Senobia to the stage," and he winked at her. Understanding her husband's intentions she waved Senobia to come forward. Visibly shy and uncertain the young girl was hesitant to comply. Once again Serou hushed the crowd, "May all your gods smile upon you for being with me tonight. It is a wonderful blessing to become a father in just one day. It is a greater blessing to have your son on the brink of marriage. Not only have my gods smiled upon me tonight. They have decided to stand by me. Those of you that know me well also know that this is not the same Master of Public Works you've known in the field." Senobia was then on stage looking nervous and unsure. Serou continued, "All of you know that the steward of my house is Tremiyo. His only daughter is a gem many suitors have sought. She has finally found the right suitor to fulfill her life. My son is to wed the lovely Senobia in the near future. Wedding plans are being made and the date will soon be set. I promise you such a wedding has not been seen in all of Judea. The gods will sing to each of you, on that day for being with me." Serou gently brought Onofrio and Senobia together with a hand on each of their shoulders. "Have you ever seen a more handsome couple?" Serou asked the crowd, sincerely proud of the addition to his family. The answer was a unanimous round of applause. "All of you will be made to know the exact date and time." So openly on display the couple was visibly nervous and ill at ease and wishing to be elsewhere, alone.

From somewhere in the room a familiar face materialized. Komar, son of the richest diamond and gold house in Judea. Elegantly dressed and dripping with glittering jewelry made his presence known. "I would not want my son to start his married life in poverty so I brought a few gifts," And he took off a rich trinket from somewhere, then another from elsewhere, then a rich earring and a set of diamond rings and gently tossed them to the couple on stage. And flauntingly asked the crowd, "Anybody else have something to contribute to the young couple's future?" He invited and people obliged surprising the couple on stage. Soon there was a minor parade of guests coming by the stage and dropping off precious trinkets. Komar with a deep bow touched his abdomen, his chest and his brow and saluted the young couple then simply sauntered off into the crowd.

Keen on gold, the young couple found themselves collecting precious trinkets from the floor with a visible lack of dignity. They were clearly heard giggling like happy children gathering toys and cheers from the crowd. A tablecloth was soon provided and the couple quickly piled their treasure on it. As Onofrio went to pick up an expensive bijouterie, a leather pouch made a loud landing before him. No doubt heavy with gold coins. "Even Rome smiles on you on the day of your betrothal," a smiling Centurion Clemidius was heard to say. He was well dressed but still looked rumpled and unkempt.

Onofrio rose to his full height, leaving the purse untouched. Seeing Onofrio ignore the purse, Senobia followed suit and stood at her fiancé's side. She raised her chin high and looked down on the centurion with cool disregard. Clemidius stood before the stage with cold calculating eyes surveying the couple. Onofrio took Senobia's elbow, gave her a look up close, then pointed her to her father and she obeyed. Onofrio broke the ice by coming off the stage with the heavy purse in his hand and greeting the centurion with a Roman forearm clasp. He tossed the purse back to Clemidius. "Keep your gold. We have enough for our simple needs,"

Trying hard to smile convincingly, the centurion, never one to refuse gold, was taken aback. "You're refusing my gift?" he slurred out the question. "Is my gold not good enough for you?

You sneer at Rome and its good wishes for your future happiness?"

Onofrio patted the centurion on his shoulder, "No I don't but it would make me happier if my friend, the centurion accepted my gift on the day of my betrothal."

The centurion weaved a bit and muttered softly, "You always were a clever bastard. I would like to meet the bride. I'll bet I am the only person here that has not met your future wife."

Onofrio found Senobia looking at him and motioned her to floor level next to him. "Senobia, this is my friend, Centurion Clemidius. Clemidius, this is my future wife Senobia, daughter of Tremiyo; Steward of the House of Serou."

With an effort the centurion straightened himself to full height and literally surveyed the lovely Senobia with hands that itched to hold her. Somehow he managed a semi graceful bow and enviously commented, "So this is the fair dove of snow white feather, amber golden hair and eyes the color of the Mediterranean Sea. No wonder you prefer the house of Serou to the Spartan villa. Serou always manages to gather unto himself the best of what there is to have. He is generous in the way he scatters the crumbs from his table." With remarkable control or perhaps truly awed by the beauty before him, he seemed to clear his speech. "I am happy to at last meet the object of Onofrio's secret. Gossipers were unjust and totally devoid of details. I was only told you were a nice looking girl with the speech and manners of a princess." Clemidius walked around the couple slowly inspecting her every curve and imagining how beautiful she would be without all the fabric on her. Without forethought, Clemidius lecherously commented, "I may even suggest you let me teach her a few lessons I learned from my vast experiences. I will return her in a few days, well trained and no doubt with interest." The centurion was wishfully serious in his lewd suggestion and although he intended his comment partly as a joke, it fell short of acceptance as such.

"The wine betrays your manners, Clemidius. Do not impose on our friendship by trespassing unto ground where such talk is not welcome. On this day and in my home I can be gracious and forgive what the wine has said." Onofrio had a tight set on his jaw as he took Senobia's waist and led her to the stage where her father waited. She felt safe in the company of Serou's family and her dad. Serou had not missed a word of the centurion's proposal and filed it in his mind.

"In my home, I can be gracious," the thought finally made its meaning clear to the centurion. Onofrio was no longer some lost brat that would make a good recruit and win the centurion praise and promotion from the emperor. He was now a man of means, the only son of a powerful and wealthy Egyptian, Serou. The thought was disturbing.

Once clear of the centurion's leering eyes she felt safe in the company of her father and Lady Clavenia. She felt insulted and was furious by his close scrutiny of her body. It disturbed her that he should be so forward. He behaved as though she should be pleased by his attention.

Shortly thereafter Serou came from the stage followed by a muscular black slave carrying the couple's treasure in a table cloth. Clemidius toyed with his heavy purse, tossing it up and down with his eyes still on the graceful stride of the lovely Senobia. Wishful thoughts clearly showing. Serou caught the heavy purse in mid-air and tossed it to the quick handed black slave. "Put that in there also." Clemidius made a vain effort to recapture the purse but he was too slow.

"My son is new to all this. He is yet to learn that one must accept all gifts from all friends." With visible effort the slave heaved the loaded tablecloth onto his shoulder and serenely waited for instructions. "Take it to the big table in my work-room and stand guard until I come see about it." Without a word the slave wandered off through the happy crowd. Serou then spoke to Clemidius, "Don't worry. Soon you will regain your winning ways. Lady luck is a fickle friend and she's temporarily deserted you. But, she'll return. She always does. You look like a man carrying an overload of worry and that may be the reason for your losing streak." Clemidius grunted an incomprehensible something and walked away to the wine table. There were other ladies here with willing flesh to offer besides fickle Lady Luck.

The long evening continued without event worthy of mention. The guests all enjoyed themselves. Food and drink were delicious and abundant. The music was good, the dancing girls outdid themselves and the acrobats were a very entertaining group. The magician performed numerous tricks that kept the audience suspensed and awestrucked. Joyous laughter and applause followed each performance. Nobody would leave this night in discontent. When the guests were almost gone, the centurion reappeared to Onofrio, seemingly rested and somewhat sober. Senobia and her father had left. Serou and Clavenia were seen at the door bidding their guests goodnight and giving each of them a small gift for attending. The centurion was drinking juice from a big mug. With a towel over his forearm he had a large plate full of cold roasted lamb and bread. Seemingly in a mood to talk, he started to unload the fruit of his concerns.

"There is much trouble in Judea. Later tonight, I have orders to go search of a Jew that's been causing trouble for the governing council. Some rabble rouser called Jesus, Jesus of Nazareth. And who in the hell wants to be from Nazareth, anyway? Frankly I say, leave the man alone. He will talk himself into a grave sooner rather than later. He's going to run out of tricky miracles and lose favor with the crowd that follows him. The people are going to prove him a fake and dispose of him by stoning or exile. Either outcome serves the same purpose. People are saying that this Jesus character is the Messiah. Do you know who or what the Messiah is supposed to be?" Clemidius asked with a mouthful of food and obvious disconcern.

Considering the hour and with mild disinterest, Onofrio felt obliged to answer. "I've heard rumors that sound like old wives tales, that the Messiah is the long awaited deliverer of the Jewish people. A living force that will set them free of oppression."

"That's what I've heard too. I have been in private conference with leading members of the Jewish council. They are outraged that this ragged son of a meaningless carpenter should dare suggest such things, let alone speak publically about a kingdom to come. Worse of all, this tricky carpenter is said to be a son of God. If I were a son of God, I damned sure wouldn't want to tell a Jew. Jewish knives cut into living flesh just as easy as all others. This carpenter travels surrounded by a group of men that protect him wherever he goes. Most of them are low caliber men with no visible means of support. They're probably thieves also. One or two are said to carry concealed swords and one is a retired fisherman. They have successfully eluded my scouts and informers several times. They're a tricky bunch, I'm telling you. They disappear at will and sprout elsewhere, while this Jesus continues to talk about a heavenly father and the kingdom to come. We keep Rome up to date on all of this. The Emperor will not stand for another god to run around loose in raggedy old Judea. There are enough gods already, there's no need for another. I say Jupiter, God of Rome is enough God for all people. Look where Jupiter has brought Rome. Jupiter has led his chosen leaders to build the mightiest empire known to man. Now, that's a real god. He's no hokus-pokus, will-of-the-wisp promiser of things he cannot deliver. Jupiter and Rome are the power of the earth." Sober, the centurion made a sound oratory he was proud of.

"That being the case, why is Jupiter and Rome so worried about some Jewish carpenter running around loose in raggedy old Judea?" naively Onofrio asked and then continued, "This Jesus character, as you call him, has some convictions and he is simply voicing his thoughts and ideas. I do not know of what he speaks of or to whom. But, if he is breaking the law that keeps peace within the people, then he should be stopped. I have not heard of any law his cures, miracles or speeches have broken. I seldom have time or interest in such things. I'm too busy living my own life to bother with personal gods, divine beings and such as that. Nature is the only force that controls the earth and the works of man. Nothing is more powerful than nature. You have your Jupiter, the Greeks have their Zeus and in the end all of them become discarded for one reason or another. Only nature remains constant. Learn nature's rules, live by them and nature can be very generous." The rules of nature had been precious childhood lessons from his father. In his mind and heart gods were an invention of mankind. By this time only the gods themselves knew how many of their own kind floats in the minds of men, if they existed at all. Reverence to nature did not need gold plated altars, impressive temples and it did not require one to go to his knees in prayer. He lived with the spirit of nature as his daily companion and rejected all other so called all mighty gods.

Insistent to be heard, Clemidius continued. "The Jewish council wants this troublesome Jew dead. Straight and simple, dead. So, I prepared a fatal accident to befall him. The council insists on an accidental death to avoid suspicion. The council must not have blood on its hands and he chuckled a bit on that. "Besides, what is one Jew less? They're all donkey dung anyway and equally useless."

Onofrio was quick to advise, "You would be wise to keep such thoughts to yourself. You could be charged with murder."

"Murder? What murder? There's no murder. Rome's responsibility in Judea is to maintain the peace. This rabble rouser is causing dissention, disrupting the peace and he's a lawbreaker. I, as an officer of Rome have a given duty to keep the streets free of trouble making outlaws. Given to the Jewish council's opinion this Jew is guilty of blasphemy, and that's a crime punishable by death. They want him silenced accidently and not put his words to a jury's decision." Onofrio looked at his friend intently and there he saw a man ready to do murder for money. As simple as one would buy a chicken for dinner. Undaunted by the young man's advice the centurion continued. "There may even be a double reward for me in all of this. This Jesus character is said to have recently raised a man named Lazarus or Eleazar same man, back to life after being four days dead in a newly hewn rock chamber. You know that after four days in a hot cave Lazarus would stink to hell and back. But he walked out crisp and clean. Now, that's a real trick. I spoke to some of the witnesses and reviewed all that happened and I came to a logical conclusion. Lazarus was not dead in the first place. He was hidden off some place and a dummy was carried into the grave for all to see. Witnesses would say they saw Lazarus properly wrapped in burial cloth and laid to rest in that cavern. Three nights later the stone sealing the gap was rolled back, the dummy taken out and the cave cleared of telltale signs and in goes Lazarus for a few hours. Then the tricky Jew comes along and with some hokus pokus he calls Lazarus out. And by Jupiter out comes Lazarus, frisky as a new born colt. Quiet a trick, don't you think? There were more witnesses to the resurrection than there was for the burial. So the story of Lazarus' trip back to life traveled the countryside like wildfire. The council suggests that if Lazarus were to meet with a public demise, it would discredit the miracle maker, Jesus. That could give reason for Jesus to commit suicide or get stoned to death by an angry mob. The council is secretly offering a reward for Lazarus' death." And the centurion laughed saying, "Only in Judea can a man die twice." Clemidius was actually happy with his simple solution.

Onofrio gave thought to it all and pensively added, "Now, supposing. Just supposing, that he really did raise Lazarus from the dead. Imagine if you can, that none of what you think is true. Instead suppose that this Jesus is truly what the rumors say he is. Imagine for a while that he was truly sent here by God as the Messiah. Suppose that he is really the son of God. Are you ready to incur the wrath of God? What then? How long will you stand upright, with sword in hand before a bolt of lightning from his heavenly father strikes you blind, impotent or dead? How long will you live to spend your gold? Answer me that. Clemidius, think about it. Turn your thoughts around. Would you plot to kill the son of Emperor Tiberius? Would you plot to kill the son of your god Jupiter? Do you question the power of your Jupiter by doubting that he could send his son on a mission to earth for reasons of his own. What godly anger would you invite with your disbelief? What life would you have with Tiberius searching for you, seeking his blood revenge?"

Clemidius, Adjutant Commander of the garrison in Jerusalem thought for a long moment. He smiled from only one side of his face to smartly answer the young man's visible concern. "From my god Jupiter, I would expect instant death. From Tiberius, a lifetime of running and hiding to finally end surrounded or treed by his bloodhounds and a fight to my death. For the death of a lowly carpenter and his deceitful friend, Eleazar? Two bags of gold and a promotion. Perhaps a promotion to Rome. I am sick and tired of Judea. I want to serve Rome with the Emperor always in my sight," the centurion had calmly stated his life's ambition.

From somewhere in the infinite darkness Bonaz's rooster crowed, rudely invading the serenity of the great hall. As good friends would do they walked to the door. Clemidius pursed his lips and let out a shrill three tone whistle towards a chariot in the distance. It was early dawn. At unpredicted times the centurion could be civil. He looked at Onofrio with a hand on his shoulder and with a notable degree of sincerity spoke to the young man, "You don't know it yet, but you are a natural leader of men. I've seen your type before. When you gather the reins of destiny in your hands, you will cause the world to stop, look and listen." Then gave him a friendly jab to the chin. The rumble of galloping horses and churning wheels came to a stop at the side of Clemidius. By the torch lights Onofrio quietly admired the centurion's newest acquisition. A handsome white chariot decorated with a golden eagle and pulled by a pair of ebony horses driven by a young man. The centurion eased himself on board and within moments, they were gone. Leaving Onofrio suddenly alone to admire the tapestry of deep purple haze and untold number of golden stars. Alone to thank the course of nature that brought him here. Alone to think about Senobia. Alone to wonder if tonight the centurion would commit murder? Possibly double murders.

> *Now when Jesus had finished these sayings, he went away from Galilee and entered the region of Judea beyond the Jordan; and large crowds followed him, and he healed them there.*
> *Matthew 19:1-2*

> *"'Lord, have mercy on my son, for he is an epileptic and he suffers terribly; for often he falls into the fire, and often into the water ... And Jesus rebuked him, and the demon came out of him, and the boy was cured instantly.*
> *Matthew 17:15, 18*

The days were long and busy as Jesus taught his disciples and the multitudes the words of God. When word came that King Herod beheaded John the Baptist, Jesus retreated to a mountain-top to meditate and to mourn for John, his cousin.

Upon his return, he learned of the Pharisee's plan to hire an assassin to dispose of him. Even though the report was disheartening, he continued to call out wrong doers within the Jewish council asking to correct their ways. The traditions the council had for so long broadcast among the people had become corrupt and immoral. What gold could buy became the scepter of power. The council had spies along with scribes following Jesus wherever he went and recording his actions individually. They did this building up the courage to dispose of the son of man by insidious scheme and eventually murder. They colored his words to appear as blasphemy and blasphemy was a crime punishable by death. As Jesus repeatedly reminded the power heads of their wrongdoing, they in turn continued to build a felonious case against him. The greatest fear among the leaders was that Jesus would soon grown entirely too powerful. Already he had an enormous following. Pilgrims and converted sinners came to him every day. The disciples were sorely pressed to keep record of how many people were in his ministry. With such an enormous following, the Pharisees felt certain that he would soon be proclaimed king. And if King Jesus reigned, the Romans would wrest from the Jewish community their lands and holdings along with their gold and their herds. Jewish sons and daughters would become slaves and concubines at the whim of Rome. And as that fear grew greater with each passing day, the faith in the God of their fathers continued to fade. It would be far more expedient to do away with the immediate threat that Jesus posed. And they could ask to be forgiven later.

THE TRIUMPH OF JESUS

Sunday awoke Onofrio with fresh, cool breezes and beautiful skies of pale blue. From behind fleecy, cotton white clouds the sun appeared in shades of muted gold, an orb of heavenly glory, waking up to bear witness to the events of the day. A sight the young man accepted with grace as a personal gift from almighty Nature. It was a day of rest for the crew of the manufacturing plant and only a lonesome wisp of smoke labored to make its presence known from a chimney top. Tremiyo and Senobia had invited him to ride into the city that morning and would come by for him.

He made tea and armed with a supply of edibles proceeded to arrange invoices, shipment notices and miscellaneous papers in daily sequence for Serou's inspection. He had been keeping a daily tab of expenses to show his adoptive father where the money was being spent. Eljazar showed clear objection to his arranging or re-arranging what he had been doing for so long. But Onofrio easily overcame the objection by declaring with unmistakable assurance, "I do not intend to always do this. I am only doing it to further acquaint myself with the overall operation. This is your realm of authority and it will do no harm if both of us know how everything is done, if you should be absent one day." With visible hesitation Eljazar accepted the young man's reasoning. And soon they were busy stacking sheaves of paper in daily sequence. Eljazar produced an abacus and commenced to do figures on paper. After a while the stacks had been added and the result posted atop each stack.

"Serou likes finding this work in order, which is why I do it on Sunday. He seldom has time to go through each stack and verify figures, although, he is subject to spot check. Will you be going into the city today?" the elder asked to end the conversation.

"Yes, Tremiyo and Senobia are coming for me soon."

"Listen well young man and adjust to what lies on your horizon; you're living through perilous times. Political and Godly forces are in open contradiction that will cause much grief. You will see historical events develop worth retelling many times to your grandchildren. Word is said that Jesus will be in the city today, to celebrate the Passover feast. Jesus will no doubt go to preaching his brand of righteousness, browbeat and tongue lash the entire council again. Now people are saying that this Jesus of Nazareth is the Messiah," Eljazar concluded with eyes glistening.

"Who and what is really the Messiah?" Onofrio asked in innocence and had no clue why he felt compelled to know.

"The Messiah is the deliverer promised to the Hebrews by God. He's the savior of all mankind. The Messiah is not this Jesus character from Nazareth where the most ignorant people dwell. The Messiah will be a strong, God-sent leader. We need a hellfire and brimstone God-warrior to expel these hated Romans from our land, to rid us of the weakness of Herod, along with the dictate of Pilate. Where is the fire of Moses? He stood off the Philistines by raising his arms to heaven. This imposter forgives whores. This son of a carpenter born under dubious circumstances from a peasant girl in an animal stall is hardly God-like material. His tricks and deeds endear him to the people. Although he is weak in his constant yammering about "love thy neighbor as thyself," "turn the other cheek" and rot such as that. The Messiah is a force of such magnitude that it can rid the world of undesirables and gather his chosen children unto his breast. That is God-like power. Not this son of an ignorant carpenter. We are being eaten on three sides. The carpenter lures our people away with promises he cannot possibly keep. The Romans take our lands and rights, along with our women, sons and relatives. And we fight among ourselves. We should at least get rid of one pest and find peace among us as a united people. The higher council members will soon have enough evidence to prosecute this imposter for his countless offenses." Eljazar breathed heavily, his eyes were on fire and he had to sit down to calm himself. Onofrio listened silently to the fiery rhetoric from an otherwise mild-mannered man. The spirited speech projected Onofrio's range of interest into a whole new field of curiosity. He looked forward to seeing and hearing Jesus up close. There was much wrong with the world that needed correcting. However, he doubted that the Jesus, which Clemidius, and now Eljazar, described could change anything. Man made the laws of survival among men and surviving made the man. Nature did precisely the same thing. Nature and man ruled the world, exactly in that order. That Rome had risen to such awesome power had a simple explanation. The biggest and the strongest live off the smallest and the weakest. It's the law of nature. Awesome and simple.

The shiny black surrey arrived, rolling on white and grey wheels and pulled by a pair of well matched black and grey mares. The vehicle sported an azure and light gray awning to protect the riders from the Judean sun. It boasted two seats with a compartment at the rear to carry anything they wished. Father and daughter dressed elegantly and both appeared glad to see the young man. Without hesitation she took his face and tenderly kissed each cheek but Onofrio was more anxious for the berry stain on her lips. His arms went around her waist and she in turn fitted herself to his body with her lips on his. Tremiyo looked on quietly. The happiness he had long waited for his daughter appeared close at hand. The lovers remained in a clinch as he cleared his throat several time to no avail.

"Got something caught in your throat, old man?" Onofrio quipped.

"Old man? Old man?" Tremiyo retorted. "This old man is going to drag you off in the bushes and horsewhip you if you don't keep your hands off my daughter. And you're going to know who the old man is around here."

Onofrio poked him in the ribs with one finger and made the older man twitch. "I'm not worried, I can run faster scared than you can mad." And the happy trio rode the elegant surrey towards Jerusalem at an easy pace.

Soon they began to merge into legions of people going to the city. They came in pairs, in groups, alone and from all regional races. There were wagons full of people. There were convoys of camels and donkeys. Some people were carried on litters while others hobbled on crutches. The hills abounded with humanity heading for the city. They looked like ants whose nest has been disturbed. Style and color of apparel ran to infinity. Herders pushed their lambs and sheep with added caution that they not lose an animal. Calls of confused animals echoed from all directions and a few dogs mingled within the swarm of people. Children were seen playing and chasing each other in gay abandon while mothers struggled to keep their children in check.

Suddenly Senobia screamed in horror with her hand over her mouth pointing to an old woman run down by a rude horseman. The old woman's crutch went flying in one direction while the bundle she carried flew elsewhere. Tremiyo stopped the surrey while Onofrio jumped off and ran to the old woman's side. She could not stand without her crutch. Onofrio finally located the crutch, it was mangled by many careless feet. He picked up her bundle, her crutch and the old woman, then brought her to the tailgate of the surrey. Gently he laid the woman there with her bundle close by. From inside the surrey he took a water bag and gave the woman a drink. She sipped gratefully and wiped her chin with her shawl. Her ankle was badly swollen with black and blue patches of skin. Promptly Tremiyo and Senobia helped make her comfortable. On a clean old cloth they poured water and sponged the woman's face and arms. There was no need to question her destination. "May Allah smile on all the days of your life," she said to them in a raspy tone. "I travel to the city to hear him speak and be close enough for him to heal my ankle. I have suffered with this painful limb for fifteen years," the old woman sighed.

Tremiyo's eyes lit up and promptly volunteered, "We've come to hear Jesus speak also. My daughter and I are faithful followers and hear him speak often. If you can get into his presence, he will heal you." Tremiyo finally felt the tug on his sleeve from Senobia as they both saw a befuddled Onofrio listening and binding the old woman's crutch with leather tongs.

The young man chose not to question. Instead he gave the old woman her crutch adding, "It's not a permanent fix but I did the best I could with what I had," He proceeded to help Senobia into the surrey, while the near frenzied multitudes continued all around, nonstop.

In noticeable silence rode the four passengers, each lost in their own thoughts. The crowd continued to push and shove visibly disturbing the natural gait of the horses. Tremiyo was hard pressed to control his animals. A stranger grabbed the reins and called out to Tremiyo, "They're not happy among so many people. If you'll let me, I'll walk with them and calm them down." Tremiyo nodded approval and the man spoke to the horses and petted them with experienced hands. He walked with a casual stride and began to hum. Like magic the horses settled down to the easy pace of the stranger. From everywhere voices rang out in many languages as the city gates loomed ahead. Onofrio noticed that many people appeared oblivious to those around them. Each seemed mechanically driven to reach their destination before all others. Shortly before the gates he noticed the cheerfulness and laughter previously present dissolved into an eerie tension of push and shove.

With considerable effort Tremiyo navigated through the crowd to an empty alley way and finally to an out of the way barn-like place.

Greeted by a man he knew from previous visits, and after a brief chat, the man took charge of the surrey and horses. But not before Tremiyo spoke to the old woman, "The one you seek will come into this market place, I am almost certain. You are much closer to your goal from here." He then helped her down from the surrey.

"I will no doubt have to sleep on the streets tonight. A bedroom will be hard to find and the prices are outrageous." Onofrio tore off a willow branch and applied it to the ill mended crutch. The old woman thanked him, straightened herself up as good as she could and adjusted the mended crutch under her arm. She gathered her raggedy bundle as something precious, ready and anxious to go find Jesus. Tremiyo admired her stony resolve, then added, "We will be here late afternoon or early evening. Whichever way your quest goes we will meet you here and if you need a place to sleep we'll take you with us and provide your needs. Muster your faith and strength to the fullest and you will find Jesus. I pray to see you walk without pain when I see you next."

"May Allah sweep a place in heaven for you and yours." the old woman spoke and set her limping pace in the direction of the market place. She was the only one that knew the strength of her resolve to be close to Jesus.

Tremiyo and Senobia went in pursuit of what her father wanted and Onofrio would meet them later at a well known eating place beyond the market square. Since his curiosity had been peaked he was anxious to find this Jesus and hear him speak. But, he wanted to do it alone and decide for himself what this Jesus man was all about. He muscled his way through the crowd and was not surprised to see and hear angry vendors vainly protesting the careless abandon of the mob. Crates of fruits and vegetables got spilled and rolled down the street as if escaping captivity. Soon he was running with the crowd to keep pace among vandals and frenzied zealots. They ran to meet a procession headed this way. On a stone step at somebody's door Onofrio rose head and shoulders above the crowd. Unfamiliar anxiety gripped him as he caught the first glimpse of such wild interest. A man rode on a pale tan donkey. He was a well favored Jew with brown hair and a full beard. According to the crowd, it was Jesus clad in a simple brown mantle devoid of presumptuous decorations. Onofrio could not find logical reason for such fanatical behavior at the sight of such simplicity. The man did not possess the arrogance of a conquering hero. His posture on the donkey was not a show of grace. Jesus did not raise his hand in meaningless salutes to win approval. Nor did he search the crowd to favor a stranger with an empty smile. He did not appear to yearn for or relish adulation. To Onofrio, the man appeared weighed down with a heavy burden. Eljazar was right about one thing, this man was hardly god-like material. Even though he appeared taller than most, he did not display the expected kingly manner. He seemed humble yet fortified with inner strength. Onofrio felt and saw a man on a mission, devoted to reach his goal and to his work. He appeared to be in meditation but still aware of everything around him and accepting it with deep calm. He was here to mend all the patients he could reach and then Onofrio thought, *"Not even kings can do that."*

Onofrio stretched himself high to see what was blocking the pale donkey's progress. For a short while the entire forward movement came to a halt. The chanting and shouting stopped and a hush fell over the crowd. Onofrio felt a cold chill touch his heart. It was Centurion Clemidius, astride a tall reddish-brown mare. He looked almost elegant, in a splendid bronze breast plate, with a blue and gold cape draped casually over his shoulder. He had been groomed, clean shaven and sported an impressive shiny new helmet. It made an excellent portrait of Roman power. He rode expertly, guiding his animal with reins held up high while his free hand rested nonchalantly on his sword. Clemidius faced the Jew astride the donkey with cold eyes. With the point of his chin, he gestured Jesus to continue bringing his ride to a stop and giving room for Jesus to go his way. But he studied Jesus as he passed by like a hunter would study his prey. Onofrio was not very far away and heard the centurion speak to his men. "How proper it is to see the King of the Jews riding an ass to the city in homemade clothes. It all goes so well together"

Jesus appeared to recover from his contemplation as he re-positioned himself on the donkey and surveyed the multitude with a deep sigh. As if ready to face whatever lay before him, while the crowd continued to gain momentum.

Reviewing Eljazar's rendition of the expected Messiah, Onofrio surmised that some people were here wishing this man would dispel the aggression that suppressed their spirit, name-ly Rome. This man was no threat to the empire. If Rome so wished it could smash him dead by the twitch of an eyebrow. He appeared to harbor no kingly aspirations. The crowd had not ceased to yell and shout at him except Onofrio. He felt alone with his silence and studious observations. This man was not to be yelled at, if he was here on a Godly mission. It was a time for reverence. A time for joining spirits to help him complete his divine mission.

Should that be the case, this was certainly not the time for maniacal demonstrations. The moment called for quiet resigna-tion. Gradually, as if in deep thought Jesus moved his brooding eyes over the people. And he saw them all; those on the walls, in the windows, those that begged for his touch and those that looked upon him as a circus come to town. He even saw the ven-dors and hawkers that profited from his presence. His eyes finally came to rest on Onofrio, perhaps because young man was the only calm face in a sea of rampant hysteria. Onofrio felt isolated by his own silence as Jesus momentarily looked at him with calm appraisal. The young man felt captured by a calm gaze so strong he felt powerless to move. His mind heard strange words that went beyond friendly concern although the eyes that held him did not smile or change. A strange power negated all his thoughts and fell upon him like a chilling breeze of calm acceptance. He had visions beyond the poverty and slavery around him, and beyond the illness, the suffering and the plots and schemes of men. Onofrio experienced a fusion to this man riding a pale donkey, with an inner glow he never knew before. He shivered from the power that held him and before he knew it, he was blinded by a flood of tears, with pains in his chest, and he knew not why. Something within him urged him to break loose and run, to leave this place immediately. With brute force he muscled and shoved his way out of the crowd and ran away like an animal in panic with no positive direction. He found himself not long after in a small park-like alley, alone except for the cooing of doves and a leafy tree overhead, exhausted and panting for breath. With considerable effort he came out of his crying jag. He felt weak, perhaps from running. First he heard, then he found, a little fountain musically splashing into a lavabo and there he cooled his face and hands until he felt renewed again. He would proceed to the meeting place and wait for Tremiyo.

Before he knew it, he got swept into the melee again. The streets were covered with palm fronds and people were seen throwing garments off their backs into the frightened donkey's path. While all this was happening in a crazy uncontrolled fashion, Jesus continued on his journey with calm resolve. Never faltering or disturbed by such wild adoration. "Hosanna! Hosanna!" The word rebounded like echoes bouncing from the walls. "Blessed is he that comes from the Lord of the Most High. Make way, make way, the King of the Jews is arrived." Chants and shouts rang from all directions. "Glory to the son of David," others were heard to yell. Many screamed for mercy and salvation from their pains. They even fought each other fiercely to be close to the rider of the pale donkey. The clamor was deafening with no relief in sight. Only once did Onofrio see Clemidius riding quietly but methodically on the fringes of the crowd; noticeably keeping an eye on Jesus, it seemed probable Clemidius had orders to only patrol the mob. Onofrio was relieved to know the

centurion had not carried out his threat of last night. Perhaps
his quarry had eluded him again. Soon he was carried along the
many languages and dialects ringing within the crowd. Greeks
and Hebrews, Arabians and Egyptians, Syrians and African even
Iberian and Islamic all merged into a single objective. All anxious to be close to and see firsthand the son of God, Jesus. He
was not a stranger the multitude came to see. He was known
and recognized by scores of people. Recipients of his cures had
seen his face and heard his words firsthand. They felt his touch
rejuvenate their tortured bodies with infinite compassion.

Mayhem still reigned supreme everywhere. Only within the
circle of his escort was there a semblance of peace. His disciples
dressed moderately and all wore sandals. Most were fair skinned
with decent features. As they stayed close to Jesus it was easily
noticed that at least one carried a sword under his outer robe.
Struggling through the crowd Jesus made numerous stops to pray
for and lay his hands on the sick, stopping a short distance from
the temple steps. He dismounted, gathered his clothes about
him, seemed to meditate for a few minutes, then proceeded with
calm assurance up the steps to the house of God.

Onofrio had decided to follow Jesus and his men to the
temple with no reservation. "You would be far wiser to wait here,"
a familiar voice said behind him as a calloused hand held him
back. It was the ugly Syrian. "If he goes in there and proclaims
himself King of the Jews, all hell is going to break loose. Roman
legionaries are ready to cut him down the moment he makes
that claim, along with anybody that gets in the way, orders from
Pontius Pilate. Casually look around without causing suspicion
on yourself. There are soldiers posted everywhere. Notice how
they're armed with shield armor, lance and sword at the ready.
Rest assured there's more we don't see. It's safe to say that someone inside the temple will give the signal when Jesus makes that
claim. Its best you be calm and watch from here."

"That man has no intention to be king. You know that and I know that." Onofrio released himself from the grip still looking at the temple.

"But Rome is not taking any chances. Come on let's get a cup of wine," the Syrian invited wanting to be at a safer place. "We can see better from the balcony over this tavern and not be mobbed. Come on. Once up there nobody can accuse you of being involved," he pointed to the shaded balcony above.

Onofrio debated momentarily and reluctantly proceeded to the tavern lost in thought. They were hardly settled at their seats when unholy mayhem broke loose at its wildest. There was suddenly a flock of sheep, lambs and goats running free throughout the hundreds of people. Screams, yells and shouts mixed with clattering hooves and crashing noises resounded. Now some camels, donkeys and even a few colts were scampering away with nowhere to go. Horned bulls and beeves created awesome fear among those close to the danger. Soon thereafter a swarm of pigeons and doves flew out of the roof momentarily darkening the sky. People in panic were running from equally terrorized animals while others ran after their flocks. In spite of the hazards others tried to gather their stock into a unified fold with no success. There was a riot going on inside the temple. Loud angry shouts, vulgar curses and wild screams rang out from the agitated multitude below. Children were running in all directions.

The wine finally arrived and the Syrian acquired an animated look of satisfaction. His prediction was visibly correct but looks alone would not suffice. He had to voice his thoughts. "I told you there was going to be trouble," and he poured them some wine. "This is just the animals. We have yet to know about this fellow, Jesus." Onofrio wanted to leave the tavern and go see what was happening inside the temple and made ready to go. "Don't let your curiosity overload your common sense. There's trouble brewing in there that even Serou cannot fix. You best stay right here because I don't want to answer to your daddy if you get hurt." And he looked ready to hold him back physically.

"Look over there," and he pointed to a group of armed men moving toward the temple. It was not apparent if they were armed citizens or henchmen of the council. "Those men are intent on doing physical damage to somebody. Best it be somebody else rather than you or I," the Syrian announced seemingly proud of his decision. Sipping wine, happily enjoying the show going on and laughing hardily when a young boy was dragged down the street holding on firmly with both hands to the tail of an escaping ram. Onofrio was sorely vexed to know first hand what was happening inside the temple, while the Syrian never missed an opportunity to toast a sip to the recapture of a runaway animal or the retrieval of spilled produce.

Two men took the table next to them discussing the issue at hand. "This man Jesus has performed a series of amazing miracles and cures, he's also adhering firmly to the laws of Abraham and Moses. He had to put a stop to the council using the temple as a business center instead of a house of prayer. And he's right." The Syrian urged Onofrio to listen by nodding towards the men.

"What about my losses," asked the second man, seemingly driven by greed or perhaps by righteous indignation? "I fatted and cared for those two lambs for an entire year, counting on the profit to help sustain my family. My two sons are out there now looking for them. Those lambs will never be found and if they're truly lost, who will reimburse me for my loss? This Jesus may be right in what he does, but why should it cost me?"

The first man made an effort to console his friend. "Your lambs are afoot out there and they will be found, so calm yourself. I lost ten cages of doves and my losses are gone in the wind. Where they land nobody knows. I will never retrieve the money I invested in them. The fault lies with the council. Had they obeyed the scriptures and adhered to the law. All this would have been avoided. A modest fee is extracted from each merchant using temple space to conduct business. People depending on that income are now deprived of it. The losses suffered all around are enormous. But, I still say the initial fault lies within the council."

"We can agree to all that. Now, you go out there and tell those people that suffered losses to have the council reimburse them for what they lost, since it was their fault in the first place."

"And while I'm doing that, you want me to mention the loss of your three lambs?"

"Of course," the second man replied. "I want my four lambs or I want the money they would bring."

"My, my, my," the first man chuckled softly in his wine, "how fast those lost lambs multiply."

Although Onofrio was devoid of any Godly convictions, he was nonetheless repulsed by a palatial house of worship and prayer desecrated with the smell and permanent stains of animal dung. Onofrio keen on the conversation found comfort and continued to listen.

"The righteousness of Jesus is unquestioned. The fact remains that the council is not going to stand idly by and simply say we were wrong in allowing business to persist in the house of God. They are angry at their losses and Jesus will be made to pay for the council's wrongdoing. Mark my words."

The greedy man regained attention to ask, "'Do you really think the council might reimburse me for my four lambs?" Then joyfully added, "You know he overturned all the money changer's tables, huh? There were coins of all kinds rolling all over the floor and everybody scramble, gathering what they could get, and so did I."

"I'm not surprised," his friend commented. "I'm not surprised. Did you gather enough to pay for your missing lambs?"

"No! What I found on the floor has nothing to do with my four lambs."

Onofrio was strangely struck to know, that mellow Jesus could be sufficiently incensed to wreck havoc in the temple, the very house of God. The man Onofrio previously apprised as not being God-like material was now under a different light, changing the volume of his convictions considerably. Perhaps Jesus was acting under a Godly order. What if he was truly the Son of

God? A mortal man acting under a Godly mandate to put right what other men have done wrong could act with such reckless abandon. Why else would he behave in such a way if he didn't have some very powerful support? And the support of a heavenly God by any name was too powerful an incentive for a mortal man to refuse. The young man sipped wine only moderately as he remained consumed with the activity around the temple and more so with what may be happening inside. The previously seen armed men would now be upon Jesus to inflict injury or even death. Calmly he concluded that being inside the synagogue was not a safe place to be. Murder may happen he did not wish to see. The council was powerful enough to oversee such an event and call it "for justifiable reasons." Jesus was in fact a trespasser, an invader attacking people aggressively with a whip. The council's actions could be self defense.

> *And Jesus entered the temple of God and drove out all who sold and bought in the temple, and he overturned the tables of the money-changers and the seats of those who sold pigeons. He said to them, "It is written, 'My house shall be called a house of prayer'; but you make it a den of robbers."*
> *Matthew 21:12-13*

> *And the blind and the lame came to him in the temple, and he healed them. But when the chief priests and the scribes saw the wonderful things that he did, and the children crying out in the temple, "Hosanna to the Son of David!" they were indignant; and they said to him, "Do you hear what these are saying?" And Jesus said to them, "Yes; have you never read,*

> *Out of the mouth of babes and sucklings thou hast brought perfect praise'?"*   *Matthew 21:14-16*

THE ANGER OF CHRIST

On the day Christ ascended to Jerusalem
Singing multitudes attended
and the very Heavens were rended
with the shout of them.
Chanted they a sacred ditty, every heart elate;
but He wept in brooding pity,
Then went into the city by the golden gate.
In the temple, lo! What lightening
makes unseemly rout!
He in anger, sudden frightening,
drives with scorn the
whitening money-changers out.

Richard Watson Gilder (1844-1909)

Having decided he could be of no use to anybody and that the actions of the strange acting fellow named Jesus would resolve themselves he hastened to meet Tremiyo and be satisfied with what he had seen. After a few wrong turns and detours he found the rendezvous restaurant. Comfortably seated away from the rising crowd Senobia and her father waited. No sooner had he arrived at their table that she joyfully took his hand to ask," Did you see him? Did you get to talk to him?" Obviously hoping to hear a favorable reply her eyes beamed with childlike excitement. "Father and I were very close to him and we almost touched his hand. I was so hoping you were there with me. I desperately wanted to share what I felt with you." She placed her hand over her father's and apologized, "I'm sorry, Father dear. But I wanted to be in his presence with only Onofrio and me, that he may bless our union." With a faint smile her father nodded his approval.

Senobia was so excited her words fluttered from her lips like bees from a hive. What she said impressed him but the depth of her wish escaped him. What Onofrio saw was a self appointed priest and prophet of some kind. A man surrendered to a conviction that only he fully understood. Onofrio along with countless other people could not fathom the magnitude of his man's destiny. He saw a man astride a donkey, dressed in homespun. With new thoughts? Possibly a change from the standard of the day? Only Jesus knew. To Onofrio Jesus was no more than a mortal man, trying to clear out a place for his convictions. Why he went berserk in the temple was an action only Jesus could answer. He harbored no doubt that all his miracles had a logical explanation. So, he had brooding eyes that could captivate a man, so could an attractive woman with a lusty body.

They shared a pleasant meal, surrounded by enthusiastic conjecture regarding the day's events. The inn soon began to fill with guests from different places. Stories and rumors abounded from table to table. Someone brought news that Jesus had retired to Bethany and the city was resting well. Numerous patients received a cure and some went home with more money than they came with. Thank you, Jesus. A few animals were still free and slowly being gathered and returned to their rightful owners. That effort could be the source of countless quarrels. Another man was heard saying, "I have it on good authority that Jesus committed villainous blasphemy this very day. The council will have him arrested for it, as soon as possible. You can count on that. And it is one thing to call the Sanhedrin down for their errors in religion. It's another thing to cause them to lose money. Powerful members of the council are known to sponsor some money-changers and lenders and rely on the income derived from that activity. Written messages have been sent to Herod bringing him up to date on the carpenter's assault on the temple. It's only a matter of time before Jesus joins his headless cousin John, the Baptizer."

Through all these bits of news and horror stories Tremiyo sat quietly, sipping his blended wine and only nibbling on his dinner. He knew Jesus endangered himself by confronting the governing religious order. The high council had long held sway over the people. Jesus seriously shook the very foundation of their grip on the masses. Tremiyo also knew Jesus would not raise a sword, lead a rebellion or bid for kingship. His words and his deeds would be the power to reckon with in the future. He felt certain Jesus would not back down from his convictions and bring upon himself the full force of the governing body, perhaps even Herod. Scholars and laymen were coming to him from near and distant places to listen and learn from him. Jesus would suffer pain and possibly even death for stepping on so many powerful toes. But, it would be difficult to kill out his ideas. Worldly power can die overnight. Thoughts, words and ideas grow beyond the life span of man. A pensive Tremiyo filed these thoughts in his mind.

At early evening the trio arrived at the place that stored the surrey and horses. A crowd of strangers gathered by the barn door around the old woman they helped earlier. She was walking without her crutch. The dark patches on her ankles were gone and so was her pain. Onofrio thought she looked younger, then realizing that was impossible, he concluded it was the freedom from pain that radiated from her face. She said Jesus told her, "If this affliction returns, think of me. Believe in me and thou shall be well again." Tremiyo asked if she needed a place to spend the night? "Oh no sir, I only wanted to see you and thank you from the bottom of my heart for bringing me here." Then she looked directly at Onofrio. "Had it not been for you, I would have never been able to get close to him. I have nothing to give in return for this miracle so I must bring others to him for salvation from their pains. I have decided to make that my mission. The man that owns the barn has given me leave to stay in a room over the barn as long as I wish."

Onofrio gave the woman some money and Tremiyo contributed an equal amount. When she refused Onofrio closed her hand over the coins and said, "Words must be fueled by food. You are weak from your journey and you must regain your strength. What you propose to do will take more than just faith. Not even Jesus can live on words alone. He too must have bread to live."

There was a look of simple adoration in the old woman's eyes. "He has touched you too," she said. "You may not know it yet but He has. You have powerful convictions. When He calls you, you will come to him. You are a born leader of men. I can tell. When you gather the reins for your destiny in your hands, you will cause the world to stop, look and listen." She carefully studied the young man's face and impressive physique. "I have nothing to give you for your kindness, but my heartfelt blessings. May all the days of your life be filled with infinite health and happiness. May Allah grant you many children and may they all grow up to be exactly like you and your beautiful Senobia." The woman beamed with excitement. She made her goodbyes and disappeared into the crowd that still lingered about. And Tremiyo turned the surrey toward home.

> *And he sent two of his disciples, and said to them, "Go into the city, and a man carrying a jar of water will meet you; follow him, and wherever he enters, say to the householder, 'The Teacher says, Where is my guest room, where I am to eat the passover with my disciples?' And he will show you a large upper room furnished and ready; there prepare for us."*
> *Mark 14:13-15*

The way home was full of questions regarding Jesus. To which Tremiyo had the most answers. "Why must you meet in secret?" Onofrio asked.

"Rome and the Jewish council have many spies. Some of those spies have tried to infiltrate our society, to find out more about Jesus, the Messiah. There are those that believe the Messiah to be a worldly king that will steal power from Rome," Tremiyo stated casually mending the reins.

"This man is not a thief nor does he aspire to be king," Onofrio retorted.

"That is true. But people have labeled him as such and he has not denied it. By not refusing the title 'Messiah,' he indicates that he is. It's called acceptance by silence. The high priests do not believe the signs are correct for the Messiah to be among us. They believe the Messiah, when he comes will be a hell-fire warrior-God that will throw out Roman power with a wave of his left hand."

Awestruck Onofrio was urged to reply, "That is an enormous expectation. Jesus does not appear to have such power. And if he had it, he appears too humble to use it."

Then Tremiyo continued, "Jesus teaches us to be kind to one another. To help each other and always be of service to those in need. Senobia has written down countless stories regarding the activities of Jesus. She has recorded the miracles he's performed and all the words he has said, like a diary." Onofrio immediately asked her if he could read it, and she did not miss the opportunity to read it to him.

The conversations finally reached a weary stop. The trio rode silently within the aura of love and unity and, lulled by the muted stride of the horses, found comfort among their cargo and slept in each other's arms. Tremiyo enjoyed a sense of fulfillment from the happy sight as he peacefully drove home. The sky was a canopy of purple velvet littered with twinkling stars and a pale white moon while the vaporous heat of the day, rose from the scorched earth to cool off among the heavens. And the surrey carried home a load of happy hearts, except for the reluctance of two unfulfilled lovers having to kiss and say goodnight, then suffer with empty arms the rest of the night.

Chapter Eighteen

For Sale: Prison cells, Scourging Posts, Whips, Chains and Crosses

The thunder of hooves woke Onofrio from a restful sleep. It would soon be daylight and he expected Serou. Dressing quickly he greeted the Egyptian and after some early morning pleasantries proceeded to look over the neat stacks of papers. After some study they surmised approximately how much more money was needed for the month's expenses. They rode Serou's chariot to the manufacturing plant for an early morning inspection tour. Serou looked pleased with the amount of work done and the quality of the finished products. Even the upright cross beams deeply branded with the letter "O" won the young man much praise. Knowing well that Serou was always "Business first," Onofrio refrained from asking Serou's opinion on the near riot of yesterday at the temple. At daylight wagon loads of workers arrived following the Syrian's lead that seemed to find joy in waving at Serou's chariot.

Clearing his throat, Onofrio prepared to hear a long speech from Serou. "Herod has commissioned me to improve the water supply to the Jewish sector. Members of the councils are not pleased with the work as I recommend it. They are squabbling like children over a new toy. In reality, they fight among themselves over who will have the most water rights. Whoever controls the most water, will have control over the crops. I have surmised the final outcome and set the gears of progress in that direction. The project is well planned and the benefits will be multipled. As long as you continue to do well here, I will not worry about this place and its production. As discreetly as possible, I want you to pay attention to expenses. It seems that expenses have risen while production has remained the same or even dropped. I want you to see how we can reverse that trend. I want to see more production at less cost. Don't jump in and start making changes. Learn everything you can about the entire operation and bring me what you recommend. Be observant but do not appear overly curious."

When Onofrio sensed Serou was coming to a summation he slipped in his question," What do you think about this Jew, called Jesus that has Jerusalem stirred up in near riot?"

The question was so far off Serou's current thoughts that he was distracted for a moment. He took a deep breath to regain traction on his mind and slowly redirected his thoughts. "I think the man is courting an early death by opposing the high priests and the Sanhedrin. I'm convinced it is only a matter of time before he is tried for sedition by Rome and blasphemy by the high council. He'll be found guilty and executed. But what has that got to do with what we were talking about?" Serou was clearly annoyed by the distraction. His mind was on the business of the day and not on some penniless prophet, newly come to light. "The man is distracting the decision making process of the council regarding the water project. From my observations and informers he is a self serving preacher able to do perplexing tricks, yet to be explained. He is like a magician that performs baffling feats of magic. When the secret of his deception is uncovered the magic simply goes away. Jesus is a man, struggling to achieve his own goals, just like you and I." And so concluded the logic of Serou. Shortly thereafter he was gone to comply with the many other demands on his time.

Onofrio had been appalled from day one with the repugnant food the men were given. Equally so he was repelled by men having to fight for slop on a wooden shingle. Worst yet was to see men spitting out worms that came in the food they fought to have. But here in open view was an opportunity to up production. On a nearby crest was an abandoned hearth and the study wheel base of a old wagon. With an engineer and the Syrian in tow he asked the men to design and build a cook wagon from which to feed men that filled their quotas. Only Eljazar raised objections, claiming these men did not deserve such luxury. But Onofrio was inflexible and would not see men in these horrible conditions fight over rotten food to outlive their sentences.

That night he explained his plan to Tremiyo and asked he put out word among his contacts for a man to cook big meals and bake bread in open air. Within a week the wagon was complete and the hearth put back in service. A burly man recommended by Tremiyo was hired and he oversaw the final touches to his future kitchen. Eljazar objected even louder when asked to give money to a total stranger and provide transportation for him to go buy supplies. It was unheard of and the young man would pay a high price for his recklessness. The kitchens in the city that provided the meals were sure to raise heated objections.

Before the cook left he asked that a supply of large spoons and ladles be made from oak. He asked that a fire be started on the old hearth and have the men carve out bowls and spoons for themselves. A sideline project that fell unwelcome to the free men of the woodworking crew.

Around midmorning the man returned and asked for some trustworthy assistants. Amparo and a second man became kitchen help in short order. The cook was soon instructing them how to knead huge lumps of dough while Amparo was made to cut meat and vegetables and tend to the fire. The Syrian appeared with a wagon and four barrels of water. "Two of these are for the cook, the two under that tree are for men to scoop out water to wash their hands. And they will have to do without linen towels." He smirked, truly enjoying this while it lasted.

Eljazar was beside himself with objections and warned that the men would become lethargic and production would plummet. "You've turned the prison workshop into a paradise for convicts. And the cost will eat up the entire budget."

Onofrio remained calm and quietly told the man, "Eljazar, you've made your point clear. If the price goes over the present cost, it's not going to cost you. I intend to pay the difference from my salary. Would you like some bread and lamb stew?"

It was not long passed high noon and the smells from the impromptu kitchen were driving the men crazy. Onofrio stood on a large rock and gathered the men around while the guards rode closely by. The men were near to riot from the torturing aroma of lamb stew and fresh baked bread. He hated to make the announcement but he had a job to do. "You men that met your quotas for this morning line up to the right," and he pointed with a large wooden ladle. "Men that are shy two projects from your quota go to my left. Men that have not met their quotas will be fed last. Each man gets one bowl and some bread. There's no seconds and there's fresh water to drink. You should keep up with your bowls, your spoons and drinking cups if you want to eat from now on. There is plenty for everybody so be civil to each other. The guards are instructed to remove you from the line if you get offensive." And with that he jumped off the rock. Not exactly in civil order the prisoners obeyed. It helped to keep order seeing the Syrian taste and approve the stew to everybody that passed by.

His evenings were divided between conferences with Serou and late night visits with Senobia. Serou was pleased with the lunch wagon concept and acknowledged it was sure to raise production. In a few days the men would be far more eager to meet their quotas and surpass them for a second bowl of food. Good incentive. Only Eljazar remained adamant to the change. Every day was a renewed education for Onofrio. From the engineers and Eljazar he learned quick reading lessons. Deciphering work orders, invoices and columns of figures became routine. The young man was eager to learn and learn as quickly as possible. He consumed every bit of written matter with high gear enthusiasm. Often working past midnight to achieve a particular goal, new energy coursed through his mind. He gave no thought to his impending wedding, Tremiyo was in charge of that and made it abundantly clear that he would use his vast experience to produce the most elegant wedding Jerusalem had ever seen for his only daughter. In plain language, he did not welcome outside interference from anybody. Serou would see that his adopted son's needs were all met properly and Senobia would be the perfect lady. He was compelled to put forth a mighty effort and learn as much as he could from what was put before him by a team of learned men. In the final summation, he was happy with the end results of his efforts. He was happy that Serou was pleased and unknowingly he was happy to know almost as much as that girl he was about to marry. It would irk him something fierce if she read and counted better than he. The wily Egyptian laid an awesome responsibility on him and it indicated to Onofrio that an equal amount of trust came with it. He would not fail that trust due to a lack of effort on his part.

Mid morning Thursday, Tremiyo drove the surrey in panic haste to the home office. Before the cloud of dust settled he was swiftly ushered to a large room where Onofrio was in conference with some of the staff, Eljazar and the Syrian. When Tremiyo entered the room in a panic, the meeting came to an abrupt end, leaving Onofrio to confront Tremiyo's dilemma. Once alone with Onofrio the older man seemed to calm down but his voice was shaking, "I had visitors early this morning." Onofrio poured him a cup of wine and made him sit down. "An affluent member of the Jewish council and new to his post came this morning in the company of an ambassador from Macedonia. They came on behalf of Centurion Clemidius. The centurion has commissioned these men to come ask for the right to court Senobia. They were very diplomatic and extremely polite. They brought expensive gifts of perfumes and costly baubles as a token of his smitten affection. In the most diplomatic fashion I could muster, I declined their proposal, dumped the gifts into their bag and tossed it to them in open rejection. I then told them that Senobia was betrothed and her future was already decided. I told them I was a very busy man and they were burning my time. The Macedonian ambassador informed me that my former master had declared me a runaway slave and that I was not a free man. However he was empowered to let the matter disappear as a courtesy to Rome if I would grant the centurion his request. The centurion was not asking for her hand in marriage, as of yet. He simply wanted to acquaint himself with Senobia. He wants to know the girl better and decide if she is what he wants to fulfill his life in the service of Rome." Tremiyo continued, "The centurion claims to have been a devoted subject to the empire, thus denying him of the most precious of all human relationships, a wife, a home and a family. It may be that she is not what he seeks for his life. They even knew you had not inquired into the matter of her dowry, had not made a public announcement accepting the marriage. It is clear to them that something is amiss and gives them proper cause to ask politely, if you will, that another suitor make a bid for her hand. He promises that if the relationship blossoms into marriage born of true love, I may use the dowry funds to benefit my older years and grandchildren whom he promises will be many, if he finds my daughter suitable to his needs. If he finds my daughter suitable to his needs lit a fire in my brain. I may have committed a serious error. In anger I picked up a large kitchen knife and slashed the Jew on the arm. I held the knife at the ambassador's throat as I told him he was a cheap liar and a paid jackass carrying lies on his back for bits of ill gotten gold. I told him that his place in hell was assured by this filth. I urged them to bring the Macedonian army. He would need it. I am no easy man to deal with. I promised to cut off his ears and feed them to the dogs when he led an army against me. They left with promises that the matter was far from over. According to them, I have only scratched a pimple on the centurion's power and influence.

He has powerful friends in high places back in Rome. I decided to speak to you before I told Senobia and Serou. I am not worried about those two messenger boys. I am worried about how serious the centurion is in pursuing the matter. It would look odd if you two would marry instantly. People would talk and wrongfully assume unpleasant things. I would not have time to do the things I wanted done for my daughter's wedding day. I've had Serou's dog keeper bring a trained animal to guard my house. I gave no reason for the precaution and let him assume it's because of the gifts you received the other night." Finally the older man came to a stop, seemingly out of breath.

Onofrio had no opportunity to say a word. He weighed all he heard calmly, sipping on some early morning wine. For the first time in his life Onofrio experienced profound jealousy. It was raw, deep and gnawing at his innards. He envisioned the vile centurion pawing on Senobia's tender flesh to satisfy his wanton lust and was disgusted by the unacceptable vision. His inner rage knew no boundary and he wanted to confront the centurion with sword in hand this instant. Pacing around the room grabbing gulps of air and with extreme effort he managed to regain a sense of calm. His temples throbbed and his heart raced. A gripping sensation clutched his stomach then he became motionless, like a cold statue deep in thought. Perhaps it was a lesson from Serou that inched its way into his mind. "Weigh all possibilities with care before going into battle." For now, the most important thing was to gather all the facts and formulate a plan of attack. Without a plan, it would be like charging a hornet's nest naked. He harbored no illusion of being an instant victor over the battle-tested centurion. However, he was convinced that Clemidius would fall to his blade. With the obligation he once felt dissolved, he now had only a faint glimmer of respect for the man. This action, clearly a strike at Onofrio, removed the final vestige of regard for the centurion. Clemidius chose his own fate. The young man knew that where the centurion was an experienced warrior, he himself was far more agile than

the clumsy Roman. He respected the centurion's strength but
he was strong also and did not fear the centurion. Onofrio reviewed the centurion's maneuvers with infinite care and saw his
flaws in strategy. The centurion suffered a lack of tactical skills.
Therein lay considerable weakness as Onofrio pondered. And
so it was that Onofrio resolved to outwit the centurion and kill
him. Straight and simple. He considered himself an honorable
young man. His honor was clearly under attack by an individual
he did not see fit to be a Roman officer. He would stand and
protect the only value he owned of his own accord, his honor. His
manliness demanded it. Clemidius invited his anger. Clemidius
would boast his actions publicly. He would make obscene jokes
about the couple. He would perform physical gestures depicting
his intentions for the fair Senobia. He would laugh and cause
others to laugh with him. His death would be called "for justifiable cause" and only fools would mourn him.

Without further payments to the member of the council
and the Macedonian emissary, the matter would dissolve and
be forgotten. Tremiyo was not a runaway slave. That would be
proven publicly. Suddenly he was aware of a deep need to be close
to Senobia. Like a flash of lightening he saw her face next to his
own. He felt the sweet warmth of her breath. He felt her anxious
body flush to his. He was forced to take several deep breaths
to suppress visions of them dashing to complete their loving
needs. Forced to gather his visions into more realistic order a soul
tearing thought generated actual fear in him. What if Senobia
preferred the company of the centurion? What if she secretly
yearned for such a man? Would such a suppressed secret find a
place in their marriage? Tremiyo gave his daughter the right to
choose her life mate. The action he intended would deny her that
exercise and would she still love him if he deprived her of that secret desire. Was it possible that she was only obeying her father's
wishes since he favored Onofrio so much? Seething anger at the
centurion's actions and fear of love denied swirled in his mind
like a wild sirocco. Senobia, her father and he would discuss the

events of the day later in the evening. He would consult Serou on a second course of action. He was not ready to abandon his number one plan. He liked it a lot. He looked forward to it. For some unexplainable reason he experienced joy and excitement from the thought of killing Centurion Clemidius. He foresaw the centurion's stab at empty air as he met Onofrio's blade in his ribs. He saw the centurion's eyes wide in panic recognizing his own demise. Onofrio envisioned the centurion's gore on his blade as he slowly withdrew. He saw the action as payment due for previous offenses and the current dilemma he incited.

But his thoughts were out of place. There were programmed responsibilities he must meet. His personal problems were his to confront on his own time. Production must not suffer due to a jealous rage. Regretfully he bid Tremiyo goodbye with the promise to be at his home as soon as possible. The Syrian and Onofrio heard the thunder of hooves and saw Tremiyo whipping his horses to full speed ahead of billowing clouds of reddish dust.

"It's obvious you are needed elsewhere," the Syrian commented casually. "Being that Tremiyo is not known for torturing animals for his needs indicates something serious is afoot. You have one responsibility to fulfill and if you give me leave, I'll take charge the rest of the day. Three crosses have been ordered. Two thieves are to be crucified in a few days and possibly a third individual. You have to select the best we have, to fill the contract accordingly."

The young man gave the proposal some thought. Amparo standing close by asked with a smile, "Want me to get a horse or do you want the chariot?" The chariot won, as the Syrian and Onofrio walked the short distance to a pile of crosses in disarray. They spotted one with an "S" branded on the long beam then another.

"We'll give them the best we got. Two of mine and one of yours since I have seniority rights." They found a third beam with the blackened "O" at the base, completing the order of three. "Look, yours comes with flowers already," the Syrian pointed to

a limpid blossom struggling to survive its destiny. Momentarily Onofrio was touched by the four-petal flower struggling so
fiercely for its place in the sun. Silently he gave praise to such
tenacity; in just three days the little flower had left the darkened
bowels of the beam to claim its life again. For reasons only his
soul knew, Onofrio plucked the little white blossom and tucked
it into the left side pocket of his under robe.

The crosses were heavier than he remembered. The wood
was coarse and bit harshly on the bare skin. It proved to be
hard work moving the beams to the spot a wagon would pick
them up and transport them to their destination. From there
the convicts would bear their crosses to Golgotha also known
as Skull Hill. Secured to the cross by spike or rope, the convict
on board suffered tearing agony when his cross hit the bottom
of a readymade hole. Once upright the cross was secured to the
ground by stakes, stones and loose dirt. Convicts were then left
to die in that torturous position. Their strength would yield and
their own weight would force their bodies down. The weight
compresses their vital organs until they ceased to function. Some
men died of asphyxiation as their lungs collapse inward. Others
die of heart failure for the same reason. It's a slow and torturous death reserved for the most hardened felons. The Syrian
explained somberly and with great care to the semi-deaf ears of
Onofrio as he waited for the chariot.

Shortly Amparo drove the chariot smoothly to within a step
or two of Onofrio. The horses were in high spirits, ready to fly
wherever the reins demanded. It was joyous to ride the handsome
chariot on such a glorious day. The horse's enthusiasm sparked his
spirit. The wind refreshed his body and gave him time to perfect
his plan of attack on his tormentor. How dare that slovenly lov-
er of horse manure even think of being in the same room with
Senobia! And to declare that she may not be fit for his life, but
he wanted to know for sure, in case he was in error. And Onofrio knew well the centurion's definition of wanting to "know her
better." The very thought of it gnawed at the pit of his stomach.

The young man never recognized the root of his untempered rage. The challenge the centurion issued was the first affront any man ever made on the life of Onofrio. He never possessed anything another man could want. He never had to fight for a love that was already his. Or was it? The unacceptable thought slid out of his mind. It made an easy exit when he refused to accept that Senobia would mislead him. Senobia the genuine. Senobia the sincere, would not play games with his affection. Senobia the truthful, would not lie barefaced about loving him. Yet on this gloriously sunny day his heart was filled with rage and ready to commit murder. Only vaguely aware of how green and lush the countryside was. A soul mellowing breeze prevailed and on it, sailed the undeniable scent of flowers. Every little nook among the scattered stones boasted its own miniature bouquet of spring blossoms. Bees hummed a musical rhapsody as they visited each bud and blossom and birds among the bushes made their tuneful contribution. A symphony not held to heart by an angry mind.

Senobia, along with Camia the chaperone, waited hoping Onofrio would be close behind her father who was now busy tending to the horses and dust covered surrey. It was not long before clouds of dust announced a chariot's approach from a distance. Senobia's heart leaped to her throat in anxiety and ran to meet the chariot Onofrio rode. He no sooner had feet on ground that her arms flew around his neck and her lips were firmly planted on his with no regard to public opinion, including her stern faced father. The aroma of her presence was an instant spiritual intoxicant. The exhilarating magic of loving human flesh touched by loving human flesh swiftly propelled him to enormous joy. Her hands struggled through his arms to reach his face and encircle it with warm tenderness. Her eyes searching deep into his, she asked with enormous concern, "What is happening? Father has been terribly upset all day." Her sweet question was total innocence that touched his heart. "I've been so worried ever since this morning. Have you changed your mind about us?" she asked, her eyes glistening with tiny diamond tears. Her lips quivered and it was clear to see that her father's problems would be solved but not hers if Onofrio had changed his mind. "Tell me everything is alright between us," now crying in earnest with giant tears running down her fevered cheeks. "If you have changed your mind, please tell me what I must do to put your heart back on course." She was in near panic and Onofrio was subjected to severe pain seeing his beloved in such a state. He saw the agony she would suffer if their marriage was called off. Her open display of love brought shame to Onofrio's previous thoughts. He knew now there was no reason this side of heaven or hell to delay the wedding. Immediately was not soon enough to meet her at the altar. He tenderly put a hand over her mouth and softly spoke with borrowed authority.

"Hush now. Have no fear. There is nothing wrong between us. A minor irritation has changed our plans. Your father will tell you all about it, very soon." He took her face in his hands as was her favorite hold on him and in a quiet masculine fashion gave her the assurance she needed with his eyes. Then confessed in a whisper, "There is no dream in my life, other than you. There is no place on earth I would want to be if I were not with you. Have no doubt we will be married but there are some minor alterations to our plans. Please stop crying. There is no reason to cry."

She stood firm dropping all holds on him. Her body, arms and hands twitched to re-embrace him. Her lips were a resolved little pout. One hand wiped a left-over tear from her eye and her little fists were firmly planted on her waist. Her gaze beamed directly into his eyes as she firmly asked, "I want to know here and now. I don't want any run around answers. I demand straight forward man answers. Yes or No. Right now. You have talked all around the subject, but you have not said if you love me or not. And I want to know."

Onofrio could not contain himself and started laughing in the company of his doubting soul. Before him stood a young girl with feet firmly planted on the ground, fists at her waist demanding he say, "I love you." Right here and right now. "Yes madam, your highness. I love you this much," he said holding forefinger and thumb barely touching to show degree. Accepting his jovial lie as being far more she blissfully accepted. Having cast away their doubts both lovers filled with joyous laugher heard in heaven as lyrics for an angel's choir.

Her father stone faced and untouched by their youthful antics broke the circle of joy, "We have important matters to discuss." And pointed them to the door of the home.

"Your father has a sand fly biting on his backside. Best come see what's bothering him so." Camia sensibly added ushering the couple ahead of Tremiyo. Comfortably seated Tremiyo systematically let out the sordid events of the day sparing no detail. All through the telling of the story Camia's anger and dislike of the centurion grew by visible degrees. Ranging from shocking surprise to gnarling hissing fury. Then again to silence as if in deep thought. Senobia was shocked at such an outrageous proposal and clung to Onofrio for guidance.

Out of courtesy and allowing the older man to vent his wrath Onofrio remained silent. When Tremiyo finally came down to level ground Onofrio spoke, "I fail to see where all this is such an enormous problem. I will deal with the centurion myself. This is a personal attack on me. He may yearn for Senobia as a bedroom toy, but the proposal is an attempt to draw me out. I will arrange a safe and suitable place for Clemidius and me to meet and there I will kill him. There are no complications. It is the simplest solution to the Macedonian and new council member problem. There will be one less Roman in Judea and even Rome will be better off without him." Onofrio calmly stated, convinced of the outcome from such a dangerous encounter. While three open mouthed faces looked at him in sheer shock. Tremiyo bowed his head in prayer knowing full well what Onofrio was feeling. Long ago he had been victim to such justifiable rage.

Senobia rose in a single motion to gingerly put her hand over his lips. "NO, my love. That is not the answer. It is a mortal sin to kill, especially with malice and forethought. If you harbor such terrible thoughts you are sinning as long as you nurture such evil." She took his face and gently kissed each cheek and then his lips as if to forgive him. "I will pray to God that he forgive you." bowing her head in prayer.

"I will not have the centurion pawing all over you," he stated with youthful affirmation.

Raising her head slowly from her meditation her eyes beamed with excited joy. "You're jealous. You are pea-green with jealousy," and she broke out in childish laughter. "Oh my precious love, I've waited for you a lifetime. No flea bitten centurion is going to get in the way of my dream. I will not have blood on your hands on our wedding day. My love, your honor has been attacked and for that, there is a remedy. But, it is not murder. The centurion's own huff and bluff will blow him away like dry dung when he is not received. That will be the end of him. My father is not a runaway slave. That is easily proven with the help of Master Serou. So, there! End of the problem. When do we get married?" she asked in full command of the situation. "Has father shown you my dowry? Have you let it be known that you accept me as your bride? And if not? Why not? If you haven't, its time you did. It may be that your negligence brought this problem forth. All you had to do is tell one person and all Judea would know by sundown." A silent and mildly intimidated young man listened in amazement to the future of his life. Her father and Camia broke into uproarious laugher.

"Do you see what you have raised my daughter to become?" Tremyio accused Camia.

"I only did what you told me to do," came her swift reply. And happy laughter resounded from all four. "I agree with Senobia, when are you two going to get married? We should set a date now and let the gossip patrol have the news. It'll make the centurion look bad coming with his offer too late."

Camia loved Senobia from childhood. She was her own baby in every way but biologically. Onofrio was a recent addition to her affection but she could arrange them both with equal regard. They could be daughter in law and son or son in law and daughter. And she would be just as happy. Their offspring would be her grandchildren. She looked forward to them with joyful expectation. Camia gestured for silence and made a shocking announcement, "We should invite the centurion for refreshments late this afternoon. I think we should show him some well deserved hospitality." Three faces went ashen at the off base suggestion. Raising her hands again she silenced them and continued, "Tremiyo, have you known me long enough to trust me and my remedies for most situations?" The question dripped mischief from her artificial smile.

"Yes, I trust you but I want to know what is festering in that cranky little mind of yours?"

"I'm asking that you trust me and I promise that after this day, the centurion will never have another thought in this direction. And no harm will befall anybody, me included. We can send a fast-footed messenger to him. He will be easy to find. Everybody knows where he goes and what he does. He is to come for refreshments late this afternoon. He will only be received before dark. Plenty of daylight will make things socially correct. Leave the rest to me."

Over Onofrio's objections, the messenger was sent. Senobia was to be kind and friendly. "Not overly friendly," was Onofrio's instruction. Senobia still glowed from knowing he was jealous. It made her feel special to him. She would serve whatever refreshment the centurion preferred and partake of the same beverage. "In limited portions," according to her fiancé. Senobia would confess her deep love for Onofrio and how she looked forward to their life together. She should talk about lessons she's taken with the Lady Clavenia and her love of music, dancing and the arts. She should make it clear that there is no room in her heart for anything except her father's wishes and Onofrio. She should remain at a respectable distance at all times. Clear across her room was Onofrio's preference. She should be gracious and polite and use her manners as a shield against unwanted advances. People were made to silently busy themselves cleaning house while Camia played chaperone. She wanted witnesses to be present at all times. Camia assured that little conversation would pass after all that. Camia escorted Senobia to her rooms to receive final instructions and personal preparations for her late afternoon guest.

> *And when he got into the boat, his disciples followed*
> *him. And behold, there arose a great storm on the sea, so that*
> *the boat was being swamped by the waves; but he was asleep.*
> *Matthew 8:23-24*

> *And when he had ceased speaking, he said to Simon,*
> *"Put out into the deep and let down your nets for a catch."*
> *And Simon answered, "Master, we toiled all night and*
> *took nothing! But at your word I will let down the nets."*
> *Luke 5:4-5*

Chapter Nineteen

Centurion Clemidius Comes to Call

'Tis Midnight; and on Oliver's Brow

'Tis midnight; and on olive's brow
the star is dimmed that lately glowed:
'Tis midnight; in the garden now
the suffering savior prays alone.
'Tis midnight; and from all removed
the savior wrestles lone with fears;
E'en the disciple whom he loved
heeds not his Master's grief and tears.
'Tis midnight; and for other guilt
the man of sorrows weeps in blood;
Yet he that hath in anguish knelt
is not forsaken by his God.
'Tis midnight; and from heavenly plains
is borne the song that angels know;
Unheard by mortals are the strains
that sweetly soothe the savior's woe.

William B. Tappan (1794-1849)

Onofrio and Tremiyo went to see Serou. According to words from slave and worker alike, Master Serou was in conference with several high ranking members of the Jewish council. Word was that the meeting had been very loud and boisterous. Shortly a large contention of official look-ing individuals was leaving by various means of transport. Two men riding in a cart were striking each other with their fists and grumbling fierce insults at one another. Serou dropped all other matters to greet his new guests amiably. He looked tired and Onofrio concluded that his foster father was overworked. While Serou admired how grand Onofrio looked in a blue Chinese silk tunic overlaid by a polished, soft brown goat skin blazer. Even the bronze bracelet looked good on his wrist. Openly pleased with what he saw, he playfully roughed up the young man's hair.

"I presume, you two are here to talk wedding" and he headed for the comfort of a large couch and wine on a low table.

"No sir, we have acquired an unpleasant situation and need your advice on how to deal with it." Onofrio was first to say. The Egyptian was instantly ready to hear their plea.

"Will you men drink with me," he invited and poured drinks from an elegant Grecian pitcher. As he handed them their cups, he pointed to the elegant array of couches and low tables by a large open door. Serou gave Tremiyo his full attention and was truly awed at such audacity by the new Jewish council member. The Macedonian emissary could be bought with loose change. He was a minor problem. He left the room and soon reappeared holding a scroll and sat by Tremiyo. "Here is all the proof you need in any court to prove you have been a free man since the day I said you were. This is a document I never thought we would need. When I came upon you, I found a friend. I did not buy a slave. I set a worthy man free and gave him every opportunity to leave but he chose to stay of his own accord." Touched by the Egyptian's uncommon show of emotion Tremyio touched his arm.

"We never needed it, until this crummy Roman trespassed into our world. I was a free man when you owned me. You never gave me reason to feel like I was your property." Then on Se-rou's quiet insistence Tremiyo read the old documents again.

They gave Tremiyo absolute freedom along with his daughter, Senobia. Onofrio correctly surmised that his foster father was further driving his point home that his word never be doubted, even by his long time friend and steward of his home. Onofrio watched lengthening shadows slowly creep up the outside walls as the afternoon began to wane. Repeatedly he took nervous looks out the patio doors and using the fading sunlight to tell the approximate time. Sensing or seeing Onofrio's nervousness, he smiled at his new son.

"You need not worry, son. If the centurion so much as touches a hair on my future daughter-in-law, he will not live long enough to tell it. He is a foolish man, but he is not stupid enough to try anything out of order in front of witnesses. Your bride is perfectly safe. Camia is a far better sentry than the dogs in the front yard. I trust that woman with my life. Come, let's go inspect my villa." The sun was slowly sinking behind the hills, seemingly reluctant to leave the day. *"But Senobia is alone with that damned centurion and it will be dark soon,"* Onofrio was thinking. Twice he looked back to Tremiyo's home knowing he would see nothing but fading daylight. Neither Tremiyo nor Onofrio seemed surprised to receive swords and scabbards from Serou. He left the room momentarily, speaking to a servant by his side. Then they rode the surrey to the villa, in no particular haste. The only thing Serou said on the way was "It's time to clear out this nest of rats." He gave his companions no instructions, as though they knew what to do. As the leader of the three-man expedition, Serou presented the profile of a confident commander to his new son as he guided the horses with easy grace.

They arrived at the villa at near dark. Two skinny horses were tied to the marble columns while dogs and goats ran around loose. Chariots lay on their sides awaiting repairs. Tiles on the entry way were slick with animal dung. The stench of urine hung heavy in the air. Clearly men had urinated on the flagstones regularly. Saddles, riding gear and dirty clothes lay all about the front yard and entrance. When the trio made their way inside, they met a drunken officer with a woman in each arm, equally intoxicated.

"Who in the hell are you people? Centurion Clemidius is gone to fetch his sweetheart. He should be back soon. You can wait over there," a``nd he gestured with his chin to the only clear area in the cluttered room. "Oh and there's some wine over there somewhere. Help yourself." The officer's attempt at hospitality fell on deaf ears. "This place looks like a mess now. But, the centurion is bringing his sweetie and she's going to fix up this villa as pretty as her father's. This is going to be her home while the centurion is in Jerusalem. The owner of this property is a close friend of the centurion and gave my commanding officer full use of this entire estate." The officer concluded, urging his companions to a room in the far corner, and surveyed the trio with misguided contempt.

Onofrio went to draw his sword and Serou gently laid his hand on the young man's forearm. Hawk-eyeing the officer intensely, he spoke clearly for all to hear, "Men of honor do not fight drunken dogs that bark without knowing their own ground. I am Serou, Master of this property. Are you sober enough to take orders?"

Undeniable authority stirred the drunken embers in the officer's brain. He labored briefly, digesting the introduction and following the question. Slowly he released the women and gestured them to go to the room behind him with a silent hand. "Yes sir, what do you want me to tell Centurion Clemidius?"

"You are to take your companions and you are to leave these premises immediately." Serou called the women back, "You ladies come this way this instant." They stopped in their tracks, timidly looking back at the tall Egyptian with the booming voice. They came forward sheepishly clinging to each other for protection. At another time in another place they may have been attractive. Tonight, they were overused objects of wanton sex.

The officer was making a desperate attempt at being dignified. "What is the problem, sir? Why are you ordering us out of the centurion's home?"

The Egyptian was running short on patience and promptly retorted, "This is no longer the centurion's home. He will be leaving tonight along with you, your playmates and anybody else in this house."

"Oh, there's nobody else. They're all gone to arrest some worthless Jew that's hiding out in a olive grove not far from here. The Centurion could not go. He was invited to sip tea with his sweetie then he's going to bring her here for an introduction to her future life." The officer laughed a little bit while Onofrio was having an awful hard time staying calm. With borrowed dignity the officer slurred his words out slowly, "Don't worry sir. We'll go. We've been thrown out of better places than this. You're the master of the house and what you say goes." And he peeled out his sword and charged Serou.

Onofrio tripped him neatly and before the officer hit the floor he whacked him on the skull with the pommel of his sword. Tremiyo looked at the young man with a full smile, while Serou looked at his son with reserved pride. "Well done, boy" and he grinned happily. Onofrio only gave him a boyish shrug of his shoulders, looking down at the big mouthed officer. The women drug their disabled companion to the nearby wagon. They grumbled and complained but they complied since their only source of protection was sleeping soundly. Soon they were leaving the estate and a woman was clearly seen searching the officer's purse.

> *And they went to a place which was called Gethsemane;*
> *and he said to his disciples, "Sit here, while I pray." And he*
> *took with him Peter and James and John, and began to be*
> *greatly distressed and troubled.* Mark 14:32-33

Slowly the trio walked through the empty villa, each assessing the damage done to the once elegant home. Much to their surprise they soon heard muted voices and soft music from behind a closed door. Onofrio took the lead ever so cautiously he gently pushed the door open. A giant knot of apprehension trapped in his throat along with the hated question, *"Had Clemidius brought Senobia to this room? Were they now, behind this door?"* He fought the vile feeling of wanting to know and his inability to open the door fully. When the door was half open the sounds of merriment emerged along with very pleasant odors. Fully open, the door fanned out into a spacious well kept room, superbly furnished, well lit and ventilated. A room filled with the fragrance of flowers and costly incense. Fresh food and drink decorated an elegant table. A large handsome bed with elaborate trimmings and abounding with cushions and pillows waited for its occupants in the center of the room. *"The honeymoon suite!"* thought Onofrio as anger and other unrecognized emotions swelled up in his mind. The smelly dog, the would-be friend was a conniving son of a filthy sow. He laid those plans to rob the young couple of their first night of virginal love as was rightfully theirs, leaving an unforgotten blemish on Senobia's life. And for no good reason other than his wicked lust.

> *While he was still speaking, there came a crowd, and the man called Judas, one of the twelve, was leading them. He drew near to Jesus to kiss him; but Jesus said to him, "Judas, would you betray the Son of man with a kiss?"*
> *Luke 22:47–48*

No less than half a dozen individuals lounged around the room. Elegantly dressed and merrily talking around a low table surrounded by plush cushions. There was wine and fruit abundant along with a large pipe and smoking tubes, the participants having taken turns at the pipe were dreamy-eyed. They appeared relaxed in the spirit of God-sent euphoria. One of them rose from his cushioned seat when he saw guests enter, motioning his companions to rise and stand behind him as he greeted the arrivals. "Hail, the conquering hero that brings his virgin bride to her rightful throne." And he bowed profusely to Onofrio and his companions, swirling his gossamer robes aside with a flourish of feminine grace. Tremiyo heard the man's voice and cautiously pushed his way forward. His disbelieving eyes methodically examined this person that had earlier been his painful tormentor. Here was the Macedonian ambassador. Except this man was no more an ambassador than Tremiyo was a Jewish midwife. He was stunned to realize that this was a theatrical company. Actors hired by the centurion to disrupt his life. Tremiyo swiftly drew his sword and before anything could stop him, he neatly pricked the man's ear. An instant flow of crimson rushed down his face and clothes. The actor screamed in pain and equally from panic as he recognized Tremiyo and remembered the older man's earlier promise, now partially delivered. He cringed lowly, holding his ear as the crimson flood continued; fearfully looking up at Tremiyo as if expecting the final blow. Another person, apparently the leader of the troupe, stood before Tremiyo, also recognizing the older man. He played the part of the new Jewish council member on his first mission.

"Be not so harsh in your judgment, brother. We are all slaves to a higher order. What we did was simply act out a request. We do our work as an honorable profession. We are a company of actors and entertainers. Our humble troupe is widely known for our portrayals and theatrics. Our specialty is to imitate the actions and reactions of famous people, without insult or injury. One day soon you should allow us to demonstrate my impression of Herod beheading John. It is awesome. It is absolutely gruesome. We have enjoyed remarkable success with that skit. That slender man over there is practicing the seductive dance of Salome to add flavor to the performance. But the highlight of the act is the beheading scene. People love the sight of blood except him." And he pointed to the actor being attended for the injury to his ear, which was still bleeding. The effeminate leader and would-be member of the Jewish council was unafraid and lightheaded from the effects of the pipe. He was nonetheless in command of his faculties since he was speaking to a possible client. "Our work of this morning is now a previous episode. We are waiting for the centurion to pay us for our services. Our task here was to clean and decorate the bridal chamber. It is said that he is bringing some sweet loving thing he is smitten by. A mere slave girl, I'm told. I've never seen the girl. So I don't know what the little whore looks like and I could care less. I think she's the daughter of one of the slaves that works under you." And he pointed at Tremiyo who still had blood in his eye. Only the Egyptian remained his usual calm.

"And how much are you owed for your services?" he asked.

The troupe swiftly gathered at the prospect of *pay*. "I believe the current rate for this type work is thirty pieces of silver." Serou reached for his purse and counted out the equivalent in gold. "Each!" the greedy eyed troupe leader stated pleased with his share. "Except for him," and pointed to his companion now holding a bloody rag to his ear. "He deserves a bit more. Medical expenses, you know." Serou paid them all, one at a time. Onofrio smiled to himself, remembering an ancient near forgotten thought the lovely red haired, green eyed Ruth Ann always said, "All it takes is money."

Watching the troupe ride out amidst happy waves and shouts, Onofrio was struck with a welcome thought. For the centurion's misled foolishness he had plotted murder. He felt relieved he did not pursue his plan to kill and felt the awesome weight removed from his mind. Clemidius contracted a wicked and traitorous plan and saw to its delivery. All for the sake of adding a virgin to his list of dubious conquests. Such high profile risks could account for his being transferred to this troublesome and faraway place, second or even third in command with little or no chance for promotion. He still felt a grisly anger at Clemidius and he would not soon forget the reason for it. The report of all this complete with a bill for damages done to the villa would go to Pilate and then to Rome. Reasonably inflated, of course. It would leave an indelible mark on the centurion's record, perhaps denying him a higher rank.

Serou patted his son on the back, pointing to the surrey, "Go see about Senobia. Tremiyo and I need to walk and talk about your wedding." Onofrio was not at all surprised to see the dog keeper posted with other men watching Serou and the villa. Several guards were having a rip-roaring laugh. The obnoxious odor of fresh human feces filled the air. From behind some bushes came Clemidius, gripping his abdomen and running for the villa. He was the source of the offensive odor. He reeked of it as he ran past the surrey with the tail end of his tunic visibly stained and dripping. That powerful anger Onofrio felt earlier evaporated seeing the man in such an embarrassing condition. He knew not why Clemidius was torn with such agony. He only knew that whatever it was rendered the man incapable of executing his plan for Senobia. Filled with laughter, Onofrio was subject to wonder how descriptive the centurion would be, explaining his absence from duty to his superior. The true answer would be comical, any way it was told and subject to long term memory. Onofrio remembered what the drunken officer at the villa said, "They've gone to arrest some worthless Jew that's hiding out in an old olive grove not far from here. It won't take long to get it done. He's got some of his gang with him, but they're no challenge." Onofrio only vaguely speculated it might be the man called Jesus of Nazareth. Be that as it may, it was no concern of his. His mind was far keener on reaching and being close to Senobia. He would learn who they arrested tomorrow. For now, he was hungry and Senobia was near.

Two grown men experienced and wise in the complexities of social order walked home through a familiar darkness. They discussed and arranged the future lives of Onofrio and Senobia. Each wanting this wedding to be an event not soon forgotten, they collaborated on every detail and even allowed for changes the couple might want.

Anxiously Onofrio pushed the horses to reach Senobia, meeting with much gaiety and unusual freedom when he drove into the compound. Countless people gathered around their front door laughing and exchanging stories while children frolicked around in carefree abandon. It seemed a holiday had been declared. The young man from parts unknown was even more surprised to be hailed as a returning hero. People he knew, and people he didn't, all cheered and waved as he slowly drove through. And he didn't have the vaguest idea why. Senobia, Camia and other women were exchanging laughs and great merriment when Onofrio arrived unexpectedly. Anxious, he went directly to Senobia and without ceremony wrapped his arms around her and bent to kiss her, only to have her shy away, astonished to see him. A faint smile and gleaming eyes joyfully reverted to coy appreciation instantly. "Not now, love. Not in front of all these people. What would they say if they saw us like that?" Senobia's little giggling statement was the signal to disband this brood of cackling hens. Women were soon leaving, looking and snickering over their shoulders. Contemplating, they may have missed seeing a passionate love scene in full session.

Camia saw the last woman out the door and propped herself exhausted against the closed door frame. "Those gossiping old biddies will have the story all over Judea by sunrise," she said still giggling.

Feeling happily reunited Senobia wrapped her loving arms around the object of her dreams. "I have never had so much fun in all my life. It was hilariously funny the way he tried desperately to fit into a realm where he did not belong." Although completely left out of their private merriment Onofrio was captured by their laughter. It seemed like hours before they finally slowed down enough to relate the events of the evening.

"We received the centurion cheerfully when he arrived promptly on time and looking his best. Clean-shaven, finely dressed and reeking of costly body lotions. He even brought a man to see about his chariot and tend to the horses, while he got acquainted with the fair Senobia. He oozed with synthetic charm so clearly a bad act. He even made a clumsy effort to demonstrate his vast knowledge of music stemming from his tours of duty. He sang to Senobia songs that turned out to be bawdy barroom ballads and military hymns. Senobia served the wine he claimed to favor while she sipped on her favorite mixture. Clemidius was never one to refuse good wine and, showing his good manners, drank what was put before him. They sipped and chatted about meaningless things while he obviously longed to put his twitching hands on her. But he was stymied by her beauty and lady like manners." Camia remembered and then continued. "Suddenly, he was stricken with a panic urge to discharge his bowels. Clattering flatulence was loud and clearly heard as offensive gas filled the room, which Senobia and I made abundantly clear was intolerable. We openly urged the Negro manning the feather fan to hasten his pace. Clemidius managed to go out back to relieve himself. He made a second attempt at being civil apologizing profusely and blaming the terrible food in Judea as the cause. The second onslaught allowed no time to reach the latrine in time. Many saw his humiliating condition and laughed hardily while children giggled, holding their nose and pointing their fingers in shame. I had flavored his wine with a powerful powdered herb that induces immediate and violent bowel movement. Senobia was made to nibble on fruit and allow ample running room and she complied not knowing what to expect. Everyone in the compound was asked to be outside not only to witness any undesirable action Clemidius may take but more so to see him leave. Nobody was told of my plan, therefore the centurion's behavior came as an unexpected surprise. With our story fully told, we all three broke out in non-stop laughter. People outdoors heard us because from the outer darkness came corresponding hilarity."

In between random chuckles Onofrio tried to explain how he saw Clemidius emerging from the bushes and still smelling offensive. Then added in joyful jest, "Camia, I will always trust you. But I'm telling you now, whatever you give me to drink or eat, you will have to sample first." And it gave reason to renew their joyful laughter.

Onofrio had not the slightest idea which god these three loving people revered and prayed to, but recalling how close he came to committing murder and how he was prevented from it, he was compelled to say, "Thank You, God. Thank you."

CHAPTER TWENTY

MIDNIGHT AT GETHISAMANE AND AT THE HOUSE OF SEROU

Then those who had seized Jesus led him to Caiaphas the high priest, where the scribes and the elders had gathered ... Now the chief priests and the whole council sought false testimony against Jesus that they might put him to death, but they found none,   *Matthew 26:57, 59-60*

And as soon as it was morning the chief priests, with the elders and scribes, and the whole council held a consultation; and they bound Jesus and led him away and delivered him to Pilate. And Pilate asked him, "Are you the King of the Jews?"   *Mark 15:1-2*

Public conduct unbecoming an officer of the Roman Empire.

Wanton vandalism of private property.

Setting standards for subordinate officers not acceptable to the community as a whole.

The afore mentioned further contributes to the existing problems between our countries, snarled in a conflict of human values as we are.

Under the rule of Rome, the community is entitled to respect for their property by officers of the Empire, that right is well lodged within Roman law.

The community is due the right to men of honor and integrity as keepers of the peace through these troublesome times.

Serou's disclosure would be heard in Rome. Onofrio struggled with many of the words but now he had Senobia close by to help him read the document. Onofrio was to deliver the document to Pontius Pilate the next day. Enclosed was an added note that the matter be brought to Herod's attention also. Governor Pilate would read the document and have the story verified by his staff before forwarding it to Rome and Herod. Serou, having inspected the villa, added a slightly inflated bill for damage done to his property. The inflated difference being for negotiating purposes. He included the cost of the troupe with a lengthy account of the Macedonian and Jewish council impersonators, and specifically a detailed account of the reason for the deception. The account did not condemn the actors since they were simply earning a living. The guilt rested on the patron of their talents. The intent and purposes of the scheme reflected on the purpose of Rome's presence. Was it Rome's design to rule by malicious deception or by rightful law?

Tremiyo came home full of joy and embraced the couple with heartfelt affection. Surprising them both by next taking Camia in his arms and kissing her cheeks then whispering in her ear, "I have to go out again tonight. There is trouble brewing at the old olive grove and I need to to see if I can avoid a disaster." And he held his hand over her mouth to keep her quiet. Then instructed Camia openly, "Keep an eye on that young man. Don't let him out of your sight."

> *Then they seized him and led him away, bringing him into the high priest's house. Peter followed at a distance; and when they had kindled a fire in the middle of the courtyard and sat down together, Peter sat among them. Then a maid, seeing him as he sat in the light and gazing at him, said, "This man also was with him." But he denied it, saying, "Woman, I do not know him."*   *Luke 22:54-57*

Swiftly Camia responded, "Oh, he'll behave or I'll feed him some of the centurion's wine." And the budding family had reason to laugh again. Events of this day would not be soon forgotten and Tremiyo left, going to the abandoned olive grove to help avoid a disaster.

Reluctantly leaving the compound Onofrio noticed lights still glowing from Serou's workroom. And so he went to bid goodnight to the Egyptian and possibly extract a bit of information. "I see the blush of love is still bright on your rosy cheeks," laughing hardy Serou tossed Onofrio a clean cloth. The cloth was vivid from Senobia's berry stained lips.

Seeing his foster father come to a partial halt in his work, Onofrio posed his question, "Would you know a man that is master at keeping records and wise to discover cheating, if cheating is at hand?"

The question brought Serou to an instant halt, raised an eyebrow and asked with a faded smile, "Do you smell a mouse in your granary, son?"

Shy to show his ignorance the young man answered thoughtful reserve, "I discovered a few differences on some papers I am not happy with. I am inadequate to understand why the differences exist and would like some outside help to guide me to a rightful answer."

"What exactly did you discover?" Serou asked seemingly anxious to hear.

"I promised not to bring you into this until I have a clear answer. I cannot be running to you every time I do not understand something. I want to learn for myself why these discrepancies exist and bring you facts in hand." Serou hawk-eyed him, pleased with the young man's resolve. Serou was alerted to trouble and spared having to make an investigation. The water project was of prime importance. It was going to take longer than he anticipated due to the infantile squabbling of grown men. "Tomorrow I will have a man sent to you. Tell him all you have found and listen well. His is known for finding fault, if fault is truly the case. He is very good at finding flaws in record keeping. He is a master at money management and you're going to learn much from him." Serou finalized with an affectionate jab and the young man's jaw.

Onofrio stood still searching for an inoffensive way to continue. "I hope he's not Jewish."

Serou thought for a moment before answering, "No, he's not Jewish. In fact, he is Greek and well versed in Jewish ways. He's going to be good for you."

> *When Judas, his betrayer, saw that he was condemned, he repented and brought back the thirty pieces of silver to the chief priests and the elders, saying, "I have sinned in betraying innocent blood." They said, "What is that to us? See to it yourself." And throwing down the pieces of silver in the temple, he departed; and he went and hanged himself.*
> *Matthew 27:3-5*

> *The Lord is my shepherd I shall not want.*
> *He maketh me to lie down in green pastures.*
> *He leadeth me beside the still waters*
> *He restores my soul,*
> *He leadeaeth me in the path of righteousness*
> *for His name's sake.*
> *Yea, though I walk through the valley of the shadow of Death,*
> *I will fear no evil, for Thou art with me.*
> *Psalm 23 (KJV)*

The young man from parts unknown woke up before the birds fluffed out their feathers. Even though it had been a short night, he felt wonderfully rested and there was music stirring in his soul. The world was a wonderful place in which to live and nothing short of death could change that. He admired a faint tint of pink and mauve softly touching the eastern horizon, while the near side of the hills and mountains were still embedded in deep shadows. Deep purple ravines, trees and bushes sprinkled with shades of motley gray. He bathed and groomed himself at leisure. He was going before Pontius Pilate today to deliver a written complaint and make public his marital intentions. He was to meet with a Greek mentor at a popular patio inn to discuss a disturbing issue. He would have dinner with his fiancé and her father. By day's end he would be closer to being a married man. By whatever gods he had been so lavishly blessed, he acknowledged their generosity. Having no favorite god, he thanked all the gods he knew about. "Good politics" he smiled to himself. Acknowledge them all, praise them all and thank them all equally. And he laughed to himself filled with unfathomed joy. There were no storms brewing on his horizons. There was only a smooth path to happiness fulfilled, to which he would be a grateful host.

He dressed all in white. Among the many gifts from Serou, he found a pair of masculine copper bracelets along with a wide leather belt fitted with bright buttons of Cyprian brass. In his tan and copper boots he decided to wear a turban since he found a handsome brooch to finish off the headdress. If he felt elegant because he was dressed elegant, that made sense to him. It all made a good choice for the rider of such a handsome chariot and team of horses. Already the sky was tinted with amber gold and fiery reds. It would be a hot and clear day without a single cloud to mar the canopy of brightening blue. No rain in sight. He saw a flock of white egrets gently floating across the flawless sky. Headed for the wetlands by the sea, he thought. There would be cool brackish waters with abundant food and shady trees. Smart egrets, he thought, then remembered something about a God that "so loveth the birds of the field that he provided for them." He didn't know which god did that. He would have liked to thank him for the scene that was provided this morning. The clatter of wagons announced the arrival of the labor force at the plant. He would have the Syrian overlook the day while he was gone and went downstairs. It struck him strange that Eljazar was working so early. Eljazar claimed to have just arrived, but the drawn window shades, fresh ink drops and candles burned low, said otherwise. He was brief with his greetings and claimed to have business in the city today. He appeared sick and acted uncommonly nervous.

"Are you sick? You don't look well." Onofrio questioned with genuine concern.

"I don't feel well. And I have some awful business to tend to. There is a terrible injustice being done this very moment. I have to see what I can do to alter the horrible wrongs being dealt to a good man. They are wrong. They have been wrong for years. They have become corrupt and no longer live by God's law. What they do is murder. Plain, unmitigated murder. With mocking ceremony, but murder no less." Eljazar concluded shaking as he spoke. "Please forgive me, I must go." And now he was in tears, clearly seen by Onofrio as he stood aside to let the older man pass. Receding echoes followed Eljazar's footsteps down the metal stairway. Almost immediately, the rumble of his horses faded out of the compound ahead of a cloud of glowing dust in the early morning sun.

The Syrian was speaking to the workers and had their full attention. "The hills of Judea are countless. Among them all he spoke to the people about God's plan for mankind. He is a messenger from God, on a mission to correct the errors of our ways. And for that, he was arrested last night. I heard all this at the inn where I stay. He was lashed, bound, then dragged off by a horde of would-be righteous and law abiding citizens. This morning he will go before Pilate. According to the law he is guilty of blasphemy. Pilate, as governor has no choice, but to carry out the law, like it or not. They will vote for the death penalty. Rest assured they are going to kill him."

A man asked, "But is he really the son of God or not?" The crowd grumbled in unison.

The Syrian thought for a moment then slowly answered, "I think not. I think he is a God-sent messenger, a Divine healer and reminder to correct our sinful ways. But this raggedy man cannot possibly be the son of any god. No self-respecting god would send his son to earth looking as he does."

Another unidentified voice rang out from the crowd, "He has healed many people, and surely for this he can be forgiven and be set free. He has done entirely too much good to deserve the death penalty."

Still another voice offered, "Say what you will but Rome and the Jewish council rule here. And if they say he dies. He's dead. All his fine works will not save him. Son of God or not, God's messenger or not. He's as good as dead."

It surprised Onofrio to hear the Syrian lead such a debate. He knew of the man they discussed. He had seen Jesus of Nazareth, no less than a week ago. He saw no reason for the man to be arrested and condemned to death. He knew of at least one miracle Jesus performed. Surely, this debate like so many others was a pointless exercise to delay going to work. He saw no solid base for the discussion. It would prove nothing. It would solve nothing and most importantly it would contribute nothing to the day's end result. Onofrio clapped his hands loudly and briskly walked among them. Immediately the men moved toward their work stations. "Stoke up the furnaces, men. Break out the saws and hammers. There's work to be done. All of you have quotas to meet. Come on, Come on. Let's move lively."

Struggling with his ankle chains Amparo, the roadside bandit, had cleaned the chariot spotless before he was taken away.

Now it was the day of Preparation of the Passover; it was about the sixth hour. He said to the Jews, "Behold your King!" They cried out, "Away with him, away with him, crucify him!" Pilate said to them, "Shall I crucify your King?" The chief priests answered, "We have no king but Caesar."
John 19:14-15

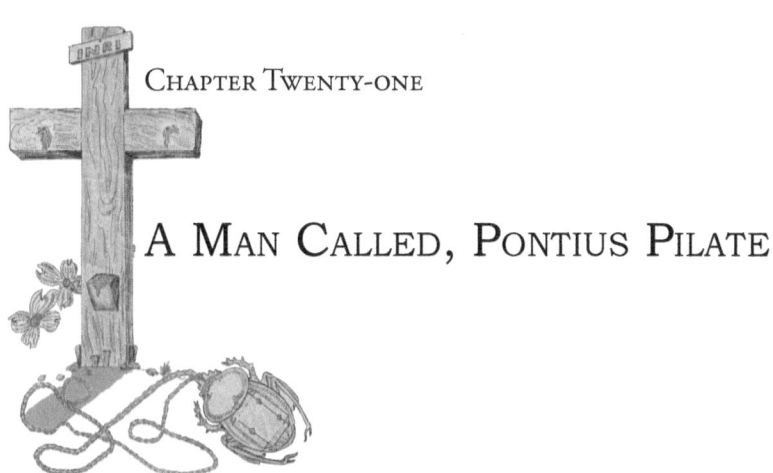

CHAPTER TWENTY-ONE

A MAN CALLED, PONTIUS PILATE

Pilate said to him, "So you are a king?" Jesus answered, "You say that I am a king. For this I was born, and for this I have come into the world, to bear witness to the truth. Every one who is of the truth hears my voice." Pilate said to him, "What is truth?" After he had said this, he went out to the Jews again, and told them, "I find no crime in him. But you have a custom that I should release one man for you at the Passover; will you have me release for you the King of the Jews?" They cried out again, "Not this man, but Barabbas!" Now Barabbas was a robber.   *John 18:37- 40*

Then Pilate took Jesus and scourged him. And the soldiers plaited a crown of thorns, and put it on his head, and arrayed him in a purple robe; they came up to him, saying, "Hail, King of the Jews!" and struck him with their hands.
John 19:1-3

The horses gleamed with good health and careful attention. As they smartly pulled the show piece chariot over stones and road bumps the grey spots on their rumps seemed to bounce freely with their stride. Onofrio even practiced the graceful way Serou held the reins at mid-chest, head held high as he reckoned with obstacles ahead. An unprecedented joy seemed to shorten the distance to Jerusalem. Such happiness he had not felt since he was a child in the company of his parents. That fading memory now seemed so far away and only visited him in his dreams. Those joy filled thoughts soon found their way to Senobia. He must find the ragged jeweler and have him create a masterpiece wedding ring. A ring like no other. A ring to last a life time. Two life times, his and hers. There was no greater companion in the roomy chariot than his happy thoughts.

He came close to a place called Gethsemane. An abandoned orchard often referred to as the Garden of Olives. The age worn trees no longer produced fruit and nobody knew who owned the forsaken old place. A number of people were gathered looking over a steep incline and speaking in excited and perplexing tones. Knowing he had ample time to conduct his business Onofrio eased the horses to gentle stop. He asked the first person he met, "What has happened here?"

Solemnly the man answered, "Those people discovered a man that has apparently hung himself."

"When did it happen?" Onofrio inquired paying little attention to the answer as he fidgeted with the anxious horses.

"Some time during the night. A passerby found him at first light."

"Who is the man, do you know?" as Onofrio asked the question he first gave thought to Jesus of Nazareth. He expected the roadside stranger to say Jesus.

"Some say the man was called Judas Iscariot, a follower of the prophet, Jesus. They seem to think that this Judas hanged himself to avoid prosecution, since Jesus was arrested last night." the roadside stranger concluded.

Never having heard of Judas Iscariot, Onofrio quickly lost interest but calmly went on to say, "It seems to me that this Judas has prosecuted himself and has passed the ultimate sentence."

The roadside stranger was almost cheerful at the simplified deduction. "That's not the way I would avoid prosecution," he

laughed. Because it was the day of the Passover, work of this nature was forbidden. A person committing suicide was considered
unholy. And so Judas stayed untouched all day in the hot Judean
sun until his expanding weight broke the rope or branch from
which he hung.

It was entirely too gorgeous a day to waste mulling over
senseless suicides. He heard the cooing of doves from the underbrush, apparently having found a cool place away from the
relentless sun. "What would drive a man to commit suicide on
such a lovely day?" Onofrio quickly decided to dump the question from his mind. Call it a mystery, that need not be solved.
He never heard of Judas Iscariot. And it was too late to meet the
man and ask him, "Why did you hang yourself?" He prompted
the horses to Jerusalem trying to recapture his previous joy.

The streets were a riot of happy celebrants. Every nation
seemed to be represented by members of their state, clan, tribe
or family. The crowds extended to the far horizon causing near
traffic jams. With considerable effort he found the place to house
the horses. Insisting with coins in hand that his horses be given
good feed and fresh water, the barnkeeper needed no such reminder. He knew of the new son of Serou and friend of Tremiyo
as did most of Jerusalem. After an exchange of news and local
trivia, the young man proceeded to where Governor Pontius
Pilate was conducting office.

One must consider the terrible position of Pontius Pilate.
He was literally torn from four sides. The expectations of Rome
on his performance were enormous. The squabbles and demands
of the Jewish council were perplexing and demanded he expend
extraordinary effort to reach an acceptable compromise. Pilate's
wife, Claudia Procula, had a dream and begged him with a written note not to pass judgment on the Nazarene. And then there
was the burden on his conscience. When all was said and done,
he was condemning a man to death because the Jewish council
was jealous of his ever growing popularity. Political expedience
wore a black shroud of victory that day. And Pilate washed his

hands of the obnoxious affair. He had a cruel side of his dual personality that history would record. He was known to fling a darted barb when his ire was aroused. Now he was faced with liberating the well-known bandit Barabbas as demanded by the yelling mob and set him free then wash his hands again.

The release of Barabbas came by traditional choice. This Jesus Ben Joseph had been declared to be the Messiah by ignorant groups. The savior the Jewish community had been forecasting for countless years. Members of the Jewish council forced and coached their followers to demand the release of Barabbas, and in so doing denied that Jesus was their expected Messiah or King of the Jews. When the final line was drawn, the people preferred the good times Barabbas offered as a worldly blessing. Barabbas offered good times, food, drink and gold. Here and now. Jesus promised an elusive place in faraway heaven after death, provided a person gave up having a sinfully good time while still alive on earth.

Cordially Pontius Pilate received Onofrio, being familiar with the name, since he signed his adoption papers only days ago. He read the document Serou prepared in haste. Clearly accepting what was written as being fact, he gave the document to someone nearby by. The governor looked intently at the well-dressed young man. "You're a handsome addition to your father's house. Why did Serou not present this grievance to me himself? It would appear he sent a grown boy to do a man's work," he chided and bowed courteously.

Onofrio smiled respectfully at the procurator of Rome and ignored the casual dig. "I am well acquainted with the case, having lived on the premises during the time this incident unfolded." Onofrio responded gathering every ounce of respect he knew how to use. "And a man to be married within the month is hardly a boy, sir."

"Married?" Pilate asked in wonderment. "You were just adopted as a baby a few days ago." Laughing good-naturedly he continued, " Well, so it is that you conduct your father's business, present yourself to the governor and bring news of your impending marriage. All in one clean sweep. Concisely done. Who are you marrying?" Pilate asked and rinsed his hands once more appearing to be far off in thought.

"My bride is Senobia, daughter of Tremiyo Steward of the House of Serou."

"Ah yes," the governor answered with a gleam in his eyes. "The gem of Jerusalem, so I hear. I have never seen the girl but it is said that she is a rare beauty of impeccable character and Divine grace. Congratulations, son. Tell your father, I will see to this matter myself. And I'll have him a reply in a few days." He said that over his shoulder by way of dismissal and was rinsing his hands again.

And as they led him away, they seized one Simon of Cyrene, who was coming in from the country, and laid on him the cross, to carry it behind Jesus. And there followed him a great multitude of people and of women who bewailed and lamented him. Luke 23:26-27

Chapter Twenty-two

And on My Cross He Died

And he [the criminal] *said, "Jesus, re-member me when you come into your kingdom." And he said to him, "Truly, I say to you, today you will be with me in Paradise."*   Luke 23:42-43

When the centurion and those who were with him, keeping watch over Jesus, saw the earthquake and what took place, they were filled with awe, and said, "Truly this was the Son of God!"   Matthew 37:54

Onofrio got unexpectedly rushed into a mob of people. They were pushing, shoving, crying and even cursing the rude pack. He tried several times to break away and go for the chariot only to be forced into the opposite direction. Struggling uselessly against the uncivil herd. From out of the faceless mob appeared the only person he recognized, the old woman whose ankle Jesus healed a week or so ago. She was walking straight and at the sight of Onofrio, came directly to him. She was crying, bewailing in a highly animated state. Her face was a roadmap of wrinkles flooded with crystal tears.

"They're going to kill him!" she screamed at Onofrio. "Do something! By all the gods in heaven, why him? He does not deserve death. He's my savior!" the old woman was consumed with sheer hysteria. And she forcefully pushed Onofrio in the direction of the wild mob with borrowed strength. A small group of soldiers shuffled passed, forcing their way with shield and lance to the head of the procession. Onofrio got captured by the mood of the crowd, as he heard the old woman's screams drown within the unruly pack. Unconsciously he fought everybody for a single view of what was happening. Although he stayed close behind the onmoving soldiers, it was still hard going. Finally the street opened up to a wide avenue and he could see what was happening. Jesus of Nazareth was struggling with a heavy cross, precariously draped over his shoulder. He had been brutally lashed. His back was an ugly crisscross pattern of torn and bleeding flesh. Onofrio was shocked to actually feel the agony of the lashing on his own back. It was not imagined, it was excruciating pain and it was real. He looked at his hands momentarily and they were shaking uncontrollably. The pains he felt were like nothing he ever experienced before. His agony was equal to the man struggling with the cumbersome cross. Something griped his heart and there was terrible anguish coursing through his mind and body. He leaned his back against the nearest wall and remained magnetized to the unfolding drama.

Vaguely aware of two strangers beside him, Onofrio honed in on their conversation to help him break away from the inhuman spectacle before him. The strangers were unconcerned and disconnected from what they saw. "They gave him thirty-nine lashes," one of them said.

"No." the second man responded. "They gave him forty two. I got word from one of the men present that the Raven, miscounted by three lashes."

"Who in the hell is the Raven?" the first man asked unconcerned and craning his neck for a better view.

"He is the official scourger and delivers legal punishment in most cases." the second man responded as he nonchalantly looked around somebody's shoulder. "Some young man was granted the privilege of giving the Raven three good lashes for his mistake. You know, they say the man cannot count. Why then have a man doing that kind of work? I would not want my back lashed. I would learn to count." the stranger concluded without the slightest concern for the agony of Jesus of Nazareth.

"Look!" one of the strangers called out seemingly delighted and pointing at Jesus. "Some thoughtful individual platted a wreath of thorns with which to crown the King of the Jews."

Onofrio then focused on the crown of thorns Jesus wore. How could he have missed it before? New anguish flared within the young man from parts unknown. The crown was a thick circle of fierce thorn bush entwined together. Mighty thorns pierced the skin around his head as streams of scarlet coursed down his pain-drawn face. *What senseless brutality is this?* questioned Onofrio in silence. Experiencing a budding sense of anger and helplessness, kneaded into a perplexing and choking sensation.

The crowd was pushing everyone along like an angry river. Shoving and screaming as the final vestiges of civilized men fell into the raging torrent to later stain their souls. Nobody from within the crowd made an effort to stop the maniacal cruelty. And there was sinister laughter from within the mob that had a diabolical tone. Unmercifully a soldier lashed Jesus to make him speed up the pace. Only an act of God could alter the pre-destined ordeal of Jesus Ben Joseph of Nazareth.

Someone yelled from an upper balcony, "If you're really the Son of God, why then do you not save yourself?"

From another unseen voice came "You run out of miracles too soon?"

And still another anonymous heckler rang out, "Son of God or not, he bleeds like a man."

Onofrio pushed forward with the relentless crowd. The odor of sweaty unclean bodies filled the air. Above, not a single cloud marred the flawless skies. Only a black buzzard slowly circled the endless blue like an ominous symbol. With wings spread open the bird was too far away to be touched by the actions of misguided men. Suddenly a man accosted Onofrio. It was the ragged jeweler from Mecca. He was panic stricken and his features so distorted Onofrio hardly recognized him. His face a flood of tears gushing down his beard.

"Onofrio, these idiots are going to kill the Son of God." his blabbering hardly understandable. "There will be such fury come down from heaven that the earth will never be the same again. Make your peace with all your gods for the end of the world is upon us all, for those that plotted to condemn him and for us that had not the courage to prevent it." The jeweler looked to the infinite blue expecting fire to rain down. Struggling he stretched his arms out and openly prayed, "Allah, Supreme God of the world and all the heavens, make this nightmare be a horrible illusion and save this man from this terrible wrong." Visibly the jeweler was a living portrait of hysteria. "I searched for this man for ten years and what he speaks of is already known to me. He is truly the Son of God. I have never known a man so pure in spirit, mind and body. He is flawless and in so being, makes him the Lamb of God. But Allah, not this murderous way! Allah, not this murderous way!" And the jeweler wove himself into the ruthless crowd ranting as he went.

Onofrio was more compelled than ever to follow the frenzied mob. He rolled with their abusive shoves and inflicted shoves of his own. He would do what he could to save Jesus and take him to the house of Serou. *We have an army of men there to protect him until Serou hires a clever lawyer to defend him.* Onofrio was sincere in his belief that Serou could fix a scar on the ocean. Earlier the young man heard that the Jewish authorities hired false witnesses against the Nazarene. Those falsehoods could be proven in court and a retrial would net more favorable results. Naiveness often being the fuel of error, the young man decided to put his plan to work. As he shoved someone out of his way and propelled himself forward. He saw Jesus fall. The crowd stopped in its tracks as each individual looked on silently, without the slightest effort to help. As if frozen with fear or anticipating his rise to walk away unblemished. Onofrio made a supreme effort to reach Jesus and help him escape through the senseless mob. Suddenly a soldier clumsily pushed him back and stood defiantly before him blocking his path and view. When Onofrio tried to force his way around the armored Roman, he met with a stronger shove backwards. The blow soundly delivered by a shielded elbow aimed to his chin and jaw sent him reeling backwards. He landed in unwelcome arms and fell helpless to the ground. Sandaled feet tripped over and stepped on him and all around. With brute strength he fought to regain his feet, realizing he was well behind the herd. He felt a warm trickle creeping down his cheek and saw the front of his elegant white robe stained with vivid crimson. He unfurled the turban and used it to wipe blood from his cheek and mouth. Anger boiled within him instantly. No idiot, low life soldier was going to do that to him and simply walk away. He started grabbing people by their clothes and shoulders projecting himself forward through an ocean of unruly human flesh. With all the strength of a virile young man, he shoved and even kicked his way forward, determined to help Jesus. The mob was so dense it was a pliable, living wall that gave no leeway. His head was reeling and he shook it to clear his swirling vision. He was panting for breath and ached terribly from the blow and from being stomped on. His mouth still bled a bit and the once snow-white turban was now a mottled rag of scarlet and dirty grey. From somewhere in the noisy confusion a hand grabbed him and pulled him back to a safe alcove in front of somebody's home. It was the Syrian. And all he could think to say was, "What in the hell are you doing here? You're supposed to be working."

"Watching over you," replied the Syrian scanning his face. "Here, let's see about that bleeding." The Syrian unceremoniously took Onofrio's face in his hard, callused hand and examined it. "You've got a nasty cut between jaw and big mouth." The Syrian tore off a piece off the turban and poured some wine on it. "Here, hold that over the cut, tightly. It'll help stop the bleeding. You need to stop and catch your breath; you look like you've been run over by an elephant." Too far back to see what was happening the Syrian had an instant solution. "What we need here is a spy. He picked out a small, wiry man and stopped him. "Hey you! You want to see what's happening up front?" Bewildered by the Syrian's size, the man meekly nodded. The Syrian picked up the man and made him straddle his shoulders. Then gruffly told him, "Damn you, don't just sit there. Tell us what's happening." From his elevated position the wiry man started reporting what he could see. "Jesus has fallen. Wait! There is a woman coming to his aid. No, she's not helping. That one is his mother. Yes. That is Mary, widow of Joseph of Nazareth. Wait, they're talking. I'm too far to hear what they're saying. Mary Magdalene is there also. They are talking to Jesus. He is still fallen. But wait. He is getting up. Yes, he's gotten up. He's taking the cross again." Onofrio could plainly see the Syrian was intent on hearing all the small wiry man had to report. Strangely, Onofrio remembered the old woman with the blackened ankles and wondered if she had gotten close to him again. He wondered what would happen to her if Jesus died, since he promised to heal her if only she thought of him. The Syrian managed to free the wine skin from his shoulder and took a swallow. "Here, you look like you could use this," and he tossed the wineskin to Onofrio. Onofrio caught the full wineskin and was surprised to learn how dry his throat was. He noticed his lip bleed had stopped and the headache slipped away. The Syrian planted a big foot in the middle of the person ahead and gave a mighty shove. More than a dozen people started falling in all directions like dominoes, taking many others down with them. He then looked at Onofrio and without having to urge the young man, they worked their way forward over fallen and cursing bodies. Soon the mob grew thick again and the wiry man asked for the wineskin. Onofrio felt newly refreshed and neatly caught the returning wineskin to take another sip. The small, wiry man continued reporting.

"Jesus has fallen again. A soldier just grabbed a black man and he's making the black man carry the cross for Jesus. They just made Jesus lead the black man. The black man has the cross over his shoulder. Another woman is coming to help Jesus. I know who that is. That woman is Bernice. She's taken her veil off to wipe his face then gave it to Jesus. Jesus is wiping his face with it and is giving it back to her. She is kneeling before him because Jesus is down again. He is up on one knee now. He's up on both legs and he's limping. He is weak. He has lost a lot of blood and looks drained. He is reeling. He will never make it to the top of Skull Hill. That hill is also known as Golgotha, you know. That hill is treacherous for an able bodied man and more so for Jesus as weak as he appears. The black man with the cross has stopped. He is waiting for Jesus to recover." Onofrio and the Syrian were glued to the report. Approaching from behind another group of soldiers came pushing their way through. Onofrio instantly decided to duplicate his earlier tactic. He poked the Syrian in the back urging the big man to look back. "Fall in behind them when they pass," Onofrio instructed.

"Some women have come to his side. They are talking to him and trying to give him some help and perhaps courage. The women look Jewish. But I can't tell for sure. I think they're just local women. This man Jesus has every woman in Jerusalem crying out for him. If I had that many women crying out for me, they wouldn't ache for long. Jesus is leaving the women now. He's shaky. He's fallen again. That is his third fall. He'll never carry that cross up the hill." Comfortably perched above all heads the small wiry man asked, "Is that wineskin dry?"

Onofrio shook it and it still had plenty of the stuff that moves willing tongues. "Save some for the brute that has you up there, he drinks more than you do."

A tap on his shoulder made Onofrio turn to find the swollen but kind and gentle face of an older man. "It's a terrible day in Judea," he said. Then added, "But it's a fine day in heaven, the Son of God is coming home."

Onofrio was mechanized to move into the opening left by the passing soldiers. No longer plotting to rescue but pulled forward without a will of his own. The Syrian and his rider moved right behind him. The young man looked back to the elderly man, in time to see him cleave a sign of the cross in midair, like a blessing. Intently they followed the passing troops for what seemed an eternity, slowly moving with the now dwindling crowd. Many people were returning to the city as they were well out of it by now. "We're going up the hill to Calvary," the wiry man reported. "Some call it Golgotha. Oh, I told you that already."

As they approached the top of the hill, the soldiers parted in unison to the left and right in equal numbers. It left the trio almost directly in front of the unfolding scene. The black man still had the cross on his shoulder. The Syrian put the wiry man down and frantically started pointing to the cross. "Look, Onofrio Look! That's the cross you made. Look on the bottom of it. It's got your letter "O" on it.

It took a short moment for the young man to regroup his thoughts and grasp what the Syrian was saying. When the Syrian's cryptic statement came clear and he focused on the bottom of the cross. Onofrio was horrified. Sheer terror swept through his body and he shook violently for a moment. He heard his soul scream within him, "Heaven, have mercy on me." Clearly stamped on the bottom of the beam with branding iron precision was a large circle. The letter"O." Vividly he remembered the Syrian stamping the red-hot iron on the timber. Memories of that day flashed through his mind. He even remembered the persistent little white flower that kept growing back on the rough hewn pillar. With considerable effort the black man hoisted the rough-hewn cross off his shoulder and dropped it with a resounding wallop where a soldier indicated. He saw the spot from where he pulled off the little white blossom and when he made the effort to get closer and make sure, he was stopped by a red-eyed soldier. Onofrio looked again at the foreboding cross and the scorched letter "O" seemed to grow more clear in the sunlight. He remained magnetized to the bottom of the fiendish cross. The fearsome instrument of torture and death lay glowing in the sun ready to receive its intended victim with no regard for friend, foe or family. Jesus spoke painfully to the black man. The bearer of his cross was crying profusely. Streams of silver tears washed down his ebony face, now a contorted map of agony. The Syrian patted Onofrio on the back cheerfully stating, "Well, one thing for sure this man Jesus got the best of what we had to offer. Your cross got put to good use today. Your cross got a Son of God, mine only gets two thieves. Some people are just born lucky, you know." Onofrio demonstrated profound aversion to the Syrian's cheerful statement. He quickly discharged his displeasure to refocus his attention on the horrible burned circle on the bottom of the cross. His cross. The cross on which Jesus of Nazareth would surely die today.

Slowly the trio moved forward with the crowd around them. Troopers kept everybody from getting too close to the unfolding scene. Small hazy clouds began to invade the horizon moving slowly towards Golgotha. A storm was brewing in the far away hills and many witnesses were already accustomed to seeing crucifixions. They were common occurrences to most sightseers. The name "Jesus" was simply one more name soon to be forgotten, like so many others. The festering rainstorm in the distance was inching forward. No sensible reason to get soaked over some criminals getting their just reward. Disgruntled, disappointed or bored thrill seekers found reason to leave the scene. The oncoming tempest slowly dimmed the day like an evening out of place, while brave hearts surrendered to suspenseful apprehension by the eerie silence of the birds and whispering voices in the wind.

Two men, both thieves were already secured to their penitent crosses. Jesus stood facing Calvary, looking down to the cross at his feet. All the while Onofrio remained galvanized to the man called Jesus of Nazareth, unflinching not wanting to leave the scene. From all he knew of the man, he failed to find one sensible reason why he should endure the ordeal before him. A trooper came forward and stripped Jesus of what clothes he wore, leaving him naked with only a cloth draped around his waist and loins. Onofrio felt his insides freeze when a trooper produced a handful of sharp spikes and threw them on the ground making a metallic ringing sound. Onofrio wanted to step forward. He wanted to stop what he knew was about to happen. Yet, hard as he tried, he was physically immobilized. An unknown power rendered him paralyzed in body but, keen of mind and sight. Jesus saw the spikes, took a deep breath and his face conveyed a portrait of calm resignation. Harshly Jesus was positioned on the cross. The lacerations on his back still bled yet he received no mercy. Not a sign of pity showed in the cold eyes of the trooper, well accustomed to the sight of somebody else's blood. A soldier stretched an arm out on the traverse and with only two precisely aimed blows drove the sharp spike through the wrist close to the palm of Jesus' hand. A task performed with the efficiency born of experience. The soldier stepped over Jesus, took the other arm and repeated his skillful performance with cold indifference. Quickly he placed one of Jesus' feet on the wooden block attached to the upright beam and the second foot on top of the first. He took only a moment to mentally calculate the trajectory of his hammer. With swift competence he secured both feet to the wooden block with two blows on the metal spike. Onofrio shivered in horror. His breath failed him and he could almost scream in agony as he clearly heard the sharp ring of steel hammer on steel spike passing through living human flesh. A deathly grip choked him and he was sure he felt the pain himself. Onofrio was openly crying as he found himself completely alone. The Syrian and the small wiry man were gone and he didn't know when they left. Thunder was booming and clattering closer in the dimming horizon. Through all this Onofrio finally noticed that although he was certain he felt the pain of the spike passing through his own flesh, Jesus was abnormally quiet. He had not let out a whimper or a shout. He demonstrated only silent agony. He did not give his enemies anything from which to rejoice. Only steadfast devotion shone from a face that looked intently to the heavens. Even an enemy with the coldest heart would have to respect the silent devotion reported by the paid scribes. Workmen materialized and carried the cross up the few steps to the summit of Golgotha with Jesus nailed to it. With a resounding wallop the cross landed at the bottom of the excavated pit. A loud thud echoed from the bowels of Golgotha joined by the clap of far away thunder. Black clouds roiled in the distance like an angry bull gaining momentum to charge. The cross was erect now. Men used stones, dirt and wooden wedges to secure the instrument of death precisely upright. The living body of Jesus shook from torment. Blood flowed freely from his hands and feet and still not a moan. He hung limp on the crude timber, breathing with measured effort. Some stout hearted sightseers still lingered along with the Jewish council's paid scribes and soldiers on duty. Jeers, shouts and insults fell without meaning from his ear. Instead he made an effort to give comfort to the two thieves on the adjoining crosses. He told one that before his day passed he would join him in Paradise. After an eternity, during which time Onofrio did not take a breath, he heard Jesus ask for water and he made an effort to comply but was forced back. A trooper took a sponge on a hyssop and dipped it in vinegar then put it to the mouth of Jesus.

But Jesus refused it. Jesus looked to the heavens and painfully said, "Forgive them Father for they know not what they do." The thorny crown continued to dig its spikes into his flesh as new streams of scarlet flowed down his agonized face. Above the head of Jesus was a rough inscription quickly done on a rude plaque in three languages. It read *"King of the Jews."* Rude laughter followed and soon there were other such cheers. "If thou be King of the Jews, then save yourself." His helplessness gave license to other stone hearts to fling their crude arrows at the Nazarene. And their lewd humor multiplied among the senseless crowd bordering on insane laughter.

Onofrio looked at the sun as his habitual timepiece, it was close to noon. He noticed a grayish veil began to fill the sky. Not like the coming of sunset but as an encircling gloom, approaching from all directions. Hardly noticeable at first but the bright clear day of before was slowly fading, like an evening before its time. The caustic merriment of a few moments ago transferred to apprehensive awe and disquieted whispers. Still Onofrio remained magnetized to the man nailed on the center cross. Slowly the smell of fear invaded the area and Onofrio recognized it. He then saw tempered soldiers gazing at each other in wonderment while others grew pale. And the light of day continued to fade into the gloomy veil of an unexpected evening.

Two thieves and a Jewish rabble rouser were secure on their crosses. Their orders had been carried out and so the soldiers began departing from the stony hill. The weird storm in the distance inching forward with no hesitation gave them ample cause.

"He that cannot save himself would destroy the temple and rebuild it in three days." jeered a man, whose scorn was apparently born of his association with the Jewish authorities. Since their task was done, the soldiers retreated a short distance away. It freed the remaining people to throw their voices like stones at the helpless Nazarene. Suffering tremendously and totally helpless, he endured their foul mockery. While Onofrio stood by, gazing in total amazement at the devotion and strength of this slender man. A man of greater strength would have long ago cried out shamelessly in pain. Yet Jesus, with absolute resolve, languished on the cross, bearing jeer, insult and agony with equal silence. Another cowardly voice came through the countless others. "If thou be King of the Jews, or the Son of God, come down to us." Onofrio calculated Jesus had been there no less than two hours. Jesus asked for water, again. Someone came with a sponge on the end of a long slender stick and poured vinegar on the sponge and raised it to the mouth of Jesus.

After this Jesus, knowing that all was now finished, said
(to fulfil the scripture), "I thirst." A bowl full of vinegar stood

there; so they put a sponge full of the vinegar on hyssop and held it to his mouth. *John 19:28-29*

When Jesus had received the vinegar, he said, "It is finished"; and he bowed his head and gave up his spirit. *John 19:30*

Onofrio, first born son of Horacio and Maria Elena de Iberia had only once in his entire life suffered pain of long duration. He was a child of seven summers, living wondrously happy days in the bosom of his parents. On this day as he bore witness to the atrocities of man, he was suddenly bathed in a warm love such as he had not felt since childhood. Slowly he luxuriated in the clear memory of parental love without limit. Memories lost in the black catacombs of his forgotten past became crystalline views of what seemed to be only yesterday. Coarse hordes of men dressed in animal hides; brandishing axes and swords came from a long ship anchored in the river, not far from the home and farm of his father and uncle. They ravished and pillaged and burned and killed and took what they wanted. Horacio had fought these hordes before in the service of his King, as well as protector of this region and his own belongings. It was for services rendered that Horacio was granted his lands and title. Onofrio had listened to battle stories his father and uncle shared as they worked in their fields and barns. Onofrio was experiencing the clearest pictures of his previous life he ever had. And although his mind was now a crystalline vision of his past to the present moment, he failed to recognize it as a miracle. He was far more engrossed by the scene unfolding in the gloom of a noon day night. In only minutes he silently recalled every minute detail that brought him to this place without a single blemish; as graphic as the picture of this man that hung painfully by his bleeding hands and feet on a cross Onofrio built. This man of healing miracles, a teacher of his God's laws was as innocent of criminal activity as was a newborn lamb. A man devoted to the path of righteousness. A man of such spiritual strength as no ordinary person could ever hope to match. And Onofrio was not surprised or intimidated when he felt and heard the earth shake and tremble under his feet. Somehow he knew that the God of Jesus had a right to anger.

It was now past the third hour of Jesus' ordeal. Although many people lingered nearby, obsessed by what they saw, others came to see and weep anew. Some stone hearts lingered about to throw insult and jeer at the helpless Nazarene. A separate group in hooded robes was solemnly on their knees, praying in earnest before the Son of God. Still Onofrio remained honed into the pain and agony of this man called Jesus of Nazareth. An innocent man condemned to this torturous death by the masters of plot, ploy and scheme.

> *It was now about the sixth hour, and there was darkness over the whole land until the ninth hour, while the sun's light failed; and the curtain of the temple was torn in two. Then Jesus, crying with a loud voice, said, "Father, into thy hands I commit my spirit!" And having said this he breathed his last.*   *Luke 23:44-46*

> *When the soldiers had crucified Jesus they took his garments and made four parts, one for each soldier; also his tunic. But the tunic was without seam, woven from top to bottom; so they said to one another, "Let us not tear it, but cast lots for it to see whose it shall be." This was to fulfil the scripture,*

> *"They parted my garments among them, and for my clothing they cast lots."*   *John 9:23-24*

> *And when evening had come, since it was the day of Preparation, that is, the day before the sabbath, Joseph of Arimathea, a respected member of the council, who was also himself looking for the kingdom of God, took cour-*

age and went to Pilate, and asked for the body of Jesus.
Mark 15:42-43

And Joseph took the body, and wrapped it in a clean linen shroud, and laid it in his own new tomb, which he had hewn in the rock; and he rolled a great stone to the door of the tomb, and departed. Mary Magdalene and the other Mary were there, sitting opposite the sepulchre.
Matthew 27:59-61

MARY'S ORDEAL

Beyond the intricacies of politics, away from religious dictates and contradictions, including Roman law and order, down in the heart of the frenzied mob was the mother of Jesus. She was rudely shoved and pushed aside as she struggled to see her son being spiked to hardwood timbers. There to suffer excruciating pain until her son's last breath was forced from his tormented body. The thoughtless mob was geared to achieve the best view and had no concern or mercy for the grieving mother. Finally a strong somewhat friendly face pushed people aside and let Mary and her companions pass. An angry individual pushed aside had to ask," Who is that and what is she doing in this crowd?"

"Shut up, you idiot. That's the mother of the one on the center cross," someone volunteered. Cheers mixed with catcalls filled the air. Obnoxious name calling with hoots and hollers rang throughout the uncivilized mob.

Imagine then the agonizing torment of Mary, coming painfully through that unholy crowd to witness her son's death. Enormous trauma wrapped in supreme apprehension clutched her heart. The child she carried in her womb was now the subject of insane scorn and ridicule. Imagine the frightful helplessness of a loving mother forbidden by law to help her child. With human strength drained from her body, she accepted the helping arms from her companions. At the summit and in full view, she waited with painful anxiety for the end to come and prayed for the moment not to arrive. Mary had witnessed many of her son's miracles. Can we not speculate that on this fateful day she would pray wholeheartedly that the Father of her son would intervene and stop this insanity? Of course. Imagine then, the super inner strength of this little woman to forge ahead half in prayer and half in acceptance of this pre-ordained fate. Through this terrible ordeal she suffered a thousand deaths and was held together by a power she did not know, let alone understand. In humble solace she had long ago accepted this cruel and unwelcome destiny. Not until the third torturous day would she know peace when word would come that her son had risen from the dead and was seen ascending to heaven. But that was three painful days away. Today, clouds were gathering in the hills and her son had seen his final throes. A lance was driven into his side to prove without doubt that he was truly dead. There was still the arduous task of bringing him down from the cross and carrying him to safety in the approaching storm. Black rolling clouds menaced the scattering multitude angrily. It was already raining in the hills nearby.

When Onofrio saw Mary in the company of her other sons and companions, their eyes met for a fleeting second. Neither of them knew each other so Mary nodded gently in acceptance of his tortured face and sympathetic bow of his head. His mind raced to his conviction that she was still another victim of the cross he built. Her unfathomed anguish and pain was clearly visible on her gentle face and limp body. His sense of guilt amplified tenfold at the sight of her despair. Part of her grief transmitted to Onofrio instantly. The pain of her ordeal traveled through his mind and body in a sweeping flash. In that fleeting moment and in painful bond Mary and Onofrio became as one in shared agony.

Without warning an enormous sense of guilt swiftly filled Onofrio; stemming from the undeniable fact that Jesus died impaled to a cross he had built. It was the cross Onofrio built that became the instrument of Jesus' death. The Nazarene never did anything to harm Onofrio and so Onofrio experienced overwhelming guilt for the saintly man's demise. Added to his torment was the sight of a soldier driving a lance into Jesus' ribcage to insure his death. Stranger still was the water that flowed with his blood. A few soldiers and a tribune were tossing dice from a leather cup for the robe of Jesus. A seamless woven garment, colored with walnut stain. He could not fathom how men could be so callous. Jesus was barely dead and these men contested for the spoils. Onofrio realized that it was the way of their lives that made them so. And this is what Centurion Clemidius had in mind for him in the service of Rome? Suddenly the bowels of the earth heaved in convulsions, forcing the world to shake in unmeasured violence. Tongues of angry fire flashed across the purple sky. Horrendous thunder clapped and roared with savage fury. Each crashing boom louder than the last and close enough to strike fear into the bravest heart. He knew it was mid afternoon, yet this storm discharged the day into the dark of night. As if the gods willed this day to cease just like his friend the ragged jeweler had earlier predicted. It was easy to believe the gods were infuriated because one of their kind was put to death. Brave men ran like frightened children seeking shelter. The mob dispersed as fast as scared legs could carry them. A few of the braver men stood around the crosses looking amazed at the display of Godly fury upon the land and sky.

A young soldier standing by Onofrio visibly scared and deathly pale looked at the limp corpse of Jesus and said,"This man was truly the Son of God." Hearing that, Onofrio fell to his knees expecting the next bolt of lightning to strike him dead on the spot. And rightly so. He justly deserved God's revenge for it was he that built the instrument of his son's torment and demise. Rain fell from the darkened heavens in furious gushers. The hill became awash with mad, dashing streams taking debris, twigs and small stones down the incline. He arose and with difficulty made his way down the rocky knoll. No man has known fear as Onofrio knew it on that tempestuous day. Lightening struck nearby and a small bush instantly ignited with hellish blue and white fire. Only to be quickly extinguished by the heavy downpour. Onofrio knew the angry gods were aiming their bolts at him and he did not expect to survive the noon day night. His sense of guilt so deeply embedded that he resolved to accept his rightful punishment, which he expected would come with the next bolt of furious lightening. Silently with a heart filled with fear, he asked Jesus to forgive him. The tempest raged all around him and still he did not run. His heart pounded furiously and he cursed the day he built the villainous cross. Emblazoned in his mind were the horrible images of Jesus' tribulation. An ordeal that may not have happened had he not built the damned cross. Slowly he picked his way down Calvary, going to the city. He wanted to run but knew that to run from a god was futile. If a god sought revenge upon you, he would find you. Another bolt of lightning struck a water puddle very close to him and gaseous blue tongues of fire raced across the sodden earth. Then another bolt struck equally close and deathly frightening and still he walked resolved to meet his doom when it arrived. The incline gave way to level ground and he did not hasten his pace. Fear measured his steps and put his dimmed vision unto the distant city lights. He was drenched to the skin. His clothes were heavy with water and he gathered the dragging hems to lessen the burden on his stride. He walked upright although it was with borrowed courage. There could be no shame in being struck dead by a god. Even gods have a right to justice, and the young man knew that if someone killed a child of his, he would hunt that person down and claim his right to justice. A life for a life. And the father of Jesus had a right to the life of Onofrio. From somewhere in his tormented mind came the vision of Senobia. If an angry god claimed his life today, Senobia would become the wife of another man. If there was an after-life as some people claimed, it would add to his punishment to look back from wherever dead people go and see his intended bride; his dearly beloved (for now he knew better than ever that he truly loved the fair Senobia.) married to another man. Now he walked as if he dared the gods to strike. He still felt awesome fear and anxiety for his life. But, he began to believe that if the father of Jesus really wanted him dead, he would not have missed with his deadly bolts from heaven. And Onofrio el Segundo de Serou would now be dead.

Deafening thunder roared and clattered all around him, dispensing clutching heartfelt fear. Then another bolt of blue and white fire struck a few steps ahead of him burning a hole in the ground. It split rocks with such power that made Onofrio stop in his tracks to see smoke rising from the shattered stones. He heard the rocks sizzle in the downpour as the hole quickly filled with rain and floating debris. Stunned, weak and amazed he finally came to the barn that kept the chariot and horses. As cool as the rainfall was, he felt uncommonly warm and held fast to his determination to reach Senobia and home. The barn keeper was not happy to see him. He behaved frightened and ill tempered allowing his feelings to show freely. In the soaking rain the man hitched up the chariot, fearfully cowering from each echoing thunder and shocked by every flash of lightening. The man strongly advised Onofrio remain indoors until the tempest subsided. "It's not safe to ride out in the country. Lightening will surely strike you dead," the man warned and quickly ran into the barn.

Onofrio yelled out, "If the gods want me dead on this noon day night, they will not hide their intentions in a thunderstorm."

There is a green hill far away.
There is a green hill far away
without a city wall,
where the dear Lord was crucified,
who died to save us all.
we may not know, we cannot tell
what pains he had to bear;
but we believe it was for us
he hung and suffered there.

He died that we may be forgiven,
he died to make us good.
That we might go at last to heaven,
saved by his precious blood.
There was no other good enough
to pay the price of sin;
only he could unlock the gate
of heaven and let us in.
O, dearly, dearly has he loved,
and we must love him too.
And trust in his redeeming blood,
and try his works to do.

Cecile F. Alexander (1823-1895)

CHAPTER TWENTY-THREE

ONOFRIO, ON TRIAL

Next day, that is, after the day of Preparation, the chief priests and the Pharisees gathered before Pilate and said, "Sir, we remember how that imposter said, while he was still alive, 'After three days I will rise again.' Therefore order the sepulchre to be made secure until the third day, lest his disciples go and steal him away, and tell the people, 'He has risen from the dead.'   Matthew 27:62-64

And behold, there was a great earthquake; for an angel of the Lord descended from heaven and came and rolled back the stone, and sat upon it. His appearance was like lightning, and his raiment white as snow. And for fear of him the guards trembled and became like dead men.   Matthew 28:2-4

While they were going, behold, some of the guard went into the city and told the chief priests all that had taken place. And when they had assembled with the elders and taken counsel, they gave a sum of money to the soldiers and said, "Tell people, 'His disciples came by night and stole him away while we were asleep.'   Matthew 28:11-13

And when the sabbath was past, Mary Magdalene,
and Mary the mother of James, and Salome, bought spices,
so that they might go and anoint him. And very early on
the first day of the week they went to the tomb when the sun
had risen.   Mark 16:1-2

And they found the stone rolled away from the tomb,
but when they went in they did not find the body. While they
were perplexed about this, behold, two men stood by them in
dazzling apparel; and as they were frightened and bowed
their faces to the ground, the men said to them, "Why do you
seek the living among the dead?   Luke 24:2-5

And he said to them, "Do not be amazed; you seek Jesus
of Nazareth, who was crucified. He has risen, he is not here;
see the place where they laid him. But go, tell his disciples and
Peter that he is going before you to Galilee; there you will see
him, as he told you."   Mark 16:6-7

The way to Senobia was riddled with fearsome flashes of godly fire and the unnerving, crackling booms of thunder. The horses spooked several times and he had to fight them to regain control. Then he remembered a common saying among shepherds. "When lightning strikes, the sheep do not look at the lightning, they look to the shepherd for guidance." These were good obedient horses so Onofrio descended the chariot and soothed and reassured his prize animals. Patiently he spoke to them calling them by name stroking and patting them with assurance until they calmed down enough to continue their journey. Ominous black clouds wrestled each other across an eternal darkness casting angry bolts of lightning on the earth, while the rain continued in gushers from an angry sky and threatened to inundate the entire world. The terrible sense of guilt still filled him. Although he was clear of mind and felt almost well, something was wrong. He shivered and shook in recurring spasms, his vision blurred several times and he urged the horses to reach home and Senobia. Finally he came to the compound and drove the chariot directly to the barn behind Tremiyo's home. His head was reeling. He was barely able to find the door on which to knock. Camia met him visibly shocked to see him weaving to stand erect. He was distressed, soaked and splattered with mud and blood.

"Where is Senobia?" he asked more like a demand then a civil question. Camia turned to bid him follow her. He was brought to a small room, devoid of decoration, hosting a few tables and some strange pieces of furniture with a small low platform on which to place their knees and a cushioned elbow rest. On these strange pieces of furniture knelt Senobia and her father. Camia took the third bench next to Tremiyo. They were strangely quiet and did not acknowledge his presence, not even Senobia. Instead they continued their silent meditation. There were no idols, no images, no incense or effigies of any kind. Only this silent empty room in which to pray or worship a god or gods. Noticeably was a sense of deep devotion heavy in the air. He veered uncontrollably and grabbed a prayer bench to support him. Slowly he struggled to reach Senobia's side and touched her shoulder. She looked up to him with her lovely eyes awash with glistening tears. He was torn to see her crying and in a distant silence wondered why.

"To whom do you pray, my love?" he asked in a voice not like his own.

From Tremiyo came an answer strained and close to choking, "We pray to the Father of he that was crucified today. We pray that God relent and not destroy the earth for the murder of his son. We pray to the God of Abraham and of Moses. We pray to the Master of all creation. The storm outside is witness to his anger. Have you not noticed or has the wine destroyed your vision?" thinking Onofrio was nothing more than drunk, Tremiyo lowered his head and continued his appeal to God.

The older man was near frantic and Camia patted his shoulder to pacify him.

Suddenly, it came clear to Onofrio that if the father of Jesus sought revenge on him, he would also destroy anyone associated with the killer of his son. He was guilty of building the cross on which the Son of God died. Onofrio came to these people, whom he dearly loved and now he endangered them all with his presence. He felt ill. He shivered and shook. He felt helpless. More than all else, he experienced powerful, engulfing fear. He feared the wrath of an avenging God and needed to put distance between him and the people he loved most. He would confront his avenger by himself. He would not endanger the dearest living beings in his life. He started to leave in haste and his legs felt like columns of ice. Frantically he realized his legs would not move. He fell, almost directly on his face. He experienced great terror. A horrible clutching hand moved through his body. This had to be the revenge of God. First his legs froze, now a frozen rock filled his stomach. His legs would not move in spite of his effort. He heaved and clenched his teeth to move and nothing would. The revenge of God had truly found him. He was convinced of it. He looked to where Senobia knelt but she was now by his side. He did not see the tenderness and devoted concern on her lovely face. He did not see her amazement by his fall. He only saw a Senobia in grave danger. God would surely strike her dead for loving the killer of his son. Tremiyo materialized from the shadows and came to help. God would strike him too, if he so much as touched him. Panic struck he yelled as loud as he could, "Get away! Get away from me, He'll kill you too. All of you get away from me." With super human effort he came to his feet. Unsteady and by near stumble he awkwardly reached and stood attached to a prayer bench. His once handsome face was a distorted look of horror. Making a clumsy effort he waved them away and yelled again. "I killed the son of the God you worship. I built the cross on which Jesus died. It was I that caused his death. God is chasing me now to avenge His son. You have to get away from me or He will strike you also. His curse is already upon me, I cannot move." The icy clutching fear continued to dominate him. He fought to reach the door only to fall again. He turned on the floor and began to propel himself away with his hands and arms while on his buttocks. He shouted at them insanely loud, "Don't touch me. If you touch me, God will strike you also. What I did, I did on my own." And he looked to heaven in deep lamented appeal. "Strike me. I did it. I built the cross on which your son died. Strike me. Not them. They are innocent. It was I. It was I." Then without warning, there was only deep, silent darkness as he melted onto the floor.

He floated into a tortured landscape of scalding sand and drought. Tongues of hellish red and yellow fire shot to an orange sky from unpredicted places. He walked through the coals of an enormous furnace. The air was so grossly hot, he could hardly breath. Sprigs of white, four petal blossoms began to sprout all around him. Hundreds of them, even thousands as far as the eye could see. Only to quickly wither and die away. As they withered, they slowly froze. In this hellish enferno? Their petals then melted into teardrops. The heat seared his senses torturing him without mercy. He fought to escape the hellish fires that raged within him. Then he peacefully glided on mellow breezes before a limitless sky of soft, cooling blue. Traveling through time and space to gently land on soil his feet had not touched since childhood. It was the soil of home, his home. Horacio de Iberia, his father and childhood mentor, his one and only God took him by the hand and silently they walked to a nearby stream, where crystal clear water rolled musically over stone and fallen branch. Overhead a luxurious canopy of bright and muted green bathed in glowing sunlight gently waltzed to a musical rhythm that only the wind can make. A mountain scented breeze brought the mellow fragrance of ripening wheat. The combined odors filled his senses. No, wait. It was not ripening wheat in the field. It was the smell of harvested wheat on a wagon, going home. He remembered his developing muscles aching from work he did with his father and wanted to sleep in the invigorating aroma of their harvest. And he did in blissful serenity.

He was a little boy again, comfortably sleeping secure in the knowledge his father was nearby. Without warning, the wheat ignited and he was burning on the wagon going home. He screamed in torment. In a flash, he knew the agony Jesus suffered was far greater than his own. A review of every moment he spent with Jesus on the cross passed through his mind precisely like reliving the experience, and he sweltered in the oppressive heat that governed his existence. Then from somewhere, or nowhere, Maria Elena, his mother touched his face with cool hands. He rose to join her as she walked peacefully in a dimming sunset to a grass covered knoll and by a large stone she laid down and went to sleep. His father took him by the hand and led him away from her peaceful slumber. Together they walked to a refreshing pool of silvering water. There his father took him and gently dipped his entire body into the medicinal, silent swirls of melted snow. He did not mind the eternity under water nor did he suffer to breath. An emotional release coursed though him and all his torturous thoughts left him to sink into the still waters. He clearly saw the man above the surface that held him. It was his father. It was not his father. It was Jesus. No. It was not Jesus. It was somebody else. He broke in sheer panic as he realized, the father of Jesus was trying to drown him. He struggled to rise from the water. Then he heard his father's voice, clear and unquestioned, "Be a righteous individual and all you seek will come to you." He sensed his father's joy to hold him by the hand as they walked by each other again. Together they walked out of the cooling pool. He was hand in hand with his only God and all was well. They sat on the grassy shore green and soft and refreshing, each happy to be in the other's presence. Horacio laid back and his face was bathed in golden sunlight. His hazel green eyes were like effervescent jewels. His amber colored beard sparkled with little drops of water that gleamed like tiny diamonds. His eyes peacefully surveyed an endless sky of blue and white birds floated gracefully like silent kites. Filled with peace and tranquility such as he had not known since boyhood, he basked in the precious ointment of unity. Across the silent pool of peace, a raging fire broke out. The trees were suddenly ablaze. The underbrush was an inferno of twisting, swirling red and yellow tongues of fire consuming the vegetation in violent gulps. Yet, his father lay silently appraising an endless cerulean sky. While fleecy white clouds mingled with the birds across an endless serenity, Onofrio felt the heat from the blaze raging across the pool and he was near paniced by it, searching frantically for an escape route. The peace and tranquility conveyed by his father calmed his fears. Horacio laid in comfort and immune to the fiery violence beyond. And Onofrio listened to his father speak again, in that clear fatherly tone he heard as a boy, "The storms of men will be countless. The peace of heaven will always be one."

Horacio de Iberia rose to his enormous height. Onofrio like a child looked up to his father and when their eyes met there was a silent exchange of mutual love promised for eternity. Strangely he felt their unity stem from their dip in that cool crystalline pool, in the wilderness, close to his once happy home. He knew his childhood was gone forever and he could no longer live in the fantasies of that time. He also knew his father no longer walked among men. He did not know how he knew. He just knew. He labored to overcome the enormous sense of loss and finally cried out in heart-tearing agony. And when his grief was at its peak, his father laid a hand on his shoulder and said, "Come home, boy." and they walked down a long familiar path to their home.

Onofrio looked back at the fire in the forest. All that remained was the charred carcasses of trees that resembled the torsos of men. The walk was pleasant and they were soon in the familiar comfort of home. His mother was busy cooking and the air filled with delicious smells that stirred his appetite. His mother looked beautiful. She was graceful in her stride. She had a loving face and a smile that could melt snowfall. The musical tone of her voice stirred unparallel happiness in the depths of his soul.

It was the choir of love with no limit. And he was home. At last he was home. Small flecks of light began to break before his eyes, like fireflies in a pleasant moon filled night. Horacio and Maria Elena were in a loving embrace by the open hearth. They began to slowly fade away. He remained galvanized to them. Regrettably knowing that oblivion would claim them and they would soon dissolve into permanent residents of his mind and heart.

His eyes came open and there was Senobia, faint and distant at first. Then she came clear as though out of a faraway mist. A deep glow of concern amplified the bluish-green beauty of her eyes. Her touch to his face was a magic elixir that aroused masculine emotions he thought were dead. She saw him struggle to focus and apparent concern became a fluid strength, urging him to move towards her. He hungered for her presence and yearned for the fragrance of her being. An arm slipped behind his head and shoulders and her body came next to his. Apparently fighting back her tears and making an effort to look happy and relieved. Her other hand caressed his face with warm loving care. And he briefly thought of his mother and father. Such naiveness was soul stirring when she asked, "Are you feeling better, Ony? We've been so worried. You've been screaming and sick for almost three days. Camia had to fight with the doctors Serou sent. She's been with you since Friday night. Serou is very worried also and has been by to see you several times."

"What day is it?" he asked still groggy and feeling weak.

"It is Sunday morning," he heard Tremiyo announce from where he took refreshments with a guest, discussing recent events including the young man's illness that took him down for almost three days.

With some effort Onofrio managed to rise and sit with Senobia. He smelled funny. He was embarrassed that she should smell his unpleasant odor. Understanding his discomfort, she was quick to explain, "It's a cooling poultice of mint and other herbs Camia prepared for you. It doesn't smell too, too bad." And she wrinkled and held her nose, giggling girlishly.

"May I have something to drink?" he asked smiling weakly.

Camia materialized from somewhere and firmly instructed, "Don't give him anything with milk. Give him orange juice or pomegranate nectar." His chest was bound with a smelly cloth and he wanted to take it off. Camia came to help, "Here, let me do it. I know how it's tied. The fever has left you, that's good. Are you hungry?" she asked with motherly concern.

"I'm starving and I feel weak," he answered gesturing to lie back down.

"You should be. You haven't eaten in two days. I'll have someone prepare a warm bath for you and get you some clean clothes. Then I'll feed you." It was only then, he realized, he was almost nude. Modestly, he covered himself and looked at her with impish embarrassment.

"Don't worry I've seen sick men before." she retorted, with a smile.

Bathed, shaved, groomed and wearing clean clothes, the young man was certain he was born again. And perhaps he was. A hearty breakfast was laid before him, enough for everyone around. The conversation slowly edged into the crucifixion of Jesus.

Instantly his appetite left him. The deep sense of guilt returned in full scale. The anguish, the torment and the pain all resurrected in one quick stroke. Everyone in the room noticed his sudden change. With his head in his hands and still weak he began to cry in earnest. So immense was the volume of his grief that Senobia's solace could not reach to touch it. It was a good while before he gained control of himself and he explained, "I built the cross on which Jesus died. I believe his Father, who is said to be in heaven will seek revenge on me. I fear his wrath may be felt by all of you, whom I dearly love. I need to be away from you if you are to be spared his anger. None of you should suffer for what I did."

Tremiyo peered at him strangely and exchanged looks with his guest.

Onofrio stood up to leave and fell back down on his seat trying to gain the strength to try again. Senobia, by his side, looked at her dad and with tear-filled eyes announced, "Where he goes, I go with him. And let the gods have their vengeance on us both." And she sat closer to wipe his tears and stroke his hair. Tremiyo saw resolve in his daughter he could not fight.

Onofrio felt weak and filled with confused apprehension and did not want to see the guest Camia said was at the door. "He's been here twice to see about you," she added. He had no response to give. Soon the ragged jeweler came before him looking prosperous and Tremiyo bid him sit at Onofrio's table.

"I saw you at the crucifixion. But there were so many people that I lost you in the crowd. It was a very upsetting event. I heard you took ill and came to see if I could be of service but I see you already have a guardian angel by your side." He smiled cheerfully at them both and rolled his eyes over the abundance of breakfast, to which he was promptly invited.

When the ragged jeweler noticed Tremiyo's unidentified guest, they exchanged courteous bows without a word being said. Their silent acknowledgement did not escape Onofrio and since it was not of vital concern, he chose to ignore it, as Onofrio correctly guessed he was one of the disciples of Jesus. The unknown guest, a tall man dressed in homespun and worn out sandals, came towards, Onofrio. He laid a gentle hand on the young man's shoulder and kindly said, "Your sense of guilt is baseless. The Lord knows that what you did was simply your duty. Had you not built the instrument of his death, other men would have. Rest at peace with that thought. Your loved ones are perfectly safe from the wrath of God as well as you. In a few days when you're feeling better, I'll come back and we will talk. For now, do your best to discharge these troublesome thoughts. Rest assured the Lord is not seeking to avenge his son through you." With a graceful bow he bade them all "Goodbye" and quietly left. The man's mellow voice and unpretentious demeanor left Onofrio with a sense of ease, vaguely bordering on being pardoned. He remained silent for a few moments and began to acknowledge how wonderful it was to be here. He closed his eyes and took a deep breath of pure Senobia. It was a aroma he could not live without. And he was still hungry and he had a guest to share a meal with, the ragged jeweler.

And so it was widely said that on the third day (or before) the corpse of Jesus mysteriously vanished from the stone crypt in which he laid. News traveled swiftly from mouth to mouth and soon the entire region was buzzing with the astonishing story. The Roman guards could not explain how they slept through the laborious effort of moving the massive stone. The more callous observers deduced that the guards were simply not at their post. They were most likely enjoying the benefit of their rewards at any of the nearby dens of iniquity. Secure in the fact that dead men do not walk away from their death chamber, no acceptable explanation ever came forth from the abundant and reliable sources of information. The fact remained undisputed in the minds of many that the long time predicted prophecy had at last become reality. And on the third day "He shall rise." Jesus of Nazareth became "Jesus Christ" on that fateful day. The Christ had arrived and touched the hearts and minds of righteous people. There he would live to this very day and beyond.

About midmorning Serou arrived to see about his adopted son. After a hardy breakfast Onofrio was napping, as prescribed by Camia. Serou's voice woke him up smiling and feeling strangely renewed, which was a welcome feeling he acknowledged right away. Happy to see his adopted son recovered, the Egyptian grabbed the young man in a bear hug, like a rich long lost relative. "Glad to see you up and moving about." And jabbed him gently on the jaw not at all embarrassed by his show of affection. Onofrio could not deny he was equally glad to see Serou. He briefly remembered Horacio, his father and their visit by a cooling pool not far from home.

As the pleasantries dwindled, the conversation grew awkward until Camia threw a friendly barb at Serou. "Had your doctors touched him, he would still be sick. Maybe even dead."

The level-headed Egyptian was not shaken by her sting and quickly responded, "It didn't hurt your medical talents one bit to personally attend to a handsome, virile young man in the nude, did it?"

Serou laughed with uncommon joy. "I would be willing to bet that you used up every opportunity to attend to him by hand, while he slept." And laughed even harder at his insinuation then looked around to see who heard him. Onofrio and Camia broke out in unified laughter to see Senobia with tongue in cheek confront the tall Egyptian. She was not impressed by his off-color innuendo. But the vivid tinge of red on his cheeks was too much for Senobia to ignore. She pointed a little finger at him and gave him a hawk-eye like his own and merrily snickered, "Look how well he blushes, the great Serou, Master of Public Jokes." And the contagious laughter of happy people filled the house.

Serou continued, "It was Joseph, the counselor from Arimathea that went before Pilate and successfully acquired the corpse of Jesus. I was close by and heard most of the conversation. Pilate had every right to be cautious, considering everything involved. Religious rituals, Pilate's duty to Rome and the family of the now deceased. Leave us not forget the unnerving possibility that Jesus may truly rise from his grave. Joseph of Arimathea with the help of some women and the mother of the deceased brought down the corpse of Jesus and laid him in a tomb Joseph had built for himself and his family, not far from Golthotha. Nicodemus is said to have favored Jesus but feared retaliation from the Jewish powers and avoided the prophet. Privately Nicodemus came to the mourners bringing much myrrh and aloes to help prepare the body. It is known that both Joseph and Nicodemus are disciples of Jesus but kept their faith in him a secret. Joseph, the counselor is being detained somewhere by the Jewish authorities until tomorrow. My informers are not clear why or where he is being held. I suspect the council fears Joseph will steal the body during the night to fulfill the prophecy of the Messiah. I'm not exactly sure of all this but my informers are usually correct. The truth about Judas Iscariot has come to light.

Judas was a self-serving man with a hunger for money and possibly recognition. He reported to the Jewish council, where the elusive Jesus would be on Thursday night. Jesus and his group were to sleep at a place called the "Garden of Olives" and Judas led his captors there. Later Judas regretted his decision and went back to the council to return his ill-gotten money. I believe it was thirty pieces of silver. However, the council would not accept his blood money and he had to live with what he did. Apparently, he could not live with his decision and went and hanged himself." Serou had been in non-stop conversation since they left the compound. They agreed that a ride in the country, some fresh air and sunshine would prove beneficial to the young man. Onofrio felt alive again and glad to be with Serou in a flashy chariot everybody recognized and hailed.

They wheeled into the manufacturing plant and rolled to an easy stop by the office building. Serou led the way upstairs to where Onofrio's Greek mentor was working. The Greek was a mellow man in mid-life. His hair had departed from the top of his head leaving only a ring of white fluff around his cranium. Paolo the Greek, had deciphered records and organized a concise review into the management of finances since Saturday. He had piles of papers with figures and descriptions neatly laid out in separate stacks. After the formalities of introduction Paolo directed himself to Serou. "It's all been a very simple procedure, well done but simple. There's paid invoices for goods not accounted for. Here are sums of money paid for supplies, food and materials inconsistent with the lesser amounts actually paid. Countless bills and receipts have been carefully altered to a greater sum. The discrepancies are never in large amounts so not to be very noticeable. Rather like a hen that fills her bill one grain at a time. The sums appear to consistently leave reason to accept as an honest mistake. Putting all that aside and concentrating on adding up the differences is a monstrous undertaking since these discrepancies go back a number of years. The system, over time has skimmed off a respectable fortune. I have some totals for you. I went through an entire year day by day and month by month. I corrected every alteration I could find. Then I added up the differences between invoice amount and actual payment. One year alone adds up to a considerable sum. The figures are on that stack." Paolo pointed to a neat column of numbers on top of a heap of invoices. "There is a number of duplicated invoices. The duplicate paid for goods never ordered or received. According to what I discovered, it all implicates a man called, Eljazar directly. Even the method of writing matches legitimate records. The man in question has proven the evidence I gathered is correct. He left this for you." And Paolo handed Serou a small leaf of paper. Serou read it in silence and gave it to Onofrio. It simply read, "I took too much, I cannot pay back." It was unsigned. Even with Onofrio's limited ability to read, he recognized Eljazar's penmanship. Serou looked at Onofrio and being of a single mind, they were on their way to the home of Eljazar, north of Jerusalem.

The wife of Eljazar met them at the gates of an impressive and well kept villa. Reflective white walls with red-orange shingles set the large home in a class of its own. Although a bit overweight, her sensuous attractiveness was undeniable. She dressed in modest refinement that did not escape the inspection of her visitors. Serou was quick to the point," We're here to see Eljazar. Where is he?" She had obviously been crying profusely. Her eyes and face were swollen and she gripped a small cloth in her hand while carrying a young boy on her hip. In a quaking voice she answered the ominous inquiry. "Eljazar is not here. He has left me and his child and his home. He came Friday afternoon and took everything of value and he left." The woman's voice broke and she started wailing loudly. After a few painful moments and in between sobs, she added. "I have no idea what he has done. It must be something terrible if he would not tell me where he was going. Another man was with him. Together they loaded camels and left through that terrible storm." Apparently she was still in shock and asked, "What has he done, that is so bad he would leave his wife and child? First Jesus was tortured and crucified and when I came home, my husband of ten years leaves me, our happy home and his child. I don't know how much more I can bear." In a near scream of anguish she asked again, "What has Eljazar done?"

Serou looked at his adopted son as if looking for an answer. Onofrio simply said, "He has done nothing that time cannot fix." And wheeled the chariot around, anxious to leave the scene.

Coming through Jerusalem, they met large crowds of people. "He is risen. He is risen, as predicted He has risen from the dead. An earthquake removed the rock from his tomb and an angel came from heaven and took Jesus from his grave. Jews beware – Jesus lives! Jews, you better run – Jesus lives!" Countless cheers in many languages bounced from person to person in contagious jubilation. A great sense of alleviation and unprecedented joy filled Onofrio to the brim of his soul. He was choked by it. Speechless, trembling and tottering on the brink of tears, he gave the reins to Serou. The Egyptian looked at his adopted son, happy with what he knew Onofrio was feeling. Exoneration in the first degree.

Being no more and no less than Serou, he embraced the young man. "I think we should confirm this. Don't you?" And he proceeded to the site of Jesus' tomb. All around the rumors ran amuck. The cross on which he died had been stolen, removed or simply vanished. Some people were saying that the corpse was never in the chamber in the first place. Others claimed the disciples of Jesus hid the body. The report given by a soldier that evidently had too much to drink was difficult to accept: "His followers rolled back the stone and stole the body." *All the while seasoned soldiers slept without a sentry posted?* Serou pondered the point in silence while Onofrio's emotions went into reverse.

He prayed he could see Jesus for himself alive and talking and only then would his sense of guilt dissolve completely. The small wiry man that rode the Syrian's shoulder came to Onofrio to state his mind: "I personally think that the followers of this Jesus man stole the body after Joseph, the counselor and the women left. They had a Jesus look-alike pose like the prophet in this early morning's light. The women were in mourning, they were scared witless and it would be easy to fool them with white flowing robes and a mellow voice. It would make a good act for somebody that knew what to do. Like tell them to carry a tale to his gang that Jesus was gone to Galilee and they would see him there. Unless of course, an angel really came, put the guards to sleep, rolled back the massive stone, restored life to the mutilated corpse and they cheerfully rose to heaven unblemished. For fear of being struck dead by a god, I'll have to say that perhaps, only perhaps a miracle really did happen here today." Shaking his head with thoughts that only he knew, the wiry man said his goodbyes and blended into the crowd.

With apprehensive calm Onofrio and Serou walked to the open sepulture. Onofrio gathered his courage as best he could and with effort walked into the tomb of Jesus. A few brave hearts lingered close to the open tomb, seeing Onofrio enter like curious children hiding their eyes behind their hands. It gave him no joy to see the cave was bare with only the lingering fragrance of myrrh floating in the trapped air. He stood alone well within the hand hewn cavity of rock. There was a shelf cleanly cut into the cave's wall on which the body would have laid. He stiffened as he sensed that Jesus was there. He felt it strongly. He felt a living Jesus. He heard the faint sound of breathing besides his own. The sensation gave reassurance. Then quickly fell away from the lack of living proof. On the stone shelf was a sizeable blood stain. He touched it. It was dry. And the stone was warm as though Jesus had recently laid on it. Still he did not feel a dead Jesus. But, the guilt that haunted him would not recede. He found pain in breathing and was happy to see the Egyptian waiting for him at the entrance. Without a word being said and Serou at the reins, they rode the chariot away.

At Serou's insistence, Onofrio came home with his foster father to finish recuperating. He ate well and then they spoke of all that happened the last few days. An obvious joy dwelled within the Egyptian to share an intimate part of the young man's life as father and son.

"Do you plan to prosecute Eljazar for fraud?"

The question surprised Serou. "Of course. Without question. I will prepare a case against him with the help of Paolo, hire a force to track him down and bring him to justice. I will also do what I can to help his wife and child through this."

Onofrio sensed that seeking to punish Eljazar stemmed partly from the fact that his reputation was shaken. He took pride in always knowing what was happening in his own pocket, Eljazar seriously shook the foundation of the conviction. With ample reason to take pride in his reputation Serou would pursue, find and prosecute Eljazar.

When the young man began to nod his head, Serou urged him to go rest and left him. The hour was late and there was much work to do. Eljazar would not be very far away tomorrow.

No sooner was Onofrio asleep, Jesus the Nazarene eased into his dream. Jesus did not call him vocally nor did he gesture with his hands. Deep within Onofrio knew to follow him. Side by side they walked to a quiet stream meandering peacefully through a lush meadow. The earthy aroma of green grass, rain drenched soil and ripening wheat drifted in the air. On a refreshing breeze, muted and sun struck, foliage danced softly over their heads. Not a word was spoken and Jesus looked relieved of all his torments. Without him speaking Onofrio heard what Jesus said from the cross, "Forgive them, Father, for they know not what they do." and He slowly began to dissolve away from Onofrio into a vast wheat field beyond him. He appeared to be inspecting a new harvest. Sun light caught in the flowing, brownish hair of Jesus and it glowed like a golden crown. And Onofrio slept in peace.

From his work in the fields of long ago he learned much of the many gods his fellow field workers revered. He concluded that there was a god for every purpose, for every season and for every need. In fact, he was convinced that there were so many gods floating around, that only the gods knew how many of their own kind dwelled in the minds of men. For whatever reason the gods chose to favor his most recent stroke of good luck, he acknowledged that only the gods could have made it so. He never imagined he would ever be in the position he found himself today. He had long ago decided to follow the work in the fields and from there he would one day find his way home. Never having been in haste since he didn't know where home was. Home had been a hazy illusion, much like a faded dream, with only bits and tatters of his youthful life routinely flashing in his dreams. Going home had always been a dream too far. And now? Now that he had the means, did he still want to go home? He felt he owed a debt, a serious debt to Serou. It was an obligation greater than his quest to go home. Beyond that self-imposed commitment was a clear road to the green fertile, valleys somewhere close to Granada in Iberia beyond the wide Mediterranean Sea. He yearned deeply to see his mother and father, to firmly hold them close to him and live again in the heartwarming circle of their love. Suddenly and with bone chilling reluctance he knew that could never be again. Horacio and Maria Elena laid in eternal rest on a grassy knoll, by a clear rolling stream close to home. He knew now that his father's visit was to tell him of their demise. His father walked him to his mother's presence that he may see her again in their home and feel again the love they had for him. His father left him with verbal lessons he would live by all his life. `A flood of painful grief overpowered the young man from the hills of Granada and he cried at length, deep within his soul and in the silence of his quarters. His was a private grief. It was covered with gold dust and he would carry it in the pocket of his heart for all his life.

CHAPTER TWENTY-FOUR

THE SEARCH FOR ELJAZAR

T here was still another obligation, one he did not fully understand. He felt compelled to tell the story of Jesus and his day on the cross. The criminal Barabbas had been set free, although openly guilty of innumerable offenses. The Son of God had been sentenced to a cruel and painful death. Jesus was a testament to the injustice of manmade justice. It was evident that the heads of the Jewish council feared Jesus far more than Rome. To Rome Jesus was a minor pest. To the Jewish authorities he was an enormous threat to their way of life. It was not Rome that condemned the saintly prophet to a scourging post, the humiliation and the agony of the cross. It was widely known that mislead religious authorities feared the humble son of a carpenter. They feared his teachings would sway the masses since their grip on the Jewish community was eroding. The earthly powers of the council were no match to the miracles delivered by this saintly man. Council members were nothing more than men lusting for worldly power and comfort. Jesus had proven that his ministry on earth was ordained from his Father's house, which was said to be in heaven. Jesus cured the sick, dissolved leprosy, saved children's lives, had restored eyesight and even made the dead walk and breathe again. No chant or incense smelling ritual could match the Nazarene's miracles. At no charge. No doctor, Egyptian, Grecian or otherwise could do what Jesus did without a medicine case. He openly demonstrated a faith in his heavenly Father, his only God far stronger than any faith Onofrio had ever known about. Jesus suffered his ordeal, in full knowledge of greater things to come.

Onofrio slept again in holiday comfort and saw himself in a dream stretched out and relaxed, viewing a wheat field not far away. The crowns of wheat ranged from amber gold to golden cream and swayed gently on an invisible breeze, held to the earth by strong stems of green before a placid sky of infinite blue. But when he looked again these were not the standard heads of wheat. These resembled the upper torsos and heads of men. Men waiting to be collected into an assembled fold united for a common cause. Powerful black storms formed nearby advancing rapidly from multiple directions. With them came fierce winds broadcasting the suffocating odor of sulfur, no doubt from the sulfur mines in the distant hills. The beautiful field of ripened wheat began to disintegrate. The stalks got yanked up by the roots with violent force and fed to the grumbling winds that sounded like fierce obscenities. Black monster clouds wrestled over each other in haste to be first at inflicting damage. Ripened heads of men or wheat were flung into the tempest with ruthless fury. Onofrio sensed hatred; he felt the hatred and did not know to whom or to what it was directed. It was real; it was alive with the will to destroy while riding on the crest of a murderous storm. The calm of Onofrio's holiday froze in place. The warmth and serenity of the previous moment was dashed into oblivion. A strange fear filled him and he knew this was all a dream, a nightmare from which he could wake up. Knowing full well it was a nightmare made the chocking fear no less real. As hard as he tried to wake up, he could not. Only Jesus remained majestically calm. He stood invincibly strong, peacefully waving the shattered seeds goodbye. He was in effect blessing the shattered heads as they gracefully sailed into every frenzied direction. They were seeds on a mission to find fertile soil in which to multiply and sparkled with the gentle glow of a distant star. The skies were filled with them and the attacking clouds had no effect on their destination.

Onofrio woke up, not frightened or confused. He understood his dream and yet he did not know what it was he understood. His heart was tranquil and he wanted to share his dream with Senobia. He had not thought of Senobia since he did not remember when. He knew she was in his heart and in his mind and yet she was not. He also knew that Senobia, her father and Camia were faithful followers of Jesus and from that he found joy.

On a leisurely stride he made his way to the home of Tremiyo. His hair tossed in the warm desert breeze that carried the scent of wet sand and flowers. The gardens of Serou were in full bloom. Beauty abounded at every turn of the path. Fresh invigorating air filled with the perfumes of life. Birds that made their homes here were busy collecting food for the nestlings. He strolled through a garden of manicured beauty, filled with the essence of reproduction and life. He would be a permanent guest in the garden of marital bliss in a few weeks. His senses swelled from knowing it. Although the occasional fear of a vengeful God still haunted him. He knew Jesus was alive and teaching somewhere.

With a smile full of boundless joy Senobia met him in the courtyard of her home. They looked at each other for a long moment without exchanging a word. Her hair had been carefully done. And she looked fresh and clean and adorable and wonderful and without a go ahead signal they melted into each other's arms. Her figure flush against his sent passions racing through his anxious body. Their kiss was not one of wild abandon. Instead it signaled a release from the doubt of absence. A love reassured. A promise still in waiting. She released her hold on his lips and kissed his face with carefully placed little pecks. Her face was flush and her eyes full of longing. When she was satisfied she had covered his entire face and with a look full of mischief she asked semi seriously, "Have you ever had a butterfly kiss?"

"Of course!" he answered much too quick with a boyish grin. "Every butterfly I've ever met cannot bear to set wings to flight without first kissing me."

"You lie." she said with a pout on her lips. "You never had a butterfly kiss. Here let me show you." Without further ado, she took his face and fluttered her eyelashes against his cheek. Tiny tingles caressed his cheek and he actually felt the flutter of miniature wings brushing his face. He was surprised how physically exciting a butterfly kiss could be. He readjusted his arms around her and said still smiling, "Kiss the other cheek before it gets jealous by the neglect."

"I better not." she said coyly. "You're liking this too much." And she turned her face away with a smile and happy twinkle in her eye. It pleased her loving heart to know she was first in giving him a gift of affection he never had before. "Enough is enough, after all our honeymoon it still two weeks, three days and ten hours away. I must consider the fact that you are still weak from your illness."

Softly he whispered in her ear, "There will be no butterfly kisses on our wedding night. Only the sweet moans of a virgin saying goodbye to the little girl she once knew."

"Weary soldiers can be made to rise again with a simple butterfly kiss." she said coyly walking to her door where Camia stood patiently waiting. And they left their unfulfilled passions to cool on the desert breeze.

EASTER MORNING

> Tomb, thou shalt not hold Him forever:
> Death is strong, but life is stronger;
> Stronger than dark, the light;
> Stronger than wrong, the right;
> Faith and hope triumphant say,
> "Christ will rise on Easter day!"

> While the patient earth lies waking
> Till the morning shall be breaking,
> Shuddering 'neath the burden dread,
> of her master, cold and dead.
> Hark! She hears the angels say,
> "Christ will rise on Easter Day!"
>
> And when the sunrise smites the mountains,
> Pouring light from heavenly fountains,
> Then the earth blooms out to greet
> Once again the blessed feet;
> And her countless voices say,
> "Christ has risen on Easter Day!"

Phillip Brooks (1815 – 1893)

Eljazar, the embezzler was nowhere to be found. None of Serou's spies and usual sources of information came up with a single clue. Eljazar, having long been familiar with Serou's suppliers of news and information, hid his tracks exceedingly well. Serou knew something about everything that moved in his territory. Like a leopard knows every odor in his domain. Eljazar had a right to fear the wrath of Serou, knowing full well that he courted dungeon time if Serou found him. He methodically covered every track and removed all clues to his whereabouts. Bits of information he left with known informers were all useless clues pointing away from his real destination. He made sure every lead was an empty trail. It was as though the earth had swallowed Eljazar. Serou relieved his informers and passed the word along that Eljazar had left the country. With the search called off, Eljazar could chance coming out of hiding. Even the craftiest fox will come out of its den if led to believe it's safe. Knowing the thief would not leave his son behind, his wife, yes, his son, no, Serou and his crew waited for the fox to leave its den and risk its life to save its young.

> *But their eyes were kept from recognizing him. And*
> *he said to them, "What is this conversation which you are*
> *holding with each other as you walk?" And they stood still,*
> *looking sad.*   *Luke 24:16-17*

Serou allowed his adopted son time to rest and fully recover, to concentrate on his wedding plans and regroup his life. Serou did not put it in words, but it was generally understood that Onofrio would not return to the manufacturing plant. Onofrio and Serou knew that if the necessity arose, the young man would not hesitate to go. Politicians, statesmen, lawyers and assorted businessmen increased their visits to the house of Serou. Onofrio offered his help in relieving the workload from his foster dad, and was consistently refused with instructions to recover fully. Onofrio was not one to be put off by overprotective concerns. So, he disobeyed and repeatedly stayed to do what work he could. He ran errands, delivered documents, picked up supplies and in general became the third hand of Serou.

> *As they were saying this, Jesus himself stood among*
> *them. But they were startled and frightened, and supposed*
> *that they saw a spirit. And he said to them, "Why are you*
> *troubled, and why do questionings rise in your hearts? See*
> *my hands and my feet, that it is I myself; handle me, and see;*
> *for a spirit has not flesh and bones as you see that I have."*
> *Luke 24:36-39*

> *Now Thomas, one of the twelve, called the Twin, was*
> *not with them when Jesus came. So the other disciples told*
> *him, "We have seen the Lord." But he said to them, "Unless*
> *I see in his hands the print of the nails, and place my finger*
> *in the mark of the nails, and place my hand in his side, I will*
> *not believe."*   *John 20:24-25*

CHAPTER TWENTY-FIVE

ELJAZAR AND CLEMIDIUS

The ultimate trick was to leave Judea with the cargo intact. Four nondescript ships fully loaded with cotton, linen, elegant fineries and jewelry idled leisurely offshore at the port of Joppa, a day's journey from Jerusalem. Through careful manipulation Eljazar converted what he stole into an enormous fortune in sellable goods. The spies of Serou failed to connect Eljazar to the remote ships. Rumors and clues carefully laid by the fugitive embezzler indicated his camel caravan went north and east of Jerusalem. By cover of night he doubled back to be safely quartered in one of the ships where even the sailors were kept ignorant of his identity. The profits would keep him living in lavish comfort for a long time with life and limb intact and free of marital encumbrances. He sold his home, slaves and his wife then extracted a condition not to take over the properties until he was one day out to sea. A dream life awaited in a new land with new friends and new wealth to exploit. New loves to enjoy until newer loves came along. His long time schemes carefully carried out would make his dreams come true. A few short weeks across the Mediterranean and he would be in Iberia or Italia to sell his cargo, intact or in segments for fifty times more then what he stole. All this hinged on escaping from Serou and his spies. Eljazar trembled knowing a tiger was stalking him. His blood ran cold thinking Serou would discover his hideout and all he stole be confiscated with himself going to prison.

Three other ships loaded with weapons and military supplies lolled impatiently on their moorings. By hook, crook and fast dealing Centurion Clemidius acquired the three ships that would sail with the vessels of Eljazar. Clemidius had done well selling weapons to Rome that belonged to Rome in the first place. Clemidius guaranteed that the swords, scabbards, lances, shields and assorted military gear were all produced in Iberia according to Roman standards. Disguised as a merchant of military goods, he would deliver the cargo to a special port in Italia. The fort commander at the designated province was instructed to pay him with gold. He would then cut his hair, shave his unruly beard and proceed to Rome as Centurion Clemidius, recently stationed in Jerusalem. There to receive his promotion and spend time in the luxury the emperor provided. Free women, plenty to eat and drink plus money-making games to double his fortune. He gleamed with the joy of being so rich that his new home would out shine the palace of Serou.

As a tribute to the newly established friendship of Clemidius and Eljazar, the centurion offered a plan to throw the tiger off the spoor of Eljazar and it would read, "In the event of my untimely demise and should my remains not be found, let it be known that only Serou, the Master of Public Works can profit from my departure from you. It was the plan of Serou I was forced to follow. Investigate the records and you will discover that Serou was always at the head of the shortages you will surely discover." Some loose details followed to add credibility and a witnessed signature. "While Serou is wresting himself free of the investigation, our ships will sail," Clemidius assured. Eljazar could adopt any name he wished to use in his new life. He might also drown at sea. Eljazar was a thinking man and he liked the plan but he doubled the guard around himself. A scribe composed and delivered the letter and the plan was put in motion. In due course a patrol would arrest the great Serou and the tiger would be caged. Heading the arrest patrol would enhance the promotion of Clemidius considerably. He gloated at how good it would look on his not so bright record and the timing could not be better.

Once the man delivered his full trust to Clemidius, the rest would be easy. A few drinks, a stroll on the deck after midnight, a little shove and clear sailing to added wealth. The god Jupiter was truly smiling upon him. They had a few drinks strolling on the deck and to gain Eljazar's full confidence Clemidius gave the embezzler his list of goods for safe keeping. Impressed with the gesture of trust, Eljazar increased his guard again.

Seven ships moored to the docks gently swayed in the ceaseless motion of the sea patiently waiting to set sail. Captain Marroquin, commander of the motley fleet was a crusty, bearded man with many years at sea. His claim to fame was simple. He delivered what he promised. He portrayed a man of dubious honor to be trusted only within sight. Nonetheless he was a man that guarded your secrets if you paid him well. In gold.

In lieu of taxes, Clemidius confiscated an excellent old villa on a grassy knoll within sight of his ships lolling on their moors. He selected a modest crew to run and maintain his current home, then let it be known that he was living with a highborn woman that had no stomach for military jargon. Secretly he smarted fiercely from Senobia's open rejection and public humiliation. That it came to happen on Serou's property added fuel to his simmering rage. Serou was entirely too lucky. He was lucky at cards, dice, with women and all the high-ranking people he mingled with. It was time to chop the foundation pillars out from under him. A disastrous fall from the heights in which he lived, would serve him well. Clemidius delighted over the prospect of placing Serou under arrest. He would bring his most efficient, smartest and best-looking soldiers with him, each one spit-polished to the ears. It would be difficult for the centurion to play the part of a calm and dignified protector of justice. Clemidius would even lament the unfortunate event and offer to help the Egyptian any way he could. What fun it would be to extract some gold from Serou for his efforts to help him out of his dilemma. The look on Serou would be absolute horror, facing chains and dungeon time. Clemidius could hardly wait since the plan was so rich in personal satisfaction. With Serou out of the way, he would claim Onofrio for Rome and have him sent to fight the savage tribes in Gaul. Senobia was young and would tire of waiting for her hero that would not return. And there would be Clemidius. He would keep her and use her in every wanton way he knew. In a month or two he would return her to Tremiyo claiming she had not been a virgin and was already pregnant. That would be the final installment for her rejection. He felt justified in his actions since he sincerely put forth a heart-felt effort to properly win her affection.

Eljazar lived comfortably in the luxury quarters of Captain Marroquin. For the present he was a well kept secret, protected and well provided for. Serou could roam the country side all he wished but would never think to look under this stone.

Chapter Twenty-six

Farouk El Kamin

Just as day was breaking, Jesus stood on the beach; yet the disciples did not know that it was Jesus. Jesus said to them, "Children, have you any fish?" They answered him, "No."

John 21:4-5

A countryman, a fellow Egyptian came to see Serou unexpectedly. Patiently the elegantly dressed man waited for the master of the palatial estate. Leisurely shifting like slow moving sand throughout the great hall, paying special attention to art works and statuary. Clearly a man of fine taste and refinement, more accustomed to being waited on and not given to wait for anyone. He was made comfortable, provided with refreshment, and his entourage outside properly attended. The Lady Clavenia made her presence known with ample apologies for her husband's absence. They spoke at length with mutual interest and appreciation of the art trends in Judea compared to those in Egypt. Music, the art of dance, even history, were topics visited by the stranger and Lady Clavenia. It was a pleasant exchange for both. More so to Lady Clavenia, who seldom spoke to her guests about her likes and dislikes. She delighted in his unpretentious knowledge of the subjects he addressed and the eloquence of his speech. A rare man to share his views and respect hers as an artistic and intellectual equal.

Serou arrived curious to meet the man that patiently waited for him. When Clavenia chose to remain and discover what the mystery man wanted, the man asked Serou if he would please provide a private place to discuss "a certain delicate matter." It was a clue for Clavenia to retreat to the upper chambers.

Refreshed the men sat comfortably before an elegant array of assorted fruits and beverages. He introduced himself as Farouk El Kamin, the product of a Jewish mother and Egyptian father, an emissary to his father's empire in shipping, importing and exporting goods.

"I recently purchased a sizeable piece of property. Along with servants, animals and ready made family. The home is modest but the foundation is solid and allows for expansion. With the proper modifications, the home will represent my father's business in Judea," the man stated.

"How soon will you be looking to expand your estate?" Serou asked, in no rush to commence a new project.

"I think you will determine when modifications should begin, after you hear how I acquired the property. As we speak, there are seven ships moored at the port in Joppa. The things I tell you are verifiable facts. I know them because it is my business to know the facts. In one of those ships is the man from whom I bought the estate. I am not to take over my property until he is one day out to sea. I have confirmed everything and legally protected myself and my future holdings. The man is a very important person in your life. He is Eljazar, your recent business associate."

Serou's senses went on instant alert and forced himself to be calm. "This kind of information demands verification and always comes with a price. How can I be certain that the man is Eljazar?" Serou asked struggling to show a calm face.

Farouk El Kamin clearly understood his fellow Egyptian's hesitation and gracefully withdrew a legal document from his garments and gave it to Serou. "Is that not the signature of Eljazar Ben Philip? Does the man not have a wife and son, you visited just days ago, at my estate?"

EASTER HYMN

Death and darkness get you packing,
nothing now to man is lacking.
All your triumphs now are ended,
and what Adam marred is mended.
Graves are beds now for the weary,
death a nap to wake more merry;
Youth now, full of pious duty, seeks in thee for perfect beauty.
The weak and aged, tir'd with length of days,
from thee look for new strength;
And infants with thy pangs contest as pleasant,
as if with the breast.
Then, unto Him, who thus hath thrown even to contempt thy
kingdom down. And by his blood did us advance
unto his own inheritance.
To Him be glory, power, praise from this unto the last of days!

Henry Vaughn (1622-1695)

*Then he led them out as far as Bethany, and lifting up
his hands he blessed them. While he blessed them, he parted
from them, and was carried up into heaven. And they returned to Jerusalem with great joy,* Luke 24:50-52

*And when he had said this, as they were looking on, he
was lifted up, and a cloud took him out of their sight. And
while they were gazing into heaven as he went, behold, two
men stood by them in white robes, and said, "Men of Galilee,
why do you stand looking into heaven? This Jesus, who was
taken up from you into heaven, will come in the same way
as you saw him go into heaven."*
Acts of the Apostles 1:9-11

Having always known when it was best to listen, Serou gave Farouk El Kamin his full attention. "The man is being hidden from your grasp on a ship lolling at the docks of Joppa. You should know here and now that I intend to acquire the entire cargo the ships hold. Legally, of course. It will set well with my father to start business in Judea with such an extensive inventory. That tiny mark, as you well know is the mark of the scribe that generated this document for Eljazar's signature. That same scribe brought me news of a plot generated by your former tenant, Centurion Clemidius and Eljazar against you, personally. I took the liberty, in your behalf to detain and closely guard the scribe. He is a valuable witness in your defense against the charges being brought against you."

Serou finally got a chance to speak, "And to what do I owe all this consideration? I know of no plot against me by Clemidius and Eljazar. Although, I put nothing past the centurion. As for Eljazar hiding out in a ship in Joppa, that is very unlikely. My spies report that he has fled the country by land. And my trackers are on his trail as we speak."

Farouk politely waved his hand to silence Serou. "Your trackers are following a ghost caravan that does not exist. People along the trail have been paid to give your men false information. While you pay your men to stay on the track, you serve your enemies well. Eljazar knows you are stubborn and he left ample reason for your trackers to believe they are on his trail." With a keen look in his eye and a sympathetic smile Farouk added, "The great Serou is not so easily deceived. It gets no simpler than this. Eljazar left a clear starting trail then doubled back by another route to the ships that hold his precious cargo. He is housed in one of those ships. The cargo is a vast collection of very expensive items that will bring high prices in Italia. Part of the fleet's cargo is military armament and gear belonging to Centurion Clemidius who incidentally, has grown a beard. It is destined to a small, out of the way port in Italia. Something about that destination does not seem right. My guess is the cargo is stolen goods. The plot to implicate you of embezzlement will keep you busy fighting the charges, while the ships sail away, without notice, since people are still focused on the recent crucifixion of Jesus and now the arrest of Serou." Instantly convinced of being so completely deceived, projected Serou into an instant rage. He had never reacted out of compulsive anger. Although seething inside, he knew that uncontrolled fury would only serve to cloud his judgment. He sent a servant to find Onofrio and bring him. While superficially calm, he sat with Farouk El Kamin to plan a viable strategy. Both men had plotted courses of action before and their minds seemed to work as one. Although habitually cautious with his emotions, Serou was comfortable trusting his fellow countryman. With Onofrio present they ate, drank and spoke at length to finally agree on the best plan to follow.

Onofrio was assigned a party of men from Farouk and Serou's personal guard. All experienced men of battle. Spies were sent ahead disguised as street vendors looking to sell items of food, clothing and even small weapons to members of the crew. They invaded the ships with cautious abandon, some pretending timidity, others apologizing and bowing profusely while others portrayed experienced vendors. They all looked dirt poor, unarmed and harmless. Still others came begging for alms for the poor and hungry. Once Eljazar's exact location was determined, the main body of men would follow. Some were curious about various things aboard, looking and making lewd jokes with the crew.

Sales were made and information extracted. Proposing to sell the pampered tenant of a spacious cabin some worthless trinkets for a pittance, Eljazar was annoyed but equally amused all at once with such outrageous offers of cheap baubles while resting on a fortune of fine jewelry and gold to stagger the peddler's wildest imagination. Feeling secure and in total absence of forethought, Eljazar plucked a brooch from his headdress and handed it to the man. With a wide smirk on his face he asked,

"Tell me my good man, how much do you think this little trinket is worth?"

The fake peddler hefted the piece in his hand and pretending amazement he stammered, "This jewel is real! It's a giant ruby." His face lit up like a child with a new toy. "Oh Master, this jewel is worth many fortunes. I may deal in trinkets, but I know genuine value. I cannot put a conclusive price on it. But it will buy the owner anything he wants." The fox had let down his caution as the guards stood idly by. The peddler returned the brooch and with countless apologies and bows made his exit. He had located the fugitive embezzler Eljazar. In short order the mob of peddlers began to leave the ships. A quick conference was held and a swift messenger sent to the waiting Egyptians.

When a rooster crowed, the assembly of men woke up and swiftly moved like silent shadows onto the ship that held Eljazar. They met with minor opposition from Eljazar's guards and the sailors on board. A few sailors and guards ended up in the water and out of commission. When they had their quarry neatly bundled along with all his belongings, they made peace with sailors from the other ships, briefly explaining their mission was complete. Damage was done during the scuffle and Captain Marroquin was raising a loud ruckus about it. So they bundled him up too and brought him along. He was no easy catch and fought like a tethered tiger. A knife to his neck kept him quiet and his sailors away. A securely tied Eljazar, Captain Marroquin and the listed inventories were brought before Serou. The wily Egyptians had hardly lifted a finger to gain this giant coup. Eljazar went silent, seemingly accepting his fate with a semblance of dignity. He expressed no regret and chose to ignore the sparkling rage in the eyes of Serou.

Before the silent assembly, appearing much like a pre-trial with Serou as judge and Farouk El Kamin as prosecutor, the captain was the most fearsome and outspoken. "You have nothing to hold and judge me for. I render a service to those that can pay the price. I have stolen nothing. Yet my men have been brutally attacked and most likely drowned. My ship was raided and damaged for no fault of mine. Even now the damage continues, since there are no men to see about my vessel. What your men have done is absolute piracy. Undeniable piracy. Rome will hunt you down and hang all of you for this." The man was a boiling pot of fury and his wrangling seemed to have no end.

Finally Serou came to him and calmly cut the ropes that held him, then calmly stated, "You are not being held against your will. You may go anytime you wish. However, if you choose to remain and bear witness in this case, your ships may be returned to you. You may even gain the transport fee without having to leave port." That statement won the captain's full attention as he finished undoing his ropes. "Secondly, should you decide to leave, your collaboration with Eljazar, the embezzler and Clemidius' cargo of weapons may not set very well with Pontius Pilate and with Rome. You could easily be seeing your beloved sea from the oar seat of a slave ship." And Serou made certain Eljazar hear the last part of his statement. Never lacking in hospitality, Serou poured the captain a cup of wine and even smiled at the man. The ring of money quickly brought the captain to calmly consider the situation. Earn the fee of transport and not have to leave the harbor was powerful enticement. Soon he was advising Farouk El Kamin how to obtain the cargo like jolly old friends. And Eljazar smiled at how quickly fate can change.

All that while Onofrio and thirteen men waited outside a tavern of shady distinction where the centurion was engaged in a winning card game. He had enjoyed the company of the best looking night lady in the place. She rendered her services free of charge and complimented him by saying he was the best she had ever had. The man that challenged him was losing large amounts of money and Clemidius wasn't even cheating. His challenger paid for Clemidius' dinner and abundant drinks claiming that he was here to defeat the reputation of Clemidius as a champion card player. Finally the centurion won the man's entire purse.

With nothing more to lose, the man called the game. And a rooster crowed somewhere in the infinite darkness.

When the centurion finally said his slobbering goodbyes to all the night ladies, wine girls, patrons and assorted bar flies, he managed to find his chariot. He enjoyed an enormous high having maintained his championship, been properly treated by the choice night lady at no charge and a large purse full of gold coins. Life didn't get any better than this. The challenger requested Clemidius come alone and bring plenty of gold to lose. He sent a gold coin of large denomination to sweeten the invitation. The challenge had been too great to ignore. He was no sooner in his chariot adjusting the reins when a body of reticent shadows sprang from the bushes and quickly overtook him. Without hesitation Onofrio plucked the heavy purses. They were Serou's monies. The centurion was bundled up in a burlap bag reeking of barnyard droppings. His sword confiscated and given a hard rap on the head for good measure. After that he posed no problem, in fact he slept well.

At first light the maligned duo stood before Serou, Farouk El Kamin and a body of armed men. A pre-trial so to speak. Only Eljazar remained disturbingly silent. It gnawed at Serou to see his long time friend and associate remain so determined and terribly quiet. He refused to answer questions after making his solitary comment, "You have all the evidence, the scribe, the record of my acquisitions and the testimony of Captain Marroquin. What else do you want? You will not see me grovel and beg."

And he went silent again, except for when Serou told him, "I seriously thought of challenging you with a sword to quell my anger."

And Eljazar simply stated, "You would do murder for your vanity? I think not."

The captain was uneasy knowing an armed force was on his ships. Sailors were allowed back on board and were busy tending to ship's business. Guards were posted everywhere and almost every sailor had an escort. Marroquin having calmly weighed his options adjusted to the facts and made peace with his predicament. Playing the game right would net him the transport fee and a reward. He took charge of his ships, yelling orders and ignoring the armed guards, as though they did not exist.

Centurion Clemidius was properly chained. The man would pose a serious threat were he not bound and secure. He answered no questions. Serou calmly read the orders and list of goods out loud proving the cargo belonged to Clemidius. It was destined for Italia to fill an order from Rome and be shipped back to Judea, paid for as though coming from Iberia. When Serou was satisfied that whatever legal entanglement might await him could easily be overcome, he and Farouk went to see Pontius Pilate. They brought along the scribe that witnessed the birth of the plot for good measure.

"You're the son of a filthy sow," yelled Clemidius to Onofrio. The young man flinched at the insult and the centurion kept on. "You cut me lose and give me a sword, you bastard. Give me a chance to defend my honor. You won't live long when my men discover where I'm held. They'll storm this damned place and rip each of you apart. I taught you everything you know, you ungrateful son of a jackass. Turn me loose, you bastard." Never once did it occur to the centurion that he could not rip chains apart. He kept fighting the manacles that held him.

When Onofrio had enough, he had two men hold the centurion while he stuffed a dirty rag in his mouth and tied it in place. Calmly Onofrio asked the centurion to listen to something of importance. After hearing the request twice the centurion calmed down and made ready to listen. "Your commander has been informed of where you are and why you are being held. He has been given the choice to interfere or wait until the matter is cleared up and him given the credit for recovering the inventory and finding you out. I feel safe to say, he will choose the latter. Should he choose to interfere and attempt to rescue you, these men have instructions to help you commit suicide with your own sword. The end result will be the same. You'll be dead and he'll still have the glory." The room went deathly silent except for the ragged ramblings of the centurion and the near insane giggling of Eljazar.

Onofrio made certain the men understood Serou's instructions, he saw to Eljazar's comfort and checked the chains holding Clemidius. Then he cheerfully announced he was going to get something good to eat and spend some time with Senobia. Hearing that, the centurion was rankled something fierce, shaking and swearing maniacally. Onofrio never intented to antagonize the man but if he chose to take it as added torment, so be it.

A few hours later when the young man returned berry stains and all, the men met him at the door. Some of the men were rested from last night's adventure, knowing the prisoners were secure. Eljazar found a way to slash his wrists while pretending to bathe. He was searched, but the guard overlooked a seemingly innocent shaving mug and razor. That Eljazar chose to commit suicide did not surprise Serou. It was easier than facing his wife and son. He would not have lived in peace anywhere within the Jewish community. Even the seasoned centurion remained quiet and pensive, adjusting to what fate had in store for his dismal future. He laughed within himself and said, "Goodbye, Emperor. We could have had such great times together."

The following days were filled with exciting events and the young man was kept terribly busy. There were endless rumors of Jesus being slighted by countless people. Some even said He was seen rising to heaven on a cloud. Serou was quickly cleared of any wrong doing. Farouk El Kamin was hassling with the port authorities over the cargo. Rome demonstrated appreciation for the recovery of the arsenal with a sizeable reward. Serou instantly gave half to his adopted son and the other half to the men that helped bring Clemidius to Roman justice. Suddenly the young man had enough gold to charter passage to Iberia for two with a certain sea captain that he knew. First and foremost in his mind was learning more about Jesus from His disciples. After the wedding he and Senobia would travel to Iberia and share their stories of Jesus to all that would listen. Onofrio had a strange illusion visit his dreams one night. He saw Jesus blessing grains of wheat that glowed with an effervescent light as they gently floated away to land on fertile minds and Onofrio decided he would do that for Jesus in Iberia and beyond.

As if his blessings were not enough Senobia and he were cast into a dance of exhilarating joy to learn that Tremiyo and Camia decided to make it a double wedding day. Knowing how Tremiyo always wanted things done legally and proper, Serou threw a friendly dig at the mature couple, "It's about time you two gave your daughter a legal name." Laughter filled the house. Along came the captain looking for a landside meal and to wrest an invitation to the weddings and perhaps drum up a little business. The not so ragged jeweler brought a prize winning wedding ring in a golden box for the young man to approve or improve.

AWAY

I can not say, and will not say
That He is dead – He is just away.
With a cheery smile and a wave of his hand,
He has wandered into an unknown land,
And left us dreaming, how very fair
It needs must be, since He lingers there.
And you – O you, who so wildly yearn
for the old-time step and the glad return,
Think of Him faring on, as dear
in the love of there as the love of here.
Think of Him as the same, I say;
He is not dead – He is just away.

James Whitcomb Riley, 1849-1916

EL FIN ?

www.ingramcontent.com/pod-product-compliance
Lightning Source LLC
Chambersburg PA
CBHW020535020726
47494CB00006B/1778